The Flaming Sword

The Flaming Sword

By Thomas Dixon

With an Introduction and Notes by
John David Smith

THE UNIVERSITY PRESS OF KENTUCKY

Publication of this volume was made possible in part by a grant from the National Endowment for the Humanities.

Scholarly publisher for the Commonwealth, serving Bellarmine University, Berea College, Centre College of Kentucky, Eastern Kentucky University, The Filson Historical Society, Georgetown College, Kentucky Historical Society, Kentucky State University, Morehead State University, Murray State University, Northern Kentucky University, Transylvania University, University of Kentucky, University of Louisville, and Western Kentucky University.

Editorial and Sales Offices: The University Press of Kentucky
663 South Limestone Street, Lexington, Kentucky 40508-4008
www.kentuckypress.com

Frontispiece: Thomas Dixon. From *The Flaming Sword* (Atlanta, Ga.: Monarch Publishing Co., 1939).
Illustrations by Edward Shenton.

05 06 07 08 09 5 4 3 2 1

Library of Congress Cataloging-in-Publication Data

Dixon, Thomas, 1864-1946.
The flaming sword / by Thomas Dixon ; with an introduction and notes by John David Smith.
p. cm.
ISBN 0-8131-9129-7 (pbk. : alk. paper)
1. White supremacy movements—Fiction. 2. African American criminals—Fiction. 3. Anti-communist movements—Fiction. 4. Murder victims' families—Fiction. 5. Back to Africa movement—Fiction. 6. New York (N.Y.)—Fiction. 7. South Carolina—Fiction. 8. Lynching—Fiction. 9. Racism—Fiction.
I. Smith, John David, 1949- II. Title.
PS3507.I93F57 2005
813'.52—dc22
2005002741

This book is printed on acid-free recycled paper meeting the requirements of the American National Standard for Permanence in Paper for Printed Library Materials.

Manufactured in the United States of America.

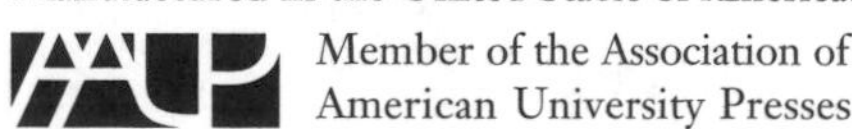

To Madelyn

Across this path stands the South with flaming sword.

—W.E.B. DuBois

Contents

Letter from the Author xi
Note to the Reader xiii
Introduction xv
A Note on the Text xxxi
Part I
The Crime 1
Part II
The Search 151
Part III
The Solution 311

Raleigh, North Carolina.

To All Purchasers of the De Luxe Edition:

The Flaming Sword is more than a novel. It is the foundation and justification of a crusade to rid our country of influences and activities which, for years, have been secretly dynamiting the pillars of the nation.

The Flaming Sword discusses the problems of the future which have grown out of the conditions of the past. A dramatic story of historic, social and racial facts. A candid camera picture of American life from an unusual angle. A STOP, LOOK and LISTEN signal for every man who loves his country.

I have given the publishers authority to issue this De Luxe edition in advance of the regular one, not for the purpose of review, but to furnish a hand-picked group of our citizens the chance to read and study the story before the date of official publication, with thc hope that each one of you will join with me in meeting the threat which now menaces our nation, endangering our liberty and progress.

I am informed by the publishers that they will furnish me with a handsomely bound book containing the name and address of every purchaser of the De Luxe edition. I shall highly prize this addition to my library and will write to every subscriber and keep you informed on the steps we are making to meet the conditions.

To each of you I send patriot greetings.

Sincerely,
Thomas Dixon

To the Reader

A novel is the most vivid and accurate form in which history can be written. I have tried in this story to give an authoritative record of the Conflict of Color in America from 1900 to 1938. To do this I have been compelled to use living men and women as important characters. If I have been unfair in treatment they have their remedy under the law of libel. I hold myself responsible.

Thomas Dixon

Introduction

Writing from London in 1938, the black nationalist and pan-Africanist Marcus Garvey commented on the response of African Americans to the writings of the famous white supremacist and novelist Thomas Dixon Jr. (1864–1946). "Mr. Dixon's presentations up to the present," Garvey wrote, "have been regarded by a large number of Negroes as being doubtful as far as their interests are concerned. Another number of us have not given sufficient thought to the work to place it in any particular category, and still there are some of us who regard his work as being expressive of the white man's desire to make plain what he sees to be a dangerous matter." Garvey added that he was "very much interested in Mr. Dixon's new work and more so when he has stated that his desire is to work in behalf of the repatriation of Negroes to Africa—that is, that section of them who would willingly leave for such a domicile. I wish Mr. Dixon all that is good and do hope to be able to correspond with him leading toward that object."[1]

The following year, in his "new work," *The Flaming Sword*, Dixon lauded Garvey as "a man of striking personality, a coal black whose face bore the lines of a born fighter."[2] In writing *The Flaming Sword*, Dixon, then sick and nearly penniless, was on a mission to evangelize the colonization of Negroes and to save the New South from the triple threats of racial mixing, socialism, and communism. Following the publication of *The Leopard's Spots* in 1902, Dixon portrayed African American men as servile, bestial, and sexually threatening. Premising his earlier books on the essential inferiority of the Negro, Dixon identified three possible scenarios for future race relations in America: blacks could accept Caucasian superiority; the races could separate; or blacks could be annihilated. *The Flaming Sword* reaffirmed Dixon's commitment to this ideology but framed his old arguments within the context of the Great Depression, the New Deal, the rise of Soviet Russia, and the looming world war in Europe and Asia.

In *The Flaming Sword* Dixon also responded to his longtime critics, mostly blacks, by using them as characters in the book. "I have tried in this story," Dixon explains in the preface, "to give an authoritative record of the Conflict of Color in America from 1900 to 1938. To do this I have been compelled to use living men and women as important characters." Aware of the risk he was taking in imbedding real persons in his fiction, Dixon adds confidently: "If I have been unfair in treatment they have their remedy under the law of libel" (xiii). In doing so, Dixon had brazenly thrown down the gauntlet to his early black critics, including Howard University mathematician and sociologist Kelly Miller, Atlanta University historian and sociologist W.E.B. DuBois, and novelist and poet James Weldon Johnson.

The Flaming Sword remains among Dixon's most obscure, least analyzed, yet most interesting works, especially for students of southern race relations. This grim, neglected text brought Dixon's saga of interracial conflict in America from the Progressive Era up to the age of Franklin D. Roosevelt and gave Dixon an opportunity to underscore what he considered the cancer of communism infecting American life and the apathy of white Americans to that threat. Though *The Flaming Sword* is more reactionary than his earlier novels, the work's graphic, pathological ugliness offers an extraordinary window into how Dixon's racial ideology remained constant from 1902 to 1939.

In the limited, deluxe edition of *The Flaming Sword* issued prior to the release of the standard edition, Dixon proclaims:

> *The Flaming Sword* is more than a novel. It is the foundation and justification of a crusade to rid our country of influences and activities which, for years, have been secretly dynamiting the pillars of the nation.
>
> *The Flaming Sword* discusses the problems of the future which have grown out of the conditions of the past. A dramatic story of historic, social and racial facts. A candid camera picture of American life from an unusual angle. A STOP, LOOK and LISTEN signal for every man who loves his country.[3]

In this book Dixon responds to what he considered the central role of blacks in a new menace—the subversive Socialist-Communist-criminal threat. *The Flaming Sword* also provided the feisty seventy-five-year-old author with a venue to answer his black critics of more than three decades.

Though Dixon had supported Roosevelt in 1932 and had spoken throughout the nation in 1934 on behalf of the National Recovery Act, by

1936 he had abandoned the Democrats, having become increasingly uncomfortable with Roosevelt's liberal agenda and having been convinced that Communist subversives were infiltrating the New Deal.[4] In 1938 Dixon informed the white supremacist and emigrationist Earnest Sevier Cox, a fellow Garveyite, that the National Association for the Advancement of Colored People (NAACP) was "all powerful at the White House through Mrs. Roosevelt."[5] In *The Flaming Sword*, "the wife of the President" appears at an Alabama meeting of a Communist front group established "to stir in the deep South the ugliest phase of the Negro Problem by a brazen demand for social equality" (405). Here Dixon referred to Eleanor Roosevelt's 1938 attendance at the Birmingham, Alabama, meeting of the Southern Conference for Human Welfare in which she defied the state's segregation laws.[6]

Years before, Dixon had published a trilogy of books—*The One Woman* (1903), *Comrades* (1909), and *The Root of Evil* (1911)—outlining what he considered to be the evils of socialism. Dixon spoke of socialism and communism interchangeably—never distinguishing between the two—convinced that the systems "were signs of racial degeneracy."[7] Responding in 1919 to Dixon's diatribes against socialism, Wilfred A. Domingo, a Jamaican Socialist who served as an early editor of Garvey's weekly *Negro World*, reminded African Americans "that the very men like Thomas Dixon . . . who are fighting Socialism or as they maliciously call it Bolshevism, are the same men who exhaust every unfair means to vilify, oppress and oppose Negroes."[8] After abandoning the Democrats over what he considered their sympathy to Communists and blacks, Dixon broke with the New Dealers and campaigned for Republican nominee Alfred M. Landon in 1936. "The increasing influence of Communistic advisers around" President Franklin D. Roosevelt, Dixon railed, "has steered Roosevelt more and more into radical channels. I have no use for them—the devil take them!"[9] Isaac M. Meekins, a Republican judge, rewarded Dixon for his new political allegiance by appointing him clerk of the federal court for the eastern district of North Carolina.[10]

Dixon's new day job supported his real work—writing *The Flaming Sword*—a book that he informed Edward Young Clarke, the former imperial kleagle of the Ku Klux Klan, was "the most important thing I have ever done." It was to be "bigger and far more sensational" than his previous works, Dixon said, predicting that it would "certainly sell a million, if pushed with faith and enthusiasm."[11] To do his part, Dixon spent as much as sixteen hours a day researching and writing the book.[12] He charged that Doubleday, Page, the press that had published *The Clansman* (1905), rejected the manuscript because they were "afraid to antagonize the Negroes." Dixon feared contracting with one of the major presses because "they could lie down before a savage Negro attack and crucify me." Instead, Dixon sought "a daring young house, fearing neither man or the Devil, who will DRIVE the thing for all it is worth." He wanted publishers "who believe as I believe on the Race Problem." Ultimately Atlanta's Monarch Publishing Company published the book.[13] The renowned artist Edward Shenton (1895–1977), whose work appeared in books by F. Scott Fitzgerald, Ernest Hemingway, and William Faulkner, illustrated *The Flaming Sword.* The stark and linear style of Shenton's pen-and-ink drawings emphasized Dixon's increasingly somber, sinister, and foreboding narrative.

Raleigh's *News and Observer* announced that *The Flaming Sword* was a sequel to *The Clansman*, drawing for its inspiration upon "the Scottsboro case, the rise of Red Communism among Negroes and scores of interracial incidents blazed across 20th century newspapers." The newspaper predicted that Dixon's new book would have all the power of David Wark Griffith's *The Birth of a Nation* (1915), the immensely popular film adaptation of Dixon's *The Clansman.* Dixon explained that his new book would begin where *The Leopard's Spots* ended "and bring the romance of the South from Reconstruction Days down to 1937." He promised to include "strong, dramatic characters" and to portray contemporary race relations, especially the spread of communism among Negroes under DuBois, whom Dixon characterized as a "Red radical preaching dictatorship of the proletariat."[14] Dixon stated that his book title came from a passage in DuBois's *Black Reconstruction in America* (1935),[15] a text he branded "a blazing manifesto of Communism,"[16] "the Negro Bible of Communism."[17] Dixon assured readers that in his book he would depict the Costigan-Wagner Antilynching Bill (designed "to put the South back under bayonets as in Reconstruction") as the work of DuBois's "Negro Communist Society" and the NAACP.[18] In fact, though in the late 1920s and early 1930s DuBois admired Soviet Russia, both he and the organization opposed American Communists. DuBois had left the editorship of the NAACP's *The Crisis* in June 1934.[19]

Dixon's 562-page *The Flaming Sword* appeared in mid 1939, soon after he had succumbed to a crippling cerebral hemorrhage and as war was breaking out in Europe.[20] The novel, according to literary critic James Kinney, "combines the threats of socialism and racial equality, presenting blacks as communist dupes attempting the overthrow of the United States."[21] Literary historian Lawrence J. Oliver explains that in the work Dixon "dramatized, for the final time, the recurring theme of his fiction and nonfiction: that Reconstruction had let loose upon the land a savage black beast who would, if unchecked, 'Africanize' the United States and destroy the greatest civilization that the world has ever known."[22]

While *The Flaming Sword* builds upon many of the themes and set characters introduced in *The Leopard's Spots* and *The Clansman*, in 1939 Dixon updated them to reflect his obsessions with miscegenation, Communist-inspired black revolt, and race war in the South. Like Margaret Mitchell in *Gone With the Wind* (1936), in *The Flaming Sword* Dixon revived the race melodrama. But whereas Mitchell situated her book in the nineteenth century, Dixon set his in the recent past and present—"allowing him to make a full-scale assault on Reds as well as Blacks." The book, Oliver concludes, "reflects in dramatic fashion the virulent racism and right-wing 'Americanism' that pervaded the 'Red Decade.'"[23] It also signifies, according to Stephen Joseph Karina, the closest student of Dixon's last work, Dixon's last ditch, reactionary warning to Americans—"his surrealistic view of history since 1900, which condemned the entire black race for individual criminal offenses and supposed that all blacks waved red flags because a handful of their leaders turned to Communism."[24]

The Flaming Sword begins in idyllic Piedmont, South Carolina, early in the new century.[25] Though hardworking whites are transforming the New South into an industrialized society "without violating the community's natural innocence,"[26] racial tension hovers over the land. Almost on cue, Dan Hose (presumably the brother of Sam Hose, the black man lynched in Georgia in 1899), a sex-craved, beastlike Negro, savagely murders Dave Henry, an upwardly mobile yeoman, and his infant son David; Hose also rapes and murders Dave's sister-in-law, Marie Cameron.[27] Hose was inspired to rape Marie by reading James Weldon Johnson's 1915 poem "The White Witch," originally published in the NAACP's magazine *The Crisis*, then edited by DuBois and, according to Dixon, was "a vile bundle of poison" (123).[28] "A nigger in Harlem," Dan says after raping Marie, "sent me a little book dat say I got de right ter marry a white gal ef I kin git her. Can't marry her down here, but by God, I got her" (136). Upon learning that Hose had a copy of Johnson's poem in his coat pocket, John Lovelace, one of Dave's friends, remarks: "That's the sort of damned stuff given to Niggers to read. There's the match that fired the powder." Marie's rape, Dixon adds, "was a blow of race." It was "a challenge to the existence of the white man and his people" (142).

Unquestionably, by 1939 standards the detailed rape scene was obscene. After Dan threatens to kill baby David, Marie agrees to succumb to his lust if the baby's life is spared. "He gripped her wrist," Dixon wrote, "and dragged her unresisting into the large bed room, crushed his naked sweating body against hers, and pressed his bulging thick lips into her mouth until she gasped for breath. For half an hour he played with her as a cat a mouse, raped her with brutal violence and ordered her to get up, while he stretched his huge black body full length on the bed, his mud covered wool socks staining the white linen." After Dan orders Marie to sit in a chair, she begins to slouch. "'Straighten up—damn ye!' he grunted. 'I want ter see all of ye. Jist like the devil made ye ter lead men ter hell and damnation. Straighten all the way against the wall, and put yer hans behin' yer head and keep 'em thar till I tell ye ter come back ter me.'" When Marie begins to slump again, Dan whips her (136–37). "For another half hour he subjected her to the agony and shame of indescribable sex atrocities until she sank unconscious to the floor" (138).

Commenting on Dixon's rape scene in 1966, historian J. Zeb Wright remarked that "no more lewd picture can be found in inexpensive paperback novels today."[29] Karina correctly notes that Dixon's "preoccupation with black sexuality assumed almost pathological proportions" and raises "questions [about] his very sanity."[30] "Reverend Dixon in fact spends three pages describing the rape and degradation of Marie," writes Oliver, "and he is not squeamish about providing prurient details capable of inflaming racial passions. . . . Of course, Dixon himself had to imagine the scene in order to depict it. His graphic account suggests that the lustful, violent brute is a projection of his own suppressed impulses." Dixon's assertion that Johnson's poem "idealiz[ed] the Negro's passion for white women" (214), according to Oliver, "is absurd. The poem in fact explicitly warns black males to *avoid* the snares of the white temptress."[31] Dixon also has one of his characters cite the notorious African American negrophobe William Hannibal Thomas as an authority on the male Negro's "imperious sexual impulse, which, aroused at the slightest incentive, sweeps aside all restraint" (156).[32] Dixon's gruesome and violent post-rape lynching scene—including details of Hose's emasculation and incineration—served as the author's transitionary device to the second part of the book.

This occurs in New York City, where Angela Cameron Henry, Dave's wife and Marie's sister, relocates after overcoming the trauma of their deaths. She is committed to studying Negroes anthropologically in Harlem in order to help solve the race problem. Phil Stephens, a lawyer, racial liberal, and Angela's rejected beau from Piedmont, joins her in New York and works first with the Inter-Racial Commission and then the NAACP to promote racial harmony. But gradually Angela and Phil come to see the "Negro problem" more clearly. It was, she explains, "an unsolved and insolvable tragedy" (83). Blacks are inherently inferior and degenerate; education only exacerbates, not ameliorates, their condition. Blacks are obsessed with the idea of full "social equality," making them especially susceptible to New

York's radical "Negro Junta" (Dixon's term for the NAACP), their white liberal supporters, and Communists who promise black men sex with white women in exchange for their support. Dixon included Oswald Garrison Villard, Joel E. Spingarn, Albert E. Pillsbury, and Moorfield Storey among white supporters of DuBois's "Negro Junta."[33] According to one of Dixon's characters, every member of the NAACP is "a goddam racial imbecile who thinks that a Negro is better than a white man" (124).

As she ponders the complexities of the race problem, Angela concludes that racial purity can only be achieved by separation—colonizing the blacks to Africa. Influenced by a pro-repatriation speech delivered by the white supremacist John Temple Graves in 1900, and the colonizationist ideas of black leaders Henry McNeal Turner, Lucius Holsey, and William H. Councill,[34] she endorses repatriation. "We have the ships—we have the millions. It only remains to develop the plan of a peaceful friendly separation" (186). Angela next devotes herself to studying communism. "The thing is in the air," she says (321). Angela fears that American Communists are plotting to use the vast army of unemployed and disgruntled Negroes to topple the U.S. government.

Observing blacks in Harlem, Angela sees the "New Negro" for the first time and listens to jazz. "Whether worth while or not," Dixon wrote, black music "was certainly a direct growth of the African jungle. As their dancing is an expression of sex impulses straight from the tropical forests. As is their low resistance to the poison of syphilis and alcohol, and their easy surrender to the sway of superstition which they call religion" (220). In Harlem, Angela feels "for the first time the threat of a nation inside a nation under the teachings of radicals whose hatred of whites had become an obsession. Certainly the days of 'Mammies,' 'Aunties,' and 'Uncles' had gone forever" (222). She cringes at the seemingly ubiquitous sight of black men arm in arm with white women, usually blondes, practicing "the oldest profession known to woman" (221).

While in New York, Angela, Phil, and Tony Murino, a reformed bootlegger also committed to destroying the Communist threat, establish the Patriot Union—a secret national army of whites devoted to protecting America from the Communists. According to Tony, "Communism is the collapse of the human mind under the pressure of modern life. It is a malignant, contagious, mental disease now sweeping the world as the Black Death swept Europe in the middle ages. Its victims can see but one way to safety. A return to the herd life out of which an intelligent humanity grew. This impulse to touch shoulders with the herd, to sink back into the mass for food and shelter, means the end of all progress and the death of civilization itself" (403). Convinced that Soviet-inspired Communists had infiltrated America's schools and churches, its labor unions, its communication and transportation networks, the postal service, even its military and navy, Angela goes undercover and enters the party's inner circle.

Determined to learn the date of the imminent revolution, Angela and Phil desperately but unsuccessfully try to prevent the overthrow of American democracy by radical blacks and Communists. The Negro-Communist insurrection begins during one of Roosevelt's fireside chats in 1940. In the South members of the all-black Nat Turner Legion rise up in "a reign of terror—burning, murdering and raping" (452). "Negro criminals have been detailed to fire every Southern city, rape every white woman who can be taken, and blow up the armories" (443). After a violent coup the totalitarian Soviet Republic of the United States triumphs and rules North America.

Dixon blamed the nightmarish demise of Anglo-Saxon civilization on Communists and the "Negro Junta," especially the writings of his old black critics Miller, DuBois, and Johnson—whom he charged with challenging racial segregation, demanding intermarriage of blacks and whites, and rejecting repatriation in order to enlist the black masses in the revolution.[35] Dixon believed that Depression-era blacks were ripe for what he considered the cheap and dangerous rhetoric of black intellectuals, their white neoabolitionist friends, and Communists. He judged their agenda—antilynching legislation, equal access to education and employment, and the end of Jim Crow laws—as radical steps prone to usher in the demise of white society.

Early in *The Flaming Sword*, for example, Captain Tom Collier, the conservative superintendent of Piedmont's school system, quotes Miller as saying that whites are "arrogant and rapacious, the most exclusive and intolerant race in history." This may be so, Collier explains, but he insists that one must answer the "cold blooded question: Can you change the color of a Negro, the swell of his lip or the beat of his heart with a spelling book or the use of a gang plow?" (33). Collier next alleges that "social equality with the great white race has become the passionate faith of ninety-nine out of every hundred educated Negroes in America. It is the soul of DuBois' teachings. Charles W. Chestnut [*sic*], your Mulatto Cleveland novelist, believes it and proclaims it. Professor Kelly Miller, your distinguished Negro teacher in Washington, believes it" (33). Later, following Marie's rape, Angela's friend Ann Lovelace quotes Johnson as saying that "in the cone of the heart of the African race problem the sex factor is rooted." Ann, however, informs Angela that "the physical contact of two such races is a constant violation of God's law. We pay the price of that violation. We must obey the law or pay the penalty" (155–56).

Dixon, however, reserved his special disdain for DuBois, whom he described as "the greatest Negro leader the race has yet produced in America," "the bold champion of the Dictatorship of the Proletariat" (385, 387). Dixon transformed DuBois, his longstanding critic, into *The Flaming Sword*'s "Black villain."[36] According to Wright, Dixon owned most of DuBois's books and his marginal comments in them "reveal a genuine disgust with the Negro professor." For example, "when DuBois wrote of the Negro's love of liberty, Dixon wrote '*Rats!*' Of DuBois's mention of 'ancient African chastity' Dixon wrote '*Fool or Liar—*.' Du Bois's statement that race prejudice was 'deplorable in its intensity, unfortunate in results, and dangerous for the future, but nevertheless a hard fact which only time can efface' evinced an exclamatory '*Race Imbecile!*' from Dixon."[37] In *The Flaming Sword*, Dixon refers to DuBois as "the Mulatto," "this Mulatto," or "a Mulatto Professor in Atlanta University" (19, 14). Du Bois served as the lightning rod for Dixon's most personal, racist, slanderous, and vicious attacks. Dixon blamed him for trying to censor *The Birth of a Nation* (202) and named him as an "agitator" fomenting a bloody John-Brown-like "Negro insurrection" and a Communist leader with direct ties to Moscow (270). *Black Reconstruction in America* became "the central text of the revolutionaries."[38]

Near the start of *The Flaming Sword*, Angela's grandfather, Dr. Richard Cameron, the father of Ben Cameron, Dixon's hero in *The Clansman*, denounces DuBois's *The Souls of Black Folk* (1903) as "a little black book" published "with the deliberate purpose of stirring the worst passions—a firebrand thrown into the imaginations of ten million Negroes" (14).[39] Dr. Cameron next questions DuBois's credibility as an authority on the "Negro problem." "Professor W.E.B. DuBois," he said, "was born in Massachusetts. His people never knew slavery. . . . All he knows of the history of our states and our people he drew from the imagination of Abolition fanatics who caused the Civil War." DuBois's knowledge of slavery was second and third hand—"from sources of ignorance and prejudice," Dixon explained, and "his reference to ancient African Chastity . . . stamps the writer an ignoramus on the history of the Africa from which our Negroes came" (16). Cameron later compares DuBois with "the scoundrels who first sowed hate" among the black man during "the black days of Reconstruction when Negroes, Carpetbaggers and Scalawags ruled this country" (44). Captain Collier believes that DuBois's flaws were most readily identifiable "in his glorification of Frederick Douglass, the Negro orator, whose final triumph was his marriage to a white woman." Collier charges that, like Douglass, DuBois's solution to America's race problem was "'assimilation by self-assertion and by no other means.' That is to say the making of American Mulatto [*sic*] by the self assertion of the Negro" (31).

Though Dixon openly criticized Booker T. Washington, he nevertheless considered him more qualified to lead the race than DuBois, whose ideas he judged "daring and dangerous" (322). "There was no trace of the Negro in him," Phil observes of DuBois, "except the light tinge of brown in his skin, and that was not marked. A pointed beard, dark melancholy eyes, a quiet man of culture, French looking rather than American, he gave no impression of an African. . . . It was easy to believe that he had taken degrees at Harvard and in Germany. . . . It was difficult to believe that such a man, with a bare trace of a Negro in his makeup, should be so fiercely, passionately, and insistently African as to lead a crusade of violence against the white race" (199). Phil finds DuBois's *Black Reconstruction in America* so radical that he severed ties with the NAACP when the organization's leaders refuse to censure its author. DuBois's treatment of economic issues, he remarks, was "a specious plea for the philosophy of Karl Marx" (385).

Black Reconstruction in America, Phil explains, contradicted all previous interpretations of Reconstruction. It audaciously championed the rule of blacks over whites in this period "in terms that will not bear discussion." Phil judges DuBois's book "so bitterly partisan" that it was worthless "as an historical document. His theme is that the Negro made in the tragic fiasco of Reconstruction a noble record. That his white rivals of the South were his inferiors" (385). Though DuBois was a scientifically trained scholar, in *Black Reconstruction in America* he exposed himself as a doctrinaire Marxist; his book was a "firebrand." "It is in no sense a history," Phil concludes, "in spite of its jumble of irrelevant and worthless quotations. It is a call to race riot by a man who has become a monomaniac in his hatred of whites. In every line one feels the passionate desire of the author to slit the throat of every white man in the world. His theme is merely the platform from which he rises to harangue the mob and excite them to violence" (386).

Later in the story Dixon explained DuBois's shift to the Left—into the Communists' ranks—as a pragmatic move designed to retain influence among his people. According to Dixon, "the struggle of the Red leaders for control of the race threw the amalgamation Junta in New York into a panic of fear for their future. DuBois met the situation by a sharp turn to the left in his writing and speeches. The Russian government was praised, our own denounced. Atheism was applauded. Denunciation of the white race increased in violence. Every device of insinuation and direct attack was now used to stir the hate of Negroes against the Southern people" (376). On the eve of the revolution, a member of the Communist Inner Circle informs Russia's ambassador to the United States that thanks to DuBois's influence, 550,000 armed blacks would fight for the Red cause. "DuBois is the greatest leader we have ever produced in America," he says.

"His book advocating the Dictatorship of the Proletariat has become what he designed it to be, the Bible of the Negro. We'll give the Southerners the biggest surprise of all" (422).

In the end, however, it was Dixon who was surprised by the negative and indifferent response to *The Flaming Sword.* As war loomed in Europe, Depression-era Americans found little interest in Dixon's sexual fantasies and his rant against miscegenation and Negro Communists. Writing in the *Raleigh News and Observer*, Frank Smethurst, managing editor of the newspaper, remarked that the book more appropriately deserved "news treatment rather than literary criticism." Dixon's novel, Smethurst explained, "gathers up the loose threads of the race problem . . . and weaves them into the pattern of a new national menace, Communism." He dismissed *The Flaming Sword* as generally gratuitous—"a preachment of conservative patriotism and an indictment of the liberal concept in race relations which the author scores as an invitation to the radicalism he seems to fear with something like hysteria."[40] Similarly, the critic in the *New York Times* brushed off the book as a manifestation of Dixon's paranoia, predicting that the public would judge it as "nightmare melodrama," "the expression of a panic fear."[41] Though the *New York Herald Tribune* paid *The Flaming Sword* short shrift, the proximity of the book's appearance to the signing of the August 23, 1939, Molotov-Ribbentrop Pact and Adolf Hitler's invasion of Poland nine days later, inclined the reviewer to remark that Dixon's "vehement melodrama . . . is not as wildly incredible today as it might have seemed a few short weeks ago."[42]

While Americans watched with horror the war that would quickly envelop Europe, they ignored Dixon's lurid fears of miscegenation, his pathetic and wildly inaccurate accusations of a Negro Communist conspiracy, and his erroneous forecasts of race war at home. His last book was an utter failure. Just as DuBois never responded to Dixon's libelous and malicious attacks in *The Flaming Sword*,[43] Americans rejected his hysterical, dog-eared recitations of black degeneracy, black retrogression, and pending racial doom. African Americans had always found Dixon's books "doubtful as far as their interests are concerned." Early in the twentieth century blacks had good reason to fear the harmful backlash of Dixon's malicious lies on members of their race. They understood too well the racial phobias and venomous race hatred that lay at their core.

By 1939, however, blacks considered Dixon's final warnings to be the sick fantasies of a bitter, desperate, and isolated man. As Americans braced for a second world war, the author of *The Flaming Sword* stood dramatically out of touch with the accomplishments, achievements, and self-determination of modern black Americans.[44] Shortly before that book appeared, Dixon informed Earnest Sevier Cox that "some . . . people may find sentences in my books that are hard reading on the surface. I have simply tried in all my writing to develop Lincoln's and Jefferson's views through the characters which I have created showing that separation is the only sane solution. Personally I have always loved the Negro race, and for that very reason have savagely opposed amalgamation."[45] The "Negro problem" as Dixon defined it thus had become quite literally *his* problem. African Americans long before had disproven the rabidly racist misrepresentations and predictions of Tom Dixon.

John David Smith

NOTES

I received research assistance from Daire Roebuck, Mimi Riggs, Marihelen Stringham, Ann Rothe (North Carolina State University), Elizabeth Dunn (Duke University), Randal Hall (Rice University), Alexander Andrusyszyn (Yale University), Jane Ruffin (*Raleigh News and Observer*), Hope Lorraine Murphy (University of North Carolina at Charlotte), and Charles H. Rousell and Leslie S. Rousell (Northeast Center for Trauma Recovery).

1. Marcus Garvey to Earnest S. Cox, October 6, 1938, in Robert A. Hill, ed., *The Marcus Garvey and Universal Negro Improvement Association Papers*, 9 vols. (Berkeley: University of California Press, 1983–95), 7:892–93.

2. Thomas Dixon, *The Flaming Sword* (Atlanta, Ga.: Monarch Publishing Company, 1939), 415.

3. Thomas Dixon, *The Flaming Sword*, deluxe ed. (Atlanta, Ga.: Monarch Publishing Company, 1939), n.p. Hereafter, all page references to Dixon's book will be parenthetical and will refer to the University Press of Kentucky edition.

4. Stephen Joseph Karina, "With Flaming Sword: The Reactionary Rhetoric of Thomas Dixon" (Ph.D. diss., University of Georgia, 1978), 128–29.

5. Thomas Dixon to Earnest S. Cox, December 11, 1938, Earnest Sevier Cox Papers, Duke University. On Cox's ties to Garvey, see Earnest Sevier Cox, *Let My People Go* (Richmond, Va.: The White America Society, 1925), [4].

6. See Thomas A. Krueger, *And Promises to Keep: The Southern Conference for Human Welfare, 1938–1948* (Nashville, Tenn.: Vanderbilt University Press, 1967).

7. William David Harrison, "The Thoughts of Thomas Dixon on Black and White Race Relations in American Society" (master's thesis, University of South Carolina, 1970), 25. On Dixon's fears of Marxism, socialism, communism, and feminism, see Raymond Allen Cook, *Thomas Dixon* (New York: Twayne Publishers, 1974), 80–88. These aspects of Dixon's thought cry out for systematic scholarly attention.

8. W.A. Domingo, "Socialism: The Negroes' Hope," *Messenger* 2 (July 1919), quoted in Herbert Aptheker, ed., *A Documentary History of the Negro People in the United States*, 6 vols. (Secaucus, N.J.: Citadel Press, 1951–1993), 3:262.

9. "Dixon Gets Post in Federal Court," *Raleigh News and Observer*, May 2, 1937.

10. Raymond Rohauer, "Postscript," in Thomas Dixon, *Southern Horizons: The Autobiography of Thomas Dixon* (Alexandria, Va.: IWV Pub., 1984), 322; Cary D. Wintz, "Introduction," in Thomas Dixon Jr., *The Clansman: An Historical Romance of the Ku Klux Klan*, ed. and abridged by Cary D. Wintz (Armonk, N.Y.: M.E. Sharpe, 2001), xvi; J. Zeb Wright, "Thomas Dixon: The Mind of a Southern Apologist" (Ph.D. diss., George Peabody College for Teachers, 1966), 288–89. Dixon held the clerkship until 1943. See "Dixon's Funeral to be Held Today," *Raleigh News and Observer*, April 4, 1946.

11. Thomas Dixon to Edward Y. Clarke, August 11, 1938, Thomas Dixon Papers, Duke University.

12. Wright, "Thomas Dixon," 288.

13. Thomas Dixon to Oscar, August 18, 1938, Dixon Papers.

14. "'Birth of Nation' Will Have Sequel," *Raleigh News and Observer*, October 22, 1937.

15. Lawrence J. Oliver, "Writing from the Right during the 'Red Decade': Thomas Dixon's Attack on W.E.B. DuBois and James Weldon Johnson in *The Flaming Sword*," *American Literature* 70 (March 1998): 135, pinpoints the quotation in W.E.B. DuBois, *Black Reconstruction in America: An Essay Toward a History of the Part Which Black Folk Played in the Attempt to Reconstruct Democracy in America, 1860–1880* (1935; reprint, New York: Atheneum,

1973), 707. DuBois wrote: "A clear vision of a world without inordinate individual wealth, of capital without profit, and of income based on work alone, is the path out, not only for America but for all men. Across this path stands the South with flaming sword" (706–7).

16. "'Birth of Nation' Will Have Sequel."

17. Dixon to Cox, November 22, 1939, Cox Papers.

18. "'Birth of Nation' Will Have Sequel." This bill, proposed unsuccessfully in 1934 by Democrats Edward Costigan and Robert F. Wagner on behalf of the NAACP, would have imposed a $10,000 fine on counties where lynchings occurred. See George C. Rable, "The South and the Politics of Antilynching Legislation, 1920–1940," *Journal of Southern History* 51 (May 1985): 201–20.

19. Elliott M. Rudwick, *W.E.B. Du Bois: Propagandist of the Negro Protest* (New York: Atheneum, 1972), 256–57, 283.

20. Raymond Allen Cook, *Fire from the Flint: The Amazing Careers of Thomas Dixon* (Winston-Salem, N.C.: John F. Blair, 1968), 223.

21. James Kinney, "Dixon, Thomas, Jr.," in Charles Reagan Wilson and William Ferris, eds., *Encyclopedia of Southern Culture* (Chapel Hill: University of North Carolina Press, 1989), 881.

22. Oliver, "Writing from the Right during the 'Red Decade,'" 132–34.

23. Ibid.

24. Karina, "With Flaming Sword," 273–74.

25. For a useful summary of the characters and plot of *The Flaming Sword*, see Daniel W. Jolley, "Thomas Dixon's Literary Crusade for Racial Purity" (Honors Essay, Department of History, University of North Carolina at Chapel Hill, 1992), 159–87.

26. F. Garvin Davenport Jr., "Thomas Dixon's Mythology of Southern History," *Journal of Southern History* 36 (August 1970): 361.

27. On Dixon's repeated use of Hose in his psychosexual dramas, see Mason Stokes, *The Color of Sex: Whiteness, Heterosexuality, and the Fictions of White Supremacy* (Durham, N.C.: Duke University Press, 2001), 218 n 21.

28. James Weldon Johnson, "The White Witch," *Crisis* 10 (March 1915): 239.

29. Wright, "Thomas Dixon," 277n.

30. Karina, "With Flaming Sword," 270.

31. Oliver, "Writing from the Right during the 'Red Decade,'" 140, 142 (emphasis in original). Oliver adds (page 142) that "on the symbolic level the 'white witch' that lures and destroys African Americans is not a woman at all but materialistic 'white' culture. . . ."

32. For Thomas's comment, see William Hannibal Thomas, *The American Negro: What He Was, What He Is, and What He May Become* (New York: Macmillan, 1901), 176–77. On Thomas, see John David Smith, *Black Judas: William Hannibal Thomas and "The American Negro"* (Athens: University of Georgia Press, 2000).

33. On Villard, Spingarn, Pillsbury, and Storey in these years, see Richard B. Sherman, *The Republican Party and Black America from McKinley to Hoover, 1896–1933* (Charlottesville: University Press of Virginia, 1973).

34. On Graves and his speech cited by Dixon favoring repatriation, see John David Smith, "'No Negro is upon the program': Blacks and the Montgomery Race Conference of 1900," in John David Smith and Thomas H. Appleton Jr., eds., *A Mythic Land Apart: Reassessing Southerners and Their History* (Westport, Conn.: Greenwood Press, 1997), 125–50, and John David Smith, ed., *Anti-Black Thought, 1863–1925: "The Negro Problem,"* 11 vols. (New York: Garland, 1993), 2:48–57. On Turner, Holsey, and Councill, respectively, see Stephen Ward Angell, *Bishop Henry McNeal Turner and African-American Religion in the South* (Knoxville: University of Tennessee Press, 1992); Glenn Askew, "Black Elitism and the Fail-

ure of Paternalism in Postbellum Georgia: The Case of Bishop Lucius Henry Holsey," *Journal of Southern History* 58 (November 1992): 637–66; and John David Smith, "William Hooper Councill," in John A. Garraty and Mark C. Carnes, eds., *American National Biography*, 24 vols. (New York: Oxford University Press, 1999), 5:586–88.

35. Oliver devotes considerable attention to Dixon's response to Johnson in "Writing from the Right during the 'Red Decade,'" 136–37, 141, 144.

36. Roy Stanley Flewelling Jr., "Three Voices on Race: Thomas Dixon, Marcus Garvey and Lothrop Stoddard on the Future of the American Stock" (master's thesis, University of North Carolina at Chapel Hill, 1971), 29.

37. Wright, "Thomas Dixon," 283 (emphasis added).

38. Mark Emory Elliott, "Albion W. Tourgée and the Fate of Democratic Individualism" (Ph.D. diss., New York University, 2002), 92.

39. In 1905 Dixon had remarked that in *The Souls of Black Folk* "we see the naked soul of a Negro beating itself to death against the bars in which Aryan society has caged him! No white man with a soul can read this book without a tear." See Thomas Dixon Jr., "Booker T. Washington and the Negro," *Saturday Evening Post* 178 (August 19, 1905): 2.

40. Frank Smethurst, "Americans in Black, White and Red," *Raleigh News and Observer*, August 6, 1939.

41. K. W., "A Novel of Conflict," *New York Times*, August 20, 1939.

42. George Conrad, review of *The Flaming Sword* by Thomas Dixon, *New York Herald Tribune Books* 16 (September 17, 1939): 12.

43. DuBois left no record of his response to *The Flaming Sword*. When in 1940 a correspondent asked for his opinion of the book, DuBois failed to address the question. See Mrs. J.G. Cockrane to DuBois, November 10, 1940, and DuBois to My dear Madam, November 18, 1940, in Herbert Aptheker, ed., *The Correspondence of W.E.B. Du Bois: Volume II, Selections 1834–1944* (Amherst: University of Massachusetts Press, 1976), 239–41.

44. On the context of black modernism, see Houston A. Baker Jr., *Modernism and the Harlem Renaissance* (Chicago, Ill.: University of Chicago Press, 1987).

45. Dixon to Cox, September 21, 1938, Cox Papers. On Dixon's frequent use of Lincoln as an "archsegregationist" symbol, see Michael Davis, *The Image of Lincoln in the South* (Knoxville: University of Tennessee Press, 1971), 148–52, 170.

A Note on the Text

After Doubleday, Page, the publisher that had brought out *The Clansman*, rejected *The Flaming Sword*, Dixon sought "a daring young house, fearing neither man or the Devil, who will drive the thing for all it is worth." He settled on Atlanta's Monarch Publishing Company, a publisher, he wrote, "who believe as I believe on the Race Problem." In 1939 Monarch published *The Flaming Sword* in deluxe and standard editions. The deluxe edition serves as the base-text for the University Press of Kentucky edition. To maintain the integrity of Dixon's work, the editor has not corrected the author's errors of capitalization, punctuation, or spelling. He has, however, added annotations to identify or explain persons or events Dixon mentioned. The editor's goal has been to refrain from interfering with his text. The stark, malevolent power of Dixon's racial fantasies speaks for itself.

Part I

THE CRIME

Chapter 1

Angela Cameron stood before an old fashioned mirror dressing with unusual care. She was seventeen years old—intensely modern. People never spoke of her as pretty. She was too tall and stately. Yet no man in Piedmont ever looked at her without declaring her beautiful. Her face was the perfect oval of a Madonna. Her figure full and graceful, suggested exhaustless vitality. Her soft brown hair was one of the loveliest things about her. It flashed in the Southern sun with a suggestion of subdued flame, and the sparkle in her brown eyes added to the illusion.

A year ago she had been compelled to leave the Moravian Seminary at Bethlehem, Pennsylvania, because of the failing health of her grandfather. She returned to Piedmont, South Carolina, to care for him and her twelve year old sister Marie. Dr. Richard Cameron early observed that all the boys in town were hanging around the old farm house.

Her father, Ben Cameron, had made a fortune in cotton seed oil and organized a Trust of the Mills in the two Carolinas. When the Cordage Trust smashed, and the coal bearing railroads went into the hands of receivers, the ensuing panic wrecked his corporation. He sold the Cameron town house with its furnishings, surrendered every dollar he possessed to his creditors and returned with his father to the old homestead in the country.

Dr. Cameron had given him the town house when he married and set up housekeeping, on the overthrow of the Negro regime, but held the farm. Working with desperate energy to make a living, he came home on a cold night drenched to the skin, went down with pneumonia and died within ten days.

The people who had followed him through the battles of the Civil War and the horrors of Reconstruction built an equestrian statue to his memory in the Public Square. Austin Stoneman's daughter, whom he had married on the triumph of the Klan, could not adjust her life after his passing. She had worshipped her daring husband and began to fail from the day he died. She rallied a few weeks, saw the statue unveiled and heard the eloquent tributes friends paid his memory. Then she took to her bed and in three months she was dead.

The elder Cameron fought to make a living on his run down thousand acre farm by letting it to share croppers, but failed. Their laziness, shiftless ways, lying, cheating and continuous demands brought him to ruin. The farm was advertised to be sold for taxes. A miracle saved it. His old butler, Nelse, who lived in Greenville, had made a little fortune. The moment he heard of the plight of his former master, he came to his rescue, paid the taxes and the mortgage, discharged all the poor whites, reorganized the black share croppers under an 'efficient Negro foreman and moved into his old room behind his master's. There was no more lying or cheating and the farm was now paying enough to meet the household expenses and save a little.

Dr. Cameron had made the day of annual settlement a public occasion on which he sought to bring about more cordial relations between the white and black races. There was a barbecue celebration on these days, with two long tables, one for whites and one for blacks, built under the spreading oaks on the lawn.

This barbecue and the Doctor's annual speech to assembled blacks and whites had become a custom of the County's life. And since Angela's return from college every young blade in the town of Piedmont was sure to be there, without the slightest interest in what her grandfather might say in his speech.

She was dressing for the barbecue with a haunting feeling that the day would be an eventful one in her life.

The crowd of boys who would come were of minor interest. The "crowd" had narrowed in her mind to two men. She had promised one of them an answer today. But she was not ready to give it. Phil Stephens was the catch of the town, handsome, brilliant, with plenty of money, an honoured name and the best young lawyer in the County. She liked him, and he had been her mother's favorite. Yet somehow he failed to touch to depths of her being as the other—called by many a poor white boy. He had been a tenant once on her grandfather's land before his own father's death. He was now a carpenter earning fair wages. She missed her mother this morning, yet knew what would have been her answer and frowned. Elsie Stoneman, born in Pennsylvania, had become an aristocrat of aristocrats on marrying Ben Cameron, Confederate Soldier and Klan Chieftain. The idea of her daughter's marriage to a poor white would have been unthinkable. She couldn't have talked with her mother about this even if she were alive. Her grandfather could give her no help. If she got his attention long enough he would side step the issue with a kiss and tell her to run along and not take life too seriously at seventeen. Certainly she couldn't get his attention today. He was downstairs now in his room rehearsing his speech—a thing he had never done before. He tramped the floor, stamped it and raised his voice at times to full declamation. There was something unusual on his mind. There was something unusual in the air. A tension she had never felt before. It was barely half-past nine o'clock and the crowd had begun to gather. The whites for the first time outnumbering the blacks. They stood in groups talking in subdued tones. Captain Tom Collier, the patriarchal leader of the town, Chairman of the School Board, had come for the first time and he was passing from group to group of the whites shaking his mane of long gray hair and touching his moustache nervously.

It was ominous. She hoped and prayed he had not come to badger her grandfather. The Captain was of the old, old South from the crown of his head to the toes of his fine boots. He had from the first treated the campaign of Liberals for "better race relations" with open contempt and had never before honoured one of these barbecues with his presence. Yet he seemed in the best of humor. His hearty laugh had in it a friendly ring of triumph that puzzled Angela.

She must hurry if she were to carry out a plan that had slowly shaped in her mind. There was a woman she could confide in. She had met her once on Sunday when a new minister had filled the pulpit of the First Baptist Church. She had not seen her again. Ann Lovelace rarely attended any congregation. People said she was queer. Some said she was a fortune-teller who picked up money from the people who consulted her. Angela knew this was not true. There was a look of strange power that had drawn her to the woman the first and only time she had seen and spoken to her.

The girl rose with quick decision.

"I'll see Ann Lovelace."

She descended the stairs and passed through the gathering crowd toward a path that led into the woods to a cottage on a little farm a quarter of a mile away.

Captain Collier tipped his hat and deliberately stood in her path after a graceful bow.

"Pardon me, my dear Miss Angela," he smile'd. "Let an old man tell you that you're a gloriously beautiful girl worthy of the gallant father and gracious mother whom I loved as my own children."

"Thank you, Captain," she gravely answered.

"In spotless white today," he went on, "I see in you the incarnation of the Old South for which your father fought—" he paused and dropped his voice—"and now that I've passed the time of day, my dear, will you tell me if your grandfather got the book I sent him a week ago?"

"Yes," the girl nodded. "He did. I took it to his room. It must be the book that's exciting him so this morning."

"He's excited?" the Captain inquired.

"Stamping the floor and declaiming his speech so loudly you can hear him even here if you listen."

"Good!" the patriarch breathed as he stood aside to let her pass.

She paused for a moment at the door of the little cottage, already, in May, clothed in a robe of red roses. She must tell this woman the truth about her life or not go in. She hesitated a moment at the thought of any one knowing her secret—then she sounded the brass knocker and waited.

Ann opened the door and greeted her tenderly.

"I'm so glad to see you, Angela. I've thought of you often since the day I caught your eye in church."

"And I've thought of you," was the simple answer. The older woman studied her for a minute. "What is it, darling, I can see something is troubling you."

"I am greatly troubled, Mrs. Lovelace. I've come to you because I feel you'll understand and there's no one else I could go to."

"I'm honoured in your confidence. Tell me what's on your heart. Maybe I can help. I will if I can. Sit down here."

She drew the girl to a chair beside the open window and took one beside her.

"Two men are going to ask me to marry——"

"You're sure?"

"Absolutely. I promised to give one of them an answer today."

"He *has* asked you then——"

"Yes. He's a fine boy, too. The young lawyer, Phil Stephens."

"I know him and I agree, a fine boy."

"The other some people call a poor white man. He's nothing of the kind really. He's poor, yes, but his people are the best Scotch Irish stock of the South. His family came here from the Valley of Virginia. They are of the Patrick Henrys—to a man patriots. His father, David Henry, fought in my father's regiment. He loved him and was one of his right hand men in the Klan uprising which overthrew the Reconstruction Negro Government. The son is worthy of his father. A brave clean boy, David Henry. He's no longer a tenant farmer. He has learned the trade of a carpenter and makes good wages. He has saved a little money. I've taught him to read and write."

Ann smiled. "And held his hand to shape the first letters, no doubt?"

"Why, yes, I did." Angela blushed. "And the touch of his hand made my nerves tingle."

"And you don't feel that way with Phil?"

"Mildly."

"The poor boy has asked you to marry him?"

"Not yet. But I can make him when I wish."

"And why don't you?"

"I don't know. Something seems to hold me back. I'd break with the aristocratic traditions. Yet I feel my happiness, true happiness, can be found in David. What shall I do?"

"There's only one thing, my child. Seek God—and ask His guidance."

The older woman's dark eyes searched the girl's face. Angela looked into their depths for a moment and asked with quiet intensity; "What is your religion?"

"I don't know, my dear. I haven't any by the orthodox standards, maybe. My people were Quakers in Winston-Salem. I was a Cannon, of Uncle Joe's family. I wanted to study Life and Truth and Uncle Joe gave me the money to go to College. The most wonderful College in the world, I think. The School of the Great White Brotherhood in San José, California. They are seekers after Truth and profess no religion save the purpose of discovering Truth and realizing the Presence of God in human life. When I came back to my home in North Carolina I met John Lovelace. He was a poor white man of little education, but fine character. I married him and we've been very happy."

The girl rose laughing softly; "So you advise me——"

"No, no, dear child, I don't advise you. Go into your room and lock the door and seek God's will. Be still and think about Him. That is prayer. And God in your own soul will speak to you. He will advise you and you will not make a mistake."

"Lock myself in my room, now, this morning?"

"As soon as you get home."

Angela nodded: "I'll try it."

She hurried back through the silent woods with a lighter heart. There was soothing in the presence of Ann Lovelace. A strange power came from her personality.

"Be still—be silent," the girl repeated. "I thought 'the silence' of the Quakers was just a ceremony of their queer religion. I didn't know it meant trying to realize the Presence of God. I wonder if it will mean anything to me, a silly outsider?"

The crowd had rapidly increased. She passed through them still more surprised at the increasing number of white people. Captain Collier had something up his sleeve and he had called the town to witness when he drew it out. She hoped he would not do anything to hurt her grandfather, now eighty six years old. A violent scene might kill him. The Captain's cordial smile, the friendly wave of his hand as she passed reassured her. He had never liked these gatherings for "a better racial understanding" but he was too old a friend of the family to hurt Dr. Cameron.

Marie was busy arranging the tables.

Angela walked swiftly upstairs and sought the big old nursery at the back of the house. The bolt on the door sounded ominously loud as she threw it. Never before had she known it to be used. Queer, now that she thought of it. Why Southern people put locks on their doors at all was a mystery. They were never used. Only the front door was bolted when rough crowds were in town for some public gathering and there were drunken parties passing the highway at night.

Seated beside the little cradle in which her mother had rocked her she gazed out the window over the peaceful river valley clothed in the rich green of spring. Bright clouds floated lazily in the azure sky. A Negro was plowing a mule in the nearest field of cotton. Cows grazed in the pasture below the house. The world was hushed in an unearthly stillness. She could hear her own heart beat. She began to think about God. Was He in the room with her really? Was He in her heart and life as Ann Lovelace had said? If, as they had taught her at Sunday School, He is everywhere—why, it must be so. In the sweet silence she felt it was so. A tender peace began to flood her being.

What a wonderful thought that the throb of her heart was one with the sweep of wind and cloud in the sky. One with the rhythm of the sun and moon and stars. That God was all and she was a part of His Plan. Of course if He dwelt in her Soul, He would guide her life if she would let Him.

She *would* let Him! She breathed a silent prayer of submission and yearning for guidance. Suddenly the world was a glorious place in which to live. Her heart waked to new possibilities.

The revelation was startling, and she felt herself laying hold of new forces, new courage, new strength. She felt herself mistress of life and fear vanished. The hum of the gathering crowd seemed a far off accompaniment to a song of triumph in her heart.

She could face Phil Stephens when he came for his answer and give it firmly but tenderly. Clearer and clearer became her duty. She must follow the leading of her heart. God was leading. She felt it. She knew it.

Flashes of the glory of a perfect love flooded her imagination. Dave Henry had set his heart on buying a small farm and going back to the country. All right, she loved the country.

She went to the stairs to go down and meet Phil Stephens with a calm assurance which she had not dared hope for when she had first faced the day's dilemma. She paused on the first step and looked at him a moment as he stood waiting by the mantel. His face was flushed and he was mumbling to himself. A habit she had so often chided him about. He was dressed in a pearl grey suit that fitted his tall figure to perfection. His long fingers were clinched by the thought that held him.

Her heart failed her for just a moment at the idea of refusing him. Their engagement had been taken for granted by everybody in town. She liked him, too. He was jolly, good company, ambitious, a little spoiled by too much admiration, perhaps, but it had not hurt his character. He would take her to the fine white pillared mansion his father had left him. Their home would be the center of the social life of the town and country. He would go far in his career. Only twenty-four years old, he was the most successful man in both the State and Federal Courts. He had read law under Captain Collier who backed him for a future Governor of the State. He could win it, too. He was an eloquent speaker, quick of wit, daring, thoughtful.

Why couldn't her heart thrill at his touch as it did to Dave Henry? By every law of common sense, by every tradition of her class Phil was the man she should marry. Yet she was drawing back this morning with firm decision. Why? Why? She asked herself a hundred times. Their tastes were alike. Their sympathies and convictions in harmony. He was a "liberal" who sought to break the power of the past over the lives of the Southern people. He was the friend of the poor white man. He was the friend of the Negroes. He dreamed of a new South, of an uplifted prosperous people, black and white. She admired him for his brave stand. She could fight for this by his side and help him win. Yet she was not going to marry him! She came softly down the stairs and stood by his side before he knew it.

"What are you talking about now?" she laughed.

"About you, dear," he answered soberly. "Let's sit down and talk fast before this shindig begins. There's going to be a rumpus of some sort. It's in the air."

"I've felt it too," she agreed. "What is it?"

"Don't know and I don't care this morning," he rushed on. "There's only one thing that interests me—the answer you're going to give to my question—will you marry me?"

"I'm sorry, Phil, I can't say yes."

"Why——"

"There's another man."

"Another man?"

"Yes——"

"There's no such man in town. I know them all."

"He doesn't live in town——"

He stared at her in dumb misery. "You don't mean that red headed poor white boy you've been teaching to read and write?"

She nodded.

"I've wondered about him since I heard of your one man school."

Phil rose. "He has asked you to marry him?"

"He hasn't yet. But he will and I'll accept him."

"Not if I can stop you. I'll not stand by and see you sink to that man's level."

She rose and faced him.

"I'm a woman, Phil. Don't talk to me as to a child——"

"A woman! You're just a romantic seventeen year old girl—under some kind of spell."

He stopped abruptly. She laid a hand on his arm.

"I'm sorry to hurt you. If I hadn't met this man I'd have married you. My mother always wished it. I don't mean to be cruel."

"No, but you give me up for an ignorant, red headed animal."

"Please, I won't let you talk like that."

He made no reply, but watched her intently.

"You've gone mad for a moment. You just can't know——"

He sank to a seat and covered his face with his hands. She sat down beside him and slipped her arm about his shoulder.

"Forgive me, Phil, and believe me when I tell you I cannot help this. I am sorry. You will always be dear to me. I shall never forget that you loved me."

He looked at her pathetically.

"You'll not hurry into this marriage?"

"I'll marry him when he asks me."

"I just can't realize it!"

He suddenly took her in his arms and kissed her. She did not resist or respond.

"It's no use, Phil."

He nodded blindly.

"Of course. It'll hurt but I'll play my part. There'll be no ugly scenes between Dave Henry and me. He's the luckiest man on earth."

He started to leave. She threw herself into his arms and kissed him.

"Goodbye, Phil, dear!"

His answer was so low she could hardly hear: "Goodbye, darling——"

She stood then and watched him go, tears gathering in her eyes.

Chapter 2

For just a moment a doubt stabbed Angela's heart. For a moment she felt the chill of a shadow over the future as she saw coming up the steps the man for whom she had dismissed Phil Stephens. The two passed each other on the steps, each nodding conventional friendly greeting. Dave saw nothing in his rival's features that would betray his emotions.

The big red headed six footer extended his right hand.

"Hiah this mornin', Miss Angela?"

"Fine Dave—and you?"

"Never felt better. If I did I'd be gettin' scared o' myself."

She let him crush her slender hand. He held it a moment unconsciously, blushed and dropped it in confusion.

"Everything's ready now," he said. "Will you come out and look things over before we bring your Grandpa and Nelse out on the porch?"

She nodded and followed him down the steps and through the crowd to the two long improvised tables. One for the whites and one for the blacks.

The tables were of clean unpainted boards with rows of wooden plates and spoons. Hundreds of ginger ale bottles formed a center piece extending the full length of each table. There were a few white boys tippling hip flasks on the side, but the crowd was very quiet. A low hum of small talk came from the whites and subdued laughter from the Negroes.

Dave showed the great wash pots full of barbecue ready to be served.

"Did you ever see the like?" he laughed.

"Enough to feed an army."

"Captain Tom Collier saw me yesterday and asked if I was managing the meat and bread for you. I said yes. And when I told him how much I had ready, the same as last year, he smiled:

"Double it."

"I done it and he was right. It's the biggest crowd we ever had. Twice as many Niggers and three times as many white folks. What's up, you reckon?"

"I don't know. The Captain's going to start something. He brought this big crowd here and appreciates your fine management of everything, Dave."

"There's nothing I wouldn't do for you," he answered slowly, his voice dropping to low tones. "You know that don't you?"

"Yes. I know that."

"After the barbecue's over will you do me a favor?" he asked.

"Maybe—what is it?"

"I've about made up my mind to buy the old Newberry place with the burnt chimneys and the six fine magnolia trees on that hill overlookin' the river. I'd like you to look at it and tell me if it's better than the lower farm with the bottom lands."

"You think I'm a good judge of farm lands?" she laughed lightly.

He blushed again. "No, but you're a good judge of the building site, the trees, the old rose garden and the rich vegetable garden."

"Won't it cost a lot of money?" she asked gravely.

"Nobum. You'll be surprised. There's nobody seems to want it on account of the big heavy woods that come right up to the barn. They're two miles deep and not a road through 'em. Kina scary. But I like deep woods, don't you?"

"I love them."

"I can buy the old buildin' site and fifty acres of land for ten dollars an acre. Only five hundred. And I can swing it."

"I had no idea you could buy a place so cheap. I'd love to see it."

"Fine. I'll get my buggy and drive you out there the minute the barbecue's over." He paused and hesitated. "Of course, you may not like it because there are no near neighbors."

A smile played around the girl's full lips.

"That's nothing. You're not afraid?"

"Of course not," he blushed. He had caught the flicker of the smile and wondered if he had been too bold. She had maybe guessed what was in his heart. No matter. He had made up his mind that he'd tell her he loved her before the sun set if it killed him. The place to tell her was seated on the bench beneath that magnolia looking out over a winding stretch of the river. The prettiest view in the County. The old place was so lovely, every tree and shrub and flower would plead his cause.

She threw a startled look at the crowd that was now taking their seats on the board benches in front of the porch.

"My, Dave, it's time to begin. We must hurry and see that Grandpa and Nelse are ready."

Dr. Cameron was already on his way to the door when they entered. His snow white hair and dark shining eyes, with his old black butler holding his arm tenderly, made a striking picture.

"Don't try to hold me up, Nelse! I can walk as well as you," he growled.

"No you can't, neither. You look out fer dat step gwine down ter de porch. Yur foot slip ef you doan mind."

In spite of protests, the gray haired Negro guided his master gently across the door sill and down the one step.

The crowd broke into cheers. The applause came with equal enthusiasm from black and white.

Nelse led Dr. Cameron to the arm chair in the center and took his seat in one provided for him a little behind and to the right.

"Oh, you Nelse!" a Negro shouted from the crowd on the left.

"Yassah!" the black patriarch answered. "I'se right here, once mo'—praise Gawd!"

The white haired speaker of the day stood erect with remarkable poise for a man of eighty six. With more than his usual poise. From the flash of his eyes and the nervous way in which he gripped a small black book that he held in his right hand it was plain to see he was deeply moved.

When the applause had subsided the keen dark eyes rested on a shock of long white hair in the crowd on his right.

He pointed his finger and spoke in clear cordial tones:

"I see that my old friend Captain Thomas Collier, Chairman of the County School Board, has honored us with his presence today. I'm going to ask him if he will further honor us by taking his seat on the platform beside me?"

Collier rose, amid loud cheers, quickly walked up the steps, and grasped Dr. Cameron's hand.

"Thank you, Tom," the old man whispered. "You know what I'm going to say today."

"I think so."

"Sit down here and I'll speak for both of us."

He pointed to a chair on the left and his friend sat down, a curious smile playing about his mouth as his eye rested on Rex Weldon, the good looking, well-dressed Mulatto Superintendent of the Negro Schools of the County, who occupied a seat well in front among blacks. Weldon had scented trouble the minute Captain Collier had been called to the platform. It was an ominous gesture on the part of the speaker. The Captain represented the authority of the County in the control of all its schools, and he had not hesitated to express his disapproval of things which Weldon had done and particularly of one thing he had planned.

The educated Mulatto pursed his full Negroid lips and frowned. He was in for trouble. He felt it coming. He must suppress his real feelings when the storm broke, bend to it and cultivate the diplomacy of the one leader of his race whom he despised—Booker T. Washington. He guessed the secret of Captain Collier's interest in this meeting. What he couldn't guess was the bold line of attack his opponent had chosen.

The aged speaker began his talk in even low tones, his white straight hair crowning his head in the brilliant May sunshine with the effect of an aureole. From the first word he held his listeners. He seemed a spirit speaking from the shores of eternity.

"My people," he said, "for ten years we have celebrated here before this house the generous deed of my friend and servant who saved it, a shelter for my old age."

"And mine, too, Marse Richard," Nelse intoned.

"Yes, yours, too, Nelse. We've lived here together, friends and comrades as in the days before the war. I have rejoiced through these ten years in seeing better relations slowly grow between the black and white races. The crimes of Reconstruction drove us apart and the gulf that separated widened and deepened. Until under the inspiring leadership of the greatest Negro born in America, Booker T. Washington——"

He paused until the applause had subsided, applause coming equally from black and white except from Rex Weldon and a little guard of Negro School teachers who surrounded him.

"Until Booker T. Washington led the way to a better understanding between us. This great black man is teaching his race the lessons of industry, thrift, character and sterling manhood. He is teaching them to avoid politics as a pestilence. He is teaching them to demand nothing until they have proven themselves worthy to receive it. He is telling them to do their duty first as good citizens and that their rights will come in due season. He has given to both races new hope and inspiration."

He stopped short and fixed his flashing eyes on Rex Weldon.

"Now comes a new leader who would destroy all this, and array race against race in another war of hate. I hold in my hand a little black book by a Mulatto Professor in Atlanta University written with the deliberate purpose of stirring the worst passions—a firebrand thrown into the imaginations of ten million Negroes. Let me quote you a few samples of its teachings."

He opened the book, adjusted his glasses and read:

"'The dull red hideousness of Georgia.'"

"This man earns his bread as a teacher in Georgia, and thus brands the State whose hospitality he enjoys. You may be sure that no Negro born in Georgia ever penned such a sentence. That no Negro born a slave in that state could have penned it. No. Professor W.E.B. DuBois was born in Massachusetts. His people never knew slavery, at first hand, or second hand. All he knows of the history of our states and our people he drew from the imagination of Abolition fanatics who caused the Civil War. Again I read: 'Slavery was indeed the sum of all villainies, the cause of all sorrow!' This from a man who knew absolutely nothing about slavery except from sources of ignorance and prejudice.

"Hear him once more in speaking of the ignorance and poverty of the Negroes when emancipated: 'Nor was his burden all poverty and ignorance. The red stain of bastardy, which two centuries of defilement of Negro women had stamped upon his race, meant not only the loss of ancient African chastity, but also the weight of a mass of competition from white adulterers.' His reference to ancient African Chastity again stamps the writer an ignoramus on the history of the Africa from which our Negroes came.

"We are next informed that the white South is yet uncivilized. 'As the South grows civilized. The South is still an armed camp for intimidating black folks. Such a waste of energy cannot be spared if the South is to catch up with civilization.'

"He tells us that two million Mulattoes in the United States testify to the rape of two million helpless black women by white brutes."

A loud laugh from his white listeners drowned his voice.

"It's no wonder you laugh at the shameless lie. You know and I know, and every black and white man of the old South knows, that the rape of Negro women by white men is the dream of an Abolitionist fool. It didn't happen.

"And we now reach the heart of the DuBois message in an implied teaching from Frederick Douglas that the solution of the race problem in America will be found in ultimate assimilation (intermarriage) through self assertion and on no other terms."

A storm of hisses broke from the whites.

"The conclusion of this little black book is found on page 206: 'Some day the awakening will come, when the pent up vigor of ten million souls shall sweep irresistibly toward the goal!'

"Could a more devilish incitement of riot and bloodshed be put into a black man's hand than this?"

He paused, threw the book down on the table and drew his figure stiffly erect in spite of his age.

"My friends, the time has come for the old South and her children to face an ignorant world and tell the truth about the Negro in Africa and America. The truth about Southern Slavery, and the racial inheritance of the black man. This volume rests on two poisonous lies which have been repeated since the war until millions of people North and South believe them. Accept them as axiomatic truths.

"The first of these lies is the most dangerous. That the Negro was torn from a home of freedom and ancient chastity in Africa and sold into a cruel and barbarous slavery.

"What are the facts? I shall speak to you with the assurance of positive knowledge. I'm going to tell you something now that no one before me knows except the two people concerned in my story."

He paused and looked at Nelse who waved his arm and cried:

"Tell 'em, Marse Richard. Tell 'em and let 'em walk humble before de Lawd!"

The speaker nodded and went on:

"Long before the war my father went to Charleston to secure more men for his four farms. A great slave ship, commanded by a Yankee skipper, was landing its cargo. I was a boy of fourteen. He took me with him. I went to the slave market and watched the scene. Among the group of men and women to be sold I caught the bright eyes of a little black boy of my own age. He smiled at me—a winsome boyish smile. Two rows of white teeth lighted his face with a joy of life that was unmistakable. He moved to the edge of the railing, leaned over and beckoned to me. I answered his call, came close and felt a warm hand grip mine. He made quick gestures that asked me to buy him for myself when he should be put on the block. I nodded my consent and asked my father for him. He laughed goodnaturedly and agreed.

"When the auctioneer turned him over to me I caught his hand and led him to our carriage. He kissed my hand and I felt the tears of gratitude. We became inseparable companions. From the day we met there has never been an hour in his life that he wouldn't have died for me."

"Dat's de truff, Marse Richard!" Nelse intoned.

"There's never been an hour in my life that I wouldn't have died for him."

"Dat's so, too, sah!" came the low tones again.

"I taught him to speak the English language. In two years he could speak it as well as the best of the servants in our house. In long hours of play and boyish confidence he told me of the life in Africa from which he had been taken by the slave traders. From him I learned that there is no such thing as ancient African chastity. That virginity there was a thing to be bartered, an item of property to be sold to the highest bidder by the girl's father. That polygamy is the only form of marriage known. That every wife is a slave. That her husband beats and abuses her—kills her if he feels like it. That the only work ever done in the home or field is done by women. That women are the beasts of burden. That the African man spends his entire life hunting and fishing, and living off women. That ignorance and superstition rule all life. That the witch doctor was the most powerful man of every tribe. That when a member of the tribe dies, the witch doctor hunts for the witches, and sentences them to death without appeal or mercy. That more boys and girls, men and women, were murdered by these witch doctors than were ever sold into slavery.

"That the cheapest thing in Africa is human life. The business of the tribe is to make war on their neighbors, a savage war of extermination. All prisoners are killed except those reserved as slaves. In their rejoicing over victory hundreds and thousands are slain in their ceremonies. Sometimes they break their bones and bury them alive and the people dance over the still panting and convulsed bodies covered by a thin layer of dirt through which legs and arms protrude. Sometimes they are driven to a slaughter pen, their throats cut, their brains beaten out of their heads and the trunks thrown to yelling hungry mobs to be eaten at their cannibal feasts.

"The African home of the well to do is a mud cemented hut constructed of bones, skulls and skeletons. The furniture, decorations, and utensils are of human skulls and bones. For ornament they pile these in rows, squares, and triangles. Or in piles like cannon balls in our arsenals. Stick them in walls, pile them in baskets and heap the store room with them. There are skull head walking sticks, jawbone necklaces and trinkets of all sorts of bones.

"The king dances among skulls with a skull headed sceptre in one hand, a skull capped sword in the other. When tired he sits on a skull stool and drinks out of a skull. At the festivals of his tribe he pays tribute to his dead ancestors' graves by drenching them with fresh human blood. The usual tribute is fifty dead bodies piled about the grave with fifty heads displayed on poles.

"When the king of Dahomey died more than three thousand men and women were killed in his honor. The royal widows killed each other until it pleased the new monarch to stop them. The new ruler dips his hands in the blood of the sacrifices, licks them and orders the blood to be used in mixing the cement mud for his new house. The Prime Minister is the executioner and for a trinket he will cut off a man's head for the amusement of any traveller. If a traveller gives the king a new gun he sends a page into the crowd outside to kill a man to see how it works.

"The aged and infirm are knocked in the head and thrown into the brush to be eaten by beasts when they are not eaten by their own families. If twins are born, or a babe with a tooth, they are thrown into the brush naked to starve or be eaten. Their dances invariably end in promiscuous sex debauchery that cannot be described before this audience. And yet we have an 'ancient African chastity!'

"Africa is the original breeding place of human slavery. Five men and women out of every six in all Africa are slaves. The bondman is so common he is the unit of currency. Values are reckoned, not in dollars and cents, but in human bodies. Of their people sold by traders for shipment to America nine out of every ten were the slaves of brutal black masters.

"On the march to the Coast every man or woman, boy or girl, who became faint or sick was knocked down, thrown into the brush, and left to die. The slave who was lucky enough to live through the ordeal of his trek to the Coast and the milder passage of the ship, moved from hell into a paradise when he reached a Southern white man's plantation. And now the Mulatto of the North, reared on the superstitions of Abolitionist fanatics, appears on the scene today to teach our black friends the glories of savage jungles! The time has come to tell the world the truth. I have learned the truth, not only from the lips of my friend and comrade of a life time, I have read every book of African travel on which I could lay my hands and every one of them confirm and enlarge his story.

"The second poisonous lie on which this Mulatto's book rests is that Slavery in the South was a thing of unspeakable cruelty and bestiality. The truth is it was the mildest form of human servitude in all the records of humanity. It was a great school in which millions of Negroes were taught the first principles of civilization. A school which bridged for them the chasm of a thousand years of progress.

"We are told today of the cruel lash of the Southern master. The slave was whipped less than the white boy in school. It was an age that believed in the Scripture's line: 'Spare the Rod and spoil the Child.' The master who beat his slaves was in every community the exception.

"A brilliant Southern woman has recorded the facts so simply, I quote her words: 'Little Negro and little white children grew up together, played together, forming ties of affection equal to almost any strain. The servant was dependent on his master, the master on his servant. No class of labor on this earth today is as well cared for as were the Negroes of the Old South. Age was pensioned, infirmity sheltered and manhood clothed and fed with the best the land afforded.'

"When the Civil War came, and our boys were at the front, the Negro cared for his loved ones, tilled the fields, harvested the crops. And when a coffin came back home from the front he buried the dead and watered the grave with his tears. In all the holocaust of war he never lifted a hand against his master or his people. A single slave insurrection in the South would have decimated Lee's Army and ended the war. Why didn't the Negro rise against his master in this dark hour? There is but one answer. Because he loved his master and his master loved him. Poor old insane John Brown believed slavery the sum of all villainies. He raised the money in the North, bought rifles, iron pikes and oil soaked torches and invaded our soil to drench it in the blood of a servile insurrection. Yet when he captured Harper's Ferry, which commanded the gateway to the great black belt of the South, and put his iron pikes and oil soaked torches in the hands of the Negroes, not a hand was lifted against a master, not a torch was applied to a single house. This fact alone gives the lie to the slander of this book. Why didn't they strike? For the same reason that led this black man, sitting here by me today, to come to my rescue in my age and poverty. They loved their white people as mine loved me.

"The weakness of Negro character today has not come from his alleged suffering as a slave of the South. His race inheritance of six thousand years of savagery in the African jungle is the source of all his troubles. And with all his inheritance of the jungle, when uncorrupted by fools, the Negro is one of the most lovable of men. His sense of music, his laughter, his joy of living, have made my life richer and more beautiful. I thank God for having known and lived with him. I'm sorry for the cold Northerners who have never known him as I have known and loved him.

"There can be no hell too deep for the scoundrels who first sowed hate in his heart during the days of Reconstruction. There can be no hell too deep for the men who are trying to rouse in him hatred of the Southern white man today. For weal or woe our lives mingle beneath the blue skies of the South. We must work out a way of living that is sane, sound, and serene. It can not be done by proclaiming lies.

"And now I'm going to be a little personal."

He stopped and fixed his gaze on Rex Weldon who had slumped lower and lower in his seat as the speaker had scored his favorite leader.

"I see here today, the young teacher of his race in this County, the Superintendent of our Colored Schools who has made the tragic mistake of inviting Professor DuBois of Atlanta, author of this book, to address a mass meeting in Piedmont in the interest of the higher education of the Negro. Has he any explanation to make to our people? If so let him rise and make it."

Without hesitation Weldon rose and there was a moment of tense silence.

"Permit me to thank you, Dr. Cameron, for the opportunity you give me to speak a word to the people. I am sorry that I extended the invitation to my teacher of the Atlanta University. Knowing him personally, a great admirer of his solid scholarship and character, I had not read his book with the eyes of the South. To me his essay was a cry of pain from a black man's soul living under conditions that hurt his pride. I can see, however, the other side as I've listened to the caustic speech of indictment today. I will at once withdraw my invitation and substitute for the oration he would have made another parade of our school children through the streets of Piedmont which you so kindly received last year."

He took his seat to a round of applause.

Captain Collier muttered loud enough to be heard by Angela and Dave, who had sat spellbound on the steps:

"Damned smart Nigger, if you ask me. Too smart to live much longer in these parts."

Silence followed the applause and Dr. Cameron again faced the audience.

"I congratulate the Superintendent of Colored Schools on his good sense and sound diplomacy. He has done his part today to heal a breach and lead us again to more cordial relations of the races. And now let us all fall on thc food and make ourselves at home."

Round after round of cheers greeted the speaker and friends crowded about his chair shaking his hand and Old Nelse's with equal cordiality.

Angela cried:

"Why, Grandpa, you're a *great* orator. I had no idea!"

"Cose he is, chile," Nelse broke in. "You orter heard him in de ole days befo' de war. He could mop up any ob 'em dat come on de stump agin him in dis County. An I was right dar ter holler fur 'im, too, dat's me, yassam."

Chapter 3

When the crowd began to gather at the tables, the Negroes were laughing and chatting, a flock of blackbirds, unconscious of the clash of races involved in Dr. Cameron's speech and Rex Weldon's reply.

Its meaning was not lost on Weldon. His heavy jaw was set, his full lips pursing as if to suppress a torrent of words he dared not speak. His first assistant and half a dozen of his more intelligent teachers gathered around him, expressed in low tones their sympathy and congratulated him on his quick wit in meeting an ugly situation.

He merely frowned, held his silence a minute, and then spoke with deliberation.

"You people stay and see that our kids are well fed. I'm going. I'd choke if I tried to eat. We've not heard the last of this."

The group did not move and he waved them toward the table for the blacks.

"Run along now and do your best to make our children happy. Collier, the old white buzzard who roosts in the top of our School Board, approaches. I'll have to speak to him before going."

The teachers went to the table as the Captain came up.

He held the Superintendent's eye for a moment and quietly said:

"I'll hand it to you, Rex. You're a smart boy. Don't agree with you always. But still kind o' proud of your bright mind."

"I think I said all that was necessary," the Mulatto broke in.

"Sure. Sure. You did it up brown. Come around to my office at nine o'clock tomorrow morning and let's have a talk."

"You're still not satisfied with my apology?"

"Quite. But I've a lot of things to say to you about the future."

Weldon closed his teeth with a silent oath, but answered suavely.

"I'll be there at nine, sir."

"Be waiting for you—goodbye."

Collier turned abruptly and joined his neighbors at the white folks' table.

Angela and Dave passed from table to table and saw that each plate was heaped with good food. She looked for Phil hoping that he might have regained his poise and returned. But he was nowhere to be seen.

When the crowd had cleaned the tables of every scrap of food and every bottle of ginger ale, they told Marie to have the boys clear the place, knock down the tables and stack the benches.

Dave smiled into Angela's happy face.

"Shall I get my buggy? I've a good horse."

"No," she answered slowly, "let's walk."

"It's nearly a mile," he protested, "and I'm proud of my buggy. It's a brand new one."

She shook her head.

"I love the path through the woods. We go by Ann Lovelace's cottage, don't we?"

"Yes, how'd you know?"

"I know Mrs. Lovelace and I've heard the old Newberry place is not far from hers."

"Taint mor'n half a mile further on. She'll be my nearest neighbor—that is if you like the place and I buy it."

They walked along the edge of the cotton field toward the woods. The air of the Southern spring was wine. The dewberry vines in the fence corner were in full bloom. Blue birds were chirping in the edge of the woods. A woodpecker made them ring with his triumphant hammer. A mocking bird sat in the top of a cedar in the hedge and called a joyous song to his mate.

A plow stood in the furrow where the Negro plowman had left it when he had called it a day and hurried to the barbecue.

"Don't you love the South, Dave?" she cried.

"Never knowed anything else."

"I've been North. The spring up there is cold. Flowers bloom and birds sing a little, but with a kind of restraint. Down here nature laughs and tells us to laugh. The sunshine fills the world with joy and our hearts sing. It's glorious—don't you feel it?"

"Never felt it in my life as I do today when you tell me."

Ann Lovelace stood in her doorway framed with garlands of roses, and waved a friendly greeting. Angela returned it with a joyous laugh and Dave bowed sedately.

"A remarkable woman," she observed.

"She don't go to church much," was the sober answer, "but I heard a woman say the other day that she's a saint."

"She'll be a wonderful neighbor for you."

They walked in a tender silence through the woods that ringed the old Newberry place, suddenly stepping into the warm sun of the clearing and the garden.

"I reckon that's the richest vegetable garden in the County," Dave said. "They tell me the soil's two foot thick and it'll grow anything—strawberries in winter time."

They passed the iron gate still swinging with hinges from heavy stone posts and took the pathway to the hilltop where the "big" house once stood. It was hedged by two rows of dense boxwood now six feet tall.

"Aint these boxwoods pretty?" Dave asked proudly as if he already owned them. "They tell me you could sell 'em for a hundred dollars. Money couldn't buy 'em if I owned the place."

"I should say not."

"And them fine magnolias have blossoms over a foot long. They're fifty years old, bloom all summer and stay green all winter—aint they fine?"

"Fine, David."

They stopped at the ruins of the house.

"Them two chimneys—fine bricks enough to build a nine foot foundation for a new house and a new chimney with a big fireplace," said David.

"You like a big fireplace?"

"Sure. Don't you? Big enough to put a four foot cordwood log in."

"Yes, I like that too. And you'll have enough brick bats and old mortar to make a hard driveway up the hill."

"Gee, I hadn't thought of that—it's so," he agreed.

"But I see the most beautiful thing of all—the long view of the river winding through that green valley!"

"It's pretty, aint it?"

"So peaceful, it makes you think of heaven."

"You like it all, don't you?"

"It's the most beautiful building site I've ever seen, but why, David, do you wish me to like it?"

"Because if you like it, I'm going to buy it."

She looked at him tenderly and he blushed.

"You wouldn't buy it unless I liked it?"

"No."

"Why?"

She was smiling at him now, her eyes holding his.

He dug a toe into the soft earth, blushed again, looked up with a sudden bold lift of his strong body and said solemnly:

"Because I love you, Miss Angela——"

"Must you say Miss Angela?"

"No, my darling—no."

He took her in his arms and crushed her. Held her in silence for a minute and when she lifted her eyes to his he kissed her tenderly.

"It just seems too good to be true," he smiled.

"Why didn't you speak sooner? Didn't you know I love you?"

"I felt it. But you seemed so far above me, so beautiful. God never made an angel that could hold a candle light to you!"

"You'll always think that?"

"As long as there's breath in me. You see I was brought up on a farm in the backwoods, no chance for an education or to learn anything except to hold a plow, drive an ox or dig a ditch, and work like a dog since I was a little boy. Then I met you and the light of your face just blinded me. And when you put your warm hand on mine and taught me to write I nearly dropped dead with joy. Didn't you feel my heart a tremblin'?"

"Yes, and felt my own heart quivering, too."

"You so bright, so refined, so well educated, it just seemed you couldn't stoop to teach a simp such as me."

"But you are so eager and willing to learn. It's a joy to teach a man like that. We've just begun. Lift up your head and face the world. You've the best blood of America in your veins. I'll never find fault as long as you love me. How long will that be?"

"Forever—so help me God."

He led her to a seat under the magnolia.

"Sit down here, honey, let me look straight into your eyes, while you tell me some things. Phil Stephens is in love with you too, isn't he?"

"Yes. He asked me to marry him this morning."

"And you turned him down for me!"

"For you——"

"I'm not worth it, honey, but I'll try to make you proud of me."

"We'll study together. I'll get the books and we'll read them to each other."

"You'll be willing to live here with me in the woods in the little house that I'll build?"

"Yes. You can do anything in life you set your hand to. You're a poor man. What of it? Everybody in the South has felt poverty. My proud father was so poor he was hungry many a day. So poor he did his own cooking and washing without a murmur. Many men have risen to the highest place in

America who started at the bottom. Abraham Lincoln did. Andrew Johnson did. Johnson's wife taught him to read and write after they were married and he became the President of the United States."

"His wife taught him to read and write after they were married?" Dave asked.

"After they were married. You and I will go back to the farm, feel the earth beneath our feet, start from the bottom and work and grow in a world of unbelievable beauty."

"You'll begin to pick up my mistakes right away, won't you?" he asked humbly.

"Right away and we'll get married the day you finish the little house you've dreamed for me on this lovely hill top."

"I aint got enough money yet."

"Don't say aint, David."

"All right, M'am, I won't!" He laughed and kissed her. "How many rooms you want in the house and what kind?"

"I've got the plans—from a book."

"You've picked 'em out already?"

"A month ago."

"Well I'll be doggoned!" he smiled. "And me tiptoeing around you afraid to say boo!"

"You were a little slow."

He kissed her again.

"You're making up for lost time. And I like it."

"But, honey," Dave frowned. "I've barely enough money laid by to make the payment on this land for the deed. It's going to take time."

"No it will not. We'll begin to buy the lumber and haul it here next week. I've a little dowry of six hundred dollars left for my wedding day by my mother. The Trustee told me he'll begin to advance it the day I announce my engagement. He thought, of course, I was going to marry Phil."

"Now you'll not live in that grand old white pillared house!—You'll like the little one we'll build better?"

"A thousand times, David."

"All right. We begin next week. Show me them plans."

"Don't say 'them' plans—those plans."

"I get you, my teacher. I won't do that any more—see if I do!"

Marie met them at the gate.

"My, you two look happy! I'll bet you're engaged?"

Angela took her sister in her arms and kissed her.

"We are."

"Can I have Phil now?" Marie whispered.

"Why you baby!"

"I'm thirteen years old. A woman too, and you know it. I'll set my cap for him!"

"All right!" Angela laughed.

Marie seized Dave's hand.

"Congratulations. Glad you won, David."

"Thank you, Miss Marie."

Chapter 4

Captain Tom Collier held his position as leading citizen of Piedmont, leading member of the Bar for the County and the State, not because he was an aristocrat of the old regime. He boasted his democratic principles and he practiced what he preached in life. For the pretensions of aristocracy he had a genuine contempt. At heart he was a man of the people.

At sixty five, his long hair was white, but his face was bronzed a healthy tan, and he walked with body erect as firmly as the day he volunteered to fight for the Confederacy. He had never forgotten his military training in the four years of the Civil War, through which he rose from the rank of private to the command of a regiment, though he attained only the title of Captain. He won his promotion by gallant conduct on the field of battle. He would have scorned promotion on any other ground. He was a brave leader and commander.

This trait was an inheritance of race on his father's side through a long line of English farmers who had married Huguenots. He built his house on a piece of his father's plantation and became a gentleman farmer of the South Carolina hills, the country of John C. Calhoun.

He was a voracious reader of the best current literature. He made no pretensions to Latin or Greek though he had studied both at Princeton in taking his Bachelor of Arts Degree. His Huguenot wife had made him a student of French literature. He had followed with keen interest the new school of French thinkers in the development of Psychology and Social Science.

In his practice of the law and his conduct of the School System of the County, he never jumped at conclusions. He never went off half cocked. He had sent a copy of the DuBois book to Dr. Cameron before he appeared at the barbecue, deliberately calculating its effect. The bomb had exploded at exactly the time he had set. He was still smiling at the reverberations. On the subject involved he was loaded for bear. The moment he had read "The Souls of Black Folks" he began a thorough study of the author's character and history. Through his correspondents in Atlanta he secured every scrap of writing Professor DuBois had published; read and digested it. In addition he had in his desk a written report from an Atlanta investigation bureau.

He was at his big flat top mahogany desk in his law office at eight thirty arranging a pile of letters and books for his interview with Rex Weldon. His office was a pretentious one at which he laughed. When he had erected the Department Store building on a choice corner lot which he had held for years, his daughter had insisted that he build it six stories high and take a corner suite on the second floor for his office. He had allowed her to furnish the place with solid mahogany and scatter oriental rugs over the floors. She insisted on a stenographer in the outer office to receive telephone calls, his clients and callers and duly announce them. He'd be damned if he'd have any woman snooping in his business! He had never had a stenographer and didn't want one. They finally compromised on giving a job as typist and telephone girl to the daughter of an old client who had lost his farm and had no one to help him but his eighteen year old girl.

He pretended he didn't like her, stormed at her and swore occasionally. But she only smiled at the noise he made.

"Annie!" he yelled from his outer office. "Where in the hell's that last letter from Atlanta?"

The girl appeared at the door and answered in a soft low drawl:

"Right in the middle drawer of your desk, Captain."

"Oh, yes—yes. I remember now I told you to put it there."

She started back to her place and he yelled again.

"As soon as that Nigger Rex Weldon comes, show him right in. I'm waiting for him. And don't bother me with anything for an hour. I don't care who the hell comes. I'm busy. You understand?"

"Yessir."

He rose from his desk, walked to the window and looked out on the equestrian statue of Ben Cameron. The straggling little village of five hundred people had grown into a town of seven thousand and boasted a daily newspaper since he and Ben had ridden the highways in their Klan robes and restored the civilization of the Old South. A pity Ben had put his last dollar in a fool Cotton Seed Oil Trust. He had begged him not to do it. Begged him to go with him in developing North Piedmont across the river on the North Carolina side. But he wouldn't. Now the town across the river had three thousand inhabitants, and two cotton factories beside the cotton seed Mill. He had bought a five hundred acre farm before the first mill was erected, became a rich man and was getting richer every day. Ben had lost all, and died heart broken.

"The damned Camerons always lacked common sense!" he muttered.

A footstep at the door brought him sharply around and he nodded to his visitor.

"Come right in, Rex, and have a seat on the other side of my desk. It's wide enough to keep us from fighting."

The finely dressed Mulatto, bowed and smiled.

"I trust we'll not fight, Captain."

"I hope not this morning."

The two men held each other's gaze in silence for a moment, a feeling of deep antagonism between them.

The white haired Southerner of the Old School standing for a way of living and thinking utterly hostile to all the new Negroid leader of University training represented. Their antagonism was not a surface inheritance. It went to the deepest roots of life and thought.

"I had hoped," Weldon began evenly, "that the little speech which I made yesterday in answer to Dr. Cameron's challenge had fully met the crisis made by his attack."

"Yes, I know you hoped that. But I am sorry to tell you the hope is vain."

He paused and touched the pile of letters from Atlanta and a stack of magazines.

"You see I've read everything Professor DuBois has written and have complete reports from Atlanta on his history, his teachings and his character. And I don't like him."

Weldon moved in his chair, pursed his heavy lips, and settled low to meet the assault.

"The center of the DuBois philosophy is found in his glorification of Frederick Douglas, the Negro orator, whose final triumph was his marriage to a white woman. The thought which sums up your ideal leader's teaching is found in the phrase which expresses his solution of the Negro Problem in America—"*Assimiliation by self assertion and by no other means.*" That is to say the making of America Mulatto by the self assertion of the Negro."

Collier rose, paced the floor, returned to his chair, leaned over its back and held Weldon's gaze while a torrent of passionate words poured from his lips.

"What I'm going to say," he declared emphatically, "has nothing to do with individuals. Personally I like you, Rex. You're a fine boy. You've won your education and your position by hard work and the stamina of real manhood. You've a good mind. You'll go far in a career in this country in spite of all handicaps.

"What the South stands for alone against the world is the integrity of the White Race. The centuries of unbroken germ-plasma of the Caucasan Race. Personal friendships for individual Negroes, of the type of old Nelse, or Rex Weldon, the man of culture and refinement, have nothing to do with the fundamental issue. We stand for our racial purity. We have no race prejudices. What fools call race prejudice is the God implanted instinct of self preservation, the first law of nature.

"We grant to the Abolitionist children of the North, to our unthinking European critics the right to bring black companions to their parties, or their tables. But in the South, in physical contact with nine million Negroes, the color line must be relentlessly drawn, without deviation, without apology. The South has tried in business, in education, in science, in art, everywhere but in politics and society, to give the Negro a fair chance. As a lawyer I can testify that he gets more than justice in our courts. The problem of problems is to enforce the law against a Negro who commits a crime against a member of his race. There's always a powerful white patron there to defend him and secure his release. If we fall short of perfect justice in our courts, in our business, in our fields of labor, I'm willing to compare the record with any Northern State.

"In the matter of complete social separation we make no concessions. We are adamant. Negro newspapers raised a great hullabaloo over the arrest of a black man for talking to a white woman on the streets of Atlanta. The policeman who arrested the Negro did his duty. We will not allow the first step to be taken in approach between the races. If a Negro can stop any white girl on the streets and attempt to impress her, his next step will be to escort her home and sit down beside her in the parlour.

"The South must keep open, at all times without fail, an impassable social chasm between the races. She is the guardian, not only of the civilization of the Southern whites but of the nation.

"If we do not maintain this guard what will happen?

"If we eat with the Negro as our equal at our tables, receive them as guests and social equals we can not prevent ultimately the marriage of our sons and daughters to them. Once the social wall is broken down the assimilation of life would begin instantly. It might be slow, but as inevitable as the law of gravitation. First, of course, in the lower class of whites, then in the middle classes and finally at the top. Wealth and political power would form the entering wedge. As a race we would pass and a Mulatto, mongrel society be built on the ruins of our civilization. In that hour we cease to be a great nation and sink to the level of the mixed peoples of South America. War, pestilence, famine would be minor calamities to this tragedy. The South stands guard today over her racial integrity and will continue that stand so long as we are worthy to live. There are nine million Negroes in the South. A quart of ink can make black fifty gallons of water.

"The secret of progress and power in any people is not found in politics, but in the *quality* of their life. The black man has never shown constructive power. He has not built a civilization in six thousand years of authentic human history. His progress here is due to the teaching of the white man. Remove that and he sinks into savagery as in Haiti and Liberia.

"The thing that we refuse yet to face is that no kind of training, no amount of education of any kind, industrial, classical, or religious can make a Negro a white man or bridge the chasm of centuries which separate him from the white man.

"Expressed in the most brutal terms, of Anglo-Saxon superiority here is the basic irreducible fact. It may be all too true as Professor Kelly Miller claims that the Anglo-Saxon is: "The most arrogant and rapacious, the most exclusive and intolerant race in history." Even so this fact gives no answer to his cold blooded question: "Can you change the color of a Negro, thet swell of his lip or the beat of his heart with a spelling book or the use of a gang plow?"

"What is the difference between us? Its secret lies in the gulf of thousands of years of inherited progress of the white man and inherited savage life of the African. New discoveries of genius constitute the basis of progress and civilization. They are for all ages and all times, never young, never old. They bear the seeds of their own lives. They are cumulative. By this standard what contribution to progress have the millions of Africans who inhabit the earth made during the past four thousand years?

"Make no mistake. Education is the development of that which *is*. The Negro from whom our slaves descended has lived on the continent of Africa, the richest and most wonderful division of land of the earth, since the dawn of history, crunching acres of diamonds beneath his feet. Yet he never picked one up from the dust until a white man showed him its light.

"And now social equality with the great white race has become the passionate faith of ninety-nine out of every hundred educated Negroes in America. It is the soul of DuBois' teachings. Charles W. Chestnut, your Mulatto Cleveland novelist, believes it and proclaims it. Professor Kelly Miller, your distinguished Negro teacher in Washington, believes it.

"We can conceive of the assimilation of nine million Negroes only in the extinction of our race and character. We are told in reply that Alexander

Dumas[1] was a Mulatto. Exactly. And had France been peopled with enough men of the Dumas type she would have disappeared from the earth as an independent nation. Dumas possessed great talent as a writer of romance, but as a man and a citizen the story of his life is a stench in the nostrils of civilization.

"The Negro serves the South for one reason only—the white man needs his labor. But when he refuses longer to work under the white man, what then? The white man is now rapidly displacing him in the industrial South.

"Does any sane man believe that when the black man ceases to work under the direction of the Southern white man, this "arrogant," "rapacious," and "intolerant" race will accord the Negro the right to master his industrial system, take the bread from his mouth, crowd him to the wall and put a mortgage on his home? Competition is war—fierce and brutal. Will the white man stand idly by and accept this ruin? What will he do when put to the test? Exactly what his white neighbor in the North does when the Negro threatens his bread—kill him. When a white man, North, South, East or West, tells a Negro that he will give him equality, industrial, political, or social, he is a liar and the truth is not in him.

"We owe the Negro a square deal. I agree with the assertion that the conduct of the Negro in the South during the Civil War was a positive contribution to the moral wealth of the world. Yet this is no reason why we should, as a race, commit suicide. We owe the Negro a square deal, but can we give it to him on this continent? Unless we are willing to surrender our birthright and sacrifice Anglo-Saxon civilization?"

Weldon lifted his head.

"Which means, Captain, that you wish my resignation as Superintendent of the Colored Schools in the County?"

"You've guessed it. I'm sorry, too. You're a likable boy, Rex. It will not be easy to fill the place with a Negro of your brains. But your usefulness here is at an end after what happened yesterday. Your common sense will tell you that."

"Yes, I know."

"I've taken a lot of pains to make you understand fully my position. I've taken these pains with you because I like you and it doesn't seem fair to put on your back the burden of a whole race. You've been reading law in your leisure hours I understand under our brilliant young member of the Bar, Phil Stephens, whom I trained——"

1. Alexander Dumas (1802–1870) was a French playwright and historical novelist. Dumas's most famous novels were *The Three Musketeers* (1844) and *The Count of Monte Cristo* (published in serial form 1844–1845). See Victoria Foote-Greenwell, "The Life and Resurrection of Alexander Dumas," *Smithsonian* 27 (July 1996): 110–12, 114–22.

"By the way," Weldon interrupted, "would the young member of the Bar, to whom you refer, agree with all you've said to me this morning?"

"Perhaps not. I haven't asked him. He belongs to a growing group of so called "liberals" in the South. Whatever it means to be a liberal on an issue that has but one side. He means well. But nothing will come of his movement in the end. Just a lot of weak sentimentalism when you come down to brass tacks. He hopes to do something to stop lynching. I hope he can. The real way to do it is to stop the crimes which lead to lynching. Some of the men with whom Phil is associating himself are pusillanimous. As they take the lead his movement will fade."

"He has been very helpful to me, sir."

"Yes, I know you two grew up together—boyhood friends. That's the old personal equation again. A thing entirely aside from the issue. May I give you some friendly advice, Rex?"

"By all means, Captain. You have stirred me and given me a lot to think about. I appreciate the time and pains you have taken."

"All right. Go to New York, finish your law studies there, open an office in Harlem and go into politics. There's a powerful group of the sons of old time Abolitionists who have joined with the Socialists and Communists. They are filling heaven and earth just now with their clamor demanding for your race complete economic, political and social equality. They are pouring from the presses, in books and magazines, a torrent of vicious abuse of the Southern people. There has been nothing like it since William Lloyd Garrison[2] pronounced us savages and fiends of hell. These damned racial imbeciles have set the North against us once more and they will continue to poison public opinion for years to come. Until a few million Negroes move North and the Race Problem there becomes as acute as here. When your cold blooded Yankee goes on the rampage, we will not have race riots, we'll have massacres.

"But you can build a career before this happens. Jump in and take advantage of the fog these fools are raising. I wish you well. And I don't mind saying I hope to be proud of you yet—up there! You have a little money saved up?"

"A little—not too much."

"When you get there, and you find you haven't enough to see you through and set up your law office, let me know. Just send me your note for the amount you need and I'll cash it without security beyond your signature."

2. William Lloyd Garrison (1805–1879) was a leading abolitionist, a founder of the American Anti-Slavery Society, and editor of the *Liberator*. His uncompromising editorials and speeches endorsed immediate, uncompensated emancipation of slaves without repatriation. See Henry Mayer, *All on Fire: William Lloyd Garrison and the Abolition of Slavery* (New York: St. Martin's Press, 1998).

Weldon rose and fumbled his hands nervously, deeply moved.

"I can't tell you, Captain Collier, how your kind offer moves me! A curious compound of love and cruelty, you old time Southerners! Thank you, sir. Thank you. If I need the help I'll not hesitate to let you know. You wish my resignation now?"

"No, no! Just go along to the end of the term. Have the big parade of your children. Our folks will stand on the side lines, laugh and cheer and say:

"Watch those damn pickaninnies! They step high. They do themselves proud!"

Chapter 5

It was sunset before the lovers turned toward the path through the woods. A whippoorwill struck the first weird note of the southern twilight. A faint shiver passed through the girl at the uncanny sound and she instinctively leaned close to Dave.

"You're not afraid of an old whippoorwill, are you, honey?"

"Not when you're here, Dave."

"There's no harm in them. Kinda queer song they sing. But I like it. I'll run 'em off the place though, if you don't like 'em."

"No, don't. I'll get used to them if you like their funny old song."

Hand in hand they returned to the house through the gathering shadows, pausing a moment to drink in the glory of the fading purple in the West. At the gate Dave stopped.

"Think I'd better tackle the old man right off the reel?" He hesitated. "Honest to goodness I'm scared to death when I think of his black eyes boring through me——"

"No, not right off the reel," Angela smiled. "I'll see him first and talk it over. You sit out on the porch and wait."

She found her grandfather nodding before a light fire which Nelse had kindled in the living room, put her hands over his eyes, and whispered:

"Guess who?"

He drew her down and kissed her in silence.

"A little bit tired after my strenuous day——"

"You did yourself proud, Grampa," she cried. "I know you're fishing for a compliment so I'll tell you that you made a hit. Everybody's talking about your speech. They said it was like old times to hear your voice ring out as you made it several times. I am proud of you."

He looked up suspiciously.

"And what are you fishing for now?"

"Who me? I'm not fishing."

"I thought I smelled bait."

"Not on my hook, sir!" she protested. "Still I would like to know if you've seen anything going on between Dave Henry and me?"

"No, I haven't——"

"Look out and maybe you will."

She ran through the door and he called her back sharply.

"Come here, darling. Don't run away like that. You've given me a terrible shock."

Angela returned, sat on the arm of his chair and slipped an arm about his shoulders.

"Dave Henry, did you say?"

"David Henry."

"Why, honey, I thought you and Phil Stephens were engaged?"

"I've turned him down for Dave."

"Why?"

"Because I love Dave with all my heart. If that's so there could be no other man, could there?"

"I reckon not. But I never dreamed of my lovely girl marrying a poor white boy."

"And why not, Grampa?"

"After all, why not, my dear. He's an honest hard working young giant. His father was as gallant a soldier as Ben had in his regiment. Your father liked him immensely. All right, darling. It's not for an old man to stand in the way of your happiness."

She stopped him with a hug and kiss.

"You're a brick," she murmured.

"Where is he?"

"Outside quaking in his boots——"

"Bring him in."

She brought Dave in, fumbling his hat and blushing.

"So you've won my girl, boy?"

"It looks that way, sir," he admitted.

The old man extended his hand.

"Congratulations, son. She'll make you a lovely wife. I do hope you'll stay here on the old place until I go——"

"Sorry, Grampa," Angela broke in. "We must build a little home of our own. Dave's going to buy the old Newberry place."

"The most beautiful building site in the County. The view of that winding stretch of the river is entrancing. I used to watch it with joy when I'd call on the family as friend or physician. You can swing it, Dave?"

"Yes sir. I've enough to buy the ground free of mortgage."

"All right, my girl and I will help on the house."

Angela again stopped him with a bear hug.

"You're the greatest, grandest Grampa a girl ever had."

"The old place is a little far out in the country. Afraid you may get lonesome by those deep woods——"

"Ann Lovelace lives near us," the girl interrupted.

The old man chuckled.

"Oh, you're already living there?"

"Yes sir," she nodded.

"Then it must be all right, dear." He caught her hand and felt Dave's big paw close on his.

"Blessings on you, my children!"

When they reached the shadows outside Angela pressed Dave's hand.

"We got by, didn't we?"

"Now what do we do next?" he asked.

"See a lawyer, of course, about the deed to the place."

"Who?"

"Phil Stephens. He's the best lawyer in town I think. I've always liked him."

"So have I," she nodded.

The next morning they astounded Phil Stephens by rushing into his office at nine o'clock. He rose with a smile, took Angela's hand and nodded to Dave.

"An unexpected honour you young folks do me this morning. What can I do for you?"

"Don't be so formal, Phil," the girl protested.

"Forgive me. I won't," he laughed. "I see how it is and I congratulate you both. You've won the most beautiful girl in the State."

"In the world I'd say, Phil," the happy man grinned.

"We'll make it the world then and its unanimous."

Angela looked tenderly into the young lawyer's eyes.

"It's fine of you to be our good friend."

"Your best friend through life. Now what do you kids want me to do? It must be important to get you here by nine o'clock."

"We're buying the old Newberry place," Angela answered. "You'll be our lawyer, won't you?"

"I'll be glad to represent you. I'll see that the deed is properly drawn and I'll search the title for you right away. Only a matter of a couple of days and you can begin to build. All I'll charge you is an invitation to the house-warming when you move in."

Angela thanked him and held his hand in lingering tenderness as she said goodbye.

Two days later, the deed delivered and recorded, they began work clearing the site for the house. Dave was worried over the roughness of the job.

"This is no work for you, honey," he complained.

"Of course it is, silly! When two birds build a nest I've always noticed that the lady bird does more work than the gentleman. I'm going to be with you every day, do my part and watch every brick laid and every nail driven."

When the last coat of paint on the outside had dried and the last touch of varnish and stain had been made on the floors, the walls, beams and ceilings, hand in hand they inspected the job and pronounced it good. The lawn required more hard work than had been expected. There were ugly sprouts and bushes to be dug up by the roots and grass had to be planted on the scarred places. The boxwood hedge leading from the house to the garden was too high. But they had to postpone trimming it until the sap went down in the fall.

The two rows of jonquils that ran along the sides of the house, they carefully cultivated for the next spring. The long rose arbor had sagged and great masses of vines lay on the ground. Dave carefully rebuilt the arbor with cedar poles and trained the vines back in place cutting away the surplus branches.

Angela had him extend the arbor ten feet toward the house and beside the new poles she planted the species of Southern rose that blooms every month in the year. Under this section she had Dave build a rustic seat from which could be seen the view of the river valley.

By the old gate stood the two majestic sentinel pillars. On the capitals was carved the old name of the place "Grandview." Angela selected a more modern name, "Hillcrest," and the foundry cast for them a bronze plate.

Late in August they planted one garden for winter vegetables. Cabbage, lettuce, turnips, kale, collards and strawberries. Angela had gotten from Mrs. Lovelace a dozen plants of an everbearing variety.

When the last loving touch had been given the place they figured the cost and there was a balance due on material of five hundred dollars. The labor had cost nothing.

"We'll clear that off in no time, honey," Dave said. "The folks we owe are all good friends. They won't push us."

"All the same I wish we were free of debt. It's the only little shadow," she complained. "Come here and rest while we drink in the beauty of the valley. There's something we must decide."

She led him to their favorite seat and he looked at her inquiringly.

"Have we forgot anything?" he asked.

"Not here. But we must decide about the wedding in November."

"I was thinking it would be this month, in September."

"No. It will take a full month to get ready."

"Lord, I can get ready in a day."

"But not a girl. I've got to have a few clothes, you know."

"I suppose so——"

"The first question is where will we be married, in the old parlour at home or in the Church where my mother married Ben Cameron?"

"At home in the parlour," Dave gasped. "I'd be scared to death marchin' down the aisle of that Church with all the boys grinning at me and nudgin' one another——"

"I like the Church better."

"Why?" he groaned.

"Because, David, marriage is a sacred thing to me, a divine ordinance the old preacher used to say at Bethlehem."

"Can't it be just as good without going to the Church?"

"Yes, but there's more to it than the tie that binds us together. The world should witness our love and our pledged faith. I'd like the witnesses to be in God's House. They'd help us make it holy."

"All right," he gulped. "Whatever you say goes with me. I'll march up that aisle, or into hell itself if you tell me that's the way you want it."

"It's settled—a church wedding?"

"Sure."

"Then I'll have the announcements engraved."

"What's that?"

"Beautifully engraved cards of invitation to the ceremony."

"May I have a few of 'em, honey?" David asked eagerly. "I've got a few friends I'll knock dead with 'em."

"As many as you wish," she laughed. "Make out the list of your friends and I'll mail them."

The furnishing of their house was to Angela a thing of intimate joy. Her grandfather insisted that she take every piece of furniture she could use from the house. She selected enough without making a single room look bare except her mother's bed room where she had slept as a baby. This room was stripped. The wide old-fashioned mahogany bed with the heavy low rolled head board and foot board the same height, was the principal piece to set first. When Dave saw it he laughed.

"Holy Smoke! Now I know why you wanted our bed room so big."

In the living room they placed the couch straight before the fire place and close behind it drew the long heavy heart pine table Dave had carefully built under Angela's direction.

"I'd like to know what you're going to do with this long table here?" he asked in wonder. "We're not going to eat on it, are we?"

"Sometimes, maybe. But most of the time it will be piled with books, magazines and papers. You and I are going to read and study beside it."

"Oh, I see," he nodded. "And we'll sit on the two long stools I built when we're studying?"

"You've guessed it, sir. This is a living room and a school room. We'll eat in the alcove off the kitchen. The table and two benches you built are perfect."

"Glad you like 'em, M'am," he bowed.

The wedding dress proved a puzzle. She was determined to use her mother's for two important reasons. It *was* her mother's and its rich material could not be bought without a great deal more money than she could afford. But the dress was too small. Ann Lovelace was skilled with a needle and gladly undertook to fit it. But no amount of letting out could conceal the luxuriant lines of Angela's figure.

Ann laughed at the finished effect.

"It's a scandal for a bride to look so voluptuous, dear, but it can't be helped, if you're going to wear it."

Angela looked into the mirror and frowned.

"No matter, I'm *going* to wear it. You can't let it out another inch, can you?"

"Not a half inch. I'm afraid now it's going to pop open. It will if you're not careful. Breathe softly as you walk up the aisle, promise me."

"I promise and I thank you so much, dear."

"It's been a joy, child. It brought back to me memories of my own wedding—a love match like yours, too."

When the announcements were out presents began to pour in from the friends of her mother and father and grandfather. Angela was amazed at their number and value. Phil Stephens sent her a set of solid silver of a hundred pieces. Dave asked him to act as best man.

"Gee, Phil, I don't know how to thank you. I know you love my girl. Everybody in town knows it. And I don't blame you. I don't see how you could help it, seein' her so often as you did. You're certainly a square shooter."

Phil grasped his rough hand: "I'm proud to be the friend of two such people as you and Angela. I can help you a little, maybe, as time goes on."

The gift that moved Angela to deepest gratitude came from an unexpected source. Captain Tom Collier brought her a silver mesh bag containing twenty-five gold pieces that counted up five hundred dollars. She stared at the treasure through happy incredible eyes.

"Why, Captain, I never dreamed you thought so much of me. May I kiss you?"

"I'll be disappointed, young lady, if you don't."

She slipped her arm around his neck and kissed him.

"That pays me with interest," he said soberly. "And now Angela, I'm going to tell you something maybe you've never heard before. . . . I owe my life to your gallant father. He saved it twice. Once on the field at Gettysburg, the second awful day of fighting at Little Round Top. He found me wounded and helpless and carried me on his shoulders to the rear. Thirty minutes later the Yankees rolled a fresh column of troops over that field and tramped the wounded into the ground. While they held it for an hour our artillery pounded them into a pulp. There was a shell hole every ten feet of the ground where I had fallen. We went back there after the war and marked the spot. If they hadn't built a monument to him in the Square here I was going to build one on that field. But the thing I see more vividly was in the black days of Reconstruction when Negroes, Carpetbaggers and Scalawags ruled this country. They had found me a hard nut to crack and had sentenced me to die. A gang of six men, disguised as Clansmen, pulled me out of my bed one night, tied my hands behind my back and started to drag me across the field to the woods to beat me to death. Your father heard the commotion, strapped two heavy pistols around him and came to my rescue. Only two of the scoundrels who had me were armed. The four of them who had no guns ran at the first crack of your father's pistol. And before the other two could draw, Ben Cameron had put a bullet through a shoulder and broken the other fellow's arm. I never saw two devils run like they did. Near as I was to death I had to laugh. Their white fake Klan robes made a streak of light through the woods. Your father kept popping at them, a pistol in each hand. It sounded like a regiment had come to my rescue and the fellows who were running thought it was two regiments. Now you know why I was Chairman of the Committee that built the monument. I like the red headed boy you're marrying too. He raised the biggest subscription of all the canvassers I sent out. His father thought yours the grandest man God ever made. He was a cavalryman in the Army and led a squadron of the Klan under Ben's leadership. Dave Henry's a poor boy but he has character. And with you to teach him he'll go far."

"You've made me very happy, Captain Tom. How did you know we would need five hundred dollars on our home?"

"A little bird told me, maybe. And maybe I just guessed it. God bless you, child, and grant you many happy prosperous years. If you ever need a friend, you know where to find him. I'd have helped your grandfather before Nelse came if I'd known the facts. I didn't. Your Grandpa is a very proud, sensitive man. He did his own cooking and washing for a year and never let a human being know his troubles."

"He was sending me to school, too, you know," she interrupted. "And how he got the money before Nelse came God only knows."

"Well, Good-bye, darling. Give my love to Dave." He passed out the door. "When your Grandpa wakes from his nap you may remind him of what I've told you, or he may think it's too big a present."

"I'll do all the thinking about that, Captain Tom," she smiled.

When Angela reached home Marie sprang a surprise on her.

"I've a favor to ask, Angela," she said demurely.

"What?"

"I think it's time to let down my skirts a little and put up my hair, don't you?"

"Maybe, darling. But can't you wait until I go and leave you mistress of the old place?"

"No. My legs are so big they embarrass me."

"All right," laughed Angela.

"I can have a new long dress for your wedding?"

"Yes, dear. And we'll get one that will make you look stunning. I never realized it before but you're as big as I am."

Chapter 6

When Dave came and she told him the news, he stared incredulously. "Why the old white turkey gobbler! I never had any idea he thought that much of you. He never come near one of your black and white barbecues until that last one when he sicked your Grandpa on Rex Weldon!"

"Well, he's made up for lost time, hasn't he?"

"He sho has."

"Did you say 'sho'?"

"Nobum, I thought I said 'surely'" he laughed. "Anyhow that gives us a house without a dollar of debt, and that's great!"

"Isn't it? He said nice things about you too, sir, and I kissed him for it all."

"Just so you don't kiss Phil. I'm a little jealous of him."

"Yes, I know. He's the finest fellow I ever knew next to you. I expect I'd have married him if you hadn't come along."

"I bet you would, too. What else has come in?"

"Let me show you."

She caught his hand and led him to a row of tables in the dining room on which the presents were piled. Dishes, glass ware, linen, blankets, pots and pans enough to furnish two houses the size of theirs.

"Won't have to buy a thing, will we?" he murmured.

"I don't know where we'll put them all."

"I'll build a big closet off the kitchen," he proposed.

The wedding day dawned a glorious Indian summer morning the first week in November. Still and warm. The mocking birds were all singing in the hedge rows.

Half the County tried to crowd into the church. They walked down the aisle arm in arm, the handsomest couple within the memory of any one in the audience. Under Phil's direction Dave was faultlessly dressed. When his new suit was adjusted his rival surveyed him with a touch of pride.

"You're a handsome dog, Dave. I hated you for a while. But I'll hand it to you. No handsomer bridegroom will walk up the aisle of that old Church in many a day."

"Much obliged, Phil," Dave muttered humbly. "Now tell me once more what to do."

He was told how to place the ring and on which finger.

"You'll stick close by, won't you?" the bridegroom asked through chattering teeth.

The crowd drew a long breath of admiration as they stood before the preacher. Angela was stunning in the shiny satin of her mother's wedding gown. Everybody in the house was thrilled at her loveliness. A few women frowned a little at the dress but they knew how Ann Lovelace had tried to make it fit with a conventional looseness Angela's figure would not permit. The boys all nudged each other at sight of Marie in her first long skirts so much like her sister they might be taken for twins.

After the wedding breakfast, at which Angela and Dave in their excitement ate little or nothing, Captain Collier's carriage, drawn by a pair of sleek bays carried them to their "Hillcrest." They planned to spend the whole afternoon roaming over the place, and Dave had promised to show her the path that led to the great swamp. He had never allowed her to go into those woods and she was eager to explore their mysterious sombre beauty. They changed clothes and ate a light lunch which Ann Lovelace had prepared.

She sat down with them in the alcove and shared it.

The bride touched her hand timidly: "It's so sweet of you to get lunch and dinner for us to-day. And so fitting. You told me to marry him you know."

"I did not! I told you to find God and ask Him."

"Same thing, Ann," the girl smiled. "You knew exactly what God would say to me."

"Perhaps I did as He once told me the same thing about John Lovelace. I'm proud and happy to be the first neighbor to break bread with you."

"I hope you'll always be our first neighbor, Miss Lovelace," Dave ventured.

She glanced at him in surprise at his improving speech and the nice way he had turned the phrase his young wife had given him.

When they rose she announced quietly.

"I want no interference with my preparation of your wedding dinner. John will be here to help me later. You two spend the afternoon beneath the trees walking reverently through their great aisles. John and I know those woods and love them. I taught him to hear the songs of the wind in their lofty boughs. Just as you're going to teach this eager boy. God bless you!"

They walked through the grounds and as they neared the woods, stopped and looked back on the white little house gleaming in its dark setting.

"Oh, David," she exulted, "I can't tell you how I love it all. I can't tell you how glad I am you're going to be a real farmer and get our living from this rich soil. The Southern white people must go back to farming. My heart smiles with a prayer in it I can't express to you. This is ours, David, our land, our home!"

"And you'll never get tired or lonely out here so far from town?"

"Never. We'll use the town for the needs it must supply. But here among the trees, the flowers, the garden, the birds, the silver winding river and green valley—we'll *live*. What a glorious day out here—how warm and still and sweet the air! Don't you love it?"

"Of course, or I wouldn't have picked it for you. But right now I can't see the house, or trees or flowers—I can only see you."

"Beautifully said. You may not be a college bred man yet, but you've the soul of a poet."

"What do you mean 'yet'?" he asked. "You're not going to make me go to college are you?"

"Yes. But here, and I'll be the president of the college and all the professors. We'll study nature first, the woods today. And then we'll read about them. John Burroughs[1] and Henry Thoreau[2] first."

"Look, honey," he whispered. "See that covey of half grown quail running down the path toward the woods?"

"Aren't they pretty. It's a pity to shoot them, isn't it?"

"No. They raise more coveys if you thin them out."

"Don't kill this covey in the edge of the yard. We'll keep them to look at."

"You expect to keep a cat, don't you?"

"Of course, and a bird dog for you, too."

"Well, the cat will run the quail out of the yard, you can bet on that."

"I'll train the cat."

"I'm afraid not. A cat's a beast and a beast's a beast. It's the nature of the tribe and the critter can't help it."

---

1. John Burroughs (1837–1921) was a naturalist author, influenced by the transcendentalism of Ralph Waldo Emerson and Walt Whitman. He was a prolific essayist on nature and a biographer of Walt Whitman and John James Audubon. See Perry D. Westbrook, *John Burroughs* (New York: Twayne, 1974).

2. Henry David Thoreau (1817–1862) was an influential nineteenth-century author and philosopher who espoused transcendentalism. Thoreau is best remembered for his philosophy of civil disobedience, later cited by, among others, Mahatma Gandhi and Martin Luther King Jr. See Walter Harding, *The Days of Henry Thoreau* (Princeton: Princeton University Press, 1992).

"I'll use persuasion. I've tamed you, haven't I? They say you're just a big handsome brute."

She gave him a hug.

He kissed her and pointed to a clump of brown along the edge of the wood.

"Know what they are?"

"No."

"Chinquapins."

"The little round chestnuts I love so?"

"They do taste like chestnuts. I've picked many a bucket full when I was a boy."

"Get me a handful now."

He shook the bush and got half a dozen and put them in her hand. She ate one and slipped the others in her pocket.

"First fruits of our woods."

The wild cherries were still on the trees a little farther on and birds were chattering among their boughs filling their craws. Persimmons were ripe. He gathered a deep brown one and put it in her mouth. The ground was covered with hickory nuts beneath the wide spreading trees. He showed her how easily they were hulled.

"I'll gather a bushel or two of them and crack them for you before the fire this winter. And walnuts too. More of the trees in the hedges are loaded with walnuts. Do you like black walnuts?"

"Better than the English ones we get from the store. I can use them in cooking, too."

"Here's the footpath that leads all the way to the pond in the swamp. Boys make it going down to swim in the summer. The water's so well shaded, it's always cool."

They stopped beneath a clump of pines that towered above the oak and ash and hickory. There wasn't a breath of air stirring below but the pine tops above were sighing. The low sweet music caught the ear with an entrancing melody.

"Captain Tom Collier owns this tract now," David observed.

She pressed his arm to her breast a moment and looked up.

"He pays the taxes, you mean, dear. We own these woods because we have ears to hear the music and eyes to see the glory of it all."

"That's right. I never thought of it that way," he agreed.

Near the pond they found a muscadine vine to which clusters of big black grapes still clung. He reached high, brought down a branch and pressed one into her mouth.

"What a wonderful flavor! Nothing like that in a store, is there?"

"I'll say there isn't."

Farther on he picked for her a bunch of fox grapes each one as large as the largest marbles boys use at school. The small wild grapes hung in endless festoons along the edge of the pond.

"Why David, I never dreamed there was so much to eat in the woods. We could almost live out here."

"People do, sometimes, when they're hiding from officers—live here for weeks at a time, especially in the fall and winter. There's something to eat all the year round. Dewberries, blackberries, wild strawberries, blueberries, persimmons, hazel nuts, walnuts, hickory nuts, chestnuts, chinquapins, huckleberries, muscadines, fox grapes—Lord, there's no end to what you can find to eat here."

"Who eats it all?"

"Mostly the game, foxes, possums, rabbits, squirrels, coons and all kinds of birds."

"Let's not kill any of them—they're ours."

The man's laughter rang through the forest.

"You're going to raise chickens, aren't you?"

"Yes. I've got an incubator and you'll build me a chicken house and a run for them."

"You can't raise foxes, possums and coons and chickens in the same back yard, honey. If I don't kill the foxes and the possums and the coons—weasels and skunks too—there will be no chickens."

"We must have chickens and turkeys and ducks."

"That's what I say. So down with the foxes and the possums and the coons! If I can catch 'em. May I keep a good coon and possum dog?"

"If they don't fight the bird dog."

"They won't. The bird dog may fight them maybe until they make friends."

"I had no idea," she mused, "how rich life could be made by the woods. It's terrible the way saw mills are cutting them to pieces."

"We have to have lumber."

"But there's a way to care for trees and still have lumber. We're going to study forestry."

The man grinned.

"Holy Smoke, if you teach me all you're layin' out, I'll be an educated man, won't I?"

"And I hope to be a cultured woman. The only way of true culture is to make it a life work. There's so much to learn, life is all too short."

They walked most of the way back in a charmed silence. As the pathway emerged from the woods, David stopped and looked back.

"There's one thing about those woods I didn't tell you, honey."

"What?"

"There's danger in there, too."

"What kind of danger?"

"There are a few ugly bears that use around the pond. And there are a lot of wild cats."

"But you're not afraid of a cat?"

"You bet I am! You know a tiger is a big cat. There are wild cats in those woods as big as an average size setter dog. One tried to get me once from the fork of a tree. I dodged his claws just in time. If he'd landed on my neck, he'd have cut my throat in a minute."

"Really?"

"You'll never go into these woods alone?"

She smiled at him tenderly.

"All right, my husband. I'll take you with me every time. There's a lot more fun with you anywhere."

"Once more before we go inside," he smiled, sweeping her into his arms and kissing her tenderly. They lingered around the house and watched the sun sink beyond the river valley in a smother of scarlet and purple.

They peeked through windows into the living room for a few minutes and saw Ann as she set the table and ordered John about the place.

She helped him move the long table back from the couch, place the knitted squares on the wood and light the candles around a bowl of roses.

"Let's go in," David urged. "I don't want John to make the fire. I'll make the first fire in our house. It's going to be a sort of sacred fire, I reckon. You know I told you to put no andirons in the fireplace."

"And I thought it a little crazy, but I humored you."

"All right. Now I'll show you why. When I build a fire flat in the ashes—I put a few in there yesterday—the wood will burn three times as long and give out twice as much heat. Andirons make a strong flue draft, send all the heat up the chimney and burn out dry wood almost like paper. I'll make the fire on the ashes, bank it tonight and it will never go out until next spring when I let it."

"I'll believe it when I see it."

"I'll show you."

"Come right in, children," Ann shouted. "The wedding dinner will be served in ten minutes. Wash your hands and pull up your chairs."

"When David has built our home altar fire that won't go out till spring. Show them, sir."

John watched him place fat pine splinters in a pile, place some kindling wood across it, lay the first three logs on top and strike a match. The fat pine blazed, caught the kindling and then the wood and in little more than a minute the three logs were blazing cheerfully.

"Makes a fire with only three logs, too," David announced. "Couldn't do that on andirons."

John Lovelace stared.

"Where in creation did you learn that, Dave?"

"Building log fires in the woods cutting timber. You see the draft comes down to the fire and that makes the wood burn slow and hot."

John scratched his head.

"Well, I'm the foreman of a cotton mill and a backwoods boy can teach me a thing like that. Thanks, son. I'll save wood from now on."

Soon the dishes were placed on the table. An oyster soup first.

They drew their chairs up and Angela asked Ann to give thanks. Her voice was very low and rich as she slowly said:

"Let us realize, dear Lord, that Thou art very near tonight. Thy first miracle was at a wedding feast. We see now Thy dear face shining on this scene. Thy name is love and these are Thy children. May their food always be sweet as it is tonight."

When they lifted their heads Dave was staring at Ann. His wife pinched him and he bent close and whispered:

"I never heard one like that before. Did you?"

"No, but it was beautiful."

"Everything but the oysters grew on our farms and came from these woods," John announced with pride.

"I tried to get everything from the land, children," Ann explained, "but we had to have the oysters. They came up today fresh from Charleston. But everything else is home made. A platter of brown juicy quail, biscuits, cornbread, yams, turnips, greens, cabbage, cole slaw, ice cream and cake."

"For heavens sake, how many quail are piled on that platter?" the bride asked.

"Just a dozen. That's three apiece if you can manage them."

"I'll manage mine!" David chirped.

"Me too," John chimed in. "I never had enough quail in my life. Maybe the girls will divide with us, Dave, if we need more than three."

From under the table Ann slipped a bottle of champagne out of a container of ice and held it up.

"This one won't count, children, as old Rip Van Winkle so often said."

Angela glanced at the window.

"Do you suppose they'll find this out and turn us out of the Church?"

"I dare them. Jesus turned water into wine at a wedding feast. I see Him smiling at us in this room now."

She filled their glasses.

"I wonder where those tall glasses came from?" Angela smiled.

"A loan for the evening, dear. John and I used them at our wedding."

She paused and lifted her glass.

"To the fairest daughter of the County on wedding the man she loves!"

"The fairest in all the world, I'll say," David added.

John lifted his glass to Dave:

"To the luckiest man in the County who fairly won the fairest girl."

When the glasses were lowered, Angela added:

"I expect I egged him on, John. I almost had to propose to him."

"I'll say he had a great teacher, young lady, almost as great as mine."

"Which reminds me," Angela cried. "A toast to Ann—to the most beautiful soul I have ever known!"

"And so say I," John agreed.

The women ate two quail each. The men three. They couldn't finish the two left.

Black walnuts and chestnuts were served with the coffee and when the feast was ended, a dispute at once arose as to who should clear the table and wash the dishes. John and Dave both volunteered and their proposal was received with scorn.

"I'll do it all myself," Ann declared. "John can carry the things into the kitchen for me."

"You'll do nothing of the sort. I'll help," Angela said. "The men will sit down before the fire and smoke until we're done."

The table cleared, the men placed it against the couch, put the books and magazines back in place, lit the stand lamps and sat down before the fire and smoked. Dave a cigarette and John a cigar.

"Can't tell you how glad we are, Dave, to have you children for neighbors."

"And that goes double, John," the young man quickly answered.

The ceremonies in the kitchen over, Ann appeared, hat and coat on.

"All right, John. We'll be going."

"Sure," he laughed rising. "These folks have no further use for us."

"There's another day you know," the bride smiled.

"But never another wedding day I hope," the woman added.

Ann slipped her arm around her friend.

"Thank you for everything, Ann. You've been mother, father, sister, brother and aunt."

"And I've had the joy of each of them in you, dear child!" was the warm response.

Their friends gone, the two sat down before the flickering fire and held hands in a long sweet silence. At the touch of hands a bright flame

rose through each strong young body and glowed in their eyes. For an hour they talked of the deep things of life and death. Dave gazed at his bride with increasing wonder at her knowledge and wisdom. And she at him with increasing tenderness and love.

At last she said:

"The fire's getting low."

He rose quickly.

"I'll put on another log."

"No. Let me see you bank it now. So I'll know how."

"It's easy."

He drew the last glowing piece of wood forward with the shovel, making a deep bed in the ashes, pressed it back and covered it.

"You haven't covered it all," she warned.

"That's enough. As it burns slow it will settle, the ashes on top, and in the morning I'll have a bed of red hot coals and put on more wood. And so every morning until next spring when we close the fire place for the summer."

"It's wonderful, if it works."

"It'll work," he answered as he sat down again on the couch beside her.

The girl watched her lover from the corner of her eye. She wondered if he would ever suggest it was bed time. She knew that he wouldn't. He was too much in love, too timid and worshipful. She would have to take the initiative, as she had before. She had placed his clothes in the spare bed room. He knew this and blushed scarlet as she looked toward the door.

"It's bed time, David," she said in a matter of fact tone.

"Yes, I know," he gasped.

"Why are you trembling so?" she asked tenderly.

"I don't know. I reckon I'm scared a little."

"Don't be, dear. You undress in your room and I'll be in our room waiting for you when you come. Stop trembling."

"Can't help it, honey," he whispered.

"Let me recite for you lines from a wonderful poem entitled 'The Prophet,' out of an unpublished manuscript, sent me by a Bethlehem schoolmate."

"All right. Maybe it'll help," he shivered.

"Listen:

"Love has no other desire but to fulfill itself.
To melt and be like a running brook
That sings its melody to the night.
To know the pain of too much tenderness
To be wounded by your own understanding of love;

And to bleed willingly and joyfully.
To wake as one with a winged heart
And give thanks for another day of living.
To rest at the noon hour and meditate love's ecstasy.
To return home at eventide with gratitude;
And then to sleep with a prayer for the beloved in your heart
And a song of praise upon your lips."

He gazed at her in awe.

"You feel like that about me, darling?"

"Yes, David. Exactly like that."

"Then I'm not afraid any more."

He drew her to her feet, lifted her from the floor into his arms and carried her into the bed room.

She looked into his shining face and cried:

"Why, David. How wonderful! You're so strong and so tender with it all."

She drew the covers down from the wide bed and touched each pillow lovingly.

"I'll be waiting for you, dear."

He strode from the room and she heard him throw his clothes on a chair, and his shoes dropped.

It seemed but a moment before she felt him enter the moonlit room.

CHAPTER 7

The week that followed their marriage brought to the lovers happiness and contentment. Angela insisted that her husband give at least two weeks to waiting on her hand and foot. Dave was eager to get to work. The fields cried for fall planting. She wouldn't hear of it yet. The Old Testament allowed young people a whole year free of toil she stoutly maintained.

"How in creation did they live?"

"The Lord took care of them."

"Yes, and He takes care o' those that take care o' themselves. But, all right," he agreed, "I'll work around the house. I can have my hound and bird dog right away?"

"Yes. They'll be good company. I love dogs."

At the end of two weeks the chicken house was built on the new scientific plans and Dave helped Angela unload into it the first hatching of two hundred chickens. He was astounded to find that his wife had installed the incubator at Ann's house a week before they were married.

Angela was in ecstasies as she shovelled the lively chickens out of the box. They fell on the prepared food eagerly and in a few minutes were running over their compartment as lively as crickets.

"Folks say they'll be fryers in about six weeks with this new fangled feed," Dave remarked.

"How can we ever kill the cute little things?"

"Can't eat 'em alive——"

"No, but you'll have to do it. I couldn't after feeding them once."

"You have to feed me, too, you know."

He built the dog kennels and bought the hound first. The dog lifted his soft serious eyes to his new mistress, came close and gently thrust his nose into her hand. She laughed at his long ears that almost dragged the ground when he lowered his nose.

"Didn't know a dog could carry such ears around," she smiled. "What's his name?"

"Boney."

"Why? He looks fat enough."

"Napoleon Bonaparte if you say it all.—a great fighter. A coon dog's no good unless he's a fighter. As a rule a full grown coon can whip three dogs. You'll laugh your head off when I tell you where I got him."

"Where?"

"From old man Adam Spake."

"Why he's on charity. He can't keep dogs!"

"That's why I got him. They gave the old man forty dollars for a month's supply for his family. He took thirty of it and bought this hound. Says he's the greatest coon dog ever born in the County. Gave me his pedigree a mile long. He cried when the Charity Inspector made him give him up. I promised the old duffer I'd take him hunting with me the first time I could go. Adam says Boney has the sweetest voice that ever called a coon trail."

"I want to go too," Angela cried.

"Now, honey, you can't scramble through the woods for three hours at a time, and in the dark too."

"I've a pair of overalls. I'm going."

"Never heard of a girl goin' coon huntin'——"

"You're hearing about it now. I want to hear old man Spake brag about the hound when he trails the coon. Poor old fellow, he must love a good hound. But it wouldn't be right for him to take all that money from his family to buy a dog. There's something pathetic in his sacrifice going without food to hear the music he loved. That's the old South in him coming out in these days of money grubbing."

"It'll be worth a scramble through the woods, I expect, for you to hear him yell when the dog opens. I went with him one night when I was a little boy and I never heard such a yell come out of a human being. There was joy in it. There was fight in it. There was something in it that stirred your blood. That's where the Rebel Yell came from, they tell me. The yell of the Southern hunter in sight of game. It was dark. The hound was a mile away, but the old man could see through blackest night. He was there in his soul if he hadn't caught up with the dog. All right I'll let you go once, just to hear the old man yell."

He brought the setter next day to keep Boney company and the table supplied with quail. He was a Llewellyn, a year and a half old, and had hunted half a season. From the moment Angela saw "Spot" she loved him. And he loved her. In violation of all good dog manners he rose gently, put his paws on her shoulders and kissed her cheek, his great human eyes pleading for her love. She stroked his head and pressed her cheek against it before Dave's command "Down, Sir," brought him to a realization of manners. He nudged his master's leg and apologized with a shamed look.

"You mustn't do that, sir," Dave scolded.

Spot wagged his tail and promised he wouldn't.

"He's beautifully marked, isn't he?" Angela said with enthusiasm. "One big brown spot on his back like a saddle. White boots on fore and hind feet, face white, ears deep red and little red spots all over his finely shaped body."

"He is a beauty," Dave agreed. "And the sweetest disposition. He'll romp and play with any kid that'll play with him. He'll get down on the grass or floor with 'em and wrestle just like another boy. He'll make a good watch dog for you, too."

"Can I go quail hunting with you?"

"If you'll let me get a few out of the two coveys in our field——"

"Not that covey we saw in the path the first day we went into the woods!"

"They'll raise more birds if you thin 'em out a little."

She shook her head. "We'll save all that covey. They're so close to the house."

"The chickens'll be right in a house and you're goin' to have me kill them——"

"Yes, but we're raising them for the table. And they don't sing. A bob white does."

"All right, Boss. I can see now I'm going to be a henpecked man. Let's take a little whirl with Spot in the lower field right now and get a few birds for dinner tomorrow. Phil Stephens is coming you know."

She flew into the house and put on her overalls while Dave got his gun, field shoes and hunting coat. He looked at her fine shoes and laughed:

"You're not going to wear those ball room slippers on a quail hunt are you?"

"What'll I wear?"

"The high top rough ones you worked on the house in."

She was ready in a jiffy and when Spot saw the gun he leaped into the air and gave a shout of joy. He didn't bark, he shouted, ran in circles, came back, leaped in the air and shouted again.

"He knows where we're going, doesn't he?" Angela laughed.

"As well as you do."

They walked into the lower field and Spot stood for a moment, his head high as he surveyed it. His keen intelligence saw in a glance the one

spot a covey of quail should be using. He crossed the field a straight streak of brown and white his head still high. He circled the place he had spied, his head erect and came to a stand, his tail straight, his body stiff.

"What's the matter with him?" Angela cried.

"He's found the birds. He's on a close point. There isn't much cover. The birds will flush if we don't hurry."

He quickened his pace and she trailed behind him. When they reached the dog his whole body seemed frozen, his long fine nose pointing straight into a clump of briars and matted grass.

"Come up!" Dave ordered, "And don't you be scared when they rise. If I don't get two birds on the flush you may kick me."

She moved closer and the covey of eighteen or twenty quail rose with a roar that brought a scream of fright.

The skilled huntsman took his time, picked a bird with each barrel and brought them both down.

"Did you get one?" she asked.

"No—two." He walked toward the place where they had fallen in the tall grass and called to the dog.

"Dead bird!"

Spot circled the place, found one, brought it to his master and laid it at his feet.

"Isn't he smart?" Angela cried.

In a moment he had found the other, brought it to his mistress and let her take it from his mouth. She hugged him.

"You're a beautiful dog, Spot—beautiful!"

He wagged his tail in agreement. Then Dave held Spot in until they reached the distance he had calculatedd for the flight and waved his hand:

"High on, sir."

The dog circled carefully and froze on a point. They came close.

"Why he's looking right down at the bare ground not three feet away," Angela said. "No bird there."

"Yes, there is," Dave smiled. "He's under a leaf."

He had scarcely spoken when the quail rose with a roar. The gun answered the challenge. And in a minute Spot laid the dead bird at her feet.

"He's fallen in love with you, honey. He won't even bring the birds to me."

She stroked his beautiful head. "He knows I love him."

"Of course, he does. Knew it the minute he looked at you."

They got three more and quit.

"Enough for a grand dinner tomorrow night. Six is enough."

As they walked home Angela studied Dave's shock of red hair for a minute and said: "No wonder you like to hunt quail—I like it too."

"The fun's all watching your dog."

"I can see that. Come here, Spot."

The dog ran to her side and jumped up on her again. Dave slapped his head: "Down, sir. Bad manners!"

"You shouldn't hit him, Dave."

"He don't jump on me. His muddy paws will ruin your clothes. You'll spoil him if you don't remind him of his training as a gentleman dog."

Angela stooped to pet him but Dave drew her back.

"Mustn't pet him now, dear. I've just scolded him. I wont be able to do a thing with him if you do that."

"I think it's a shame you hit him——"

"Must keep him in training. A dog is easy to spoil." They walked along a few minutes in silence.

"Isn't it wonderful, David, this life in the country, don't you love it?"

"I've always loved it, honey. And now that you're here, I'll never want to go to heaven."

"We're there now, darling," she breathed reverently.

When he spoke again his voice had a whimsical note in it.

"Tell me. How come Phil Stephens to dinner with us to-morrow night. Did you ask him or did he ask himself?"

"Not jealous already, are you?"

"No, but I was wondering——"

"To tell you the truth he hinted so for an invitation that I had to ask him."

"Must have something on his mind. Phil's too square a shooter to butt in so soon when he must know we want to be alone."

Angela nodded. "He told me he had something important to tell us."

"We'll be good friends with Phil," Dave said heartily, "I've always liked him."

"I'm glad."

They gave him a royal welcome when he rode up the drive on a splendid black horse. The hound barked. Spot barked and Dave shouted: "Light, Mister, and look at your saddle!"

Phil sprang from his mount, threw the reins over the hitching post and took Dave's hand.

"It's fine to see you kids looking so well," he greeted them both.

"And you don't seem to be going into a decline," Angela observed.

"Why should I?" he laughed. "The two people I like best are happy. That makes me happy."

"Spoken like a scholar and a gentleman, Phil," she responded. "Come right in. We've a quail dinner for you."

"Quail! That's great."

"Dave and I got these especially for you from our own field yesterday."

"Then they'll taste better than ever."

Dave showed him the hound and setter before following Angela into the house. Phil laughed heartily over old man Spake's investment of thirty dollars out of the Charity allotment of food for his family.

"Just like a damn fool Southern white man," the lawyer exclaimed.

"Hit shore is," Dave agreed dropping back into the vernacular of his early life when his wife's back was turned.

When the men entered, the table was set, the candles lighted and a steaming hot dinner was ready. They chatted pleasantly of current events, the beautiful fall weather and the transformation their skill had wrought in the old Newberry place. There was a lull in the conversation as Phil toyed with his second bird. He laid down his knife and fork and looked at Dave with concentrated appraisal. Angela caught the expression and spoke with a little annoyance.

"What's on your mind, Phil?"

"Something big and important for you children."

"There now," Dave broke in. "Didn't I tell you he had something up his sleeve?"

"Let's have it," Angela said quickly.

Their guest remained silent for a moment, tapping the table with one of the knives he had given them, and then began with a deliberation that was trying especially to his hostess.

"I suppose you've been too busy making love to notice what's been going on in the County for the past six months."

Dave grinned. "Couldn't be anything bigger than being in love, could there?"

"After all, maybe not. But I've come to tell you that the whole South is stirring with a new life that means the revival of our wealth and power. The nightmare of poverty is passing, and we're getting rich. It's a revolution. And the leader of it is one of the greatest men in the nation. I'm proud to call him my friend. D.A. Tompkins[1] of Charlotte is the evangel of industrial power for the South. I represent him in the County. He has been here three times and he's the most inspiring man I ever talked to. You should have heard him telling in low eloquent tones of the new era that has dawned

1. Daniel Augustus Tompkins (1851–1914), a South Carolinian, earned a degree in civil engineering from Rensselaer Polytechnic Institute in Troy, New York, and became a leading force in the southern textile mill industry in the 1890s. A successful businessman, newspaper publisher, and author, Tompkins was a vocal and influential proponent of the first New South. See Paul D. Escott, *Many Excellent People: Power and Privilege in North Carolina, 1850–1900* (Chapel Hill: University of North Carolina Press, 1985).

since the rubbish of slavery has been cleared away. Slavery held us back for two hundred years, exhausting our soil and provoking passion. Scientific inventions and discoveries are revolutionizing the world. The South is the richest undeveloped spot on earth today. You and I are young, David. We must open our eyes and keep up with the times and do our part as leaders."

"Just tell us how, Phil," Angela broke in.

"I will. But I want you to know and believe in our leader first. Tompkins was born right over here in Edgefield, of moderately well to do Scotch Irish people. Your people and mine, Dave. His mother was a cousin of J.C. Calhoun.[2] When he couldn't get the kind of education down here that he wanted he went North to the Polyclinic Institute at Troy, New York. When he graduated he went into the Bethlehem Iron Works and served an apprenticeship. He set up machinery in Europe and took a good look at the old world. He was offered big jobs in Bethlehem, Chicago and Philadelphia. But his heart was with us. He loved the South and he believed in its future. He opened his office in Charlotte and proclaimed the year of jubilee had come. The farmer must be taught new methods of agriculture and unite with the manufacturers. The Old South once led in industry. It was the center of manufacture for the nation until Slavery and politics closed our mills. In 1810 the manufactured goods of Virginia, the Carolinas and Georgia were greater in value and variety than all of New England and New York State combined." He stopped and smiled triumphantly.

"We're going to lead again in spite of the Negro Problem. The South is the most fascinating spot on the Continent today. Yankees, who drift down here to look us over, hear our birds sing and drink the wine of our air, build homes and never leave until they die."

"But what can we do, Phil?" Dave asked anxiously.

"Keep our eye on the future, not on the past. Forget politics and to hell with the Negro question. Keep our shirts on and saw wood."

"Meaning just what?" the wife asked in practical tones.

"I'm getting to it. Now listen. You're going to run this farm yourself, Dave?"

"Yes, sir. That's what I aim to do."

"You have one horse?"

"That's all I can manage."

"A one horse farmer can work about twenty acres of land and make ten or twelve bales of cotton——"

"He won't plant all cotton," Angela interrupted.

---

2. John Caldwell Calhoun (1782–1850), a South Carolinian, served in many federal posts, including congressman, secretary of war, senator, and vice president. Calhoun championed states' rights and charged that South Carolina and the South were threatened and discriminated against by a rapidly industrializing North committed to free labor. See Irving H. Bartlett, *John C. Calhoun, a Biography* (New York: W.W. Norton & Co., 1993).

"Good sense. Still it's a one horse farm and you can make a bare living working from daylight to dark with an old fashioned plow. Get out of the old farmhand ways and be a modern scientific farmer. Your land under cultivation lies beautifully. There's not a stump or a rock or a gully on it. I've been over it hunting many a time. Why plow one horse when you can drive a tractor over your fields dragging a gang plow that will throw three deep furrows at a time while you sit comfortably in your driver's seat and enjoy the landscape?"

"But thunderation," the young farmer broke in, "how much does a tractor cost?"

"About twelve hundred dollars."

Dave snapped his fingers.

"Twelve hundred dollars, just like that, he says, honey."

"Then you need a sulky plow that will take two rows of cotton at a time, while you ride instead of walk. And machines for planting the seed and sowing the fertilizer at the same time. The whole outfit for a modern farm will cost you about four thousand dollars. And I've dropped in to show you how to get it."

The young farmer rose.

"Say that again, man!"

"I mean just what I say. I've organized a new railroad company to build a line from Piedmont to the Great Falls of the river. There's horse power enough going to waste to drive a million spindles. Mr. Tompkins and I have organized the new mill. You'd be astonished to know how eager our people are to develop their own country. They are subscribing every dollar they can lay their hands on, and the native subscriptions are more than the sum of the outside capital——"

"But where do we come in?" Dave insisted.

"On the railroad first. I'm in charge of letting the contracts for grading the sixty miles from here to the Falls. If you want it, I'll allot to you a ten mile section on a contract to finish the grading in four months. You'll still have time for spring plowing with a tractor doing the work of six horses."

Dave's hand trembled as he ran his fingers through his hair. "Can I make grades right?"

"Of course. The Chief Engineer will lay them all off to an inch and give you the blue prints. You built a home by blueprints sent from a publishing house in New York. You can work a blue print on the road with the engineer to help you."

"And there's four thousand profit in ten miles," Angela asked breathlessly.

"At the lowest figure five hundred dollars to one mile. And a great deal more if he works all Negro help——"

The red head shook suddenly.

"Couldn't do that, Phil."

"Not if you makc ten thousand dollars instead of five?"

"Not if I make twenty. I'll hire my own people and take less profit."

"Oh, come out of it, Dave," Phil pleaded. "I just said keep out of politics and to hell with the Negro problem. We've got to get over our old race prejudices and make the world a better place for both races to live in."

"There's never been any prejudices down here," Dave said, "against a Negro working at anything he wants to, no matter how many poor white men go hungry. That's what's been the matter with our people. The Nigger can under-bid us on any job. He lives on less. He sleeps anywhere. He has been driving my people to the wall ever since he was brought here from Africa. It's not right. We've got to give our folks a chance."

"That's what we're doing in all these big mills. There's not a Negro in them——"

"But you pay damn low wages and you're bringing Yankee money down here on the promise of lower wages than in the North. It's not right."

"I know it's not, Dave, and in time we'll remedy it. I'm for giving every man, black and white, a chance to make the most of every talent God has given him. It's certain that the Southern white people have always been the best friends the Negro ever had."

"You mean the Southern aristocrats. They have been good friends to the Nigger. And forget the people of their own blood. I wont take the contract unless I can give the jobs to white men.

"All right. It's up to you. You'll make less money, but you can decide that for yourself."

Dave smiled.

"Just you wait. I'll pick a gang of white men that will throw more dirt in a day than any gang of Niggers you can get together this side of hell."

"You can rent a steam shovel from the company if you want to use one——"

"I'll rent it. Save me one. I've got in mind right now an engineer that will handle it like a toy."

Angela rose from the table and joined the two before the fire. She put a hand on Phil's arm and looked up at his tall graceful figure through tears.

"Thank you. Thank you for this. It's fine of you. I thought I was so happy I couldn't be happier. You've made us both happier."

Chapter 8

The day after Phil's visit, Dave began to select the men he would direct as foreman on the ten mile section of the railroad allotted him. It was the first ten miles out of Piedmont. Angela smiled when told of the allotment. Her old sweetheart had added this little touch out of consideration for her. It would make Dave's work easier. He wouldn't have to move to a section bunk house. He could work from his own home and she would see that he had the best food.

But the bunk house was the cause of their first quarrel. Her husband insisted that he could not keep his hands on the job unless he slept with the men and felt their pulse daily.

"I tell you I won't have it!" his wife stormed.

"I gotta make good in this job, honey," he quietly persisted.

She burst into tears at last and he took her in his arms and promised anything on earth if she'd not cry any more.

"Then the bunk house is out?" she asked through her tears.

He hesitated and finally said:

"I tell you what we'll do. I'll stay home at night as long as the horse will carry me to the men by sunrise and back home by dark."

She smiled.

"Good. When you build the old bunk house on the far end, I'll get a girl to stay here, take care of the house and feed the chickens and the dogs."

"And you?"

"I'll go to the bunk house, cook and serve your meals——"

"Darling, you can't do that," he moaned.

"And why not?"

"The bunk houses are built for men only. The whole gang lives in one big room."

She stopped his protests with a soft hand over his mouth.

"Please build us a little room for our own, darling. You build a lovely house. Please. I love you. I've just got to be with you every night. I'd die of loneliness if you're gone. Please, dear!"

He nodded and she kissed him.

"Gosh, I'm henpecked! And the funny part is I like it."

"I want my own little stove and kitchen sink. I can have it, can't I?"

"Everything you want that I can get, honey. You've got my goat, world without end!"

"Good. Now it's all settled I'll show you the mail. We've subscribed to the Daily Charlotte Observer! Here's the first copy with a letter from Phil. He says this is the first Southern newspaper to break from politics and go into business. D.A. Tompkins bought it and made J.P. Caldwell the Editor. It's the herald of the New Era. Read it and see what's going on in the industrial world."

Dave scanned the front page eagerly.

"By Jeminy, that's nice. I'll keep up with the times now that you've taught me to read. Bless your darling heart. Of course I'll build a little bunk house all for you when we have to go far out, paint it white and put green blinds on it if you say so!"

In three weeks, his men were selected, the steam shovel had come and the first dirt began to fly on the section just out of town.

Angela was there to watch him boss his men the first day, her heart swelling with pride. She liked the way he talked to them in his quiet tones as comrades and fellow workers. He had roused their pride in the work before the first pick had broken ground. A prize had been offered for the best finished section. He had made up his mind to win it and they had promised to a man.

As she watched these good natured, nice looking boys in overalls work with quick efficiency, her heart went out in deep sympathy for them and their people. They had not had a square deal. Neither before the war when Slavery had held them down, nor since the war when the Negro had been made the ward of the Nation, while they had been neglected. She recalled Dave's stand for them with a growing sense of his manhood and his rapidly developing character. He had stood his ground against Phil squarely and without a minute's hesitation. She was with him too. Together they would work for the uplift of these men.

When Dave blew his whistle to knock off work for the first day, she slipped her arm through his and they walked home in the gathering twilight. As they passed through the old pillars at the entrance, she stopped and looked at the little white house shining in the shadows and whispered:

"It's beautiful—isn't it?"

"Finest little house in the County."

"Well, Mr. Boss Contractor, I'm going to tell you some news as a reward for your letting me hen peck you."

"What you up to now?" he asked suspiciously.

She looked up at him.

"You'll soon be a father, David. I'm going to have a baby."

"You're sure, honey?"

"Absolutely."

He drew her close.

"Lord, I'm the proudest and happiest man in the world! And ain't I glad I said I'd stay with you every night just for your own sake before you told me this! You'll still try that little bunk house with me?"

"Of course. I'm so strong. It'll be months, you know."

"Man alive, we've got another one to work for now, haven't we?"

"I'm so happy I had to tell you right away——"

"I wish the days were longer that I could work harder for you both," he whispered.

"They're just long enough to love, David. And we always will."

"Always!"

The knowledge of her condition brought to Angela's mind a poise and dignity and eagerness for service she had never felt before. There were a lot of things she had planned to do and in her selfish happiness had not begun. She would begin them at once. The first thing she would do was to help the school in her district. The teacher had bitterly complained to her of the small attendance. The new brick building and the longer school term had made no difference. There were scores of children in the settlement who never darkened the doors. The truant officer was no good. Angela stayed but an hour with Dave on the railroad works next day, hurried to Captain Collier's office and secured a new truant officer.

The new man began work the next day and created a sensation in the community. He didn't get them all in, but he did add about a dozen to the roll call. In a week he had rounded up a dozen more. The teacher was grateful and Angela was proud of her work.

Ten days later, she saw a tiny stream of smoke curling through the tree tops on the edge of the deep woods and she wondered what it could mean. She had a vague suspicion. It was too ridiculous to put into words. She said nothing to Dave, but against his positive orders never to go into these woods alone, she made up her mind to investigate. She waited until he had gone to work and quietly reconnoitered. The smoke was barely visible. Still it was there. She drew closer and found it coming from a spot but a few feet from the edge of the woods. She crept close and heard a girl's soft laughter. A child's voice it was and then a mother's crooning.

Peering carefully through the bushes that grew from the woods into the field she saw lying under an oak a mother with a little girl about six years old. They had been sleeping on a quilt and using another for cover.

The child's voice changed to complaint.

"Where's my breakfast?"

"Here it is. A fine lot of hot roasted chestnuts."

"I can't eat any more chestnuts or walnuts or berries. I want. something hot. Something nice to eat."

"All right, baby, we'll slip home tonight and see if that man will let us alone."

Angela suddenly appeared on the scene and the young mother sprang to her feet and drew the child into her arms.

"What on earth are you doing out here in the woods with your little girl?" she asked.

"The school man came to take her from me, ma'am, and I couldn't stand to let her go. So we took to the woods. They tell me they beat little girls."

"It's not true. They don't beat children in school any more. They certainly wouldn't beat your sweet little girl. Come here, darling."

The child came timidly and leaned against Angela's skirts. The woman followed in a helpless sort of way and watched a soft hand caress her child's hair.

"Don't you want to go to school, dear?" Angela asked.

"No'm. I'd rather stay home with Mama."

"Don't you want your little girl to learn to read and write, mother?"

"I can't give her up. They might do something to her. I love her."

An arm slipped around her waist and she began to cry softly.

"I can't give her up! She's all I've got. They'll beat her. I know they will."

"But you can't let your child grow up in ignorance."

"I can't read and write. I got along. Why must they drag her away from me now?"

"Because she must have a little chance in life more than you've had, poor dear. If I go with you to the school and the teacher promises to treat your little girl nicely, won't you let her go to school and learn things like the other girls?"

The voice was so sweet and low and persuasive the mother couldn't resist.

"If you'll go with me, all right. The teacher'll do what you say I reckon. You're Dave Henry's pretty wife, aint you?"

"Yes. I'm Mrs. Dave Henry. And I taught him to read and write after he was grown. It was so unfair that he didn't have a chance like other boys. You must give your little girl a chance."

"All right. If you'll help me, I will."

The day after this Angela devoted the afternoon to welfare work among the poor white people in John Lovelace's mill town. John had built under his wife's direction the first mill village with complete modern conveniences. Each house had four rooms and a bath with toilet, hot and cold water and a kitchen sink. The front of each had an enclosed flower yard and a vegetable garden in the rear.

Not half of the yards had flowers and less than half of the gardens had any vegetables. John showed them to her and shook his head.

"Ann made me believe that God was in every one of these lazy bones when I built the places for them with so much care. Just look at 'em!"

"It's sickening, isn't it? I'll get acquainted and see if I can interest them in flowers and gardens."

She rapped gently on a door and to her surprise a neat colored woman answered.

"May I come in?"

"Yes, M'am, walk right in and have a seat. I'se sho glad to see ye. I know who you is, too. I seed you lot o' times at de barbecues at Dr. Cameron's. You'se his gran'chile dat married Dave Henry."

"That's right. Where's the mistress of the house?"

"She's in de mill workin', an' her husben and two boys. I'se de cook."

"How old are the boys?"

"Dey say one's fourteen and tother one sixteen. But twixt me an' you—" she dropped her voice— "Dey des say dat ter git 'em in de mill. Ain't nary one ob 'em fourteen. Dey caint work in de mill less dey's fourteen. And dey des say so."

"I see. Have you any children?"

"Yessum. I got two chillen myself. An' dey's bofe at school. An' dey'll stay dar, too. Dey gwine ter be edicated. I aint gwine let 'em grow up ignerent like so many o' dese po white trash."

The white welfare worker winced at the ugly thrust at her people. Her mind flashed to the look on David's face when he had told Phil flat footed no Negro should work on his section. In the sharp accents of the black woman she caught the clash of race in unmistakable terms. How could two such races live side by side in the same government, a democracy in theory at least. How could the black race build a nation within a nation and keep the peace?

The new Negro woman and her outlook on life held her with a feeling of pain. She had never encountered it before. In her sheltered home with her grandfather, and the spirit of love and comradeship which Nelse had inspired, there was nothing of this. She realized now fully for the first time that neither Nelse nor his old master belonged to the new world. There were forces at work deep beneath the surface that were digging a gulf, an impassable one, between white and black.

She went home and cooked Dave's supper with a heavy heart. Tired as he was she persuaded him to go with her to call on this family before they scattered to the picture shows in the two Piedmonts. They found them all at home just getting up from the table.

Ross Hoyle, the father, knew Dave and gave them a cordial greeting.

"Come right in, folks, and make yourselves at home. Ceily, you make Miss Henry take off her bonnet and stay awhile."

Angela extended her hand to the older boy, smiled at him tenderly and he responded with an awkward nod. The younger one held back until she beckoned.

"Come here."

She drew him close and ran her fingers through his blonde hair. They were pathetic little figures. Their bodies thin, their faces tired and pale from lack of sun and wind.

"You don't go to school?" she asked softly.

'No'm," the father put in. "The mills are short o' hands and the foreman asked me to help him out."

Angela knew this was not true. John Lovelace had done nothing of the kind. He had done his best to make his people send their children to school. Under his inspiration the mill school was one of the best in the state, a fine brick structure with every modern convenience.

The younger boy was no longer shy and held the warm hand of his visitor tightly in his own. She drew him closer with one arm and turned pleadingly to his father.

"I'm going to ask you to do me a special favor, Mr. Hoyle——"

"Ef I kin, M'am," was the prompt reply.

"This little blonde one——"

"Oh, he's fourteen year old all right," Hoyle hastened to explain.

She knew he was lying but didn't contradict him.

"Anyhow he's such a slim little boy. It's a pity to shut him up in the mill every day. Won't you send him to school, just this one, anyway?"

"He's been to school a lot," his father defended. "He can read and write, can't you, Jimmy?"

The blonde head nodded to the sweet face looking down at him. "Yes, a little."

"Don't you want to go to school?"

"Oh, yessem, if Paw and Maw kin spare me——"

Angela felt for the mother's hand and pressed it.

"You'll let him go?"

"Yessem, ef Ross says so——"

"What do you say, Mr. Hoyle?"

Dave nodded to him. He hesitated. a moment, rubbed his hands awkwardly and finally agreed.

"All right, m'am. Jest 'cause you ax it we'll send him. You married Dave Henry and I know you're one of our folks now."

In two weeks she had persuaded a dozen parents to slip one child from the mills and send them to school, and she had induced a few of the women who did not work at the looms to cultivate their gardens and flowers. She bought seed and rose cuttings and helped them start. The longer she worked at the job the bigger and more hopeless it seemed. There were thousands and tens of thousands of these people in the mills of the Carolinas. Most of them had moved to town from wretched hill country farm hovels and had greatly improved their lives. Most of them had settled down into the new found luxury content with their lot, without the slightest ambition for anything better.

She made up her mind to fight for them. They were Dave's people. They had been forgotten. The Negro was the pet of the nation. These Scoth-Irish hill folks had been the back bone of the republic. Three hundred and fifty thousand of them had come to America before the revolution. They led the revolution. Left to the Tory English settlers there would have been no revolution. They created American democracy. In the South slavery had driven the white working man and small farmer to the wall. And these millions of listless men were the result.

At home that night, as they sat before the fire, she said quietly: "David, we must have a big rally for education in Piedmont and get Walter H. Page down here to make his speech on The Forgotten Man."

"Who's Walter H. Page?"

"A great scholar from North Carolina, who lives now in New York. He's calling the South to look to the future, educate her sons and build a new world."

"All right, we'll get him. And I want to hear Governor Aycock,[1] too. They say he's the greatest man the Carolinas have seen since the war."

1. Charles Brantley Aycock (1859–1912), a lawyer, was elected North Carolina's governor in 1900 on a ticket favoring white supremacy and the disfranchisement of African Americans. Aycock advanced universal education for white children but opposed such Progressive Era reforms as women's suffrage and child labor laws. See J. Morgan Kousser, "Progressivism—for Middle-Class Whites Only: North Carolina Education, 1880–1910," *Journal of Southern History* 46 (May 1980): 169–94.

"Good," she agreed. "And we'll ask President Alderman[2] of the University of Virginia. He's a North Carolinian, too."

The man looked at his wife in wonder. "Lord, honey, you know everything. How'd you find out all that?"

"Reading the papers. You keep up with your *Charlotte Observer* now and you'll know what's going on, too."

"That's a fact. Where is it?"

He took his paper and settled down to read for an hour while his wife worked on a tiny garment. He folded the paper at last.

"Say, honey, I was just thinking. We'll take time and work that meeting up for the spring when the weather's clear. We'll make it the biggest thing this Piedmont section ever saw. We'll build an arbor on the edge of the line half in North and half in South Carolina. We'll have all the big bugs there. Put the big pot in the little one and have a shindig that's worth while. The people will pile in from Greenville, Spartanburg, Blacksburg, Shelby, Gastonia, Charlotte and from the counties fifty miles around. We'll round up every poor white man from the foot of the mountains and give 'em something to think about——"

"David!" she cried. "I'm proud of you. You're using your mind. You're going to do all I dreamed you would."

"I'm going to try to do all of it, for you. You'd better see Captain Tom Collier and get him to head the Committee."

"Another shrewd suggestion. We can't afford to have him oppose it. We'll make him our leader."

The Captain agreed with enthusiasm to head the Committee. He looked at Dave keenly. "Say, did you think this up, boy, all by your self?"

"No, sir. She helped me."

"I barely made the suggestion, Captain, Dave worked it out and it was all his idea to get you to head the Committee."

"Always knew he had sense. His father was a brave soldier. We'll fix the date in May when the weather's just right for an open-air crowd of five or ten thousand. And I'll send the invitations to Page and Aycock and Alderman on time. They're big men and make dates a long way ahead. I'll ask Charles D. McIver, too. He's one of the greatest educators in the United States."

2. Edwin Anderson Alderman (1861–1931) of North Carolina was one of the South's leading educational reformers, serving as president of the Normal and Industrial School for Women (later the University of North Carolina at Greensboro), the University of North Carolina, Tulane University, and the University of Virginia. As a member of the Southern Education Board, Alderman led an aggressive campaign for the education of white southerners, not blacks. See Clement Eaton, "Edwin A. Alderman: Liberal of the New South," *North Carolina Historical Review* 23 (April 1946): 206–21.

In two months Dave had finished the first six miles of the road and built the bunk house in the middle of the last four miles. Angela engaged a colored girl to take care of the house. Her husband promptly vetoed the plan and found a white girl, old Adam Spake's sixteen year old daughter.

"She can bring her father to see the hound," Dave grinned.

"He won't eat my chickens, I hope."

"He won't. He's poor but honest. I've always liked the old fool. And that hound loves him, too. He'll get right up in his lap and go to sleep."

Angela went into ecstasies over the little bunk house that Dave built as an extension from the main dining room. The bed was as big as the one in their room at home. Lum Anderson, Dave's section boss, assembled all hands to welcome Angela to the camp. He tried to make a speech, but all he got out was: "Glad to see you with us, m'am." It was plain to see that the men were proud of the honor done them by their contractor's wife. They went out of their way to keep her stove supplied with wood.

Every day Angela spent part of her time beside her husband on the grading watching him give orders to his men. She never stopped wondering at his keen efficiency. He expected of his men the best that was in them. And they gave it to him. He paid a little higher wages than any boss on the line and they gave him in loyalty and extra service more than the difference. He was well ahead of his schedule, took it easy toward the last and put fine finishing touches on his road bed. He meant to win that prize. Phil sent him an expert on rail and cross tie laying and the rails were placed in short order. The whole sixty mile line was finished on time and the first train drew into Great Falls to the shouts of two thousand excited people. D.A. Tompkins came down from Charlotte and presided over the mass meeting.

Marie came with the crowd from Piedmont, threw her arms around Angela's neck and had a good cry.

"Darling, I'm lonesome without you. The old house is so empty. They told me to let you and Dave alone. But I'm coming to see you every day if I want to, can I?"

"Of course, dear. I'm sorry if I've neglected you. I'll make up for it."

"You're not mad at me for running away today?"

"Did you run away?"

"Had to. Grampa wouldn't let me come."

Angela shook her head but kissed her.

Tompkins announced briefly that the entire capital had been subscribed to build the first mill below the falls that would give employment to more than a thousand people. A rousing cheer greeted the statement.

He turned to Phil.

"And, now, ladies and gentlemen, allow me to introduce to you the brilliant leader of the progressive forces of this County, who will speak to you—Mr. Phillip Stephens of Piedmont."

The young lawyer stepped to the front and bowed to the chairman.

"And allow me, ladies and gentlemen, to announce to you that you have just heard the voice of the greatest industrial leader the New South has produced. The man to whose genius you owe this railroad and the mills that will rise below——"

Another cheer swept the crowd.

He singled out David Henry and said: "Permit me before I speak to announce the winner of the prize for the best ten mile section of the grading." He paused and Angela clutched Dave's arm.

"Oh, dear, you're going to win it! He's looking right at you——"

In clear tones the speaker said: "Will Mr. David Henry step to the platform?"

Angela and Marie led the wild cheering as Dave mounted the platform and stood before Phil. He took the hand of the blushing young fellow.

"I congratulate you, Dave Henry, on winning the prize for the finest ten mile section of road way, a purse of five hundred dollars in gold."

He handed the purse to the trembling man, who looked a minute at the cheering crowd dazed, then leaped to the ground and rushed to his wife who threw her arms around his neck and hugged him before the cheering people.

Dave drew her down to the seat out of sight and pressed the bag into her hands.

"It's yours, honey. I want you to spend every dollar of it for pretty clothes. I couldn't buy you any before. I want to see you the best dressed girl in the County."

"Don't be foolish," she whispered. "It's going into a bank for our baby that's on the way."

The speaker lifted his hand and the crowd was still.

"Ladies and gentlemen," he began slowly. "The South owes her vast industrial expansion to three causes, her wealth in mines and cotton and her railroads. You know the power of cotton, your ancient king. We have restored the crown to the old sovereign, a crown with brighter jewels. We have added the rich empire of the mills to the ermine robes of the field.

"While cotton and minerals are the sources of your greatest wealth, they would be of little value without quick and effective transportation. The railroad is today the South's mightiest instrument of power. In the old days, before the war, the railroads of the South were of tremendous power. From 1850 to 1860 you outstripped the North in their construction. In

1860 you had 10,000 miles while New England and the middle Atlantic States had but 9,000 miles. The war crushed you and changed all that.

"The tragedy of your building before the war was that the lines ran East and West. Calhoun's keen eye foresaw the coming conflict over slavery and opposed the trunk line running North and South. If your railroads had run North and South, there would have been no war, for Slavery would have perished in contact with free labor. The Confederacy failed at last because the Union had been knit together with threads of steel. The roads today are healing the breach between the sections. They are bringing millions of dollars of working capital to us. This railroad makes possible the erection of the mills at these falls that will give employment to thousands of our people. The railroads will not only build cotton mills, they will tap, and they are tapping, every rich mine of coal and iron in our land. Out of the blood and ashes of our past they will build wealth beyond the wildest dreams of our fathers. I congratulate you on the completion of this line, and the opening today of your regular freight and passenger service——"

When the cheers had subsided Marie whispered to her sister: "May I congratulate Phil? I want him to see how grown up I look in this long dress."

"Of coursc, silly. Kiss him if you like."

"I would if my dress wasn't so long and my hair done up like yours. I've got to behave if it kills me. I'm afraid I've grown up too soon."

Chapter 9

Dave surveyed with dismay the modern farm machinery which Phil had ordered for him. It had been delivered a week before the railroad was finished. The tractor was formidable looking. He examined every part of it with increasing dismay. Could he ever learn to work the thing? He scratched his head and looked it over the third time before calling Angela.

She was puzzled still more.

"Don't you understand it?" he moaned.

"How could I, silly? I never was much on machinery. Can barely work a sewing machine—but this thing! You'll have to get a man who's an engineer to show you."

"Sure. I'll get Alf Sanders. He's an engineer. He drove my steam shovel."

Alf looked it over and refused to put his hand on it.

"What ails you?" Dave stormed. "Don't you know all about engines?"

"The steam shovel was easy but I don't know a damn thing about this thing. There's a fellow down at the foundry that knows all about 'em. You'll have to get him."

The gasoline engineer came and mounted the tractor with a grin—a John Deere 1912.

"Man, it's a dandy! If you make a living' with this thing, Dave, damn me if I don't quit the shop and buy a farm."

The young farmer showed him the attachments that went with it. The gang plow with two bars, the disc with four wheels, a thing to mark check rows. The man from the shop gazed with increasing wonder.

"Hell, it'll do anything, won't it?"

"Guaranteed to plow, furrow, turn up rows, bust 'em open, plant 'em, work corn, cotton, vegetables, anything."

The shop man was as excited as a child with a new toy. He filled the

tank with gasoline, started and stopped it. Filled the oil tank and drove it around the place shouting with joy. He communicated to the owner his enthusiasm and gave him lessons in the care of it.

"You've gotter treat a machine like a human bein'," he announced. "Keep her well oiled. Let her rest some. You can't drive a machine to death any more than you can a horse."

In two days Dave was driving it, dragging the gang plow that threw great ribbons of soil curling into the air. He quickly turned under the sod of the whole twenty-five acres he would put under cultivation. He laid off ten acres for cotton, five for corn and ten for potatoes. He had made up his mind to gamble on the potatoes. He was late planting them and couldn't raise a big crop the first year, but he'd make a killing with them next year. He knew a truck farmer who cashed in five hundred dollars an acre on ten acres the year before. He woke up in the night dreaming of making five thousand dollars from that plot of ground. The fertilizer would cost like blazes, but he had the money to buy on a cash basis and his crop would be free. The same with his cotton. The machine to open a cotton row, sow the fertilizer, cover and plant the seed was a wonder.

He'd have to buy another horse and hire a helper in case any of his machinery broke down. He'd need a man anyhow. Five acres in corn would carry his horses without buying any feed when the first crop was in.

When he looked at his fields and smelled the good soil his chest expanded. He was going to be a leader as a farmer. He'd buy more land, hire more men, buy more machines and teach his people in the County to rise to their full height as men.

When night came he tried to beg off from his lessons but Angela wouldn't listen.

"Change your clothes, darling, take a bath and I'll rub you down with alcohol and then we'll work on the fractions."

"Let me off tonight, just one night, honey, I'm so tired and excited I can't study."

She looked at him steadily and he surrendered.

"All right, you win, there ain't no help for it."

"*Ain't* there?"

"There *is* no help for it. But you watch my smoke I'll make you proud of me yet."

"I'm proud of you already——"

"I'll make you prouder, and I'm going to make you happier, too."

"I don't see how."

"I'll show you in the morning. Got a surprise for you."

"What is it?"

"Wouldn't be a surprise if I told you."

She tried her best but could not wheedle it out of him.

The next day a new automobile stopped in front of the door and the driver blew the horn so loudly Angela dropped a dish. She rushed to the door and saw the surprise. Without awaiting an announcement she climbed in beside the man.

"Show me how to drive it, quick. Dave Henry's a fool to spend all this money for a car, but I love him for it, bless his heart!"

"Hit's a Dodge, M'am," the man smiled. "Best little car on the market today. It runs so sweet it just makes your head swim."

She made him work two hours until she was so tired she had to give up for the day.

She waylaid Dave when he came in from the field, threw her arms around his neck and smothered him.

"Oh, you dear, dear foolish man!"

"Like it?"

"Prettiest car I ever saw. I'll make the people in town sit up and take notice. I'll make my rounds in the mill village in no time. And we'll drive all over the County, too, you and I, David. We'll drum up a crowd for the big educational Mass Meeting that will make Captain Collier proud of us."

Dave bought a new gayly painted two horse wagon and did all his own hauling. The fertilizer came first. The bill staggered him a little. When he had paid for fertilizer and seed there wasn't much left to carry them through the summer.

"Don't worry, dear," Angela said. "I've five hundred in the bank."

"Thought that was for the baby."

"It is. For my big baby if he needs it."

The cotton, corn and potatoes were planted, up and growing before they began a Sunday campaign for the Mass Meeting. Captain Collier had printed a handsome leaflet telling of the distinguished men who would address the people of the two States from a platform built across the Carolina State lines. Every man and woman in ten Counties were invited and he expected them to be there. He signed his name as Chairman of the Committee and began to write personal letters to the leaders of the towns and Counties near Piedmont. What was more he began the preparation of a speech in which he meant to explode a bombshell at the close of the meeting.

Chapter 10

One of the most remarkable crusades ever conducted in the history of the English speaking people was launched in North Carolina in the early nineties by Edwin A. Alderman, President of the University and Charles D. McIver, President of the State Normal School for Women at Greensboro. Fired by enthusiasm for education these two men, inspired by the leadership of Walter H. Page, conducted an old-fashioned evangelistic campaign in every County of their State, calling for more and better schools, more hours, more and better teachers.

The South was just awakening from the nightmare of abject poverty which followed the Civil War. As late as the session of the Legislature of 1884 the total assessed value of the property of North Carolina on which taxes could be levied was a little less than half a million dollars. On this pitiful amount of wealth the entire budget of State taxes must be levied including the funds for schools. That the schools were poor, the buildings old shacks, the teachers ill paid, the length of the term but 40 days was not to be wondered at under the conditions.

Then came the slow revival of industry and the sudden flaming of the crusade for the education of the people. Alderman and McIver stumped every County, speaking in ramshackled school buildings, in Odd Fellows and Masonic Halls, in churches, in the open air at crossroads, from the cart tail in towns, calling on the people to awake and lift the shadow of ignorance from their children.

The schools began to improve. Local taxes were first added to the pittance the State was giving and the movement culminated in the nomination of Charles B. Aycock for Governor. The young leader of Democracy from the Black Belt of North Carolina had drawn the Amendment to disfranchise the Negroes, and on that issue he was swept into office. He surprised the mossbacks by immediately demanding an education for every child, black and white, in the State. In particular were the Conservatives astounded by his insistance on the equal chances for an education for every Negro child. During the four years of his administration, he made the amazing record of dedicating a new modern school building for every day he was in office.

Captain Collier fixed the day of the mass meeting on the first Saturday following the closing of the schools to give every trustee, teacher and scholar a chance to be present.

On the day before, the Negro school children held their mass parade through the streets of Piedmont. The new Superintendent, trained at Tuskegee, invited Phil Stephens to make the address.

The black boys and girls and their teachers made a brave show, marching through the May sunshine from the Court House steps, circling the town, to their High School Auditorium.

The entire population of Piedmont, black and white, lined the side walks and shouted their approval of the fine clothes and the high stepping the little darkies displayed.

Angela with Marie and Ann Lovelace watched the procession. From Dave she had caught the tragic meaning of these marching black folks. They were being educated faster than the whites. Their great leader at Tuskegee planned a black industrial revolution that would make the life of poor white people harder than ever if it succeeded. She wondered vaguely what the end of the conflict was going to be. It was all well enough for Phil Stephens, secure in his aristocratic inheritance, intent on amassing a fortune to preach the new "liberalism" which meant "Let the Negro Problem alone. The Negro is here. We'll use him for all he's worth, give him a square deal in our Courts and Schools and let the future take care of itself."

Today, as she watched these laughing, highstepping Negro children she was overwhelmed with the feeling that it would not take care of itself. She felt that she and her husband were marching steadily toward an unsolved and insolvable tragedy, while fools stood on the sidewalks, laughing and cheering.

With a sense of sudden sickening she turned to her friend.

"Let's go, Ann. I don't want to stay any longer. We'll go and see Dave finishing the platform and the arbor."

"It saddens me too," the older woman admitted. "I've spent many a puzzled hour beneath the shadow that's growing darker each day. God knows and will lead us out of it at last. How—I don't know."

They found Dave, with his crew from the railroad grading, putting the finishing touches on the wide spreading brush arbor, beneath which the crowd would sit on wooden benches. They provided places for five thousand. The rest could stand on the edges. The speakers platform was draped with flags and bunting.

Early the next day the crowd began to gather. The first two thousand seats were roped off for the excursion trains. One was scheduled to come from Charlotte bringing all the teachers and their friends along the way. Ten coaches had been chartered to give them seats. A similar train was to come from Greenville with ten more crowded coaches.

The excursionists arrived in numbers far beyond expectations. Each train brought more than a thousand people who filled every reserved seat and crowded the aisles.

Captain Collier nodded in approval.

"I thought we'd need a lot of space for our visitors. Our folks are at home. They can stand."

Before the speakers were escorted to the platform every inch of the five thousand seats were packed and jammed and more than a thousand people had to stand along the edges.

Only two distinguished speakers were there. Walter Page and Governor Aycock. At the last minute President Alderman, now at the head of the University of Virginia, wired that he could not leave his post on account of a special meeting of his Board of Trustees.

"It's all right," Captain Collier said to Angela. "It'll give Page and Aycock more time. They'll make better speeches. Too many cooks spoil the broth."

He paused and looked at Dave. "Where you children going to sit?"

"Oh, we'll stand up." Angela smiled.

"You will not!" was the firm answer. "You two started this thing and damn me if you don't sit on the platform with Phil and the speakers. Come on. Climb up now."

The young wife hesitated.

"Do you think I ought to put myself on exhibition, Captain?"

"Fiddlesticks, young woman. Everybody in town knows you're going to have a baby. Let 'em take a good look. These are modern times."

"Sure. Come on, honey." Dave said, taking her arm and carefully leading her up the steps. Marie closely followed, beaming on Phil Stephens.

The railroad gang gave them a round of applause as they took seats on the side of the table.

When the two speakers mounted the platform, the young couple were surprised at a sudden move from Captain Collier. He led Angela to Walter Page, and introduced her.

"Walter, I want you to know the lovely young woman, Mrs. Dave Henry, who selected you for the first speaker here today."

Page gave her one of his genial smiles, held her hand a moment and said quietly:

"I assure you, my dear young lady, that I was never prouder of a sponsor than today."

"Her husband, a young man of the people who seconded the motion."

Page shook hands cordially with Dave and took his seat.

The next minute, before they knew what he was up to, the Captain drew Dave and his wife over to Governor Aycock and presented them.

"The two youngsters who organized this meeting, Governor."

Aycock grasped their hands with an intimate cordial greeting and they took their seats, beside Phil Stephens in a position from which the face of the speaker could be seen in full profile. Marie managed to sit beside her hero.

Captain Collier stepped to the edge of the platform and raised his hand.

"The meeting will now come to order. As your presiding Chairman, I will not take up the time of our distinguished guests by a formal address. I may have a few words to say at the close if you can stay and hear them."

A roar of applause assured him of their good will.

"I now have the pleasure and the honor," he went on rapidly, "of presenting to you the brilliant young lawyer of our County, a coming man of South Carolina, Mr. Phillip Stephens, who will introduce to you the first speaker of the day."

Phil stepped briskly to the front of the platform and lifted his hand to still the applause.

"Ladies and gentlemen. I count it a high honor to present to you today one of North Carolina's most distinguished sons, a man of whom every Carolinian is proud. A man who has won high honor in the big world, the greatest editor of the nation, whose love for his folks at home has never been dimmed by the applause of the bigger world in which he lives. A pioneer in education, the founder of the Greensboro State College, whose epoch making address at Greensboro a few years ago, gave to the South a slogan of progress. We will hear again today that great speech on "The Forgotten Man" by Walter Hines Page."

The noted speaker rose with dignity and faced the crowd which welcomed him with a liberal round of applause. He was in the prime of life, tall, erect, his dark brown hair thinning on top, his black mustache bristling with a pugnacious little twist. No man could be more gracious when met as an individual.

But as a speaker he had a mannerism of voice and gesture calculated to provoke the fighting instincts in those who differed with him. He never stooped to controversies. When attacked by mossbacks, he refused to pay any attention. He was too busy, and life was too short, to waste in bickering. He fired his bombshells and let them take effect. Once they had been fired, his duty was done. He let others do the wrangling. His speech at Greensboro on "The Forgotten Man" had not only coined a phrase, destined to become a battle cry of the South, it had provoked personal attacks by scores of old fashioned folks that might have disturbed a man of smaller mind. These attacks rolled off Page as water from a duck's oiled back. When friends wrote him about them he merely laughed in his good natured letters of reply. He was a great letter writer. The greatest, perhaps, our nation has produced.

Page rose, bowed to the applause, and plunged at once into his address:

"We have often reminded ourselves and informed other people that we have incalculable undeveloped resources in the Carolinas. In our streams, our forests, our mines, our quarries, our soil. But there is an undeveloped resource more valuable than all these, and that is the people themselves. It is about the development of men that I shall speak, more particularly about the development of forgotten and neglected men.

"In considering the level of life of any community you must not give undue value to any class of men. We are not rich because we have a few rich men. We are not healthful because we have a few strong men. We are not intelligent because we have a few men of learning. Nor are we sound in morals because we have good women among us. If the rest of our population is poor, unhealthy, ignorant and of doubtful morals. The common people are the foundations of your civilization. In the development of our institutions as we lay emphasis on a few rich men, on a few cultivated men we are likely to forget and to neglect the foundations. It is not these small classes that make the community what it is. The security and soundness of the whole body are measured at last by the masses who constitute its foundations.

"The dominant idea of education was that it was a luxury for the rich, the well born and the ruling class. When I was a boy, it was a tragedy to have a father who was not a Colonel or at least a Captain. I am not belittling our ancestors. From such stock came the men who rule the world today. We have written and spoken much nonsense about ancestors, believing ourselves in some way different from other sturdy folks, in some way better than the other common folks. Let's look ourselves squarely in the face. We're all common folks, once dominated by a little aristocracy which made a failure and left a crop of wrong social notions behind them—especially about education."

Angela led a round of applause that was marred by a single aristocratic hiss from the rear.

Page paid no attention to the applause or the single hiss but rushed on with his speech.

"What did this system of education do for the masses? In 1890 twenty-six per cent of our white people were unable to read or write. One in every four forgotten! But illiteracy was not the worst of it. The forgotten man was taught to be content to be forgotten. He became not only a dead weight but an opponent of social progress. He faithfully listened to politicians on the stump praising him for virtues he did not have. He was told that he lived in the best State in the Union. Told that other politicians had vicious plans to increase his taxes. For increased taxes we had fought Great Britain and won our independence. As a consolation for his ignorance he was told how many of his kinsmen had been killed in the war. He was taught to distrust any man who proposed to change anything. What was good enough for his father was good enough for him. He became at last a dupe who was thankful for being duped. The preachers told him that the ills and misfortunes of this life were a blessing in disguise, that God meant his poverty to be a means of Grace and that if he accepted the right creed all would be well and he would have eternal salvation.

"One of two things is true. Either these forgotten men and women are incapable of development and belong to a lower order of intelligence than any other people of Anglo-Saxon stock, or our civilization, so far as they are concerned, is a failure. There is no doubt which of these thoughts are true. Abraham Lincoln, Andrew Jackson, and Andrew Johnson sprang from them. They are capable of development, capable of unlimited growth and elevation.

"Since both the politician and the preacher have failed to lift their life after a century of trial, it is surely time for a wiser statesmanship.

"And that wiser statesmanship is now in evidence. We are in a great revival of education, the like of which I do not believe has ever been seen before in any State. The level of your life has been moved further upward in the past ten years than in any preceding fifty years. I never come back home but that I am astounded by the changes. There has been no other event in North Carolina since the foundation of the Union that compares in importance to this new educational progress. The movement has now reached such a momentum that nothing can stop it until every child comes into his own."

His voice reached a climax of emotional power that caught the heart of his audience and swept them into the first stirring round of applause. It had not died away when the speaker hurled a new bomb.

"The man who says that we are too poor to increase our taxes for education is a traitor to his people and their children. We charge each taxpayer but $2.13 for education. The poor old State of Maine pays $9.23. Iowa pays $15. Too poor to maintain good schools! The man who says it is the author of poverty. It is the doctrine that has kept us poor. It smells of the almshouse and the hovel. It has driven men of wealth from our State. Such a man is the victim of an ancient falsehood.

"The most sacred thing in the Commonwealth and to the Commonwealth is the child. Whether it be your child, or the child of the dull faced mother of a hovel. The child of the dull faced mother may, for all you know, be the most capable child in the State. The child whether born of poor parents or rich parents, is the one priceless undeveloped resource of any nation.

"You that know me will bear witness that I have not spoken of our fathers, nor of our politicians, least of all of our religious teachers in a spirit of ungrateful criticism. I have said seemingly hard things, but with all proper respect in my heart for them, for their good qualities and good works. Only to show that their systems have proven failures for our needs. Doubtless under the conditions of their life they did the best they could. But our conditions are different. We must accept them without the witnesses of the past. Today there is no North, no South, no East or West. Face our problems of today like men, forget the past and lift all darkness from our life."

There was a stir of dissent in the rear, but the speaker rushed on.

"I give you the creed which I hold with every energy of my soul:

"I believe in the full public training of both the hands and the mind of every child born of woman.

"I believe that by the right training of men, we add to the wealth of the world. All wealth is the creation of men, and he creates it only in proportion to the trained uses of the community. And that the more men we train, the more wealth we create.

"I believe in the perpetual regeneration of society, in the immortality of democracy and in growth everlasting.

"I nail this thesis on the door of my native State with the prayer that God shall bring it to pass! Whatever I may say in prophecy would be as inadequate as all that I might say in contemplation. Great changes come as silently as the seasons. I am no more sure of this spring time than I am of the rebirth of our society and the lifting up of our life. A revolution is in progress and this great nation is one of its tokens. In truth and solemnness I say it—an inspiring sight. We are laying, the foundations of a new social order. A forgotten people will rise and with them will rise all the people."

The enthusiasm of the speaker in his final burst of eloquence caught the soul of the crowd. His spirit was contagious. Cheer after cheer was given. The applause continued until Page was compelled to rise, bow and lift his hand for silence.

Angela pinched Dave's arm and whispered:

"Wasn't he glorious, Mr. Forgotten Man?"

"Great!" was the quick answer. "Greatest I ever heard. How did you know so much about him, honey?"

"Read his speeches and his editorials in the magazines he has edited."

"And you knew enough to get him for the first speaker. You're the wonder of the world to me."

"You'll hear another great man when Governor Aycock speaks. He'll lift you out of your seat."

Chapter 11

The Captain quickly introduced the next speaker.

"And now, ladies and gentlemen, I am going to present to you the greatest Governor the Southern States have produced since the Civil War, Charles B. Aycock of North Carolina."

Aycock rose with quiet dignity, his finely shaped head and erect figure marking as handsome a man as ever faced an audience. He was received with great enthusiasm, even greater than the first speaker. He was far better known to the rank and file. Many of them had heard him on the stump in political campaigns that had stirred their deepest passions. He hadn't spoken three sentences before he displayed the qualities of the supreme orator.

He made every man and woman before him feel he was voicing their own feelings, not trying to instruct them. He turned first to Page.

"I yield to no one, ladies and gentlemen, in recognition of the sterling qualities that make Walter H. Page a figure in our history, an honour to his native State and the nation. I owe to him the inspiration that gave bent to my life. I've read every article he ever wrote as a young journalist in North Carolina. I've followed his career in the North and read his brilliant appeals with increasing admiration——"

He paused and smiled, and a feeling of tension ran through the audience.

"But," he went on smiling, "when Walter Page talks to us about dead hands clutching our throat from the past he reminds me of the fellow who was looking for a black cat in a dark cellar, on a dark night, with no light—when the cat wasn't there!"

A shout of laughter rose in which Page joined heartily. Captain Collier slapped his thigh and howled with joy. And when he took out his pencil and began to scribble hastily, Angela fervently prayed that he wasn't fixing to make a speech that would break up the meeting in a riot. She looked with a feeling of nervousness at the speaker and distinctly heard him say to Page in a low tone: "Had to take that crack at you, Walter. It was too good to lose."

Page waved his hand in a good natured gesture.

"It's all right. Go on. Hit him again. He's got no friends."

"You've got one."

"But I see I can't depend on him."

Still smiling Aycock turned back to the audience and resumed his speech.

"There is a very fine and high sense, in which as our distinguished friend said, there is no North and no South. Yet there is another finer sense in which I am glad to say today that *there is a South!*"

A roar of applause greeted that remark. He was voicing the unspoken things in their own souls. The applause suddenly ended in a tense silence and the crowd hung on his next words.

"When I see before me this happy, prosperous, well dressed audience, once stricken by four years of disastrous war and six more years of still more disastrous Reconstruction, when I see the mighty work that the men and women of this section of our country are doing, I say there *is* a South, and a *glorious* South——"

Again a cheer swept the crowd and continued until the speaker stilled them.

"When I think of the history of this country of ours and recall the deeds of the people of the Carolinas when they were struggling with British tyranny, I'm glad to say there was, and there still is, a South. Nor am I ashamed of the mighty deeds which you wrought from '61 to '65!"

The crowd in a single resistless impulse were on their feet in a frenzy of cheers. Captain Collier hung on the edge of the platform, his flowing white hair shaking, shouting at the top of his voice. Page slipped a little lower in his seat. He should never had uttered that sentence. He realized it now. It wasn't the time or place. He couldn't blame the speaker. He was making his audience putty in his hand to mould them later to his will.

Aycock went on with steady purpose: "I shall forever defend these men and women. They were, and are, a great people. Sturdy, determined, hot blooded, maybe but it took the shock of four years battle from Bethel to Appomattox to cool their blood. I have ceased to talk about the fact that we are now in the Union. We never managed to get out. And if there be a State today that still wants to secede, we Southerners will tell them they can't get out. This is our Union made after the splendid minds of the Southern leaders who created it and the hearts of Revolutionary heroes wrought it out in suffering, blood and death, sustained through fifty years of a glorious peace and finally cemented in the blood shed on both sides of the Mason and Dixon line in a great Civil War. It is our Union now and forever. I speak of the South and for the South."

Another wave of cheering swept the crowd. He took up his speech in a complete change of humor and tone.

"Now do not misunderstand me in all this. I am not speaking to you as a man of the past. I am speaking to you as a Democrat of Democrats moving steadily forward to what I believe will be a great future. In my political career I have always believed in utter frankness in meeting every issue. I drew the Amendment to our State Constitution disfranchising the Negro. Not because his skin was black but because he had proved himself incapable of sustaining good government under the conditions of our life. Through his vote our electorate was degraded until that degradation became unbearable. Had he been capable of self government he had ample opportunity to show it.

"Not a single leader of the Negro race, so far in South Carolina, proved himself worthy of his people in the trial of fire from 1868 to 1875. We have solved our Negro problem in North Carolina by taking the black man out of politics, and thus laid the foundations for the development of both races. We have secured peace and rendered prosperity certain.

"Let me add some things that should follow. After this, let the Negro alone. Quit writing about him. Quit talking about him. Quit making him the white man's burden. Let him tote his own skillet. Quit coddling him. Let him learn that no man, no race ever got anything worth the having which was not earned. That character is the outcome of sacrifice and worth is the result of toil. That whatever the future may be, the present has in it for him nothing that will not be the product of industry, thrift, obedience to law and uprightness. That he cannot by resolution of councils accomplish anything. That he can do much by work. That violence may gratify his passions but cannot accomplish his ambitions. That he may eat rarely in this country of the cooking of equality, but he will always find when he does, that 'there is death in the pot.' The Negro must learn once and for all that there is unending separation of the races——"

Again the crowd rose and shouted. The speaker quickly quelled them and went on: "The two people may develop side by side but they cannot intermingle. Let the white man determine that no man shall, by act or thought, or speech cross this line and the race problem will be at an end. These things are not said in enmity to the Negro but in regard for him. He has always been my personal friend. As a lawyer I often defended him. As Governor I have protected him. But there flows in my veins the blood of the dominant race. The race that had conquered the earth and seeks out the mysteries of its heights and depths. When the Negro recognizes this fact we shall have peace and good will between the races.

"Universal education is the imperative and only remedy for our ills. We must build on this foundation of character and inherited traits. We must not repudiate but develop. We must put away vain glory and boasting and take an impartial inventory of all the things that we have and are."

Page suddenly lifted his hand and led a round of applause.

"When I was a little boy I was shocked one day to see my dear mother sign a deed by making a cross mark. I did not know that she could not write. Then and there I breathed a solemn promise to Almighty God that if I could bring it to pass every child born of woman should be trained to develop the best within them.

"We are entering upon a new day. We stand tiptoe on a mountain height and see the morning sun make purple glory in the East. A new day. A day of equal opportunity. Equal. That is the word. On that word I plant myself. The equal right of every child born on earth to have the opportunity to burgeon out all that there is within him."

He turned suddenly from the crowd sitting so enthralled they did not realize he had finished.

And then they rose and cheered and sang: "My Country 'Tis of Thee." The first man to congratulate the Governor was Walter Page who did it without words. He slipped his arm around Aycock and gave him a hug.

Captain Collier allowed the ovation to wear itself out before he attempted to command order. At the end of five minutes he walked to the edge of the platform and the crowd settled into their seats in a silence that brought to Angela's heart a renewed prayer that her beloved old timer would say nothing to mar the success of the meeting. His first sentence was reassuring.

"Ladies and gentlemen, I find I cannot make the little speech I had planned for today. I could have answered the political trend of Walter Page with a sharp word or two. I can always discount Page's political message. I knew his folks. His father was a staunch old line Whig—never was much of a Democrat. Walter inherits some of this and I always expect to see this in his hoof when he kicks up his heels. He did very little of this today. He brought us a message we should take to our hearts.

"I cannot make you the speech I had in mind because of what Page told you. It's this other man who has played the devil with my plans. This handsome silver tongued speaker from the Black Belt of the Carolinas who has today stolen our hearts."

He was stopped by another wave of cheers and then went on evenly: "Because of him I'm offering a resolution which I hadn't composed when I stepped on this platform. 'Resolved that it is the sense of this mass meeting of the Carolinas that a modern school house be erected in every township of every county and a full term of eight months be established for blacks and whites alike——"

A man in the first row jumped up and shouted: "I move its adoption!"

A chorus answered: "I second the motion!"

"All in favor, say 'Aye'!"

A roar of "Ayes" rose from the crowd.

"Opposed—No——"

Not a single negative voice was heard. A dead silence followed and Captain Collier squared his shoulders.

"The thing I like, ladies and gentlemen, about this meeting is frankness. Walter Page was utterly frank. Governor Aycock was the soul of frankness. As an old fashioned man of the South let me be equally frank.

"I believe if we have chosen a leader we should let him lead and we should follow. This meeting today has unanimously chosen Charles B. Aycock as our leader——"

A rousing cheer left no doubt about it.

"All right. I introduced the resolution for which he stands. Now let my gray hair strike a note of warning if not dissent. When Governor Aycock says there shall be no social mingling of the races I understand and applaud him. When he says in the next breath that we must give to the Negro a training in every way equal to that we give the white race and that will solve the Negro problem, I cannot follow his reasoning. To my simple old fashioned mind the equal education of the Negro will complicate, not solve the problem of race. When he says let the Negro know this, let him know that, I mildly inquire who is going to teach him these restrictions once he is given the powers of self assertion?

"I also mildly raise the question of book learning as a panacea for all our ills. Let me read a few paragraphs from the latest book out of France, sent me by a Huguenot kinsman of my mother. For more than a hundred years France has been the barometer of modern civilization. There is something in the French mind that finds the inner truth of things before other nations have faced it. Says Gustave Le Bon, the great modern philosopher and psychologist:

"Foremost among the dominant ideas of the present epoch is the notion that instruction is capable of changing men, improving them and even of making them equal. Being constantly repeated this assertion has been a steadfast democratic dogma.

"On this point, however, democratic ideas are in profound disagreement with the results of psychology and experience. Many philosophers, among them Herbert Spencer, have no difficulty in showing that instruction neither renders a man more moral or happier. That it changes neither his instinct nor his hereditary passions. And that at times when badly directed it is far more pernicious than useful. Criminality increases with a certain kind of instruction, and the worst enemies of society, anarchists, and communists, are recruited from the prize winners of our schools. At present three thousand educated criminals are met with for every thousand illiterate delinquents. In fifty years our criminals have increased from two hundred and twenty seven to five hundred and fifty two in every hundred thousand inhabitants, a rise of 133 per cent. Criminality is particularly on the increase among the young for whom free and obligatory schooling in France has replaced apprenticeship.

"Learning lessons by heart is a ludicrous form of education where every effort is an act of faith admitting the infallibility of the master, belittling ourselves and rendering us impotent.

"Were that sort of education merely useless it would be bad enough. But the system presents a far more serious danger. It gives to those who have submitted to it a violent dislike to the state of life in which they were born and an intense desire to escape from it. The working man no longer wishes to remain a working man, or the peasant to continue a peasant. While the humblest member of the middle class admits of no career for his son except that of a State paid official. Instead of preparing men for life our schools prepare them for public office, whose success can be attained without self direction or the slightest glimmer of personal initiation.

"The State which manufactures by text books all the people possessing diplomas can use only a small number of them and is forced to leave the others without employment. In consequence it must fear the first class and combat the others as its enemies.

"There are twenty thousand school teachers in Paris without employment in the department of the Seine alone. All of them persons who disdained field and work shops and took to the State for their livings. The number of the chosen being few the number of the discontented is immense, ready at a moment's notice for any revolution no matter who are its chiefs or what its goal.

"It is now too late to retrace our steps. Experience grim and savage must show us our mistakes. Experience alone will teach us to replace our odious text books and our futile examinations by industrial instruction that will return our young men to the field, the workshop and the Colonial enterprise, which they avoid today at all costs.

"And so we have today an army of the discontented, ready to obey all the suggestions of dreamers and soap box orators. In the school rooms of today we are creating the Socialist, the Communist, the Anarchist."

The Captain stopped and removed his glasses.

"Thus speaks the greatest philosopher of modern times. Surely there is food for thought in what he says. I have moved the resolution of the day, because we are confronted by an unsolved and apparently unsolvable race problem. I'm willing to try any thing once. We'll try this. What the outcome will be, when thousands and hundreds of thousands of Negro morons, laboring under the delusion that they have an education which makes them the equal of our white race, knock at your doors and demand admission, in politics, in industry, in society, presents a problem. A problem I cannot answer. Nor can you.

"The American ideal was never meant by its creators to include the Negro. A black slave handed to Thomas Jefferson the pen with which he wrote the Declaration Of Independence. And when he wrote 'All men are created free and equal' he had no reference to the Negro. The conflict of color is a legacy of the Civil War.

"This nation is great for one reason only. A race of white freemen cleared its wilderness and made its laws. On the quality of human life all depends.

"To quit discussing the race problem, to quit thinking about it, will not solve it. Nor will education by text books solve it. May the God of our fathers, who created this republic, lead and guide us is my humble prayer."

The speaker closed in a silence that was pain. The Mass Meeting was a success. The speakers won their points. But the crowd carried home with them a sense of grim uneasiness.

Chapter 12

The problem of Marie's rapid growth filled Angela with a tender alarm. The child came to see her every day and begged to stay until dark. The happiness of married life fascinated her. There was a hunger in her eyes that at times caused her sister a laugh that was kin to a tear.

"What are you brooding about?" Angela asked her.

"You know."

"I don't."

"Well, you know that this is leap year, don't you?"

"You're not thinking of proposing to Phil, are you?"

"Yes I am," she sighed. "Would it be wrong?"

"No. But awfully silly."

"Leap year's a real thing, isn't it?"

"Yes."

"Then I have a right to tell him I love him—haven't I?"

"Of course, darling, if you wish. But you know you must go to Bethlehem to school next fall."

"Not if I marry."

"No. Of course not."

"All right. I'll ask Phil this afternoon. I'll go to his office to see him about the little legacy Mama left me for my wedding day."

Angela kissed her and laughed.

"Put on your prettiest frock and give Phil my love, too."

Marie squeezed her hand.

"You're the dearest, sweetest sister a girl ever had. You're my mother and my sister and my father and my brother all in one. You don't know how I love you."

From the door Angela waved:

"Good luck, darling."

Marie threw a kiss in reply, then ran back and cried:

"Can I drive your car?"

"Yes, dear. But be very careful. You're only fourteen. Don't get arrested."

"I'll come back and tell you what he said."

She put on the white dress her sister had worn the day she rejected Phil and smiled in the mirror at the all but perfect reproduction. From the garden she cut a red rose bud.

Phil stared at her dumbfounded when she blew into his office half an hour later.

"I was just passing, Phil, and brought you a rose."

She came close, pinned it in the lapel of his coat and looked at him tenderly.

"You're beautiful, dear!" he said gently.

"You see I'm wearing long skirts now. This one's just like Angela's old one, isn't it?"

"Exactly. And you're so much like her it's uncanny."

"Am I as pretty?"

"I may be a traitor to say it, but you're more beautiful."

"I'm glad. For I've something-very-important-to-say-to-you. It's leap year you know—I love you, Phil, darling, will you marry me?"

It was impossible to smile at her. She was in deadly earnest, her cheeks flushed, her eyes misty, her voice trembling.

"I've loved you always. You're my hero," she went on quickly. "I couldn't understand Angela turning you down. Let me make up for it. I'll love you forever."

Phil found himself hesitating and blushing.

"Why, Marie, darling. You take my breath. I never dreamed it. This is the sweetest thing that has ever happened to me. I can't believe my ears."

"Then you do love me a little?"

"Of course, I do, dear."

"You may kiss me!"

He slipped an arm about her graceful figure and kissed her tenderly.

"And you'll marry me?"

"Well, dear, I can't say now. This is sudden, you know. I'll have to think."

"But we can be engaged?"

"Well," he said slowly, "we can have an understanding with each other. Long engagements are not wise they say."

"I don't want a long one."

"But you'll have to go to college next fall."

"Not if we get married."

He shook his head gravely.

"It will never do to cut out college. I'm a college man you know. My wife should be a college woman."

"All right," she agreed quickly. "If you wish it, I'll go. But you'll write to me?"

"Yes. I will and we'll have a nice time together here this summer. We'll keep it a secret, but I'll take you to ride, and to the movies. And I'll see a lot of you. And then you'll forget me when you're gone so long."

"Never, Phil, darling. You've made me so happy. Take me to the Falls Sunday—will you? I'll pack a box for a picnic."

He nodded and she held his hand as they walked to the door, where she kissed him goodbye.

"I can tell Angela?" she cried from the head of the stairs.

"Yes. Tell her."

She drove back to "Hillcrest" at breakneck speed, rushed into her sister's arms and told her the wonderful news.

"He said he loved you?"

"Not exactly. But that we understood each other and he would show me a good time until I went to Bethlehem in the fall."

"I knew he'd tell you to go to college. He's a great man, dear, very brilliant, very wise, and very gentle. You must do just what he tells you."

"Oh, I will. Thank you again, dear, for the white dress. I think it got him!"

"Don't worry Grandpa with this, darling. It's our secret. Just we three shall know it."

As the erstwhile child, now a tall graceful young woman, walked down the hill, her sister watched her wistfully.

"It would be wonderful if she wins him after all," she mused. "He deserves the happiness her beauty and sweet spirit would bring to him."

Her mind came back quickly to the problems of her own home. For some reason Dave was growing restless. At times almost unhappy.

When he came in earlier than usual she asked:

"What's the matter with you lately?"

"I'm scared, honey."

"Scared of what?"

"You know women die sometimes having babies—especially the first one."

"Don't be silly, Dave!" she said with scorn. "I'm as husky as an Indian Squaw. They have babies by the roadside, swing them on their back and go on. I believe I could. I'm so strong it's ridiculous. Women were made to have babies."

"I know, but I love you so—if anything happens to you I just couldn't go on. You've made the world new for me. Without you there wouldn't be any world."

She drew his head down and kissed him.

"That's the way I want you to feel, of course. But don't. I'm all right. And I'll give you a bouncing baby and never know I've had a pain."

"You think so?" he gulped.

"I know it. Go happy to your work every day and know that I'm all right."

Angela was taken with her first labor pains while getting breakfast for Dave. She finished without letting him know. When he had eaten she said quietly:

"You can call the doctor now, David."

"You're in pain, darling?" he gasped.

"Have been a little for half an hour."

"Oh, my God, and you didn't let me know!" He rushed to the telephone and called the doctor.

"Said he'd be here in half an hour. My Lord he's taking his time about it. Is there anything I can do?"

"Yes. Just sit here by the bed, hold my hand and smile."

He was trembling from head to foot.

"I'll hold your hand," he mumbled, "but I'm afraid I can't smile."

"Yes you can. It's going to be a boy and his name will be David Henry."

He laughed in a strained way in spite of himself.

When the doctor came he saw the husband trembling and snapped:

"You'll have to get out, Dave."

"Oh, please let him stay, Dr. Andrews," came a soft voice from the bed.

The doctor shook his head.

"Listen, child. I brought you into the world a little over eighteen years ago, and many a one since. I know this job. I can pull you through all right, but I can't promise to save this big trembling brute. He would probably prove too much for me. I might have to knock him in the head. Run along, Dave."

"I'll sit right outside the door, honey," he flung back from the doorway.

"Better go out to the barn. I'll call you when it's time to come."

He went to the barn, told Jim Beasley, his helper, the news, and sent him out to the field and ran back to the house.

He sat on the couch and listened breathlessly for the slightest sound from the bedroom. None came except the doctor's slow tread and the occasional click of his instruments on a table.

The door suddenly opened and he looked at Dave who leaped to meet him.

"Anything wrong, sir?"

"No, you idiot, but you might go up to Mrs. Lovelace's place and tell her your wife wishes her to come down."

"There'll be time for me to get back?"

"And maybe a couple of hours to spare."

"I'll bring her in the car right away."

He started to the door to tell Angela but the doctor pushed him back with a sharp shove that all but sent him on the couch.

"Stay out, boy. I'll tell you when."

Ann came at once and Dave gave a sigh of relief as he heard her crooning over the bed.

"She's a wonderful woman," he sighed. "God walks with her, she says, and I believe it. I know she'll help my girl."

He tramped the floor with a nervous tread and the third hour passed before he heard her first wild cry of pain. It pierced him and he sank on the couch with a groan. When she screamed again he stopped his ears. And the third, he fell on his knees, buried his face in a pillow and tried to pray. The cries came in shorter and shorter intervals and then a long piercing scream that tore the heart out of him.

He sprang to his feet and shouted:

"Damn it, why don't you do something for her!"

For a moment he walked the floor like an enraged tiger, and when Ann appeared at the door and called, he stared at her dumbly.

"You can come in now, David," she repeated before he caught her meaning.

He walked slowly as in a dream until he saw Angela lying limp and still on the bed and then he rushed to her side, fell on his knees, kissed her hand and muttered:

"Oh, my darling. I've killed you. I know I've killed you!"

With her other hand she ran her fingers through the shock of red hair.

"No, you've made me very happy. I'm the mother of your son. You'll see him in a minute."

The doctor brought the baby in and showed him to the father.

"A husky youngster weighing eight pounds."

Dave glanced casually at the little red face and frowned.

"Don't look like much to me."

"One of the finest babies I've ever delivered, sir," the doctor corrected, handing the bundle to Ann.

"And now children, I must hurry on. There's another mother calling me."

Dave followed him to the door, and grasped his hand.

"Hope you didn't hear me holler at you, Doctor."

"No," he laughed. "I was too busy to listen to a fool husband."

"I want to thank you."

"You needn't," the doctor smiled. "It's all in the day's work. Good luck, David."

He hurried back to the bedside and held his wife's hand for half an hour, scarcely speaking.

At last he roused from his half trance and rose hurriedly.

"I'll take the car and fetch Lottie Spake to cook and do the housework till you're well."

"And bring old man Adam to see the hound," Angela called.

She recovered in two weeks and insisted on resuming her work again. Dave wouldn't hear of it.

"No. You won't," he said emphatically. "Ann told me to keep the girl a month and just let you hold the baby and sing to it. May keep her all the time."

"All right, sir," she smiled.

By the first of August she was herself again, with a new soft beauty in her face and a new vitality in her body. Joyfully she went into the fields and watched her husband work. Sometimes she sat on the sulky plow and drove it for an hour.

The day the fodder was hauled to the barn proved an exciting one. All morning it looked like rain. And wet fodder meant a ruined crop of forage. Dave called all hands and the cook into the field and consented to Angela's coming.

Adam took charge of the baby while Lottie joined in the work of loading the two wagons. The old man took advantage of the occasion to introduce little David to the hound. He drew back when the big tongue first licked his hand, then crowed with delight as the good natured dog kissed his chubby face.

Angela helped Dave load and Lottie assisted Jim. The last load was piled high on Jim's wagon and rushed to cover, as the clouds grew blacker. Dave's wagon was in the lower field and it was a question whether the frame would hold all that remained.

Jim and Lottie ran back to help and when the wagon, piled high with its immense load, got to the little hill on which the barn stood, the horse balked and wouldn't move an inch. Jim sat on the load driving while the other three walked beside the wagon. In vain the driver urged the horse to pull up the hill. He just stamped his foot, looked back at the towering load of fodder and settled in his tracks.

The storm had been brewing for half an hour and it now loomed close in the west, huge black billowy clouds, streaked with lightning. Dave was beside himself with anxiety. He did not want to lose a single bundle of his fodder. It would barely last the horses a year if he saved every blade of it. Jim sat serenely on the load clucking in a futile way to the balky horse.

It thundered sharply and Dave yelled:

"What's the matter with you, Jim? Why don't you get down here and start the horse. You told me you could move any horse in the world when he balked."

Jim rolled off the fodder and stood beside the wagon.

"I can, too, if you let me do it my own way."

"Well, get at it!" was the sharp command.

Jim looked at Angela, grinned at his boss, chuckled and twitched the horse with the lines.

"Git up thar! What ails you?"

There was no get up. The horse never budged. Jim struck him with the whip. He kicked twice but never straightened a trace. The thunder was rolling now in terrific peals and Jim scratched his head.

"I kin start him, boss, ef you let me do it my way."

"It don't seem to work."

"I ain't tried it yit."

"What is your way?" Dave growled.

"You said if I cussed in front of the missus you'd lay me flat."

"You're a fool!"

Dave tried persuasion. There was nothing doing. The storm suddenly broke in fury but half a mile away. Across the valley they could see the long streams of water pouring from the sky. The first big rain drops struck them in the face. Dave looked in grief at the load of fine fodder about to be ruined and snapped to his helper:

"All right, try it your own way."

Jim leaped back on the load, grabbed the reins and let out a string of oaths:

"Now, you damned son of a bitch, we'll see what's what! Damn your lazy soul to the bottom of hell, get a move on you!"

The horse flicked his ears nervously.

"I ain't said nothin' yit . . . jist limberin' up my jaw to begin—You goddam . . ."

"Can you stand it?" Dave whispered.

Angela laughed: "I've sometimes felt that way myself, but couldn't say it—let him rip!"

From Jim's lips poured a stream of profanity the like of which she had never expected to hear on earth.

The horse's body stiffened and his ears flickered again as if the blasphemy was too much. He suddenly dashed forward with the heavy load, took the hill in a jiffy and swept into the barn in time to save the fodder. The last thing Angela heard above the growing thunder was Jim's flaming stream of oaths.

She laughed until she cried.

"I'll have to get rid of that heathen," Dave moaned.

"Don't do it on my account. I'll stand Jim's cussin if you can. He apologized profusely one day when I caught him, and said he couldn't help it. He doesn't mean anything by it. Just a habit of words he said."

When they got back to the house, old Adam was sitting on the steps with the baby on one knee and the hound on the other.

Angela caught the baby up and set him screaming with kisses, while the old man spoke in solemn tones to her husband.

"David, my son, you know you promised me something."

"Did I, Pop?"

"You know you did."

"Forgot all about it—what?"

"You promised me to go coon huntin' with me and this dog of I let you have him."

"We will go, Adam, the first moonlight night next month."

"Good nuff. Hit's a little early yit. And hit'll gimme time to round up a pack for my Boney to lead. More coons this year than I ever seed in my life."

"Where have you seen them?" Angela asked in surprise.

"Seed their tracks in every soft stretch of sand and mud in these woods. We're certain ter strike a bunch o' two or three coons on one trail. Boney can lick any one of them that walks on four feet. But he can't lick two at the same time. They'd cut him to strips."

He paused and turned to Angela.

"I want you to go long, too, Miss Henry."

"Not a bit of it," Dave interrupted.

"Cose she kin, ef she wants to," the old man maintained. "Ain't I seed her plowin' long side of you in overalls and gloves. Gee whiz, walkin' through the woods, listin' ter the grandest music is just play ter that."

He turned to Angela again.

"Don't you want ter hear old Boney open up on 'em, honey?"

"I certainly do!" she laughed.

Dave threw up his hands.

Two weeks later the old man appeared at the house with a pack of six good looking hounds for his beloved to lead.

"You see, M'am," he explained. "Hit takes a choir to make real purty music. You can't tell what a beautiful voice Boney has till you hear him leadin' five or six others. Then, man alive, you want to yell yer head off."

Dave carried the lantern and they entered the woods by the path along which he had led his sweetheart the first day he showed to her its mysteries and treasures. The dogs had plunged into the forest far ahead.

Suddenly Boney opened on a hot trail not more than half a mile away.

The old man leaped into the air and answered with an unearthly yell. By the light of the lantern Angela saw his eyes flashing with the fire of youth. Age had slipped from his bent shoulders and time had ceased to be. Again and again he answered his beloved dog's bay.

"Listen—by the eternal," he whispered, "they're comin' this way. The coon's making double quick fer the crick that runs through your lower field."

The six other dogs joined in a chorus and Adam listened in ecstasy.

"Lord, Lord, ain't that purty!" he exulted. "Aint thet music! They keep time the same ez ef they wuz plain' in a band o' seven pieces. Listen ter their different tones. Ye kin tell a dog's age by the notes he strikes. Old Boney's deep voice always leads the pack. He's way out in front of 'em, too. He's always there—the best coon dog that walks on four legs. Talk about thirty dollars fer a dog like that! He's wuth a thousand dollars o' eny man's money. There haint money enough in this world ter have bought him off o' me, ef I could a helt on to him."

He stopped, listened and straightened his figure and yelled:

"Git him, Boney,—git him!"

The dog answered quickly as if he had caught his master's voice.

Adam's excitement mounted as the volume increased. He suddenly slapped Dave a resounding blow across the shoulders.

"Boy, you're goin' ter see somethin' tonight, you'll never fergit. There's mor'n one coon in that trail. The dogs can't lose it fer a minute. There's two certin—maybe three. What a battle we're goin' ter have!"

They followed the creek bank for half a mile, there was another lull, and then Boney's voice rang out in the slow measured stroke of treed game.

"They've got 'em, by golly. They've got 'em!" Adam shouted. "But they're not up a tree. There ain't no tree in half a mile o' that place that a coon could climb." He paused and hurried to Jim.

"Gimme yer axe an' you run to the barn and fetch a spade and shovel. They're in that crick bank."

Jim darted back toward the barn, while Adam, Dave, and Angela hurried to the spot where the seven dogs were now baying slowly in chorus.

"Ever hear o' the battle o' Waterloo," the old man asked. "Captain Tom Collier tole me that Napoleon Boneparte fit that battle."

"Oh, yes," Angela nodded. "That was one of the greatest battles of the world."

"Well, you're goin' ter see one jest as great ter night, er I miss my guess. And old Napoleon Boney will lead this one too. You see, M'am," he nodded to Angela, "there's a feud tween a houn' dog an a coon. Ez a rule a coon kin lick eny dog. But not my Boney."

They pressed close through the dense cane brake and emerged into an open sandy spot between two slim maple trees, and, sure enough, the dogs had "treed." All seven of them were scratching in the sand like mad, now and then thrusting a nose deep into it. They could smell the coons beneath the earth. The entrance to their den was under water.

When Adam had yelled himself hoarse encouraging the dogs he stood over Boney in silence and watched him dig. Only a low growl came from him now and then.

"Here's where they are," he announced with finality. "Boney's got his nose right over 'em. I never seed anything like this dog in my life."

He had dug a hole in the sand three feet deep and there was still no sign of a coon when Jim came with a spade and shovel.

Adam took the spade and Jim the shovel and they threw the sand back five or six feet to open the way for a deep cut straight down. When the spade finally broke through to the den the hole was five feet deep.

The old man bent low and threw the rays of the light into the cavern. Two pinpoints of glittering eyes could be seen reflecting a steady light from the darkness below. The opening was not more than a foot across but Adam decided it was enough. The dogs had gone wild with excitement as the smell from the den flooded their nostrils. They circled the hole barking madly, but not one would thrust his nose near those glittering eyes. They had been on coon hunts before and showed a lively memory of bleeding ears and slashed heads. In the open a dog had a chance. With a coon on his back in such a hole, with four terrible claws in action, claws as sharp and strong as steel needles, no dog with good sense would venture within reach.

In vain the old man screamed his orders.

"Go in I tell ye! Fetch 'em out! Fetch 'em out!"

The dogs merely circled and watched and barked savagely. Even Boney crept down close, took a long look and crawled back to a place of safety.

His retreat, cut the old man's pride.

"He ain't scared," he protested. "Jest using caution at first. You'll see."

He knelt, took Boney in his arms, moved down low into the dug out urging him to battle. The dog felt the hurt in his old master's voice and his back bristled.

Then with a sudden quick movement of his powerful body the hound plunged straight down and rose with a coon's back in his clenched jaw. He threw the long bundle of gray fur six feet into the air. Every dog of the six in the pack was on him as he touched the ground. And then another coon leaped from the hole. Old Boney's eyes had never left the spot. He was waiting, pounced on him, and the second battle of Waterloo was on. Over the writhing, snarling, snapping dogs and coons, Old Adam stood and yelled. Angela had not believed it possible for a human being to yell with such joyous power. For two minutes he stood first over one squirming, growling group and then over the other.

Angela shook his arm.

"Can't you stop them? Why don't you stop them?"

"Stop 'em, honey!" the old man wailed. "The fight's the thing we came to see. It's a battle. It's great to see a battle."

"They'll kill each other," she cried.

"They sho will, M'am. It's a dead dog now or a dead coon. We don't aim ter lose our dogs."

A third coon unexpectedly emerged from the den and stood a moment as if uncertain whether to run or fight.

Adam dragged Boney off the coon that was now covered by two other dogs and threw him on the new one that had backed into the edge of the cane. They hadn't more than clinched when a fourth pelt of beautiful gray fur leaped from the den.

The old man screamed at the top of his lungs:

"Great God! There's four of 'em. We ain't got dogs enough. They'll kill some of 'em shore's hell!"

In ten minutes it was over. Four beautiful gray furs lay full length on the sand. Adam, so hoarse he couldn't speak above a whisper, was tenderly binding up Boney's wounds.

"Wasn't that a fight!" he sighed.

"But one of the dogs is dead," Jim retorted.

"Yes. It's all in the day's work. The minute I seed we had a bunch o' coons in that den I knowed we would lose a dog. Hit can't be helped."

He paused and hugged Boney.

"But they didn't git old Napoleon Boneparte at this battle o' Waterloo, did they?"

Dave found Angela seated on a log up the creek.

"What's the matter, honey?" he asked anxiously.

"Just a little nauseated, David."

He drew her to her feet.

"I told you that you wouldn't like a coon hunt. But you're terribly hard headed."

"I didn't know it was like this."

"Don't say anything to hurt the old man's feelings. He has been in heaven tonight."

"I'll remember."

"You can look at the lovely furs and tell Adam his dog is a wonder."

He led her to the lantern, and she glanced at the gray bodies and her eyes rested on the larger one.

"One is much larger than the others."

"The mother of the other three," Adam observed.

She leaned against Dave and wept.

"There, there now, honey," he soothed. "Don't make Adam feel bad."

She wiped her eyes.

"No—I won't."

"There's four as fine skins as you'll see this year, M'am," the old man whispered. "One of them'll make you a neck piece."

"You can have them all, Adam," she answered.

"All of 'em?"

He looked at Dave for confirmation.

"Sure, Adam. You're the coon hunter."

"That's nice of you, Dave. Them skins is worth twenty dollars this year. I thank ye—thank ye, M'am, both of ye."

As they turned toward home following the lantern, Angela shivered close to Dave.

"We won't go coon hunting again, will we, dear?"

He pressed her chilled hand.

"No. And I'm ahaid you won't like fur coats any more."

"I'll never wear another one."

CHAPTER 13

After the never-to-be-forgotten hunt a tropical storm swept the State from the West Indies. The wind attained a velocity of sixty five miles an hour. All night long the crash of trees could be heard in the woods. Limbs were twisted from the great oak in the yard and one fell on the roof of the house. No leak followed. No damage was done.

"I saw you set those rafters, David," the wife smiled. "Your work was well done."

"You bet it was. No wind can push them out of place and they'll shed flying limbs like a duck sheds water."

Until past midnight they sat beside the open fire and listened to the howl of the wind without the slightest desire to sleep.

"It's wonderful to feel human again at night," Angela said at last.

"What do you mean by that, honey?"

"Just what I said. You didn't break your back with beastly farm work today and tonight you are your old sweet self. People keep talking about solving the problems of our rickety civilization in a return to the farm. They've forgotten there's a farm problem to be solved. I'm finding out in our County that a farm hand leads the most benumbing, lonely life of any human being on earth except maybe a small farmer's wife. More of those women go insane than any other class and it's no wonder. After my first rounds in the country trying to do welfare work the wonder is to me that they don't all go crazy."

"I've thought of that sometimes, too," Dave agreed.

"The flight of these people from the loneliness, and degrading dirty work of a small Southern farm into the light and cheer of the towns is no accident. It's a move to a saner life."

"What can we do about it?" the man asked in puzzled tones.

"Do our part in leading to a human kind of farm. Its hours of work must be shortened. Its workers must be given time to see a sun rise and set. They must be given time to hear birds sing and feel the beauty of nature. While you've been driving yourself to death on our little place you've eaten your breakfast before daybreak. You've never lifted your head to see a sunrise or a sunset. You've never heard a bird sing. All these things are here, but you're too driven and tired to see or feel them . . ."

"You can't make both ends meet," he interrupted, "unless you work like a horse. With all my getting up before day I've only cleared about nine hundred dollars. I'll do better next year."

"Yes, you will. I'm going to see to it. What's your machinery for except to shorten your hours of work."

"Why, to make more money I thought."

"But not at the expense of a wasted life. The endless days of murderous toil through which you've been passing degrades both soul and body. We're going to have a change. We'll shorten hours and get more done. You're going to have your breakfast by the light of day. You've got to read and study and think. What's the use to live if it's the life of a mere plow horse?"

He stared at his wife in amazement and admiration.

"Lord, honey. You're a wonder! The sweetest woman God ever made. I'm a lucky man. I say that to myself every time I look at you. And every time I look at you I'm saying a prayer of thanks to God for giving you to me. You tell me what to do and I'll do it."

"You agree then to the new order of life at Hillcrest?"

"Tickled to death. I'd a never thought it out like you but I can see it when you tell me."

There was a long silence and they listened again to the fury of the storm. "I love to hear it," she murmured. "It means no work in the fields for you tomorrow. You can stay home with me and the baby."

"He's growing, isn't he?" was his proud interruption.

"He's crawling all over the place. He'll be walking before we know it."

"And talking, too!"

"All right. We'll take a little time and get acquainted with him. As soon as the storm passes I'm taking him over to see his Grampa. He's prouder of him than you are."

"He couldn't be," came the quick protest.

"This welfare work I've volunteered to do in the County is terribly depressing," she continued.

"Quit it. You're too young to take all that on yourself. Tend to me and the baby for welfare work and let it go at that. They say charity begins at home, don't they?"

"Shallow selfish people, yes. But I believe that the more we give of

our lives in trying to make others easier the richer our own becomes. The more you give the more you have. A rich man said the other day that as he walked down the hill of life he found that the only things he really had were the things he had given away."

"That don't quite make sense to me, but maybe you're right."

"I know I am. It's bed time now, way after twelve. We'll have breakfast at eight in the morning. The storm will still be blowing."

The next morning she received a telephone call from her grandfather.

"Come to see us, darling, as soon as you can."

"Anything the matter, Grampa?" she asked in alarm.

"A plenty, yes. But they say you're doing great work among our share croppers. I've a few poor white trash on the farm that I put on last year. I'd like you to try your hand on 'em the earliest possible minute. Come over at noon. The storm is passing."

"What did he say?" Dave asked.

"Says he has some poor white trash on the farm who need my best skill as a welfare worker."

Her husband frowned.

"It's not like Dr. Cameron to call my people poor white trash."

"They're not your people, David. In my trips through the County I've seen some who are not your kind. Two thirds of the poor white people of the South are your kind. The best English, Scotch-Irish and German blood of the nation. But there is a lower class of real trash. The Lord only knows where they came from and how they got here and what can be done about them. History says they came over as indentured servants or were shipped by the authorities of the old world because they were habitual criminals. Of course the word criminal is a broad term when applied to the people who settled our wilderness. I've no doubt old Adam Spake was one of them. But his crime consisted in shooting rabbits on posted ground. For game poaching men were hanged in England. But we've a much lower class of trash than old Adam's kind. We've a lot who are too lazy to shoulder a gun or carry a lantern on a coon hunt. Too lazy to yell once, to say nothing of yelling themselves hoarse over a coon fight."

"Guess you're right," Dave admitted. "What can you do with them?"

"Nothing much for the old ones. But we can save the children by teaching them. It's a long tough job but it can be done."

"Want me to go with you to your Grampa's?"

"No. You play with little David. I'll go alone. I can manage them better by myself."

She found her grandfather in a blue funk seated by the fire with a copy of the Charlotte Observer lying in his lap.

"I'm at the end of my row with three share croppers on my place. I've got to get rid of them and put Negroes in their place who will work under Nelse's direction. Talk to them and see if you can put any sense into their thick skulls."

"Who are they?" was the business inquiry.

"Old Peter Quinn, Ransom Russ and Ed Holly."

"Tough customers, I hear."

"You hear right. See what you can do. Old Quinn raised but one bale of cotton and owes for all his supplies. His share of the cotton didn't pay for the cash I advanced him. He wants me to stake him for another year. I would if he'd work. But he won't."

"Wasn't he a soldier under my father in the war?" she asked.

"He was under your father, but he never was a soldier. Every time he got in a battle he turned tail and ran like a turkey. He was court martialled and sentenced to die for cowardice. Your father got his pardon on his solemn promise to stand his ground in the next battle. He ran again before he smelled powder. Your father talked with him an hour and wound up an eloquent plea with the words: "Peter, it's sweet and honorable to die for one's country." "Yes, I know, Colonel, but I ain't fond o' sweet things," was the answer. "Try to get him to move without my throwing him off the place."

"I'll try."

"Dick Hollys' got two good looking girls who have gone to the devil. I won't have a house of prostitution on my place. Get him off. Old Ransom Russ made a fair crop, stole my share and hid it with his and threatens to sue me for the falsification of his account."

She began with old Quinn. He was good natured and willing to promise anything.

"Ef you'll jest lemme stay on, Miss Henry," he pleaded. "I'll do better next year. I didn't hev but one gal to work in the field this summer. My littliest gal's big enough to work next summer. The two kin raise six bales o' cotton and pay out all I owe."

"How old are your girls?"

"Come here, Sue. Come here, Jen!" he called.

Two pale tow headed scrawny children came timidly to the door. They wore kilts of cotton bagging and were bare footed. It was hard to tell, looking at them, whether they were boys or girls.

"How old are you?" Angela asked the smallest one.

"Ten, ma'am."

"And you?"

"I'm twelve."

"Are you going to school?"

"Ain't got nothin' to wear," they piped in chorus.

Angela turned to the slatternly mother who now stood in the doorway.

"If I can get you a grant of forty dollars a month from the County to see you through the winter will you send the girls to school and work your cotton in the summer, all of you?"

"Yes, *M'am*," old Quinn put in quickly. "I swear we will. God bless you. You're a angel."

As she left she knew he was lying when he said he'd work. But she'd give him one more trial.

The Holly house was perched on the top of the hill. As Angela drove up she saw the two girls dressed in neat cotton dresses that showed their plump figures. They were smiling, pert, ingratiating in their manners. Yet there was something pathetic in the look in their bright blue eyes. They were just silly, healthy, untaught children, one of them sixteen, the other eighteen.

"Do both of you girls work on the farm?" she asked.

"Yess'm," they smiled.

"Who else helps you?"

The older one drew closer. "Our daddy and two brothers, one fourteen and one twelve. They're all good workers, and we are too. We made a fine crop for your Grandpa. Paid him all we owe and have some money left. And we want to stay on. The house is good. The land is good. And we like it here."

"Why does he want you to leave?" Angela interrupted.

"Just because we're good looking and the boys come to see us. We'd just die the long nights if we didn't have a little fun. We couldn't stand it, workin' like we do. Can you blame us?"

"Not for feeling lonely and wishing to see the boys, no. But you don't have to go the limit with them, you know."

"Lord, M'am, we don't!" broke in the younger one. "I've never done a wrong thing with a boy in my life, I swear it."

"I haven't either," the older one stoutly lied.

Angela studied them a moment.

"If I get you a teacher who will give you lessons at night, bring you good books and put in a music box for you, will you promise me to behave?"

They crowded closer, two eager children, and solemnly promised on their honor. Angela had grave doubts of the outcome but the trembling gratitude of their hard pressed father and mother warmed her heart.

Old Ransom Russ proved a harder nut to crack. He was loud mouthed and insulting. He swore and blustered. Angela let him rave for a while and then quietly asked: “Did you take the entire crop before it was divided?”

“I did, by God!” he shouted, “and I’m goin’ to sue old Cameron for five hundred dollars more that he owes me for swindling me on my account——”

With a quick turn of her body Angela slapped his mouth a stinging blow that knocked the quid of tobacco he was chewing down his throat. He staggered back in amazement, spitting, choking and gagging until he swallowed the wad. And then, purple with rage, his long stringy reddish hair flopping about his face he bawled at her:

“I’ll make you pay for that, my pretty Miss, pay well I’ll promise you that——”

The girl took a step closer and he retreated.

“But you won’t slander my grandfather again in my presence, you piece of dirty trash!”

He quailed before her and his tone took on an injured whine. “I got the corn, all of it and it’s mine, until your Grampa shows me that his account of provisions and clothin’ and cash is even with mine. I’m a suin’ him fer five hundred dollars to pertect myself. I know my rights in court and I’ll stand fer ’em.”

“You know that you can be put in jail for removing the crop before it had been divided, don’t you?”

“Hit’s been divided.” he yelled. “It’s all mine and a lot more thet I’ll git in court——”

“There’s not a lawyer in Piedmont who’ll take your case against Dr. Cameron,” she warned.

“No. But I got a good lawyer in Spartanburg. He’ll be here tomorrow.”

“You’ll need him. If you don’t put all of that corn back in a pile in the barn yard by three o’clock tomorrow I’ll have you in jail before sundown.”

He threw both hands above his head and howled: “You try that, goddam you—try it—an’ I’ll show you somethin’.”

His poor wife and six daughters who worked for him as slaves crowded through the door.

His wife shook her head.

“Paw, Paw, you mustn’t talk like that to a lady.”

“Lady, hell,” he snorted. “Didn’t she haul off an’ knock a chaw er terbacer down my wind pipe? You call that a lady?”

The oldest daughter came down to her mother’s side. She was crying.

“Paw, Paw, do be quiet now.”

“Be quiet? Hell and damnation, I know my rights and the court’ll give ’em to me.”

Angela's heart went out to the seven female slaves the old devil held in ugly bondage.

"I know how you feel, Mrs. Russ. If I can ever do anything for you let me know."

"You can't do nothin', damn you," the old man raved. "We folks don't take charity. All I'm askin' is justice and the law'll give it ter me. You git off my place and stay off!"

Angela turned to go and flung back at the shabby figure: "Till three o'clock tomorrow to pile the corn back in the barn or I'll swear out a warrant for your arrest."

"Swear it—swear it!" he screamed. "You'll not put me in jail. Hit's been tried before, but hit didn't work. I'm not afraid of you nor none of your damned folks——"

"Keep your tongue off my folks or I'll have Dave Henry come over here and thresh you within an inch of your life. He could do it with one hand tied behind his back."

"Send Dave Henry over! I'll meet him with a shot gun and blow his head off. Send him!"

The wife saw Angela frown and hesitate. She shook her head and smiled: "He won't, child. Don't worry. He never had a shot gun in his life. He's too lazy to go huntin'."

He raised his hand to strike his wife and the six girls crowded between them.

"You hit my Maw again," the older one hissed, "and we'll kill you. I've warned you."

"To hell with all of you. You're all agin' me. But I know how to take care of myself."

Angela drove straight to Phil Stephens' office and told him of Russ. He filled out a blank warrant for his arrest and Angela signed it.

"If he doesn't put the corn back by three o'clock I'll have him in jail in an hour."

He asked her to stay and chat awhile. She couldn't. She had been away from home the whole afternoon. He followed her to the door.

"Happy, dear?" he asked softly.

She whispered: "Happier than I ever dreamed it possible for a human being to be."

"I'm glad. You know that."

"Yes, I know, Phil. You've been great to us and I'll always love you for it."

"Thank you, dear," he said in tones so low they could scarcely be heard.

"Have you heard from Marie lately?"

"I hear once a month. They won't let her write to me oftener."

"Thank you, Phil, for the way you've managed her. I'll always love you for that too——"

"I may marry her yet," he laughed.

At three o'clock next day Russ was arrested. He had not returned the corn. All the way to jail he cursed Dr. Cameron, cursed his uppity granddaughter, cursed Phil Stephens and started to curse the deputy who put a big fist in his mouth and advised caution. For the first time in his vicious, worthless life he spent a night in jail. It cooled his temper. His lawyer had failed to come over from Spartanburg. Russ sent him a wire collect. Late the next afternoon he appeared and bailed him out.

Nothing would do but he must issue a warrant for the arrest of Angela Henry. The lawyer protested.

"Arrest a beautiful young woman, what for?"

"Assault and battery. I know my law——"

"What did she strike you with?"

"Her bare fist, knocked a chaw er terbacer right down my throat——"

The lawyer couldn't keep a straight face and laughed aloud.

"Say," Russ growled, "are you my lawyer or hern?"

The shyster put on a solemn look and was back on the job.

"Ten dollars in advance on that action, Mr. Russ."

"I ain't got it."

"Get it."

"Right now?"

"Before I move an inch. You've made up your mind to arrest a woman for assault and battery."

"My mind's made up——"

"All right. I'm your lawyer. But I'm going to give you some advice you haven't asked for. You're a damned fool to swear out that warrant. There ain't a magistrate in the county that won't laugh at you and at me, too, for appearing for you. Ain't you got *any* sense?"

"Are you my lawyer—er ain't yer?" Russ snarled.

"Ten dollars in advance."

"I'll have it fer you in an hour. I'll choke er beat it outen my gals. They got money hid somewhere."

An hour later the fee was paid, the warrant was issued and when it was served on Angela, Dave laughed.

"Now you'll go to jail."

"Will I, David?" she asked with a quiver in her voice.

"Of course you won't, honey. We'll call Phil."

Stephens stepped before the Magistrate and laughingly pleaded guilty. The Magistrate fined Angela a penny and the cost, rose and bowed gallantly.

"Permit me, Mrs. Henry, on behalf of the County to thank you for knocking that tobacco down this old fool's neck. You have done us all a service."

Russ turned to his lawyer when the roar of laughter had subsided and spluttered: "Bring a suit for slander for a thousand dollars agin that magistrate. I know my rights."

"Oh, step to hell will you!" the lawyer sneered.

Chapter 14

The new regime at Hillcrest farm was inaugurated without hitch. The husband rose now at daylight, fed the horses and chickens, brought in wood for the day and had a little time to read the paper before breakfast was served. They ate with the baby in his tall chair, his bib tucked under his chubby chin, and watched each sunrise.

"Look at those scarlet and purple clouds, David," his wife cried one morning. "A world of enchanting beauty."

"It is when you show it to me, darling," he agreed.

"Aren't you getting just as much work done with fewer, saner hours?"

"I'll say, more, and everything seems easier. I'm not on a strain. I've got time to think and make plans. I'm going to make a pile this season. You watch my smoke on white potatoes. It sounds foolish, but if prices hold, I'll cash in five thousand dollars on that ten acres."

"We'll be happy with half that."

Little David crowed and said: "Da-da."

"Did you hear that now?" his father smiled. "Calling his Daddy already."

"He doesn't mean it yet but he soon will."

She made no further effort to ride a plow but gave the farm job to her husband and his efficient if profane helper. Jim was cutting down on cuss words. He was getting his dinner now in Angela's kitchen.

Lottie was a fixture as cook and maid, which gave Angela full time for her reading and welfare work. She got every book on her chosen field she could find and read them with care. The mills now maintained a corps of trained workers and her whole time was devoted to the far out lying rural districts. It was a trying task, the distances were long. Many children had to walk three miles over ragged bypaths and through deep woods to get to the school house.

They tried all sorts of excuses to stay at home but Angela talked with their mothers and fathers with such earnestness they couldn't withstand her. She organized a parent teachers association in each township and spoke and read to them until she made them feel their responsibility.

Her leadership became a thing of community pride. Her husband was one of them. He was running a model farm and they were watching him. He'd teach them big things before he was through. They believed in him. They were proud of him. And they were proud to know his beautiful wife who put on no airs and made their humble homes her own.

Soon she took little David with her everywhere. She would shut him up in the car with his toys and he'd play contented until she returned. As he grew her heart expanded in happiness.

Her first great sorrow came with the death of her grandfather. He had gone to the train to meet Marie on her return from College, got his feet wet, caught cold, developed pneumonia and died in three days. His funeral was the largest the County had ever seen. Five thousand people stood outside the Church among them at least a thousand Negroes.

Angela and Marie had Nelse watch beside the casket in an arm chair. The old Negro was utterly crushed. He made no response to the eloquent sermon the preacher delivered, just sat and stared at the casket. He took no notice of the condolences of his friends, black or white. The next morning he was found dead in his chair beside the fire place. Dr. Cameron had asked that Nelse be buried in the family plot where Eve, his wife, had been laid to rest years before. And his wishes were carried out.

When the family returned to the house after her grandfather's funeral, Marie in trembling eagerness seized her sister's hand.

"I can live with you and Dave. and the baby now, can't I?"

"Of course, dear. The spare room is yours. I'll try to be both your sister and your mother."

She had grown in spiritual beauty in the past year, a little more slender, her eyes graver. She greeted Phil with embarrassment at first and finally made up her mind to have a new understanding with him.

She asked Angela to invite him to dinner and he was enchanted with her new found dignity. The child had passed, the beautiful, poised young woman had arrived.

While Dave and Angela put the baby to bed she had a heart to heart talk with her girlhood hero.

"I want to thank you, Phil," she began a little awkwardly, "for your sweet tolerance of my infatuation——"

"I told you that you'd forget me at College!" he broke in.

"But I didn't. I thought of you with a new admiration for your fine character——"

"Oh, darling," Phil smiled, "come down off your high College horse and talk to me in your old sweet way."

She looked at him and laughed.

"Never in the same way, I hope. I was a very fresh child. I wonder you didn't spank me. But I did love you——"

"And now?"

"I still love you in a quite sensible way but I release you from all obligations. You don't have to marry me, or court me, or pay the slightest attention to me."

"But if I wish to?"

"You may, of course. But I'll be going with boys my own age now."

"You'll give me a fair chance with the other fellows?"

"Don't try to tease me, Phil dear. I know you love Angela. You've always loved her. You always will. And I admire you for it. You were very sweet, very wonderful to me and helped me over a hard place in my girlhood. I was foolish. You were wise. We'll always be friends, I know that."

He looked at her through a mist.

"You're so like your sister at her age. I could love you and be happy with you. But it wouldn't be you, darling. It would be the dream I was cherishing. You want to be loved for your own sake. And you will be. It won't take the boys long to find the way to this little white cottage on the hill. It has made my life sweeter to have known you, darling——"

She rose, smiled and kissed him.

"Good bye, my Phil. We'll always be friends."

"Always."

She called Angela and Dave, and Phil explained.

"Marie has given me my walking papers with quiet dignity."

"We'll never forget the part you played in helping her," Angela smiled. "She's the joy of our hearts. I never had half her beauty, or her mind. We're going to be very proud of her when she finishes College three years from now."

The young lawyer left early after promising to probate their grandfather's will and act as their attorney in settling the estate.

Marie fitted her life into her sister's household with joy. The baby was an endless source of happiness. And when the boys of the town commenced to call she received them with a skill that was an endless wonder to Angela. There was no danger of a sudden mad love upsetting her life and studies. The precocious experience had steadied her imagination and strengthened her character.

The young welfare worker returned to her tasks with renewed interest.

The program of better schools and longer terms announced at the

Mass Meeting had been faithfully carried out. Captain Collier was proud of the fact that he had built, school for school, black and white, and had a decent building for each race in each township of the County and each district in Piedmont. The length of the term was full eight months. The colored teachers, however, were not paid the same salaries for the same time as the whites. Their pay was based on the lower cost of housing and living. There was a persistent demand coming from some unknown source that all teachers pay should be made absolutely equal. It enraged the Chairman of the School Board, not so much by the demand, as the fact that he could not find the people who had begun the agitation. He employed a detective from Atlanta and stole a march on his enemies by engaging an intelligent Negro. If he did not get results he would change to a white man. He was confident he would put his finger on the real trouble before many months. And he did.

The intelligence man posed as a "progressive," a graduate from Atlanta University. He became a leader in the colored church and attended all parents and teachers meetings.

He walked into Captain Collier's office two months after his arrival smiling.

"I think, Captain, that I've located the Nigger in the wood pile."

"And what kind of a looking varmint is he?"

"Read that, sir, and I think you'll find out."

The Captain nodded and picked up a radical magazine.

"Come back tomorrow morning after I've studied every line of it, and we'll talk it over."

The next morning the Chairman of the County School Board greeted his detective cordially. "Good work, Mr. Intelligence Man. You put your finger on the trouble the first time. This is a vile bundle of poison. Every line of it is planned to stir the hatred of blacks against whites. It's a determined effort to provoke riot. What is the thing that publishes this magazine?"

"A group of radical Mulattos and Whites in the North who are trying to destroy the work of Booker T. Washington. When he spoke in Boston recently, these people planned and carried out a riot that stopped Mr. Washington's speech and broke up the meeting. They scattered cayenne pepper over the platform and through the audience until the place was emptied. The leader was arrested and served a jail sentence for this disorder, but he boasted himself a hero because of it."

"This crowd then has organized a Negro Junta to attack the South?"

"That's about the size of it."

"There must be some white men among them?"

"Yes. Among the organizers are Oswald Garrison Villard,[1] J.E. Spingarn,[2] A.E. Pillsbury and Morefield Storey."[3]

"Whew!" the Captain snorted, "I know those fellows. Every one of them a goddam racial imbecile who thinks that a Negro is better than a white man."

The Captain paid off his detective and called a meeting of the colored teachers of the County.

It ended in a feeling of ugly tension which spread to the Negro population. Two months later the Captain learned that six copies of the magazine were still coming to colored teachers. He located one of them and sent for the subscriber, a Mulatto woman graduate of Atlanta. She was bristling for a fight.

"I understand you are still a subscriber to this Magazine?"

"I am," she snapped.

"You heard my announcement as Chairman of the School Board two months ago."

"I did. And I'll tell you flat-footed that I'll not be treated as a slave. You cannot prescribe to me what I shall read. This is a free country. I'll read what I please."

"I'm sure you will," was the quiet reply. "But you can't teach a colored school in Piedmont at the same time."

"That suits me, sir. Here's my resignation. I've saved you the trouble of asking for it. I'm leaving this damned town to take a position in New York."

She threw her resignation on his desk and stalked from the room.

The incident closed the subscriptions to the magazine on the part of the teachers. For a time there was ill feeling between the blacks and whites. Ugly looks were exchanged and a rising tide of Negro insolence was evident. But it subsided. At least there was no surface sign of its existence.

The parade of the colored school children came off as usual, with the same good natured greetings from the white people who had lined the side walks.

---

1. Oswald Garrison Villard (1872–1949) was a reform journalist who opposed the Spanish-American War and who, along with W.E.B. DuBois and other activists, founded the NAACP. Villard also campaigned actively for women's suffrage. See Michael Wreszin, *Oswald Garrison Villard: Pacifist at War* (Bloomington: Indiana University Press, 1965).

2. Joel Elias Spingarn (1875–1939) became secretary of the NAACP in 1914 and collaborated with W.E.B. DuBois to mend divisions between African Americans in various parts of the early civil rights movement. Spingarn also acted as president of the NAACP throughout the 1930s. See Barbara Joyce Ross, *Joel E. Spingarn and the Rise of the NAACP, 1911–1939* (New York: Atheneum, 1972).

3. Moorfield Storey (1845–1929), a distinguished Massachusetts lawyer, combined a successful corporate law practice with a lifelong commitment to racial equality. In 1910 he became the first president of the NAACP. See William B. Hixon Jr., *Moorfield Storey and the Abolitionist Tradition* (New York: Oxford University Press, 1972).

The day after the parade Angela drove down town, the baby's hand in hers at the wheel, to see Phil give a big cheer to the departure of a Negro preacher for New York. He had been a slave of the Stephens family. His daughter had gone to Harlem, made a fortune as a singer and sent for her father and mother.

The space in front of the station was black with Negroes. The departing preacher was making his farewell address, Phil standing beside him. He was making a remarkable speech.

"I am goin' away from you, my good frien's," he said, "to take up de wuk o' soul savin' in de great city er New York. In dis country de Negroes are better treated dan in the Norf. Dey are trusted, give work, advised and hepped forward in every way. Dere's here de good feelin' between us dat's hard to describe. De respectable Negro down here, specially ef he is a minister o' de Gospel, can borrow any fair amount from de bank on his own note. He couldn't borrow a nickel in the Norf on any such a paper. When my character was once jump on in dis County, your Chammun of the School Board, Captain Collier, defends me and took hit as a fight on hisself. Goin' Norf today I has my pockets full of blessin's from de best white people in de County. De Norf sees de South too much by its fire eaters, and not enough by de peaceful kin' hearts who are helpin' my people and who are loved of dem. I has never had an unkine word spoke to me in the South by a white man who knowed me. A better day is comin', my people. God bless you!"

Angela waved a greeting to Phil and drove home. On reaching it she found Dave and Jim in high fettle. The crops were all in. He had gotten $6.50 a barrel for his white potatoes and put into the bank five thousand three hundred dollars from a ten acre field. The peas and tomatoes had added nine hundred dollars and the cotton five hundred. When the bills were paid for supplies and labor he had a net surplus of four thousand five hundred dollars.

He swung his wife around the room, threw the baby in the air as he gasped "Daddy!" and then danced a jig before the fire.

"What more can I ask?" he cried, "I've the prettiest wife in the County, a two year old kid that has red hair like my own and calls me Daddy. I've money in the bank and more on the way next year. My neighbors are making a living and they're coming to see my farm and call me their leader. You've spoiled me, honey, I'm getting proud."

She laughed and kissed him.

"We've a lot to be proud of, my man."

And then from a clear blue Southern sky the thunderbolt fell that transformed a happy peaceful country side into a flaming hell.

Chapter 15

Marie won the highest honor of her college, being elected President of her class for the Senior year opening the next fall. The Piedmont Herald carried her photograph on the front page with a sketch of her brief, brilliant career, comparing her with Mrs. Angela Henry, her accomplished sister.

The boys, with Phil Stephens leading, turned out in force and gave her a crowded reception at the station as the train arrived. She became a sensation of the town. Angela was very proud of her and Marie's raptures over the baby still more endeared them to one another. The younger sister never tired of the care of little David. She won his heart the first hour. The toys she spread before his sparkling eyes gave him endless delight. He'd stop playing with them to hug and kiss her.

"You'll spoil him, dear," Angela warned.

"He couldn't be more spoiled than he is," was the laughing reply. "I'll teach him. I'll make him love Nature and the songs of our birds as I do. You'll see. He'll be reading in no time."

David had promised to go to Spartanburg and bring Angela supplies for her welfare work, but the late May sun and wind had dried the ground so rapidly he was sure he could go back into the fields with his cultivator after the noon hour. He told Jim to stick around until lunch time.

But when they walked out into the field and tested it there was still too much moisture in the soil.

"You can run along, Jim," Dave said. "We'll get back to work tomorrow morning. No use miring down today. Three days of rain were good for us. We shouldn't complain. We're going to make another bumper crop."

"Damned of we aint," Jim agreed. "Want me to come back and feed the stock tonight?"

"No, go to town and see a good picture. You'll work all the harder tomorrow. And stop cussin—will you?"

"Shoreshell I will. Promised ye, didn't I? So long boss."

Dave made no reply save an uplifted hand. He was smiling at the waving green of his fifteen acre field of potatoes. He had increased the acreage and cut out the peas this year. If the market held he'd bank seven thousand dollars on potatoes. That was the lowest figure he would think. By the looks of the crop the yield would be greater than last year. He thought with pride of his wife and boy. He would soon take his place as one of the first citizens of the County. No longer a poor white man. A man of property. A leader of the people. His boy was growing so fast he'd soon be going to school. And Marie was the toast of the town. He was waked from his reverie by his wife's voice.

"Come on to lunch, big farmer. You know it's still too wet to cultivate."

He hurried to her side, slipped an arm around her waist and walked toward the house in silence.

"Why so glum?"

"Not glum, honey," he smiled, "just too happy for words when I see that big crop coming on and know what it'll mean to you and the boy."

"Don't get avaricious, David. Too much money may not be good for you. I was just as happy when we had nothing."

"No you weren't," he corrected. "You love pretty things."

"Certainly I do. But I love you and the boy more than all the money that could be piled in our house. You know that, don't you?"

"Sure."

"After lunch," she went on briskly, "I want you to read the history of the United States."

"I sho will, teacher. I like that book. I like to read how poor and spunky our fathers were when they made this country. I like to read how they loved liberty and hated tyrants. I like to read how they wanted to build, here in the wilderness something bigger and better than anybody had ever seen in the world across the seas. It makes me proud and strong to know that Patrick Henry was one of the leaders who forced old Virginia, with all her rich and proud men, into the revolution."

"Yes," Angela broke in softly. "If it hadn't been for Gadsden of South Carolina, Patrick Henry of Virginia, and Sam Adams of Boston, they might have made up the quarrel with the King, compromised and settled down into a rich Crown Colony."

"But old Patrick Henry's "Give me Liberty or give me death!" set their hearts afire!"

"And you're a Henry from old Virginia and South Carolina, David."

She stopped before entering the house and turned toward the river valley clothed in the glory of a perfect Southern spring.

"Isn't the wind sweet?" she sighed.

"Yes, it smells like flowers. I wonder why?"

"Because it's full of the perfume of flowers. That wind's from the tropics and it has passed over and kissed every flower in Florida and Georgia before it got to our fields."

"You reckon?"

A blue bird flashed across the yard. A red bird answered his mate. A blue jay called his challenge from the woods. And a mocking bird struck the first note of the love song to his mate nesting in the old rose trellis. Marie was pointing them out to the baby. He would crow an answer to their calls.

"Oh, David," she cried, "it's a world of aching beauty!"

"If we have eyes to see, and sense to feel it," he answered soberly. "I didn't till you began to teach me, darling."

Lunch over, the man seized his book and faithfully read as he had promised while the wife sewed and the boy played with Marie and his toys on the floor.

Now and then the reader would slap his thigh, rise, walk to the window and look out.

"What is it now?" came the gentle inquiry from the work basket.

"By gum, honey, our fathers in Philadelphia were some pumpkins when they passed that Declaration of Independence and flung their dare of war into the face of the King, the greatest ruler in the world!"

"And faced a civil war at home at the same time," his wife added. "Half the colonists were still loyal to the crown."

"And did they fight for the King?"

"Sent as many men into the King's army as we sent to fight under the new flag and the men who signed the Declaration knew it would be so."

"But we ordered old George Washington out to meet 'em, our commander in chief of the Army and Navy. Boy, that was what I call spunk!"

"Especially when we remember that he had no army, no navy, and no money to equip an army or build a navy. And while our fathers were making out his commission as commander in chief, Lord Howe was landing on Staten Island his army of invasion from 144 war ships guarded by ten thousand armed sailors."

"Still George Washington went out to meet them!"

"Yes. It was madness. But it was magnificent. Our boy has a great inheritance, David."

The man settled back to his book, nodded and murmured: "You bet he has."

A moment later the child carried three blocks and spread them at his father's feet. "Ook, Daddy. A-B-C- Marie gimme."

"Well, can you beat that!" David cried. "He'll soon be catchin' up with me, if I don't watch out." He paused and beamed with pride. "All right, brother, catch up with me! Me and you and your Mama and Marie will all work it out together!"

The child dropped his blocks, climbed up on his father's lap, hugged and kissed him and put his hands over his eyes.

"Play, Daddy!"

The mother lifted her finger in reproof. The boy slipped down and went back to a book Marie had given him, squealing his recognition of the horse, the cat, the dog, and the cow.

Dave watched him and turned to Angela.

"I wonder if you'll ever know," he said "how proud I am of you? Everybody's talking about your work. Do you know what they're calling you now?"

"No, what?"

"The Angel of the County Roads. You're always on the go, always bringing joy to poor folks."

Angela raised her finger.

"That'll be enough now, little boy. Get back to your book."

"All right, teacher," he grinned.

A half hour passed and the crunch of wheels sounded on the gravelled roadway. Angela hurried to the window.

"Why, it's Ann and John."

In a moment Ann was at the door.

"I won't come in, dear. John and I have come for you to take charge of a parent's teachers association tonight at his Mill School. He says you're the only one to do anything with them."

"All right. I'll be ready in a minute. Come on in and see the baby and his new nurse." She swept her hand toward little David and Marie on the floor.

Ann greeted David, Marie, and the baby and called.

"Hurry up, Angela. Your nose don't need any powder. We're late."

She turned to the door and called to David.

"I'll bring her back by ten o'clock."

He nodded and buried himself again in his book.

Angela kissed the baby, and said to Marie:

"Put him to bed when he's tired, dear. I let Lottie go to a movie with Jim tonight."

"I'll take good care of him and his big daddy, too," Marie called. "Run along and fight it out with the mill folks."

"And watch that leg of lamb I put in the oven for the lunches tomorrow. Bye, David!"

"Bye, honey," he said softly as he bent over his book again absorbed in the story of the freezing river and the daring crossing Washington made the night he moved his ragged little army of thirty five hundred on the division of Hessians at Trenton.

When the twilight had deepened into the full shadow of night, a huge black figure came out of the woods, stood for a minute in the bushes on the edge and looked in every direction. Looked carefully and waited before moving again.

Spot barked and the hound echoed it.

"Damn them dogs," the prowler growled. "But I'se ready fur 'em."

The dark form moved carefully in a wide circle around the house and approached the dog run from the back. He softly opened the gate and called in a low voice:

"Boney!"

The hound approached, wagging his tail at the sound of his name, thrust his nose through the gate held open and a hand stroked his head.

"Come on Boney, old boy, we'll git a coon tonight."

The gate swung wider. A heavy cord slipped over the hound's head and the gate closed. The huge figure led the dog to the edge of the yard a hundred feet from the run and dropped to his knees softly stroking the hounds silky nose.

"Good old Boney!"

The cord was suddenly drawn taut until the dog's eyes were popping while a heavy knee pinned the writhing body to the ground. The cord was now twisted tight in the left hand while the right drew a hunting knife and plunged it through the heart of the struggling animal. A huge fist turned the blade. The hound's body quivered and relaxed. He was dead. Not a sound had disturbed the silence of the night. The wet soft soil gave no noise of the struggle.

The cord was slipped from the limp neck and the heavy but careful footsteps moved back to the run. The setter was at the gate lonesome for his companion and he whined a welcome when the same voice called:

"Come on, Spot, old boy." The setter wagged his tail and pressed the opening of the gate.

When it was slowly opened the dog ran his neck into the noose without suspicion of foul play and was led loosely some fifty feet from Boney's still form where the same grim tragedy was enacted for the second time.

The thing stood still in his tracks for a long time, listening for approaching footsteps. No one had heard. He had removed all danger of interruption. A full moon had risen over the river valley showing the water a winding ribbon of silver in the distance.

The figure approached the house with more confidence, yet with caution, seeking the shadows of the trees.

Fifty feet from the door, the black bulk stopped still and listened. The silence was broken only by the chirp of a cricket and the distant weird call of a whippoorwill.

The thing moved directly toward the house now with the soft sure tread of a leopard. It stopped at the porch and looked through a window of the living room from which poured a flame of light. The figure of a man was bending over a book. He sat on the couch which stood before the fire place.

"Damn him!" the voice muttered. "He didn't go to Spartanburg wid his wife lak he said he wuz at de lodge meetin'. But she's gone ter town. I seed her go——"

Then it moved with slow carefully planted steps to the other window which commanded the opposite end of the room.

"Nobody else in dar."

The dark figure stiffened with caution. Where was she? Supper was over long ago. The cook and the helper had gone to the picture show. He saw her before he left town and entered the woods. He listened intently and heard the laughter of the baby in the kitchen. And then a woman's voice came through the long hall that led to it. They were both in there and she was trying to put him to sleep with a lullaby. He was screaming and laughing in protest. What the hell were they doing so long in the kitchen? Cooking. He could smell the roast lamb. It was eight o'clock. Cooking should be over. Well he had work to do before they came back into the living room.

He measured carefully the distance from the door to the end of the couch on which the man sat crouched low over his book. He would have to take two steps from the door to reach the end of the couch. He had covered his heavy shoes with thick wool socks, but his weight on the floor would make a noise, his victim would leap to his feet and it wouldn't be so easy. He made his plan of action quickly. There was risk of a noise that would bring the woman into the room unless he was accurate in his throw. He would be. There wasn't a Negro in the County who could throw a short handled axe with the deadly accuracy that was his.

He crept to the steps leading to the front door, stopped, listened and then reached the porch by placing his knee on it and swinging his huge body. The step might creak under his weight.

He reached the door. He could plainly see the door knob by the light of the moon. It would not be locked at this early hour, if at all. He had figured on that. He drew the keen edged axe with a handle but six inches long, from thc leather socket of his belt and gripped the handle in his right hand. With the left he touched the door knob with care. He gripped it firmly at last and slowly drew the door against the facing. At the same time he turned the knob noiselessly and the door opened without a sound.

It was easy. The man was bent still lower over his book chuckling over something he had read, oblivious of danger. The huge figure squared itself, the axe rose high and was hurled at the back of the man's head. The keen edge struck squarely and crashed through the split skull. The victim slouched low and slid to the floor. The strong young body stretched full length, quivered from head to foot, and was still. The hands still gripped the volume of the history of the United States. An ugly pool of blood settled on the polished floor. It was mixed with brains.

The black figure then bent low, drew the axe from the skull and thrust it back into the socket of his belt. He took off his coat and threw it across the dead man's blood soaked head. He'd show it to the girl when he was ready.

The baby was pattering around in the kitchen and would probably be back in the room in a minute. What he would do was to crouch beside the hall door leading from the kitchen, slam and lock it when she entered, or she might escape the back way.

Suddenly the child ran down the hall crying at the top of his voice.

"Come back here!" Marie called. "I'll tell your Mama when she gets home!"

"Good nuff!" the thing grunted. "I'll git him fust."

The baby ran squarely into the big arms as he turned toward the fire place, and a black hand closed over his mouth. It was the work of a second to place a gag and tie it tightly. The arms were quickly pinioned with the cord used to strangle the dogs and he threw the helpless limp body on the blood-stained couch.

There had been no noise but the girl would suspect the silence and come in from the kitchen at any moment. The figure suddenly bent and the coarse cotton shirt was torn off and thrown to the floor. He believed that she would faint at the sight of his great black muscles. He weighed 210 pounds. If she fainted his task would be easier. If she didn't, all right, his naked flesh would burn hers. He had dreamed of this moment a hundred times. It had come.

He crouched beside the door leading from the kitchen, immobile, as still as the head of a snake ready to strike.

She called.

"Baby! Where are you? Come back here!"

There was a moment's silence. He heard her steps approaching and every muscle grew tense. As she entered the figure leaped to the door, slammed it, turned the key and put it in his pocket.

Marie was so shocked by the sudden lunge of the half naked Negro she backed away, her hand to her mouth to repress a scream. Stunned with horror at the approaching figure she had not seen the body on the floor nor the squirming form of the child on the couch.

"What are you doing in this house?" she gasped.

"Just drapped in ter see you, purty lady."

He moved closer and Marie backed to the wall.

"Keep away from me you—you—black devil. You'll die for this!"

"Mebe I will," was the steady answer. "But I'll git you fust."

"I'll die before you do—Dave—Dave—where are you!" she screamed.

"You won't die—not till I git fru wid you tonight."

She lurched toward the front door. He leaped between, locked the door and pocketed the key.

"Hit's no use fightin'. You're mine!" he grinned. She saw for the first time in the light of the lamp his thick black bulging lips from the corners of which saliva was trickling and a wave of horror swept her.

"Where is David?" she shouted.

"I'll show ye, purty lady, so's we won't have no mo trouble. He wuz en mah way en I had ter git 'im out. You kin take one look and den I'll tell ye what ter do."

She saw the still body on the floor beyond the couch for the first time, uttered a scream, fell by his side, tore the dirty coat from his head and saw the hideous wound that had split the skull. Her hands instinctively clasped the head as she moaned:

"Oh—poor David—poor David!"

She lifted her eyes, blind with tears, and saw the gagged child tugging at the cords that were eating his flesh and threw herself from the body of the man to the child.

"Baby! Marie's here. Don't be afraid. I'll save you."

A steel claw gripped her arm, drew her to her feet and hurled her violently against the wall. The beast followed.

"Git this thing straight now, my purty white witch. Yo man ter pertect ye is dead. Dar's a better man here ter take ye. De baby aint hurt. I tied de rag in his mouf and tied his hands ter keep him still. Yo do exactly what I tells ye now an' he won't be hurt. Try ter keep back frum me an' I'll pick de brat up by de heels and smash his brains out on dem flag stones en de hearth. Do ye git dat?"

The girl stared in horror at the beast towering over her. She could smell his stinking body.

"Come in de bed room now an' take off yo clothes."

Her strong young figure stiffened.

"I'll die first!"

"Oh, no yo won't!" he laughed, gripping her arm in his claws.

She drew back and suddenly saw the short handled axe in his belt. She had seen workmen throwing such axes and burying them in trees. With sudden mad strength she took her assailant completely by surprise. With a quick lunge of her body she pushed him against the wall, snatched the axe from its sheath, tore loose from him and stood six feet away clutching the handle with grim purpose.

"Well, I'll be damned!" he grunted. "Ef ye jist knowed how ter throw hit ye mought git me but ye doan know."

He moved closer with cat like tread.

"Another step and I'll kill you!"

Her eyes flashed a defiance that sent a chill down the Negro's spine for a second. He stopped, then grinned and took another step.

Her body stiffened and she hurled the axe straight at the bowed head thrust toward her.

In her excitement she had not held it in true position, straight up and down. The beast dodged, and the blade merely clipped a piece from his right ear, burying itself in the door leading into her bed room.

The Negro lifted his body and wiped the blood from his face and neck and plunged toward her. She dodged, circled the couch and moved toward the axe. He leaped the couch and confronted her, the whites of his eyes glowing from the setting of his black skin. He was so close now that she could see the coarse yellowish veins that criscrossed them.

She backed to the end of the long table behind the couch, watching his movements intently. Her foot struck the heavy stool which David had made. It was tall, and if she could grip one of its legs it would make a deadly weapon if swung with power.

As the Negro's crouching figure came closer she suddenly bent, gripped a leg of the stool, leaped at her assailant and before he could straighten his body dealt a crushing blow on his head. The stool broke as if hitting a rock. The leg came off in her hand and she continued to rain blows with it as he closed on her.

He plunged again and she slipped below his arms and rose with both hands on his throat, her sharply manicured nails cutting the roll of flesh around his neck. He tore them loose but the fingers left their mark in blood.

He gripped her arms in a final struggle that circled the long table. There was no cry from her set lips. He dragged her at last to the bed room door, held her with one hand and with the other fumbled the knob to open it.

Her back against the wall, she suddenly hurled him across the room. He stumbled over David's body and fell across the couch, but quickly rose to his feet. She realized with a sudden rush of half mad joy that she was strong. She had once heard that a frail demented woman had overcome two guards. She would use the strength of insanity. She felt it throbbing in her muscles.

Her eye rested on Dave's double barreled shot gun in its rack over the fire place. It was loaded. She had seen him place two shells in it. If she could only get it down and to her shoulder before the beast could leap on her she might blow his head off at short range. She knew how to push the safety forward to loose the trigger. Dave had shown her in a vain effort to get her to shoot a rabbit.

She edged slowly toward the fireplace, the two eyeing each other. With a quick leap she seized the gun, fumbled the safety device and got the stock to her shoulder when the Negro, catching the deadly purpose, leaped on her and caught the gun barrel in time. With the speed of a tiger he gripped the gun, wrenched it from her grasp, extracted the shells, threw them across the room and hurled the gun after them.

In unloading the gun he had loosed his hold on her. She backed again to the table, this time to the other end where another heavy pine stool had been placed. Before he could reach her she had lifted it but the blow was dodged, he closed on her and they struggled once more around the couch. Her foot slipped in the pool of blood beside the body on the floor. With a cry of horror that brought a sense of momentary helplessness she fell across the stiffening body.

She forgot to fight and uttered a low moan:

"Oh, David—David——"

With a triumphant leap the Negro was on her. His coarse hands found the neck of her dress and ripped it from her. Before she could recover her strength he had torn every shred of clothes from her body and she cowered in a panic of shame and horror before his blood shot eyes.

"Now, my purty lady, will ye be good and do what I tells ye?"

"Never!" she breathed.

"Still full o' fight are ye?" he sneered. "I thought that ud fix ye. All right, I'll do what I tole ye. I'll smash de kid's brains out on dat hearth."

Before she could move or reply he caught the child's pinioned legs and swung him high until the little curly head touched the ceiling.

With a cry of terror, she flung herself on him and caught the child.

"I give up!" she gasped. "Don't hurt him!"

He lowered the little body, dragged the head through the blood and brains on the floor, and smeared some of it on the chubby face.

"Take a good look and see what I'll do to him unless—you—do—jist—as—I—tell—ye—will ye?"

"Yes—yes—now please take that cruel gag out of his little mouth."

"Nuttin' doin. He'll yell his head off."

"Not if I tell him to be quiet."

"Nuttin doin—I tell ye." He threw the child back on the couch. "The rag's soft, it's not tied tight enough ter hurt him. You come wit me."

He gripped her wrist and dragged her unresisting into the large bed room, crushed his naked sweating body against hers, and pressed his bulging thick lips into her mouth until she gasped for breath.

For half an hour he played with her as a cat a mouse, raped her with brutal violence and ordered her to get up, while he stretched his huge black body full length on the bed, his mud covered wool socks staining the white linen.

"Sit down on that chair," he ordered.

She slumped down into a chair and crouched low.

"Take off yo shoes and stockings," he growled.

She removed her shoes and stockings and crouched lower.

"Straighten up—damn ye!" he grunted. "I want ter see all of ye. Jist like the devil made ye ter lead men ter hell and damnation. Straighten all the way against the wall, and put yer hans behin' yer head and keep 'em thar till I tell ye ter come back ter me."

With drooling lips and fixed gaze he gloated over her beauty.

"A nigger in Harlem," he said, "sent me a little book dat say I got de right ter marry a white gal of I kin git her. Can't marry her down here, but by God, I got her. An' ye ain't de fust one. I'se had two fo' you. Dey wuz a long way outen de country. I didn't have ter kill nobody and nobody never knowed about dat. Dey kept their moufs shet. Dey didn't want no disgrace nor no hellabuloo."

He paused and stared at her.

"Stop slouchin' down!"

He sprang suddenly to his feet and drew an ugly raw hide whip from the inside of his trousers.

"Thought I might need dis," he muttered. And before she realized his purpose the cruel lash came down across her bare shoulders and legs in stinging burns that drew the blood.

"No mo' slouchin'!" he commanded.

She obeyed mechanically and stared at his black bulk, shivering. Her eyes rested again on the mud soaked socks smearing the clean sheets. She started instinctively to protest and choked back the folly of it. Strange that she should think of such a thing in such a moment! She saw his eyes devouring her and wondered dully what he would do next to torture her.

A grin opened his lips, and his teeth shone white in his black face, as he spoke:

"Dat White Witch poem say . . . "an' I kiss her red, red lips . . . round me she twine her arms . . . an' bind me wid her yaller hair . . . yas, honey chile, I has kissed yo red red lips . . . an' my fingers feel yer yaller hair! Yas, Lawd, I'se goin ter kiss ye again. . . ." He rose and pressed his ugly mouth on hers . . . and dropped back on the bed with a laugh:

"Dey got mah brother, Sam Hose, down in Gawga. But he git what he wanted fust. I'se a gittin' what I come atter, too. But de white debbils won't catch me! I knows dat swamp. Dere ain't no dog in dis county kin trail me. I'se fixed er place."

She ceased to hear his triumph. Her mind was covering her own life in rapid vivid flashes. Why had she been born into luxury and culture to end life in this leperous shame? Where were the officers of the law? Where were the soldiers and their guns? Where were the ministers of Jesus Christ who proclaimed the law? She saw her beautiful sister walking down the aisle of the church on her wedding day to marry the man lying dead on the floor. She heard again the murmurs of admiration from the crowd, their laughter and their joy. She recalled her boasts to the girls in school of the beauties and glory of the South. And this was the South! How could this awful thing happen to her? It was unthinkable. It couldn't be real. It must be a nightmare from which she would wake. Her blurred eyes rested on the graceful roll of the mahogany head and footboard of the fine old bed in which she and Angela had been born. A refinement of civilization. Civilization! There was no such thing. A world witnessing a thing like this was not civilized. And God didn't live in it.

A dull stupor stopped her thoughts and was broken by a mockingbird striking the first note of his dropper love song. From the top of a cedar he called to his mate and began to drop from limb to limb, his ecstasy growing with each dip of wing as the song mounted in tenderness and passion until on the lowest limb it burst into the climax that rang over the fields. From her chair she could see the shimmer of the full moon on the green of the trees. The perfume of flowers mingled with the night's sweetness and floated in the open window at the head of the bed.

What mockery, these symbols of the South! Birds, flowers and perfumed air! The gallant heroic South—and this! Her father's career, the saga of Piedmont, and this the end!

She covered her lips to suppress a scream and saw him glaring and lashing the bed with the whip in warning that his commands must be obeyed.

For another half hour he subjected her to the agony and shame of indescribable sex atrocities until she sank unconscious to the floor.

He flopped again on the bed.

The sudden shriek of an automobile horn came from the gate and the crunch of wheels could be heard on the drive.

He ran over the prostrate body, crushing her outstretched neck. The shock roused her to consciousness. She heard the grating wheels and screamed.

He hadn't a moment to lose. He heard some one scramble from the car and a voice called.

"Are you there, David?"

"For—God's—sake—help!" Marie called feebly. "Don't—let—him—kill—the—baby!"

A heavy shoulder was smashing against the door.

With a muttered oath the beast sprang through the open window as a man's footsteps crashed on the kitchen steps.

Marie lay gasping and bleeding on the floor.

"My God! What has happened?" John Lovelace asked her.

"Go—quick—and—see—if—he's—killed—the—baby!" she managed to say.

He rushed into the living "room and saw the child dead on the couch smothered to death by the heavy gag that had slipped over his nose.

He reached the back door in time to halt Angela.

"David—the baby?" she gasped.

"You can't see them now. You can do nothing. We must try and save Marie—come to her!"

He led the dazed woman to the girl, still lying naked and bleeding on the floor. Angela gathered the bloated face into her arms.

"Tell me darling—tell me——"

"Oh, yes, I must before I go mad and can't. A—big—black—Negro—named—Hose——"

The story sobbed from her bloody lips in all its stark unbelievable horror. Every detail of shame until the man standing by cried out and covered his ears. The girl's head suddenly dropped, blood gushed from herr lips, and she was dead.

Ann entered and they led Angela into the living room. She saw the bodies of her baby and husband and crumpled to the floor.

Lovelace lifted her in his arms and carried her to the car.

"Take her home, quick and call the doctor. Don't let her come back here tonight. She may go mad if she sees them again."

"I'll keep her if I can."

"There's no "ifs" about it. Keep her! Tell the doctor to put her to sleep. I'll come when I can. I've got work to do here tonight."

Ann started the car and he rushed back into the house and seized the telephone.

In less than half an hour a dozen men crowded into the house of death and shame and heard the story in all its hell-lit details.

John turned to a neighbor.

"Jump in your car, and get old Adam Spake to locate the blood hounds. He'll know'where they are, and he's the man to lead the trail. Bring 'em!"

An engine roared and the car shot down the drive.

"Did you phone the Sheriff?" a man asked.

"Sheriff? Hell—no!" Lovelace answered. "We won't need a sheriff. Every man in this County and the adjoining ones will be in the hunt before daylight. It's only eleven o'clock."

He stopped, bent down beside the couch and drew the Negro's coat from under it, where it had been kicked during the struggle.

"Here's the damned beast's coat. The dogs'll never lose this trail."

Chapter 16

By twelve o'clock a hundred men had passed through the stricken home. Jim arrived early with a dozen of his friends from the railroad construction crew. He waited outside with them, until the last man of twenty-five who lived in the town and nearby countryside had arrived. Then he led them in to view the mutilated body of the man they loved.

They made a circle around the two bodies and gazed for a minute in silence. And then a sob shook a tall figure, and the whole crowd were crying and cursing the beast who had killed the father and child and outraged his beautiful wife's sister.

Jim turned to John Lovelace.

"I'm going ter ask ye now ter let our crew take charge of the hunt. Anderson, our old foreman, we've elected Captain. He's six foot three and can lick his weight in wild cats. We'll follow him ter hell and back. How about it?"

"It's all right with me," came the quick answer, "if the Sheriff don't butt in."

"The Sheriff's a good man. But he won't bother us none," Anderson put in.

Adam Spake pushed his way through the door and stood a moment in silence with his head uncovered looking through tears at the man's gaping skull and his dead baby.

He turned at last to Jim and asked in husky tones:

"Where's Boney and the Setter—didn't they bark?"

"Nobody's seen 'em," was the quick answer in chorus.

"Hell—why didn't ye look?"

The old man broke for the dog run, a lantern in hand. The place was empty, the gate wide open.

"Damn him—he's kilt my dog, too!"

He lifted his lantern high and called.

A faint echo came from the woods and he moved toward the echo.

In a minute his voice pierced the air.

"Here they are, boys. Both dogs stone dead."

Half a dozen men rushed to the spot and saw the old man on his knees with his head against the cold nose of the dog he loved.

"Look at this, fellows," he whispered. "See that ugly hole right over his heart? There's where the black son of a bitch stuck the knife and turned it." He paused and leaped to his feet.

"Jist let me git my paws on him—damn him ter everlastin' hell!"

Jim grasped his arm.

"Where's them blood hounds I told you to bring?"

"They're comin'. I didn't have no car. I got a fellow ter telephone fur 'em. They orter be here now."

"Do you know how to handle blood hounds?" Anderson asked.

"Son, I know how ter handle any hound that ever drawed the breath o' life. This'll be the hottest trail ever struck. They can't lose it when they smell his coat and find the tracks he made when he jumped through that window."

They went back to the house. A car was arriving every minute now. The lawn was jammed and they overflowed into the first field.

Every telephone in a white man's house in Piedmont was buzzing and along every road leading in headlights blazed from automobiles and trucks loaded with determined men.

Anderson approached Lovelace.

"Did you go through the pockets of the Nigger's coat?"

"Yes, and found pieces of a magazine."

"Look through 'em."

Lovelace turned its leaves.

"It's marked here. Look. A piece of poetry called "The White Witch," by James W. Johnson——"[1]

"Read it aloud," Jim demanded.

John slowly read:

"And I have kissed her red, red lips
And cruel face so white and fair;

1. James Weldon Johnson (1871–1938), influential author and civil rights activist, published his best-known fictional account *The Autobiography of an Ex-Colored Man* in 1912. He joined the staff of the NAACP as a field secretary in 1916 and supported young African American talent in the burgeoning Harlem Renaissance, influencing writers such as Claude McKay and Langston Hughes. See Robert E. Fleming, *James Weldon Johnson* (Boston: Twayne, 1987).

Around me she has twined her arms,
And bound me with her yellow hair.
I felt those red lips burn and sear
My body like a living coal;
Obeyed the power of those eyes
As the needle trembles to the Pole:
And did not care although I felt
My strength go ebbing from my soul."

"That's the sort of damned stuff given to Niggers to read. There's the match that fired the powder." Lovelace frowned. He turned to Jim. "Take this to Captain Tom Collier and tell him what's happened. Wait a minute. Here's a ticket to N.Y. between the leaves. Tell him to keep them in his safe. And get back here quick. We'll start the minute the dogs come."

Jim hurried to obey the order.

By one o'clock five hundred men were crowded about the house. There was no shouting. No drinking. No loud threats. Only the low hum of an undercurrent of deep feeling. The mind of every man held a single thought—the safety of his own wife, mother, sister, and daughter. The deed done was a blow of race. A challenge to the existence of the white man and his people. As such it was faced.

There was no punishment adequate for such a crime. The old Hebrew law, an eye for an eye, a tooth for a tooth, rang out as child's play before the thunder of hundreds of beating hearts.

A mud covered car dashed up the drive and five sleek mild looking hounds scrambled out followed by their master.

Adam greeted them with a low growl of joy.

"Ye brought 'em, son, good boy—may I take 'em?"

"Sure. They'll follow you ter hell and back."

The old man stroked each shining head and they followed him into the house. He pushed his way to the couch.

"Where's that coat?"

Every dog sniffed it, growled and barked.

"Now show me the window he jumped through."

The dogs led the way following the hot trail of the Negro's footsteps through the hall into the bedroom. With steady yelps they leaped through the window, picked up the scent and made for the woods.

Five hundred men followed and spread out in the forest, lanterns flashing in the shadows.

Old Adam led the crowd close on the heels of the hounds. He answered their deep steady bay with a long hunter's call that sent shivers down the spine of more than one in the crowd. His answering cry was more than human, it was elemental in its stark racial passion. It was an answer to the challenge of his people. Into it he put every ounce of his manhood. It quivered with a madness that was contagious. A half dozen young men caught and echoed it.

The dogs made straight across the forest toward the Lake, whose shallow waters stretched a mile into the trees before it deepened into the two mile width of the open stretch.

At the water's edge the trail was lost. A long deep silence followed, broken only by the one great yell from Adam. He was there urging the dogs into the water. He led them in at last wading until the hounds were swimming in circles in a vain effort to locate again the trail.

"Damn him" the old man growled to the crowd. "He's took ter water. But we'll git 'im. We'll circle the Lake an' see ef he come out, enywhere."

It was ten miles around the water, but he called the dogs and led them in a careful search of every foot of the water's edge. It would be daylight before they could complete the circle. No matter. It was the thing to do. If they struck no trail coming out of the Lake the black devil was in a tree top somewhere in the edge of its waters. They'd get him.

Anderson heard his plan with approval and commanded the crowd to follow his lead.

While they slowly circled the Lake Captain Tom Collier drove his car first to Ann's cottage.

She met him at the door.

"The doctor put her to sleep the minute he came to stop her raving. He says it's a question of saving her reason."

"You think it can be done?"

"I think so, Captain. I've resources a doctor doesn't use, I'll try them."

"Call me, Mrs. Lovelace, if I can help."

"Thank you, Captain, I will."

The Sheriff had spent the night in Spartanburg at the Lodge Meeting which Dave had promised to attend and did not reach the place before noon.

He summoned the Coroner who viewed the bodies and rendered his verdict: "Murdered by the hands of a Negro known in the County by the name of Dan Hose."

A crowd of a thousand men were now milling around the edge of the Lake, trying in vain to pick up the trail again. The Sheriff arrived just as old Adam faced the crowd under Anderson and announced his new plan of action.

"Now listen, fellers," he began in low tones. "We've gone clean round the Lake and the hounds have covered every foot of the way. He went in that water. He didn't come out. He's in thar now."

"But where?" Anderson interrupted.

"There ain't but one place. He's waded out into water too deep fur dogs and climbed a tree. We got ter wade through the edge o' that deep water, find that tree and bring him down!"

"One hell of a job," Jim remarked.

"Cose it's a hell of a job. But we've got enough men ter do hit and there'll be a thousand more here fore night comes again. We got ter tree him by daylight and of we don't find him we'll circle the Lake agin fore daybreak ter see of he's come out."

The Sheriff stepped forward.

"And remember, boys, when you find him, he's my prisoner and I have to protect him."

"We'll remember that," Anderson said with a deadly quiet that was not lost on the official.

A hundred men volunteered to wade into the deep water studying the top of each tree. They spread out and plunged in the water while the main body of the crowd followed outside the water's edge.

The sidewalks of the town were now impassable as excited crowds milled and trouped in a tense aimless sort of frenzy. And still cars poured in from every direction.

On the third day of the search fully six thousand men were hunting the Lake and searching every tree. More than five hundred had volunteered to plunge into the deep water. Some of them had field glasses with which they swept every pine top.

At three o'clock in the afternoon a shout from old Adam's throat rang through the woods.

"Bring the dogs in here!" he screamed.

Anderson and his men rounded up the hounds and splashed their way to Adam.

The dogs were lowered into the water, and began immediately to sniff its surface. One of them looked up and gave the long deep bay of treed game.

"I knowd hit, by God, I knowd hit!" Adam yelled. "I seed a straw on the water. He's made a nest up in that pine tree."

A man focused his field glass on the bunched limbs far up in the sky.

"He's there, shore's hell!" he cried. "I saw the pine needles quiver. He's covered himself completely."

Two woodsmen began the steady blows against the big trunk.

Adam turned to Anderson.

"Git to the house now and have the chains and lightwood ready."

The news that the Negro had been treed and they were cutting down the tree in which he had hidden spread quickly. Every telephone buzzed, and a thousand more automobiles swung into the highways and headed for the scene.

The steady crack of axes on the trunk of the pine tree brought no response from the animal concealed in his den of closely woven limbs.

Waist deep in water the crowd pressed so close Anderson was compelled to drive them back out of danger.

The Sheriff pushed his way to the base of the pine tree and made a futile gesture demanding the custody of the Negro.

Anderson whispered to a lieutenant and then spoke to the Sheriff.

"All right, Mr. Officer of the Law that didn't work, my men will take you back to dry land and we'll bring the Nigger to you."

He turned and followed his guides.

"See that you do," the Sheriff called back.

The moment they had cleared the water the two men leaped on the Sheriff, disarmed, and tied him securely to a tree.

"No hard feelings, Sheriff!" one of them said. "Just carrying out orders. Keep your shirt on and we'll come back and let you go when we're through with the Nigger."

When the tree was ready to fall, Anderson pushed the crowd back and lifted his big hand.

"Now men, a word of warning. I'm in charge of this lynching and it's going to be done as I've planned and not as some fool rushes in to do it his way." He drew his revolver. "I'll shoot any man who puts his hands on that Nigger or draws a gun on him till I give the word. A dozen men of my crew will take and chain him. The rest of you stand back!"

The tree fell into the water with a soft splash, the top only half covered. A black bear-looking figure plunged out of the den and a dozen men were on him. In a moment his hands were tied with cords and chains held by six men on a side.

A wild shout rose from the close pressing crowd. The Negro stood in stolid silence as if he were not interested.

"Just a minute," Anderson called. "I want to look into his den."

He emerged quickly holding up a tow bag half full of provision and a pair of spiked shoes for tree climbing.

"He'd hid enough grub to last him two weeks and had his spikes ready for climbing."

On reaching dry land, they shackled the prisoner's ankles, kicked and dragged him back to the scene of his crime.

There were two thousand men in the crowd that came out of the swamp. There were five thousand more swaying around the little white house on its hill.

At the sight of the Negro in the edge of the woods a fierce shout came from the greater mob that was answered by his captors. An attempt was made to rush and tear him to pieces.

An uplifted revolver and a determined voice held them fifty yards away.

"Not another step closer. My men are running this thing. I know what's in your mind. The same that's in mine. You're thinking about your homes, the women God's given you to guard. So am I. We're going to make this lynching one no Nigger will ever forget. We're not going to bungle it."

He ordered the beast chained to a slender pine on the edge of the woods. The crowd of seven or eight thousand could see from the incline of the ground.

Phil Stephens pressed his way to the side of the leader.

"Anderson, I've got to talk to this crowd. Make them hear me."

"All right, Phil," was the ready response. "You're the one man I'll let talk to this crowd." A big hand was lifted and Jim placed a box on which the speaker stood.

"Men, Mr. Phil Stephens, you all know."

"We don't want to hear no damned lawyer stall for time!" a voice yelled.

"To hell with lawyers!" another shouted.

"All the same you're going to hear him," Anderson thundered from his box. "This lawyer you're yelling at was the best friend the dead man ever had. He loved him. He gave him a job that made his fortune. He gave me and my men a job. We'll hear him."

A moment's silence followed while Stephens took his place on the box and looked over the mob of flushed faces.

"My friends," he began slowly, "if you do this awful thing you disgrace our community, our County, our State and proclaim the end of civilization."

"Civilization, hell!" a voice shouted angrily. "That ended in Dave Henry's house three days ago!"

"To hell with your civilization!" another cried.

Phil lifted his hand and went on.

"The crime committed was horrible beyond the power of words to describe it. What good will come of your trying to match it with another?"

"We'll protect our homes, by God!" came an answering shout.

"The courts only can protect your homes. This Negro will be tried before a white jury, a white judge. A white solicitor will ask for his life and get it. Surely with these safeguards you can let justice take its course."

"Justice be damned!" screamed a man. "We're not here to ask for justice. We're asking vengeance. The vengeance of an outraged race——"

"And we'll have it!" shouted another, "as long as red blood flows through our veins."

"We are defending our women. To hell with lawyers!"

"We're men—not beasts. And we won't live on the same earth with beasts as our equals——"

"Shut his damned mouth!"

Stephens lifted his hand in a commanding gesture of silence. The shouts ceased again and tense silence held the crowd which listened intently for his next sentence.

"You say that in lynching this Negro you are defending your homes and your women——"

A roar of approval drowned his voice.

"That's right!"

"We are, by God!"

"That's *just* what we're doing——"

"And yet," shouted the speaker, "more than half these lynchings are for murder not rape."

"It's the same thing!" cried a man in the front line. "The Nigger who kills a white man strikes at our race. He's on the way to rape a white woman."

A roar of approval greeted the heckler.

"My God, men," Stephens cried in despair, "can't you see that you are reducing our community to barbarism, where no human rights can be respected."

The man in front interrupted.

"The beast who killed Dave Henry and his baby and raped Marie Cameron has already brought barbarism. We're in it. There is no law, no peace, no religion, no civilization. The damned beast has pushed us all down into hell. It's race against race. And we're going to fight to a finish!"

A shout of applause greeted the words, while a low growl ran through the crowd. Anderson caught its import. They were going to rush the speaker.

He drew Phil down from the box.

"It's no use. You'd better go. They're going to rush you in a minute. They'll trample you to death."

Jim took Stephens by the arm and led him through the edge of the crowd to his car.

"Get away, Phil," he urged. "We don't want to see ye hurt."

The lawyer climbed into his car muttering.

"I'll call the Governor and get troops."

The Negro stood staring at the crowd with a curious impersonal gaze. The chains that bound him to the tree were securely held by long staples drawn so tight they cut into the flesh and blood was trickling from the wounds. He seemed oblivious to pain or to the fear of death.

Fifteen cords of wood had been heaped around the tree in position to be piled about the doomed man when the leader should give the order. Only a mass of yellow fat lightwood full of rosin had been pushed close to the mud covered stocking feet.

Anderson mounted the box.

"Now, people, there's no question of his guilt. We have his coat that matches his britches, found in Dave's home. The dogs trailed him into the swamp and treed him in the pine top den. There's twenty five armed men standing around me to do as I order. The rest of you stand back. I'll shoot the first man that tries to interfere."

The crowd settled into a painful silence. The leader whispered to an aide who drew his knife. While two men held the the writhing figure, the prisoner was emasculated, slowly, crudely, savagely. The first wild screams of pain came from his bulging lips, his eyes fairly popping from his head.

The crowd yelled approval.

Above the sound could be heard the passionate cries of individuals.

"Right!"

"That's the medicine——"

"Good!"

"Let every damned Nigger take notice——"

When the crude operation was finished old Adam suddenly plunged toward the tree with a hunting knife held low.

Anderson saw his move, gripped his hand and wrenched the knife from his grasp.

"I told you to stand back, damn you," the leader growled.

He struck the old man a blow with his clenched fist that sent him spinning into the crowd.

"We'll take our time about this, men," Anderson grimly said. "For every drop of blood this Nigger drawed from Dave Henry and his baby—we'll draw two drops from his black carcass. For every scream from his wife's sister we'll wring two from his damned bulging mouth. I have in my hand the raw hide whip with which he cut the blood from her bare flesh as he held her his prisoner for more than two hours. We'll use this first."

He handed the whip to a stalwart member of his crew, who laid off his coat, bared his arm and began the savage lashing of the black bulk.

At first he twisted and writhed in silent agony. Then a low groan came and then a wild scream. The executioner paused now between each stroke and cut deeper and bloodier marks. Each blow brought a cry that found an echo in the frenzied crowd.

When the first man tired wielding the lash, another fresh hand seized it until the black body slumped into unconsciousness. They threw a bucket of cold water into his face, he blinked his blood shot eyes and stood again on his feet.

The milling crowd had pushed too close. Anderson called a dozen of his men and forced them back. The sun was shining hot. Not a breath of air was stirring. Three men had fainted and been carried to the barn. While they waited for the Negro to regain his senses, Adam slipped back of the tree and pulled Anderson's sleeve.

"Say, Lum, yer didn't have ter knock me in the head the way ye did. I jist wanted to turn my knife in him, once."

"Yes. Right through his heart. And he would have been out of all pain. This is not a dog lynching. We're teachin' a lesson to the Niggers of this County."

The mob began to shout again. A wave of anger swept them. A sound sinister, unearthly. Above it came cries that were savagely articulate.

"Burn the black bastard——"

"What's the matter?"

"Burn him! Burn him!"

The cry rose to a storm of sound from thousands of throats parched with emotion.

The leader now gave the orders. He was obeyed in silence, the men working steadily. They piled the cord wood about the figure.

A murmur of excited suspense swept the crowd.

Oil was poured over the lightwood at the Negro's feet and the logs soaked with it. Anderson threw a match into the mass and a blaze shot upward with hiss and crackle.

The burning of the Colored High School building was an incident that scarcely provoked comment. Captain Collier, anticipating this, had spoken in vain protest to the mob. He watched the stark chimneys from his office window softly muttering and swearing:

"They told us that Crime and Lynching would end with the general rise of our cultural level. We've raised the level. There's something the matter with the whole damned scheme! We taught this beast to read and write. But the trouble was he read the wrong book and wrote to the wrong people. The development of personality is the aim of education. Can-we-create-character-with-a-spelling-book?"

He looked again at the marked poem in the magazine, and shook his head:

"The end of this is not in sight!"

Part II

THE SEARCH

Chapter 17

A feeling of depression followed the burst of insane passion which resulted in the burning of Dan Hose. Thoughtful men and women asked themselves the question where such a Conflict of Color could end? Liberal leaders had preached the brotherhood of man and urged closer and friendlier relations of white and blacks. And just when the skies seemed brightest, suddenly from the jungle of Africa stalked a beast who blotted out civilization.

From the wrath of white men the Negroes hid and kept to their homes for days. Only a few women ventured to bring in the food needed to sustain life.

On the fourth day after the lynching a few Negro school teachers and leaders dared to call at the office of the Chairman of the School Board and ask his advice. Captain Collier did his best to reassure them.

To the teachers he had but one suggestion.

"Go back to your classes. Call your pupils. This storm will pass and the air will be cleaner for it. The High School Building will be rebuilt. I'll see to that. We'll rent a building until then."

To the leaders who were considering flight he said:

"Where will you go to better your lot? The same conditions confront you in every Southern community. You represent the best that's in your race. Decent white people respect you. Let's try again to find a way to live together in peace and order."

Most of them took his advice and life began to slowly readjust itself.

There was one soul into whose recesses no ray of light as yet penetrated. In Ann Lovelace's cottage a woman was fighting a grim battle. The first problem which confronted her physician and her friends was, could her life be saved?

Day followed day with no answer to the question. When she woke from the drug the doctor had given, there was a moment's silence, a mad stare from her reddened eyes and a lapse into convulsions that tore at the sources of life itself. It was necestary to administer more powerful drugs.

And then came the time when the drug began to lose its power. Ann had watched for this and prepared for it, spending hours in prayer. She entered the room with a light shining in her face.

She lifted her patient by the shoulders and looked into her brown eyes until they caught the message from her own. She held the gaze until the soul within responded to her command to sleep. The body relaxed and was lowered. For an hour she held her gentle hand on Angela's forehead and wept for joy as she heard the slow breathing of normal sleep. The first since she had laid her limp body on the bed in her spare room.

She was sleeping when the doctor called and his nurse refused the further use of drugs. He protested, but she was firm.

"I can manage her now, Doctor. She will live. Her soul answered when I called her from the shadows."

"If you need me, phone," he nodded from the doorway.

"Thanks, I will. We've yet some desperate battles to fight but I've won our vigil with Death."

He had scarcely gone before Angela uttered a piercing scream.

A gentle arm drew her down on her pillow again and a low voice soothed.

"There—there, darling. You were asleep. It was only a nightmare. It will pass."

And it did pass with the stroking of her hair and the touch of a soft hand on her forehead.

The next problem was to connect her mind with time. She had passed the days oblivious of any connection with the movement of life. She had not asked a single question or answered one.

It came at last from a long silence which followed natural sleep.

She turned her eyes, dim with tears, on her friend.

"Ann, darling, I remember now, Dave and little David and Marie are dead. Have they been buried?"

"Yes, dear, beneath mounds of lovely flowers beside your father and mother and grandfather."

The prostrate body shook with a threat of convulsions and Ann's voice spoke in firm command.

"Now, darling—we've saved your life—and you must help us."

The grip on her friend's hand tightened as she spoke:

"Why live? I'd rather be with my dead."

Day after day Ann sat beside the bed thinking divine thoughts, hoping to reach Angela's subconscious mind by their transfer without words. Silently she kept saying: Eternity is here, dear child! You are of the eternal. We must pledge life in the light of immortality. Things that seem beyond endurance become small in the sweep of the infinite. You must see life *now* through the perspective of eternity!

At the end of a week of patient brooding treatment, a limp hand rose from the bed.

"I've often wondered what became of the victims of these beasts, little thinking it would ever happen to my people. What does become of them?"

"The weak kill themselves."

"No—no—Ann—only a brave heart can take its own life."

"That is not courage, dear. The brave are not afraid of life or death. The weak kill themselves. Cowards flee and hide."

"There's no pit deep enough in which to hide my sorrow and the shame of my sister," Angela broke in. "Why shouldn't they hide?"

"Because there's nothing to be ashamed of. Shame can come only from guilt. You had no part in the horror through which you and your loved ones have passed."

"Marie surrendered!"

"That was not surrender. Her soul remained as white as the heart of God."

Angela looked up sharply.

"Why mention God? Where was God when she cried for help? Where was God when that beast slipped into our house and split David's head open? Where was God when he smothered my baby to death after Marie had plunged to the bottom of hell to save him? God—God—there *is* no God!"

She strangled, turned pale and began to wretch. Paroxysm after paroxysm shook her frame until she fell back from exhaustion unable to move.

Ann gave her cracked ice.

The sufferer slowly shook her head.

"Don't think I collapsed with nausea at the name of God. I've lost my faith, but I'm not yet capable of such sacrilege. It was just the thought of what happened."

"I know, dear, but we mustn't blame God for the mistakes and crimes of man. God is the creator only of good."

"And who made that Negro?" came the sharp question.

"Man made him a beast by the violation of law. God is law. The violation of law brings inevitable results. The Negro was taken from Africa in violation of the law. God made of one blood all the races of men and fixed the bounds of their habitations. Read the twenty sixth verse of the seventeenth chapter of Acts. The Negro is a man but not our kind of man and he's out of bounds. Hannibal Thomas, an educated Negro, says of his own race; 'The chief and overpowering element in his make up is an imperious sexual impulse, which, aroused at the slightest incentive, sweeps aside all restraint.' James Weldon Johnson, a more modern Negro writer, says: 'In the cone of the heart of the African race problem the sex factor is rooted. The physical contact of two such races is a constant violation of God's law. We pay the price of that violation. We must obey the law or pay the penalty."

A gentle hand soothed the sufferer's head and she sank at last into sleep.

A week later she had gained in strength and said to Ann:

"I haven't really lost faith in God. I just passed under a cloud for a little while—you understand."

"Yes, dear, and I want to tell you more about man's responsibility for this tragedy—may I?"

"Yes, please. I'm stronger now."

Ann's face glowed as she spoke:

"This nation has produced two great prophets of humanity. Thomas Jefferson and Abraham Lincoln.

"What does Jefferson, who wrote our Declaration of Independence, tell us on this question? Words could not express thought more clearly. Speaking on the sin of slavery he said: "Nothing is more certainly written in the book of fate than that these people are to be free, nor is it less certain that the two races, equally free, cannot live in the same government. Nature, habit and opinion have drawn indelible lines of distinction between them."

"Abraham Lincoln was the one unique, inspired man our democracy has produced and he said: "There is a physical difference between the white and the black races which will forever forbid them living together on terms of political and social equality." In his proclamation freeing the slaves he provided for their colonization. On the day he died he was working on his plan of removing the black race to Africa."

"You're a wonderful woman, Ann. You almost persuade me to live."

"You're going to live, my dear. Live to fight this thing out. In this tragedy God has given you a message for the people. With your youth, your beauty, your brilliant mind you will speak. And with Divine power. You come of fighting blood, North and South. You are not going to give up until the people hear your message. They must be taught the truth on this ugly unsolved problem. Sentimentalists and politicians tell us there is no race problem in the South. That if we fold our hands in patience time will settle all. Yet the ugly thing is here, menacing, supreme in its threat.

John Temple Graves[1] has expressed it with unanswerable logic and three great Negro leaders of the South, Bishops Turner[2] and Holsey[3] and William H. Councill,[4] agree with him. May I read to you Graves' speech at the Montgomery Race Conference?"[5]

"Please do."

A dreamy look overshadowed the older woman's face as she read with deep feeling:

"Man's views may differ and man's solutions may, but I call you to witness that on one occasion, in which the skies were opened for light upon the problem of intermingling races, God Almighty led the way through seas of difficulty to the definite end of SEPARATION.

"To treat this question with expedients is temporizing and useless. You might as well salve a broken limb with vaseline, or treat a cancer with catnip tea. This is a case for surgery. Surgery heroic but beneficial. The knife that severs a limb but saves the life."

"Do you tell me that social and political equality are not the natural resultants of civil rights and the laudable aspirations of the Negro? From

---

1. John Temple Graves (1856–1925), born in South Carolina, established himself as a newspaper editor and lecturer in Georgia. Rabidly anti-Negro, Graves was one of the invited speakers at the May 1900 conference on race held in Montgomery, Alabama. In his speech Graves proclaimed that "[t]here is not a hope in fact or reason for the Negro outside of separation." See *Race Problems of the South. Report of the Proceedings of the First Annual Conference Held under the Auspices of the Southern Society for the Promotion of the Study of Race Conditions and Problems in the South* (Richmond: B.F. Johnson Publishing Company, 1900), 56 (quote), 48–57.

2. Henry McNeal Turner (1834–1915), born a free black in South Carolina, served as a chaplain in the First U.S. Colored Troops during the Civil War, as a politician during Reconstruction, and as a bishop in the African Methodist Episcopal Church, 1880–1915. Turner was an early leader of the back-to-Africa movement. See Stephen Ward Angell, *Bishop Henry McNeal Turner and African-American Religion in the South* (Knoxville: University of Tennessee Press, 1992).

3. Lucius Henry Holsey (1842–1920) was born a slave in Georgia. Following emancipation, he became an influential minister and later a bishop in the segregated Colored Methodist Episcopal Church. Holsey subscribed to "a plantation mission ideology of paternalism as the best method for improving the situation of his fellow black southerners." See Glenn T. Eskew, "Black Elitism and the Failure of Paternalism in Postbellum Georgia: The Case of Bishop Lucius Henry Holsey," *Journal of Southern History* 58 (November 1992): 638 (quote) and 637–66.

4. William Hooper Councill (1848–1909) was born a slave in North Carolina. He settled in Alabama and became principal of the State Normal and Industrial School (later Alabama Agricultural and Mechanical College), before Booker T. Washington established Tuskegee Institute. Councill joined the Democratic Party and actively sought approval from whites, who in turn generally considered Councill a "good Negro" because of his acceptance of white paternalism and his pragmatic accommodationism. See Robert G. Sherer, *Subordination or Liberation? The Development and Conflicting Theories of Black Education* (Tuscaloosa: University of Alabama Press, 1977).

5. The Montgomery Race Conference (May 8–10, 1900) attracted national attention and ostensibly was an open forum to discuss such contemporary matters as black suffrage, education, religion, lynching, and "the social order." In reality few moderates were invited to speak; African Americans, including Booker T. Washington, were relegated to Jim Crow seating; and no blacks were permitted to speak. See John David Smith, "'No Negro is upon the program': Blacks and the Montgomery Race Conference of 1900," in John David Smith and Thomas H. Appleton Jr., eds., *A Mythic Land Apart: Reassessing Southerners and Their History* (Westport, Conn.: Greenwood Press, 1997), 125–50.

the center to the circumference of every intelligent Negro's heart there is the consuming desire to be equal in all things to the white man above him. Environment and conditions may suppress the desire. But at the first pulse of real liberty this passion leaps to utterance and to action. It is the one thing that makes him worthy of equality. After all the issue is equality, treat it as you may. Theorize, protest, it yet comes back to that. If you educate the Negro you increase aspirations and his chances for equality. If you lower him you degrade your own status in the world. If he has anything to work for it is equality.

"Separation, therefore, is the logical, the inevitable, the only way. No statutes will solve this problem. The evil is in the blood of race, the disease is in the bones and marrow and the skin of antagonistic peoples. Religion does not solve the problem. Education complicates it, bringing perception and reason. Ambition follows with aggressive assertion against the iron walls of a prejudice that has never yielded and will never yield. The conflict is still irrepressible, as it always has been.

"There is not a hope in fact or reason for the Negro outside of Separation. It is possible and practical. Its difficulties are not so great as those which surrounded emancipation. No great problem of human destiny was ever solved by theory or indirection. The world's crises have all been dominated by men of direct action. Let us have done with expedients and temporizing. Away with timidity and hesitation. Let us face the question like men. Let us grapple the issue thoroughly and once for all. Let us see the end from the beginning, and go forth to meet it with faith in God and in our race."

The hand of the suffering woman sought her friend's.

"Thank you, dear. You've helped me. I know now why the walls of your sweet little home are lined with books. They have spoken great thought to your soul. You have lifted me. I may decide to live."

She slept an hour while Ann sat beside the bed reading. But her patient waked with a start of terror and a futile look in her eyes.

"I'm sick again, dear," she whispered.

"You must stop this thinking in terms of flesh, my child. You are spirit. Not mere flesh. The flesh is a changing shell that holds your spirit for a moment. When your flesh has melted back into the earth, you still live in a brighter and more glorious life. Never can we be fouled by the mere touch of the flesh of a beast. The spirit must consent or there is no fault, no sin, no shame, no blame. Marie is a child of God and in Him you both live and move and have your being. Stand guard at the door of your soul. Let no ugly thoughts enter it. As a man thinketh so he is. Think only Divine thoughts. Remember that the only power and the only presence in this room now is God. You're a divine spirit, the child of God. Listen, dear, and you'll hear the beat of God's heart in yours."

An uplifted hand interrupted.

"But, Ann, if I decide that life is still worth living, what am I to do? You have stirred me with great thoughts. I feel the healing power within them. But I have died and just opened my eyes on a new strange world. I'm just an infant, with an infant's mind. What can I do?"

"I've worked it out for you, dear. I told you that I once studied in the University of the Great White Brotherhood of the Rosicrucians at San José, California. There I was born again. There you will rest and study and be born again into a richer, stronger, more wonderful life. You have four thousand dollars in the bank. More than enough for your expenses and courses of study."

"It's three thousand miles to California. I could never make the trip. I'm too weak and spent."

"I'll go with you, and introduce you to the Brotherhood."

A white hand pressed hers.

"You're an angel, Ann. God surely sent you to me for such a time as this. How soon could you start?"

"Tomorrow if you like."

"No we couldn't do that. I must get something to wear. I'll never see the little house again. I'll never touch a thing that was in it on that awful night. I'd like to burn it to the ground but that wouldn't be fair to those who helped us build it. I want you to give all my clothes and Marie's to Lottie. Old Adam is very poor. He has a scrawny little boy that can wear my baby's clothes. Jim can have everything of David's."

"He was here this morning," Ann interrupted, "and begged to see you. But I told him you wouldn't see anyone."

"What did he want?"

"To rent the place on shares. He says that David taught him how to farm. He can hire a man and make a fine yield and pay you half."

"Of course, he can have it. I couldn't sell it now. Jim's the only man in the County who'd live there. He'll carry on David's dream of farming and teach his people. Ask Phil Stephens to make out the contracts for me. He loved my man. God bless him."

She paused and brushed a tear from her eyes.

"Phil came again yesterday, you say?"

"And every day since you've been here. He can't understand why you refuse to see him."

"Tell him he'll understand some day. He'll always be the dearest man left on earth for me. But I can't see him yet. Something has snapped inside of me. I can't bear the thought of the love of man. He loves me. He'd show it. I couldn't endure it. Promise me something, Ann."

She paused and her friend bent close.

"Yes, dear?"

"Promise me on your soul's honor, if I go to California with you, no human being in this County shall know where I am until I choose to tell them."

"I promise."

"As time passes and I grow a new soul and body I may see Phil. But I can't conceive it now. Tell him this for me, and ask him for his understanding."

From the moment her decision was made Angela rapidly grew stronger. She made a list of clothes that she would need for the California climate under her friend's direction. They were promptly bought and packed in a new unmarked trunk and suit case.

John drove the car to Spartanburg after sending the baggage on a truck the day before.

They bought tickets to Atlanta to prevent the agent at Piedmont from knowing their destination. They would buy through tickets over the Southern Pacific in Atlanta.

A minute before the train blew for the station Angela seized John's hand.

"Goodbye. The memory of your face will be a benediction to me. I'll always love you as my brother."

The man looked away to hide the mist that covered his eyes.

"See Phil Stephens for me. You don't know where we're going. Your wife has not told you. You can truthfully say it. Ask Phil to settle Grandpa's little estate and deposit the money in a bank for me. Nelse gave him all he possessed two years ago and left no children. There'll be no trouble about it. He can rent the farm."

"I'll see that he does."

"I expect to remain with Angela for three weeks," Ann said. "Don't expect me sooner."

The air of California was wine to Angela's bruised nerves. There was in it a sense of exhiliration. She had emerged into a new world. A strange beautiful world without a black face in it.

As they drove from the station at San José, she asked:

"There are no Negroes here?"

"So few they are lost in the crowd. The Great Brotherhood knows no religion, no sect, no creed, no race. Its history goes back far into the centuries. I've never known a Negro in its membership in America. There may be a few. Don't worry, dear, you've left the Black Shadow in Piedmont, South Carolina."

The quiet beauty and dignity of Rosicrucian Park held Angela in a spell. There was something about the simple lines of its wide spread buildings that linked it to thousands of years of history. The stately shrubbery that rose in ever-green spires seemed part of the buildings, suggesting the minarets and towers of Mosques in the Orient.

Ann led her through each building and explained its use. The Administration structure was large, impressive. In it was located the staff of assistants and secretaries, some for recording, some for correspondence, some for executive work. Here she saw one of the largest mailing departments of any institution in America. The Rosicrucian Press is the biggest printing establishment between San Francisco and Los Angeles.

The Egyptian and Oriental Museum fascinated Angela with its relics and its reproduction of the only full sized Egyptian Tomb to be found in America. The Auditorium bore the name, surprisingly, of Francis Bacon.

"Sir Francis Bacon was a member of the Order?" Angela asked.

"One of its great lights."

The Auditorium was finished in Moorish design. They strolled leisurely through grounds that were beautifully landscaped by master artists. On them stood a stone replica of an Egyptian pylon and temple and a reproduction of one of the obelisks of ancient Heliopolis. The most appealing of all the buildings they found the magnificent Supreme Temple of the Order.

"Here," Ann whispered, "all the special and mystical contacts are held."

They stood a long time before the Rose-Croix University, an impressive building.

"Here you'll lay out your course of study," Ann said. "In Anthropology, Religion, and the History of Democracy."

"How foolish that I ever said life was not worth living," was the quick response.

They never tired until the last wonder had been explored—the tall signal tower, art rooms, studio, library, modern laboratories, lecture halls, motion picture studio, class rooms and research library.

"And all this the Headquarters of a Lodge?" Angela asked.

"A voluntary association of men and women studying the higher principles of life, Nature's laws, the Arts and Sciences. The object to perpetuate the wisdom of the sages and bring man closer to the cosmic scheme of the universe. To the end that he may live here a new and more useful, happy and abundant life, free of ignorance, superstition and mental bondage, filled with happiness, health and progress."

Angela entered her work with an enthusiasm that brought joy to the heart of her friend and mentor.

Chapter 18

Amid the universal condemnation of the South for the lynching there was a sharp utterance by a great Northern leader, born of a Southern mother.

Theodore Roosevelt said in *The Outlook*:

"Dreadful thing as it is for the mob spirit to be aroused in the community by such a crime, it would be even worse if the community did not feel the fury of indignation which produces the mob spirit."

Captain Collier read the editorial with deep interest. He had winced at the savage attacks on South Carolina and the whole South which this lynching had provoked. He showed the paper quoting Theodore Roosevelt to every member of his School Board at their meeting to pass on the resolution to rebuild the High School.

"Gentlemen," he said, "the Colored High School Building must be rebuilt immediately. Those blackened walls and ghost chimneys indict our people. They went mad, of course. But, by God, they had suffered a thing to drive men insane. No more penetrating truth could have been uttered than the words of the great son of a Bullock of Georgia. A people who could have resisted the provocation of the triple murder, and hideous rape and debauchery of one of our daughters and not gone mad over it, would have been unworthy to live. Their acceptance of anything short of mob violence would have been to mock our democracy. Mind you I'm not justifying this insanity. There's no need of argument to justify insanity. It is a tragedy which comes clothed in its own horror. It has no excuse or justification. It calls for none."

A member observed:

"I'm afraid our violence will be followed by a wave of crime."

"It will not!" snapped Collier. "The statement made by Northern Negro Radicals that lynching itself provokes an epidemic of crime in the

South is a damned vicious lie. As a lawyer I stand for law and order. As a historian I swear that a lynching such as that which disgraced the community is followed—always followed—by a long period of peace and quiet. Say what we will of their horror, they clear the air. It will be many a day before another Negro dares to lay his hands on a white woman in this County. The thing is bad enough without lying about it. There's nothing for us to do but rebuild the Negro High School, do all we can to reassure the better class of our colored people and try again to live together."

The vote to rebuild was unanimous. The bonds were sold and the contract let for the building.

The town was a center of interest for visitors from all parts of the South and many cities of the North. The little hotel did a thriving business. There was scarcely a day that it had a vacant room. Jake Borders, the proprietor, grinned and remarked that another lynching would require the addition of a new wing to his big rambling wooden structure.

"A new wing, hell," old Adam Spake scoffed. "What you need is a fire and a new building." The crowd in the lobby laughed approval.

Three weeks after the tragedy a fine looking stranger registered from Philadelphia and asked Borders to come to his room for a little talk.

The genial landlord sent a bottle of ginger ale with ice and took a flask of whiskey on his hip. The town was dry. But he considered it his business to supply the wants of his guests and this man looked like money. He was dressed well and gave the impression of culture and independence.

"Thanks for your thoughtfulness, Mr. Borders," the visitor said, with a smile at the sight of the flask. "But I happen to be a teetotaler. I'll take some ginger ale but no liquor."

The landlord looked puzzled.

"Sure thought that was what you wanted."

"Naturally from my asking you for a conference. But I really wanted a little chat."

"Glad to accommodate."

He dropped into an old fashioned split bottomed arm chair and offered his guest a cigar. He drew a silver cigarette case, however.

"I smoke cigarettes. Will you join me?"

Borders lit a cigar.

"Thanks, no. I like a real smoke. What can I tell you?"

"I'm tremendously interested in this lynching."

"Sure," nodded his landlord, "or you wouldn't have come."

"I represent," the stranger went on, "a publishing house who may issue a book on the subject. I may write it. Naturally I want to get my facts first hand on the spot where it took place."

"All right, Mr. Willis," he paused. "I see your name is Willis."

"Craig Willis, yes, sir."

"So the register shows. I'll be glad to get you a car and show you around."

"Thanks. I prefer to walk, where it's possible, and take my time. I may be here a week or two."

"That's fine. Where do I come in?"

"You can tell me who to see. I want to talk with a Liberal, a Conservative, a leader of the mob and an intelligent Negro who is not afraid to talk."

"All right," the landlord smiled. "They call our brilliant young lawyer, Phil Stephens a Liberal. He come damn near carrying it too far when he tried to stop the lynching. You'll find his office in the next block right down this street on the left hand side of the square. Captain Tom Collier, Chairman of the School Boards, is our leading Conservative. He's on the same street right across from Stephens' office. The leader of the mob was a six footer by the name of Lum Anderson. He's a workman in the Machine Shop in North Piedmont across the river. The intelligent Negro who is not afraid to talk don't live here. If he's got the sense of a clam he'll not open his mouth except to shut it."

"All the same," the stranger smiled, "I'd like to talk to one."

"Try the Superintendent of the High School that was burned. He has put up a wooden shack beside the walls of the old building where he's trying to carry on."

"Thank you," Willis said in dismissal. "I'll see Mr. Stephens first."

The landlord closed the door with a friendly nod.

"You'll find him the brightest young lawyer in the County."

Phil received his visitor with courtesy and frowned on his purpose to write a book.

"I'll be sorry to see another book on lynching. We've had several. They are hard reading for a Southerner who thinks. But I've often wondered why you Northern students of the South never write books on the crimes of Negroes which provoke lynching—rape for instance. We must stop these crimes of murder, rape, arson, all capital offenses in this State, before we can stop lynching, I'm afraid."

"Yet you are a man of the New South, a Liberal?"

"I try to be. But we must face facts if we ever intend to find a remedy for the tragedy which has shadowed this community. There's something wrong somewhere with the education which we are giving the Negro. A spelling book and geography are not enough. Our next step must be to develop a moral character. And we must give more time to that than to text books. The mass of our Negroes are good. They are kind, affectionate, gentle, lovable. But there's a large percentage of the younger generation who are going criminal. This is true North and South. The percentage of Negro criminals is far greater in the North where he has the ballot and a wider use of civil rights. Why is this?"

"Might it not come from the fiercer contest for bread?"

"Possibly. But does it?"

"I think so. The slum districts of the Negro in the North are the breeding ground of crime. We must clean up those slums and educate their ignorant masses. As it seems to me you must clean up your slums in the South and educate the ignorant masses here."

"We have tried to do just that in this County and then came the beast out of the jungle to laugh at us. It's discouraging."

"Don't you think," the visitor broke in, "that the time has come for the forward looking men of your type to assert the majesty of the law in just such cases?"

"It's easier said than done. The enforcement of law rests on the moral sentiment of the community."

"There was no demand in your County for the punishment of the mob?"

"None."

"Yet their identity was known?"

"The leaders—yes."

"Couldn't an indictment be secured against them?"

"Hardly."

"If a man of your standing demanded it?"

"A man of my standing would not undertake it."

"Not if a responsible group of law and order men offered you a fee of five thousand dollars?"

Stephens threw a startled look at his visitor.

"You represent such a group?"

"Yes. Recently organized in New York, composed of men of the North and the South."

"You are wasting your time and money."

"You decline the offer?"

"With thanks. You can't command money enough to interest me as a lawyer in prosecuting my friends and neighbors."

"I am disappointed. I had hoped your progressive ideals might make you our representative in the South."

"Not on a money basis," Phil smiled.

"No harm done," Willis laughed. "You are a good lawyer. Your name was given me as a Liberal leader."

Stephens rose to end the interview.

"Not quite so liberal as that."

At the door his visitor paused.

"If I get this answer from you I'd better walk warily in Captain Collier's presence?"

"I would not walk in that direction at all, if I were you," was the grave warning.

"I've a letter of introduction to him from Rex Weldon, his former Superintendent of Schools. I think he'll see me."

The Captain read the letter, looked up and frowned.

"So you're one of our good Yankee friends who are busy again warning the Bloody South?"

His caller winced.

"I'd hardly say that, Captain."

"If you're planning to write a book on this lynching I'd say it. The South is being slandered and lied about with deeper malice every day. How long they are going to put up with it I don't know. There's a Negroid Junta up North that's in the main responsible for it."

He stopped short and gave Willis a look of direct hostility.

"You will have to excuse me. I've an important case on my desk."

"But I'm very anxious to ask you two or three questions if you don't mind, sir."

"I do mind," came the sharp answer. "I've asked you to excuse me. I don't like you. I'll have to make it a little plainer. I don't like the sound of your voice. I don't like your face."

Willis rose hurriedly and stalked from the room.

He caught Anderson as he was quitting work and asked him to have dinner with him in his hotel room. He wanted the true story of the lynching from the only man who could give it.

"Can't go to the hotel," was the short answer. "Too tired to change my clothes. But if you'll come to my home and take a chance with me for supper, I'll talk to you."

Willis accepted with thanks and they walked three blocks to a modest cottage. Mrs. Anderson was flattered by the call of a handsomely dressed stranger and apologized for the simple fare—country ham and turnip greens, snap beans and corn pone.

The visitor praised her cooking and the men smoked cigarettes and talked while she washed the dishes.

The leader of the mob told the story without hesitation.

"You never seed nothin' like the den that Nigger built in the pine tree top. He'd hid a bag in the woods with enough grub to last him two weeks.

A hammer and nails, four pieces of pine board to build the floor of his nest. After he'd built it tight by tying live limbs into it, he lined it with an old quilt to keep out the wind while he slept, and an oil cloth to shed water."

"You think he went crazy?"

"Crazy, hell—no—he was slick as a black snake. He meant to hide in that den for weeks. The dogs couldn't trail him there. The water was too deep. He didn't figure on old Adam Spake's knowin' that Lake and woods so well. Adam found the scum on the water under his perch. He had bought a ticket for New York over at Spartanburg where nobody knew him. The ticket was in that marked copy of the Nigger magazine."

"You have the magazine?" Willis interrupted.

"It's mine, Captain Collier keeps it for me in his safe."

"An' here's a letter from Dan's pal in Harlem. He didn't subscribe to the magazine. The postmaster swore to that. This Harlem Nigger sent it to him with this letter. Read it."

Willis scanned the crudely written sheet of note paper.

"I'm sendin' you the magazine to let you see it in the papers. Why stick round down there and risk your neck after another white gal. You've had two. Come on up to Harlem. I'll get you one every night if you want 'em."

"Would you part with the magazine and this letter?" Willis asked casually.

"Not on your life, mister."

"I'll give you a hundred dollars for the magazine."

"What'ell you want it that bad for?"

"A souvenir. To put in my library in New York."

"Don't want to sell it."

"Not for five hundred dollars?"

"Cash?"

"Cash!"

"God, man. That's a temptation. I need five hundred. I'll step round to Captain Collier's house and ask him to let me have it."

"From my conversation with him today," the stranger observed, "I think he'll hit the ceiling if you let him know you want to sell it. From his remarks I gather he doesn't like men from the North."

"That's just his way of talking. He's all right after you get to know him."

"When you've seen the Captain and gotten the magazine will you come by the hotel?"

"Sure. In a jiffy. Have your money ready. I'm going to trade with you. I aint got no use for the damned things."

Willis returned from North Piedmont in a ramshackled Ford that had been turned into a hack. The more he thought of Anderson's coming conference with Collier the more uneasy he. grew. He decided to visit Stephens and consult him before returning to the hotel. His office was closed. He asked the driver if he knew the young lawyer's address.

"Yassah," was the quick reply, "dat I do. He lives in de finest ole house in Piedmont, wid white pillers an' a lawn wid all de flowers dat blossoms."

"Drive me there right away."

In a few minutes the ancient Ford rattled up to the stately front porch, and Willis struck the brass knocker with a vigorous stroke.

Phil invited him in with a look of surprise that called for immediate explanation.

"I find myself in need of a little advice, Mr. Stephens," he said rapidly before taking the seat to which he had been motioned. "Anderson tells me the marked copy of the magazine which they say was found on Hose, in his coat, is in Captain Collier's safe. Also Anderson has a letter, found with the magazine, from a pal in Harlem. I wanted them as souvenirs and offered to buy them. Finally offered five hundred dollars. He was tremendously excited, and rushed to get it from Captain Collier."

"You offered him five hundred dollars?" Stephens interrupted.

"Yes."

"Why?"

"As I told you. For a souvenir."

"I can't believe that. You'd better be frank with me. I don't think you've much time to lose."

"What do you mean by that?"

"You may have to leave town in a hurry. Pardon me now if I ask you a very pointed and very personal question. You have Negro blood, haven't you?"

"Why do you ask that?"

"Because as I study your features, white as they are, the idea has just come to me."

"Frankly. Yes. I am of mixed blood though I easily pass as white even in the South. I trust we may still confer on friendly terms?"

"Of course, I have many good friends among the Negroes. But you're in a very dangerous situation. Captain Collier is a man of hot temper and his hatred of Northern Mulatto leaders has become an obsession. The moment Anderson shows him that magazine—which I think he has already seen—and tells of your offer, he'll organize a vigilante committee to hang you."

"Impossible!"

"It's certain. We haven't a minute to lose. I'll take you over to Spartanburg in my car and, you can catch the nine o'clock express for New York."

"It's that urgent?" Willis asked incredulously.

"Urgent. Get to the hotel quick, grab your bag, jump back in the hack and meet me at my gate. My car'll be waiting."

In fifteen minutes the old Ford rattled back, Willis transferred himself and bag and Stephens caught the hackman by the coat collar and slipped him an extra dollar.

"If anybody asks, you haven't seen this man, or me, tonight. I'm getting him out of town—you understand?"

"Yassah—Yassah—Mr. Phil, I aint seed nobody. Dat dollar bill make me blind ez a bat."

Three cars were standing in front of Collier's office as they speeded by. In front of the hotel two more had stopped. Phil saw Collier's long gray hair shaking as he shouted to the landlord.

"Where's that damned skunk?"

"I tell you he paid his bill and left."

"Left how? There's no train at this hour."

"Left in an old Ford hack."

The Captain turned to one of his men.

"Follow that rattletrap we passed just now, come back and report."

A man leaped into his car and dashed away.

"Do you mind, Borders, if I take a look in that fellow's room?"

"I tell you he's gone, sir!" the landlord growled.

"Yes. I know. But he's a damned spy sent down here from the North. He may have left some letters."

The room was searched and not a scrap of paper found in the table drawer or waste basket. Collier tramped. back down stairs and encountered the man he had sent after the Ford.

"You overtook him?"

"Yes, sir. Swore he'd seen nobody. Was just going back to North Piedmont where he has a hack stand."

"All right. A fast car passed us as we drove up here. It was heading toward Spartanburg. I caught a glimpse of a man inside wearing a gray suit of clothes. It's a good lead. We'll follow it. If he's headed for Spartanburg he's going to catch the nine o'clock train. We may get him yet. Tell the other men at my office to follow the highway to Spartanburg."

On the crest of a hill with winding road over a two mile stretch, Stephens stopped the car and looked back.

"We're being followed," he said. "I've counted six cars in a procession at the foot of this hill. I think I can beat them but it's going to be a race."

He threw in his clutch and swept down the long grade at a dangerous speed.

Willis held on to the arm of his seat and laughed.

"I'd as well be killed by the Captain as to have them pick up the pieces in one of those ravines."

"Don't worry. I know every crook and turn in this road. Unless a tire blows we're all right."

From the next rise he looked back again and saw his pursuers rounding curves at as reckless speed as he was making. They had gained a quarter of a mile. The cars roared at steady top speed and the distance widened between them half a mile at the next rise.

"We're gaining on them," Phil muttered. "You're an agent of "The National Association for the Advancement of Colored People" I take it?"

"Yes," was the prompt admission. "We have determined from now on to investigate every lynching in the South."

"I can't blame you, of course," the lawyer said. "I only wish you people would use a little more common sense in your methods. Wholesale denunciation of the Southern people as traitors to the country and inhuman persecutors of the Negro will get you nowhere. The conflict of color is a great unsolved problem. We need wisdom and forbearance, not passion and bitterness in its study. I wish I could give your leaders a little advice."

"Why not?"

"I couldn't live in this climate and do it."

"Come to New York, the center of the nation's life. There are more Southern people there than in any city south of the line. Your influence from New York would be infinitely greater than from Piedmont."

Stephens looked back at the pursuing cavalcade.

"We can't talk and make that train," he muttered. "It's going to be pull Dick, pull Devil!"

His fingers tightened on the wheel and he concentrated on the roadbed. The whining wheels on the upper side of stark curves were lifted from the ground more than once as he drove with increasing speed.

He glanced cautiously at the clock.

"We've barely time to make that train. I hope it pulls out before our friends arrive. I wouldn't like to ride back to Piedmont with them tonight."

"We won't," Willis laughed. "I've confidence in my driver."

They dashed up to the station just as the express pulled in. Willis sprang from the car, his bag in hand and climbed aboard without attempting to buy a ticket.

As he stood on the steps of the day coach he extended his hand to his rescuer.

"I probably owe my life to you. Goodbye. I'd like to see you in New York."

The lawyer pressed his hand and nodded.

"Goodbye. I *may* see you in New York."

"Come!"

The conductor signaled and the train moved. It had barely gained a headway when the cavalcade of pursuers swung into the open space before the platform. Captain Collier sprang out and confronted Phil.

"So it was you."

"Yes."

"I suspected it. You got the damned skunk on the train in time to save his life."

"And you, a great lawyer, from being a murderer. You've had a narrow escape, Captain."

"For which I don't thank you, my, boy," the old warrior growled.

"You will later."

"Never. The hanging of that scoundrel would have served notice on the venomous breed that our patience is exhausted." He paused and drew Stephens apart from the men who had accompanied him.

"Look here, boy. Your speech to that lynching crowd was a punk performance. But this is going too far. You're one of my boys. I taught you the law."

"And I'm trying to honor a great teacher by living up to it as a man of the new world, a Liberal forward looking man."

"Fine words, my boy, but they've ceased to mean anything. Let an older man give you some information. There has been since the Civil War but two classes of white men in the South, Southerners and renegades. In Reconstruction time—from '67 to '76—the renegades were called "Scalawags"—men who ate, drank, and hobnobbed with our enemies. Today they are called Liberals. God save the mark! They're the same breed of pups. They stand for the same lack of principle and clear thinking. There was a sexless minority between these two classes, sentimental mush eaters. We've the same bunch of spineless fools today, who preach goodfellowship, toleration, a closer approach of the races. This goodfellowship, toleration and closer approach means but one thing ultimately, the mixture of races into a bastard breed that will end our civilization. I'd hate to call you a renegade. You come of good blood. But you're giving a damned good performance of that role. The time is coming, son, when the South is going to separate the sheep from the goats."

"And I'm a goat?" Stephens laughed.

"You're rapidly growing into one and it makes me sad. I've always loved you. I loved your good old father before you. When I see men of your type begin to falter in their allegiance to Southern ideals——"

Phil lifted a hand.

"Suppose I see a nobler ideal of the new South shall I refuse its call to worship the dead?"

"Not if it's noble. No. But is it?"

"I think so. This nation owes a debt to the Negro race. A kindlier, gentler, people never lived. They've cut our forests, hewn our rocks, tilled our soil and helped to make our country great. We refuse to give them a square deal—North or South."

"What do you mean by a square deal?" the old man snapped.

"Equal civil, economic and legal rights."

"And you can't see that equality in civil, economic, and legal rights means social equality?"

"I can not."

"You've a lot to learn, then, my boy, about our country, our laws, our life as a democracy, and above all you've a lot to learn about the Negro. You are talking of the surface of things, not their substance. The early attempts of pot house politicians to give the Negro both political and social equality in a day was crushed by the Southern revolution of six hundred thousand Clansmen. The new attempt of your Sentimentalists and Liberals is far more dangerous because more subtle and plausible. Your so called Liberals seek to gradually break down the barriers between the races. What we've got to do is to make those barriers impassable. Instead of demanding the equal civil rights of ten million Negroes you should be busy putting the Atlantic Ocean between us. It doesn't matter whether the African is our equal or our superior. The history of South America has proven that a mongrel breed of Mulattoes means the end of progress, the extinction of our race. There can be but two classes in this country, white men and Negroes. The minute you cross the line and mingle socially with the Negro you are one. You cease to be white. I'm warning you, Phil. Come to your senses, or turn your eyes to the North, join our enemies and be done with it."

"I may do just that, Captain," was the firm reply.

The incident brought Phil uneasy hours. Men began to pass him on the streets with averted looks. Some stared in an ugly way. His law practice dropped at the next session of the State Court. Friends greeted him with a coldness that was more than depressing. It became sickening. He began to avoid crowds and spent his evenings in his library reading.

The astounding report of the lynching which Willis gave to the Negro press from New York added to his embarrassment and roused his anger. When Captain Collier called a mass meeting to denounce this report as a tissue of lies, he volunteered to act on the committee on resolutions.

Willis baldly declared that the mob had burned to death a perfectly innocent man! That the blood hounds that picked up the trail from Henry's house had failed to locate the criminal. That old Spake had found the tree in which an insane Negro had built a den where he was living. That this poor insane man was dragged from his tree top, beaten and tortured and finally burned alive by a mob of fiends who had called a holiday to enliven the tedium of their dull lives. The description of the lynching was lurid in its details. Its sadistic features were described in language calculated to rouse the devil in every Negro reader. Not one word was said in condemnation of the murders and rape that had caused the incident.

That the marked copy of the magazine was an obvious plant. That the Chairman of the School Board had for three years carried on a crusade against this organ of The National Association for the Advancement of the Colored People out of pure hatred of the Negro. That every copy found in Piedmont had been confiscated, and one teacher of the public schools had been expelled from the staff for buying a subscription.

When Phil rose to move the resolution of censure, a tense and painful silence held the crowd which packed the Court House.

"Permit me," he said, "before I read the resolutions, to express my regret for the part which I innocently played in furthering the plans of the man who wrote the vicious and lying report of the tragedy that occurred in Piedmont a few weeks ago. You know my views on lynching. I have no apology for them. We must stop this madness. We will stop it. But we must stop the crimes which lead to it—and we will stop them!"

Applause shook the building and restored Phil to his friends.

He did not reveal the fact that Willis was a Negro in spite of his fair skin. The revelation would have increased the bitterness and done nothing to restore the life of the town to its normal conditions.

At the close of the meeting Captain Collier grasped Phil's hand.

"A true son of your father, tonight, my boy, I welcome you back into the fold."

The welcome was unanimous. Phil hurried out the rear entrance to avoid the rush to shake his hand. The whole thing depressed him. He had rescued a man from mob violence without a moment's hesitation. He would do it again. But this determination of Mulatto fools in the North to lie and lie and lie to their own people, and stir them continually to renewed hatred of the white race was a thing that roused his deepest anger. Unless it could be stopped there would be a dangerous reaction among the people of the South.

He left the meeting with a sense of depression and without knowing what he was doing he found himself on the way to the cottage of Ann Lovelace. His hunger to see Angela had become of late all but unendurable. This meeting and the memories it had stirred had renewed the feeling. He had called on Ann twice within a week trying with all his powers of persuasion to get Angela's address. He made no headway. He would try again tonight.

She greeted him with a gracious welcome and he sank into an arm chair beside her desk. She was reading a volume of Sir Francis Bacon. The title startled him a little in spite of the fact that he knew her to be a keen student of religion and philosophy. Her Quaker ancestry had bequeathed her a hunger for Truth. He noted again that every foot of her living room was lined with books and the shelves had to be extended into the long hall leading into the kitchen. There were book cases in each bedroom. He could see them through the open doors.

His eye rested on a pamphlet lying on her table, the cover of which was done in rich colors. The drawing showed the pillars of an ancient temple in which stood a group of students looking from the shadows through a vista toward a lake surrounded by snow capped mountains. At the lower edge of the cover he read the letters, "AMORC, Rosicrucian Park, San José, California." The truth still eluded his mind. Ann had studied there. Of course, she would take their magazine.

He listened to the soft drawl of the woman's voice as she told him of her joy in reading.

When he rose to go he held her hand with a hungry pressure.

"I don't ask you to give me Angela's address. You must respect her wishes, of course. But I can thank you again for all you have done for her and all your beautiful mind has meant to her life. I know that you saved her reason."

She looked at him a moment.

"You talk as if you were leaving us, Phil?"

"I may go North. The old town's getting on my nerves."

"John said you did yourself proud at the meeting tonight."

"On the outside, maybe—not on the inside. I'm horribly depressed."

"And it's so unnecessary. All you have to do is to open your heart and let God have right of way. He's all around you. If only you recognize His still voice."

It was strange that he never resented this woman's talk about religion. Most conversations on that subject bored him. He had long ago quit going to church.

He smiled and bowed, hurried home, and began to draw the leases for the tenants. Hillcrest he leased to Jim Beasley on half the crops. The old farm, which was now Angela's, he let to ten good Negro tenants.

He would make them all sign written leases, duly witnessed. The rents would give her a sufficient income on which to live when her cash had been exhausted.

It was not until six months later that his mind suddenly recalled the rich cover of the pamphlet on Ann Lovelace's table, and the address on the lower edge. "Rosicrucian Park, San José, California." Of course, she had taken Angela to this retreat!

The next day he took the limited from Atlanta to Los Angeles.

CHAPTER 19

As his train swept through the Black Belt of the South, Stephens mind was clouded anew with its problem. At every station crowds of idle Negroes loafed about the platform. It was cotton picking time. They should have been in the fields. But they got wages enough for three days' work to loaf the other four and as a rule they loafed. Children of the joys of an hour they took no heed of the days that stretched ahead.

He had supported Booker T. Washington's plan of industrial education with enthusiasm. Yet as he watched these idle throngs milling around the train, he asked himself the question how such a race could compete with the keener mind and urgent ambition of the white man. A few Negro students were being trained at Hampton and Tuskegee. They were drops in the ocean of ten million Negroes. The white race was training in industry far more rapidly. When they clashed, would not the results be the same as the fight in politics? The new white industrial worker was already crowding the Southern Negro out of the professions which he had held since the war and before it. The economic war that was looming was in many respects as ominous as the social and political struggle.

At Newnan Georgia the black cloud at the station was largest of all. This was the town from which the avenging mob had swept to the lynching of Sam Hose, who had committed a crime the exact pattern of the one at Hillcrest. The assailant of David Henry, and his people, claimed the same name. Whether an actual brother was not known. It didn't matter. They were blood brothers in race and race feeling. They were blood brothers in the inheritance of savagery from the jungles of Africa. He recalled now the fact that the same group of radical Mulattoes in New York had "investigated" the case of Sam Hose and proclaimed him an innocent hero and martyr to the infamy of white brutality. He wondered again what would be the outcome of this systematic lying and excitation to racial crime and bloodshed.

In New Orleans he recalled the tragedy of the city's early fall in the Civil War. Captured by the genius of the great Southerner, Admiral Farragut.[1] Little credit the Southern white man who volunteered to fight for the Union had been given in the mind of the nation. Three hundred and fifty thousand Southerners answered Lincoln's call to fight for the Union. Had this army of the bravest of the brave joined the Confederacy it might have been unconquerable. Thousands of Northern men deserted their colors in the dark days of the war which followed the proclamation of Emancipation. A Northern legislature actually voted resolutions of sympathy for the South! Not a man of the three hundred and fifty thousand white Union soldiers from the South ever deserted. They dared the hatred of friends and neighbors at home when they volunteered. They never looked back until the Union triumphed. Thomas, their greatest army leader, was the "Rock of Chicamauga," who saved a Northern army from annihilation. This grand army of the Union from the South remained true Southerners after the war. They scorned to associate with Carpetbaggers and Scalawags. They stood staunchly for white supremacy then and their children were equally as staunch today.

And yet the millions of the North were now listening to the slander, lies and vilification of the South with little knowledge or sympathy for their tragedy. He wondered how long this injustice would continue. He could see it all the more clearly because as a young "Liberal" he was fighting for justice for the Negro. Justice is broad. It should cover both races.

As his train swept across the plains of Texas, the dusky loafers at the stations thinned to a mere handful. The Lone Star State was forging ahead in population, wealth and power beyond the wildest dream of its pioneers—though Sam Houston[2] was one of them. To the stream of gold that had poured in from cotton had been added now the first rich oil gushers which would make Texas the greatest oil producing State in the world. The tall stalwart men who boarded the train were a distinct race. They had been born of select stock, pioneers and refugees from the old Seaboard Southern States. North Carolina had sent thousands from the

1. David Glasgow Farragut (1801–1870), a Tennessee native who sided with the Union, was the first admiral of the U.S. Navy. He distinguished himself at New Orleans (April 1862) and Mobile Bay (August 1864). See Charles Lee Lewis, *David Glasgow Farragut: Our First Admiral,* 2 vols. (Annapolis: United States Naval Institute, 1941–1943).

2. Sam Houston (1793–1863), a Virginian, became the first president of the Republic of Texas, 1836–1838, served as U.S. senator, 1846–1859, and governor of Texas, 1859–1861. Houston was removed from office in March 1861 for initial refusal to support the Confederacy. See James L. Haley, *Sam Houston* (Norman: University of Oklahoma Press, 2002).

ranks of the Klan. Every State of the South had sent her best young blood. And blood will tell. He could see its mark in the rugged features and firm tread.

The train stopped long enough in San Antonio to drive to the old Alamo and dream of its heroic defenders. Again he realized that the United States of America was great not because of the amount of dirt over which the flag flew or the number of names on its census roll. But because of the race of pioneer freemen who cleared its wilderness for the feet of Liberty and laid the foundations of its laws. The essence of Americanism is something inside the souls of men. Not the things on the outside.

He breathed the perfumed air of California with a deep exhilaration. The kind he used to feel in South Carolina when a sudden snow flurry swept the fields.

It was good to be here. He felt on good terms with the world. On good terms with Fate. He couldn't fail in his mission. There was no such word as fail. Something in the air of this new world lifted him in spirit.

He stopped in thronged Los Angeles only long enough to engage a limousine and a good chauffeur. He would drive up the Coast to San José and get the feel of the country.

He took the car and driver for a month, sustained by a faith that he would find Angela and tour the country with her. Why did he think a Southern girl, reared in the traditions that hedge women, would go with him without a chaperone on such a trip? There was in the thought no hint of the shame through which she had passed. He just felt that in this new exhilarating world she would do it. If she wouldn't, all right, he'd hire a good woman to accompany them.

He entered the grounds of Rosicrucian Park deeply impressed by the solemn beauty of its buildings. Surely a mysterious setting in a modern world. At the desk in the Central Administration Building he was presented to the Grand Secretary of the Order who received him with grave, simple courtesy.

He would carry his message immediately to Mrs. Henry, of South Carolina. Yes, she had been there seven months. She was one of their prize pupils. Her progress had been extraordinary. Her health was perfect. Her beauty enhanced.

While the Secretary went in person to deliver the message, his heart sank for a moment at the thought she might still refuse to see him. She couldn't! If she did he'd enter the Great White Brotherhood himself and stay there until he did see her.

She came immediately, a tender smile playing about her lips. Never had he seen her so beautiful as she crossed the hall with extended hand, wearing a simple one piece dress that nearly reached the floor and greatly enhanced her stately figure.

"How did you find me, Phil, dear?" she asked in answer to the warm pressure of his hand. "Ann didn't tell you?"

"A magazine of the Rosicrucian Order, laying on the table, gave me the clue and I am here. You are not sorry?"

"No. I'm very glad. I've gotten homesick at times. Three thousand miles is a long road."

She led him to a seat beside a window overlooking the grounds.

"I was so sure of finding you!" Phil said, "that I brought you the cash from your tenants. The year was a good one. The Negroes on the old place did fairly well. Jim had good luck with his potatoes, though the market sagged badly toward the end. Your income for the year nets fifteen hundred dollars. Here's the check and statement from your attorney."

She stared at it increduously.

"Why, Phil, I never dreamed of such an income. You must have given the farms your personal care."

"I did. It was all I could do for you. It was little enough."

"Thank you."

Looking through the window he watched a gray haired figure walk slowly past on the graveled path, and asked in surprise:

"Isn't that a Negro?"

"Yes," she smiled. "An apparent contradiction, isn't it? But not in reality. When I first saw his black face in an assembly meeting of the Great White Brotherhood my impulse was to leave."

She paused, lifted her head and went on evenly. "I said that my first impulse was to leave. I was shocked. But when I came face to face with him one day walking on the grounds, he stopped, looked at me and smiled as gently as old Nelse used to and quietly said:

"Pardon me, Miss, but you're from the old South, are you not?"

"It was impossible to take offense at his speaking to me, his voice was so gently respectful."

"I nodded and said, 'Yes, I am.'"

"I was born down there, a slave, many, many years ago," he went on. "My master was one of God's Princes. Not a mere nobleman, a Prince. He gave me my papers of emancipation long before the Civil War and enough money to begin life. I had learned to read and write. He taught me through many long happy hours of our boyhood. I made enough money to give me a living income. My master was a member of this Brotherhood. I came here to study, and stayed to work in its gardens. I've never left. I shall pray every day that God will lead you into as great peace and happiness as are mine."

"He never suspected my tragic history. I use only my maiden name now. I've learned many things from this gray haired old Negro. He says that he is nearly a hundred years old. Nelse was eighty-nine and he must be much older from the events he remembers. He is one of the gentlest, kindliest, most Christ-like souls I have ever known. I owe to him the growth in my heart of a deeper interest in the Negro race."

"An astounding thing, my dear."

"Yes, isn't it? I am surrounded now by the Peace of God. I am not afraid of people. I am not afraid of things. I am not afraid of circumstances. I am not afraid of myself. I am not afraid of the past, the present, or the future. I am not afraid of life. I am not afraid of death. I am not afraid—because God is with me."

He studied her beauty with a new eagerness. There was a mysterious light in her brown hazel tinted eyes he had never caught before. He had only seen the brown. The hazel tone gave a new tenderness to them. A wave of overwhelming love swept his heart.

"I am going to ask you to do something very unconventional, Angela," he ventured.

"Why not? The people here are not slaves of convention."

"I've a good chauffeur and a fine car hired for a month. I want you to go on a tour and show me the glories of California. I'd like to see them through your eyes."

"Alone, unchaperoned, Phil?" she smiled.

"Unless you wish a chaperone."

"I don't," she laughed. "And we'll go unless the Secretary forbids it."

"He will not. I've met him."

"I don't think he will either."

"I'm asking such a thing of you, dear," Phil hastened to say, "not because of any loss of reverence on account of the tragedy you suffered . . ."

She shook her head and smiled.

"No, my dear old friend, such a thought never entered my head. I see in your eager eyes a very different reason. A very vain and foolish one, perhaps. But you've come three thousand miles and I'll hear you—bless your dear heart."

The lover in him was chilled for a moment by the poised impersonal tones of her voice. But his heart beat high. There was a depth of tenderness and eloquence within that she had never felt. He'd make her feel it now. With a thousand voices of nature to sing the chorus of love, he'd take his chance of failure.

With the best wishes of the Secretary they started the next day. Their first stop Angela planned. There was a little retreat established by a member of the Brotherhood in the rugged mountains north of Los Angeles. The road to it was narrow and steep but a good car could make it. At least they said so. A map of the region showed the exact location on a little stream called "Gold Creek." A famous motion picture director, had a bungalow on the stream five miles beyond where he went into hiding when at work on important manuscripts.

"I didn't know you progressive Californians ventured on such roads," Phil observed. "They're worthy of trails I've followed in the hinterland of Western North Carolina."

She pressed his arm.

"It's a thrilling adventure."

At a doubtful spot the road completely disappeared in the dry bed of a stream and there was nothing to do but follow the water marked way.

The driver frowned, groaned and gritted his teeth but they finally emerged on dry land in sight of the little Inn.

The man in charge was elated at the sight of a human being. He was there alone, chief cook, bottle washer, proprietor, and man of all work.

"Married or single?" the jovial host inquired.

"Single." They answered in chorus.

"Then I'll have to give you a cottage apiece. This way please."

He seized the two bags and led them fifty yards down stream to a board walk connecting a row of cottages built over a brook whose music was a low sweet melody.

"This is yours, Ma'm," their guide announced, dropping the large bag. "You'll find candles and matches on the mantel."

"Right this way for you, sir," he called cheerfully.

They followed the board walk down stream to another weather stained cottage built squarely across the brook.

"Thank you," Phil called as the landlord and cook hurried away to prepare dinner, with no warning of guests, and few resources.

A moment to unpack and tidy up and Angela was ready for the steep ascent to the mountain peak for the sunset.

They sat on a boulder for half an hour and watched in silence. Phil had climbed the summit hoping for the inspiration of the right moment to tell his love. The right moment eluded him. The longer they were together the more difficult he found an approach. Not that she was cold. Just the reverse. She was too cordially friendly, too poised in her matter of fact acceptance of him as a brother and best friend. If he could have detected the slightest embarrassment in her manner he would have been happier.

As the twilight gathered he touched her arm.

"We'd better start picking our way down that rocky path."

He wanted to walk beside her and hold her arm. The path was too narrow, the brambles and briars too near the narrow way. He tried in the silence to figure out her real attitude toward him. Something had happened to her. He felt this from the first. He felt it more acutely in the silence and loneliness of this isolated mountain gorge. He was going to speak, of course. He had come for this purpose. He'd face it at the right time. He must be sure the time was propitious.

Their host was in high spirits. The victrola was playing a Spanish love song. The dinner was on the table smoking hot, broiled trout, long branch potatoes, a salad, cheese and crackers and coffee.

They were hungry and ate ravenously.

"Don't mind asking for more," their host urged. "This mountain air gives you an appetite."

After dinner they sat and chatted with the landlord, until he said:

"I've built you a little wood fire in your cottage, M'am, so you can have a visit together while I get things ready for breakfast."

The hour had struck! In the sweet intimacy of that little cottage with the music of a running brook below and the flicker of firelight through its shadows, fate could not have provided a more propitious moment, Phil decided.

He took the lantern and slipped his hand under Angela's arm. At the touch of her flesh his heart began to pound. She submitted to his guidance as a child. He puzzled his brain on a delicate approach. She had been a widow barely eight months. To him it seemed eight years. She could only refuse him. She couldn't stop him loving her.

By the firelight he studied her face for a hint of her thoughts. It was a mask. Beautiful but still a mask. The silence was becoming too intense. He thought he saw a dark flicker of the memory of another open fireplace in a little cottage on a hill and her mouth contracted. He must speak. Too long a silence under the conditions was not good.

"You know, Angela," he began, "why I came across a continent to see you."

She started from her memories and nodded.

"Yes, Phil, I know."

"There has been but one woman in life for me. There will never be another. I love you with a love that can't die. All that has happened to you has strengthened, not weakened it. Your marriage, I thought at first would kill me. It only made me love you more hopelessly. I thought I proved that to you in my attitude toward David."

"You did!"

"The awful thing that happened tore the heart out of me. Nothing more horrible could come to a human being. It came to murder you as wife, sister, and mother. The horror it brought to you cut me as it cut you. I suffered with David a thousand deaths. I suffered with your little boy a thousand more. I suffered with Marie more than words can tell. You fought a brave battle and saved your reason."

"Thanks to the divinely illuminated soul of Ann Lovelace."

"And now, my darling, all I ask is that you marry me and let me atone in some manner for all you've suffered. Find with me new strength, courage, happiness. If you wish to return to Piedmont, we'll make the old homestead the center of an intellectual and social life that will inspire our people . . ."

She interrupted him with a gesture of impatience.

"Surely, Phil, you don't think I could ever again wish to look into the faces of my neighbors in the old home, see their pity and feel the horror in their hearts."

"Then we'll make our home in New York. I've a friend in a firm of good lawyers there who has asked me to join them. We would both begin in new inspiring surroundings. New York is the center of the nation's life. I've thought of it a long time and it fascinates me. With you——"

She took his hand and caressed it gently.

"You surprise me with the depth, the sincerity and tenderness of your love. It's strange I feel no answering emotion. You seem to be talking to me from another world. You are in fact. The old world in which I lived has gone forever. I think my soul died. My body died. The woman you see here has been born again. I'm just a child beginning to timidly walk across the floor. The idea of sex is gone. I have lost its impulse. I have forgotten its meaning."

"I'll restore its mystery and joy in the wealth and tenderness of my love. Let me try!"

"You don't realize what you are asking. You can't understand the degrading shame through which that black beast dragged my soul. I look at you, my first sweetheart, and you seem a stranger. I know you're not. I know you're the one man in my life of deep spiritual vision, of high ideals, of fine character. But I've no desire again to be a wife or a mother or to build a home. These things have passed. There's slowly growing in me the consciousness of a mission. A search that may bring a message to humanity."

She paused and he saw a look in her eyes that put a new barrier between them.

"Let me join with you in that search and help you carry the message."

"I'm afraid, dear, you'd hinder it. You're a very spiritually minded man, Phil, I've always felt that. But you are also a very highly sexed animal with all your poise and pride and culture. I'd fail you. Thank you for your proposal.

It has helped me. You have given back to me something that was lacking. My sense of woman's power. It will help me build a stronger character."

"To what end, dear?" he persisted. "You talk of a new mission that may uplift humanity. Can you give me a hint what it may be?"

"If you wish to hear it—yes."

He settled back in his chair and fixed her with a tense gaze. She answered with a smile.

"Do relax, Phil. Your choice of the place and hour for your declaration was perfect. Seated here in this lovely cottage in the darkness and stillness of mountains, with that firelight flickering in our faces, the clean brook below babbling its music, the linen of a bed showing white in the shadows—if a propitious hour and perfect surroundings could have moved me, this surely would. But they don't move me. The woman you once knew and loved is gone forever."

"I love the new one then with all the fire with which I loved the first. And I've an idea you protest too much."

"But don't you see," she persisted, "that there's no response from me. I begin to see the possibility of a useful life. In the hideous experience through which I passed, I realized as I think no thoughtful educated woman has ever done before, the gulf that separates the Negro from the white race. I believe nothing can bridge it. Both races are human—yes. The pine and the oak are trees. They are utterly different. They can not be grafted on one another. The Negro race, in culture and character, is thousands of years removed from ours. Our physical contact is a threat to the existence of the nation. This is the sin of sins, the crime of crimes that must be atoned for. This is the first wrong that must be righted. We owe a debt of gratitude to the majority of the black race. I am beginning to believe that we must give them a nation of their own."

The man shook his head.

"You are following the will o' the wisp which haunted the imagination of John Temple Graves."

"Exactly. The same that haunted the mind of Abraham Lincoln. Except that it has been revealed to me as a student of history that such a separation is not a will o' the wisp. It may be the only solution of the problem. We have the ships—we have the millions. It only remains to develop the plan of a peaceful friendly separation. It may take a hundred years. It may take two hundred. It can be done."

"There is one thing that may make it possible—the continuance of the program of rousing race hatred now being conducted by the radical Mulattoes in the North. But they will come to their senses, and your dream will remain a dream."

"I am growing more and more," she affirmed, "to see it an ultimate reality. If I work for it I shall fight all hate, all loathing, all bitterness and see the cruelest savage black man only as a child of God who has been dragged out of the bounds of his habitation."

"If the Negro is out of his bounds in America, what about our own race who came here and claimed this as a white man's country. It was won from the Indians."

"And we have assimilated the Indians," Angela quickly replied. "I once thought that we had exterminated them. We have not. There are more Indians in the U.S. today than at any time in history. The Indian has no trace of Negro blood in him. The attempt to associate him with the Negro is infamous. This was a white man's country when we came here. The Indians, true to their treaty of peace with William Penn,[3] fought with us for the mastery of this continent. Because they were true to their pledge, Montcalm,[4] the Frenchman fell on the Heights of Quebec, and Wolfe,[5] the Englishman, triumphed. So we speak tonight the language of Shakespeare, Byron, and Burns and not the tongue of Moliere and Voltaire."

Phil looked at her in surprise.

"You have been studying. I congratulate you. I'm learning things I didn't know. You may have a mission! With your eloquence, your beauty, your deep experience, your profound religious convictions—I wonder where you got this new religion?"

"It's not new, Phil, it's older than time. It's Truth. Surely not taught in our good old fashioned orthodox Church in Piedmont, though I'm grateful for all its inspiration. Ann Lovelace, out of her Quaker heritage and her study of Rosicrucian ideals, led me to realize the presence of God in the world, in my life."

"And this order is attempting to found a new religion which you are expressing?"

"No. They disclaim any purpose to found a religion. The Brotherhood represents all sects and creeds and many who profess none. They are

3. William Penn (1644–1718) was born in London and in 1681 received a tract of land north of Maryland by King Charles II as payment for a debt owed his father. Penn's proprietorship, Pennsylvania, became a "bold experiment" based on total religious freedom, the prohibition of capital punishment except for murder and treason, and the white colonists' rapprochement with Native Americans. See Richard S. Dunn and Mary Maples Dunn, eds., *The World of William Penn* (Philadelphia: University of Pennsylvania Press, 1986).

4. Louis Joseph, Marquis de Montcalm de Saint-Veran (1712–1759) was a French soldier and military commander in the North American campaigns against the British forces. He was killed while fighting James Wolfe's forces in the battle for Quebec in September 1759. See H.R. Casgrain, *Wolfe and Montcalm* (1884; reprint, Toronto: University of Toronto Press, 1964).

5. James Wolfe (1727–1759) successfully commanded fewer than 9,000 troops against approximately 16,000 French soldiers at Quebec, defeating French commander Marquis de Montcalm de Saint-Veran in 1759. See David Robin Reilly, *The Rest to Fortune: The Life of Major-General James Wolfe* (London: Cassell, 1960).

an International Lodge. They do not prepare men and women for a future heaven. They seek health, happiness and achievement in this world, here and now, not the next. The grips, passwords, tokens and symbols, of course, are secret. But as an institution it is known over the entire world and its general activities are not secret. A Rosicrucian is known for his broad views of life, his study of Nature's laws, his happy and successful way of living. I am eternally grateful to the friend who saved me from suicide and sent me here."

He rose and looked at his watch.

"It's bedtime, and I'll leave this world of realities here in this sweet secret conference with you, and hug dreams in my little cottage but a few yards away. Goodnight, darling."

"Goodnight, Phil. I'll always love you in the sweetest possible way."

"And I'll always love you in the most intimate personal way."

She smiled, and closed her door. He listened to hear if she threw the bolt in place. There was no sound and he turned away grateful for her faith.

On leaving the retreat they drove through forests of giant trees, climbed dizzy heights to Lake Tahoe and gazed in wonder on the sublime beauty of white capped mountains mirrored in its cold surface. They raced an express train from Los Angeles to San Juan Capistrano along the Ocean Boulevard and beat the train by thirty minutes.

At the end of the month they returned to San José.

"How long will you still be here?" he asked before she started for her quarters.

"A year and four months," was the prompt reply. "I've laid out two years research in Anthropology and the History of Democracy. The library here is wonderful. And we command the use of every library in the State free of charge."

"And then?"

"I shall go to New York and devote my life to the study of the Race Problem. In Harlem there is the largest city of Negroes in the world. They live under the most favorable conditions. With full legal, civic and social rights. My conclusions so far may be wrong. I'll test them by the living facts of this Negro City. At the same time I'll enter Columbia University and continue my study of races and of nations. I'll begin there my search with tireless enthusiasm. I shall make it my life work."

"You've friends in New York?"

"Not an acquaintance even."

"Then my course is clear! I'll join that law firm and be making a living by the time you get there."

"I'm glad."

"Really glad?"

"Without a reservation. I'll use your brilliant mind and energy in my work."

"You'll call on me without hesitation?"

"I'll probably try to make of you an errand boy."

"I'd like nothing better. My office in Piedmont will still be open and at your service also."

"Thank you, dear."

"One favor I've just got to ask of you as I go——"

"Certainly," she smiled, "you may kiss me!"

He blushed to the roots of his hair at her quick reading of his mind, bent and kissed her lips with longing tenderness. They gave no response, but her smile made the world radiant.

Chapter 20

Captain Collier rang Phil Stephens' telephone and was surprised to learn of his absence. The girl asked if he would leave any message.

"Yes. Tell the young scamp I want to see him when he gets back. You don't know when?"

"Maybe two or three weeks."

The telephone came down on the desk with a bang and he turned to his efficient agent from Atlanta whom he had recalled to duty.

"There's no mistake about it—you got these copies of that damned radical magazine from two Negro School teachers?"

"They loaned them to me to read. I asked if they could use the mails. They said they were being sent through the express company and delivered by hand."

"The damned rascal! And he succeeded one of the best Negroes who ever pastored a church in this County. I had our bank loan him money on his unendorsed note more than once. He was a man of character who kept his people in order and his community at peace with ours. And now this dirty rag is imported by his successor!"

He paused and handed the undercover man his check. "You know your business. The County owes you its thanks, besides the fee you've earned. Take the first train for Atlanta. I'll call you when I need you again."

The Negro left the office and the Captain sent a messenger with a verbal call to Lum Anderson, who, an hour later, appeared.

"Lum," the lawyer began. "There's some more work for your vigilante committee. They're ready?"

"Always since that night at Dave's house."

"The new Nigger preacher has become a trouble maker. Two of my teachers have seen fit to violate my orders and subscribe to the poisonous package found in Dan Hose's pocket the night he went on the rampage. If this preacher and these two teachers could be taken to the woods, tied up, and given leisurely about forty nine lashes each on their bare backs, this County could breathe easier."

"I see."

"You think that such a thing could be done quietly by reliable men?"

"In twenty four hours."

"Of course, you understand I know nothing about it. My position on the School Board will not permit that. But I'm damned if I don't see that my orders are obeyed."

"You can depend on us, sir."

The chairman of the Vigilante Committee left hurriedly.

At nine o'clock a big seven passenger car roared out on a lonely road. The preacher slipped the cords that bound his wrists, and leaped from the car. Two pistol shots in the dark failed to stop him, but the two readers received forty nine lashes each with a warning to move Northward.

They promptly moved. And the Negro church began to look for a new preacher.

When Phil Stephens reached town a week later, the community was still tense over the incident. He received from his office girl an account of the whippings.

"I'm getting out in time to save trouble for myself again. I can see that," he muttered. "I, too, am going to fight these damned fanatics. But it can't be done from this end."

Captain Collier received him with more than his usual cordial greeting.

"Where have you been all this time, you young rapscallion?"

"To tell you the truth, Captain Tom, I've been to see a girl."

The old man threw him a searching look.

"I thought that there was but one girl for you, and she's dead."

"There is but one. But I've seen her alive and more beautiful than ever. The only woman I've ever known to rebuild her life after such a tragedy."

"Tell me, son, how is she?"

"I found her, and asked her to marry me and she refused."

"Of course, she would," he muttered. "That's what I meant when I said she was dead. Tell me all about it, boy. You'll never know how deep was the wound in my own heart over the crash of her life."

And then he told his old friend in rapid review of his visit, of their four weeks' tour, and her new vision of a career.

The Captain rose to his feet, took a turn to the window and sat down again.

"By God, Phil," he cried, "with her youth and poise and beauty and brains she may stir the nation. She *has* seen a vision. I know it. For I've seen it too, in the still hours of the night more than once. I'm too old to heed the call. She's in the glory of youth, with an experience that may give her the wisdom of centuries. That's great news, boy, the greatest I've heard in many a day. And I've needed some good news to cheer me lately. I'm getting old. I'm beginning to complain of fate and the trend of events. Youth is not a question of the calendar. It's a question of the mind and its attitude toward life. A question of the joy of things, the thrill of adventure."

"You must have had a few thrills here last week from reports I hear."

"A few, yes. Nobody seriously hurt. I tried to get in touch with you for a conference with our "Liberal, forward looking minds," what ever to hell that may mean. Tell me just what it does mean? What have you got on your mind? I confess I'm up a tree. What is it your crowd propose?"

"For one thing," Stephens answered firmly. "America owes to the Negro the stamping out of lynching."

"But above all things," Collier interrupted, "the stamping out of Negro crimes which excite the spirit of the mob."

"Certainly the two must go together. But we must give to the Negro the protection of his person and his property from violence. This is a minimum obligation. So long as the white South tolerates violence, no man white or black, can be assured of the integrity of the law under which we live. The right of all men to live under the law and be deprived of life only under law is fundamental."

"What else?"

"We owe the Negro better health."

"His health is better in the South than in the North."

"Even so the failure of the Northern people to help the Negro does not excuse us. We know him better. We like him better. They don't like him at all. We owe him better health for our own protection as well as his. A million and more domestic servants enter our homes daily. Many of them are bringing the germs of disease." He paused. "And we should give him the right to make a living."

"We are certainly far ahead of the North in this."

"As we ought to be. We are used to him as a workman. Yet we allow him to be crowded out of the professions that have always been his."

"How in the hell can you keep down the rising tide of white efficiency and expansion in industry? Would you strangle your own race?"

"No. But I'd give to the black man an equal chance. The growth of Unionism, North and South, threatens the bread of the Negro. If he is not allowed to earn a living what is to become of him? The Northern white workmen don't give a damn. But you and I, Captain Tom, still believe in the obligation of the strong to help the weak. We are the stronger race. We should help the Negro. We've known him and played with him from infancy. Down in our souls, in spite of all his faults, we love him. Why can't we still express that feeling in our economic and political life?"

"Because he has new teachers who are training him to hate us. The old Scalawag and Carpetbagger were amateurs. These new teachers, who are pouring into the South a flood of vicious writing, are poisoning the sources of Negro thinking."

"I agree that a way must be found to correct this." He paused and laughed. "I doubt, however, if the use of the lash on colored teachers in the schools of the South will solve the question."

"It will go a damn long way to solve it in this County, sir!"

"You know better than that, Captain Tom. You incite or tolerate such things because you're in a panic and don't know what to do. You used to say that the fear of Negro domination excused all violence. You know too much to try to fool yourself with such an argument today. Negro political domination was a tragic reality in the days of Reconstruction. Now it's a myth. We control the elections. We hold all but a fraction of the wealth. We are in charge of every Court. We are in charge of every legislature. To talk about Negro domination is for the superior race to confess an inferiority complex."

Collier lifted his hand in sharp protest.

"I'm not afraid of Negro domination, through elections, or courts or legislatures. The nightmare that haunts my imagination and of every thoughtful Southern white man today is the slow but sure breaking down of the barriers that separate the races. Social equality is the ideal of every Negro who thinks today. Under our laws he feels it's his right. The assertion of Southern Negro leaders that they have no such aspirations is talk for home consumption. The Negroid Junta is fast becoming a powerful social organization, establishing branches in every State of the Union."

"I agree with that. But we can never reach them by attacking their victims down here. We must get the thing at its source. I've made up my mind to move my office to New York."

"Not because of any difference of opinion with your own people, son?" the old man frowned.

"No, Captain Tom. To tell you the simple truth, Angela is going to settle there. To win her is the big motive. I'll do better in law there than here."

"Of course, you will, boy. I could have made my mark in the big town if I'd gone there in time. But I hesitated and was lost. I envy you your youth and daring. Go to it and win your place in the world. You'll do it, too."

"I may be able to reach the men who are distributing the propaganda of hate against the South and serve both races."

"Unless it's done we're in for trouble. The man you spirited out of town once may introduce you to their headquarters."

"I think he will," the younger man smiled.

"You can't join their damned organization, but you can organize a branch of your Inter-Racial Commission."

"I've thought of that," Phil mused. "If we could really apply the religion of Jesus Christ to this problem we might make progress."

"Remembering always, my son, that there is nothing in the obligations of Christ's brotherhood that should make a Southern patriot agree to let his country sink into mongrelism!"

The older man slipped an arm about his friend.

"My heart goes with you into the big town. Good luck. I expect to be proud of you. You read law under me, you know."

"I'll not forget it, sir."

Chapter 21

The first year in New York proved a trying one to Phil Stephens. He slipped into his new law offices without announcement and made no effort to get in touch with the Negro leaders. He must first adjust himself to his new home. The word home had a queer sound in New York. In its rush and roar he wondered how a sane human life could be evolved. Its immensity overwhelmed his mind the first weeks. He wondered whether he was going, to use its power or be crushed by it.

It was queer how lonely a human being could be in the waves of an ocean of humanity. The denser the crowds through which he pushed the deeper became his longing for companionship. He wrote a pathetic letter to Angela, told her how wretched he had been and begged her to write him.

He received a long cheerful reply laughing at his boyish homesickness. She promised to answer his letters and the sun began to shine again. He noticed there were a few birds hopping about on the grass in the parks, a few flowers blooming in an apologetic way.

The thing that depressed him most was the startling discovery that the average New Yorker was a small town potato. A man of narrow vision, of limited ideas, of colossal conceit. To him New York was the center of the Universe. The Stock Exchange with its howling derivishes the center of New York. The rest of the earth was merely provincial tributary soil. At heart he was a hick of hicks. The least excitement drew a crowd and held them more easily than in Piedmont.

The streets with their waves of humanity stunned his imagination. As far as the eye could reach these throngs engulfed the pavements and overflowed between the curbs mingling with the mass of cars, cabs and trucks. His offices were in the Wall Street district. On every side towered miles of business houses whose arteries reached to the limits of the earth. Behind their windows sat the engineers of industry with their hands on the throttles of the world's machinery, their keen eyes and ears alert to every sound of danger in the ceaseless roar that engulfed them.

He felt the savage challenge of this impersonal immensity. Here he would be put to the supreme test of character. Here the powers of Nature, spiritual and material, had gathered for their final assault on the soul of man. And he must answer for his life. The swiftness of progress, crushing and encircling, the greed for gold, the blind worship of success—a success that might sneer at duty, honor, love and patriotism and still be called success—the filth and frivolity of the so-called upper strata, the growth of hate and envy below, the restlessness of the masses, the waning of their faith, the creeping growth of despair, the triumph of brute force, the reign of the liar and the huckster as the heroes of society, all bewildered him.

He began to realize that he had entered the tropics of modern civilization. He must expect beast and reptile to be of greater size, and life capable of bigger things.

Certainly he had reached the center of commerce, art, literature and politics of the Western World. The feet of six million inhabitants pressed its pavements daily and three million more crowded in from suburban districts. Its walls framed the furnace in which are being tried by fire the faiths, hopes, and dreams of centuries past and to come. There could be no doubt about it. Here beats the heart of the modern world. To win that heart would be to hold the key to the century.

Yet he was amazed at the misery, squalor and poverty of the slums. He found in his trips of exploration districts in which ten men and women were sleeping in one room twelve feet square. London has seven people to a house. New York sixteen. In two houses which he inspected there were one hundred and thirty six children. It was no wonder that Death stalked daily through its crowded alleys.

Yet more men and women were coming in thousands, turning their back upon the open fields to crowd into this foul, rotting, crawling, smoking, stinking, ghastly heap of fermenting brick, stone, steel and cement, oozing pain from every pore. Crowding the crowded trades, crowding closer the crowded dens in which human beings whelped and stabled as beasts. They leave friends and neighbors who love them, leave earth for hell, and still they come. The tenement, a monster of modern greed, engulfs them and the word home is stricken from their tongue. Last year one in four of the total population was buried from a hospital, jail, almshouse, asylum or workhouse. They no longer preach hell to these people, who expect to better their condition in the next world whether they go up or down.

He stopped and looked on a row of palaces on Fifth Avenue, shook his head and muttered:

"When your bread lines lengthen a little more, your stock market collapses and the gulf between the rich and the poor becomes impassable, I see a vision. Idle thousands, sullen and desperate looking with darkened brows on your mansions. I can hear the tread of coming mobs from the shadows further down who will laugh at your flag, who know not the name of your President, your Mayor, or your God; whose rough hands upon your doors will call you before the tribunal of the knife, the torch, the bomb."

If ten million Negroes are forced into the struggle for existence with this dark mass of our underworld, what will be the outcome? His study of the North had intensified the looming tragedy of the Negro. The South, one hundred percent pure Anglo-Saxon stock, might save the nation, but for this unsolved and apparently insoluble question.

The longer he brooded over this aspect of the conflict of color the more ominous it became. The more urgent became, to his mind, the need of giving to the black man full justice as a citizen of our republic. He took fresh hold on his ideals and thanked God he had come to the center of the nation's life.

He warned Angela of the shock which she might receive in all this. But his warning made her all the more eager to breast the tides of the great city.

He had been in New York, a patient student of its problems for a year before he got his head above water. He had not appeared in court in a single case when, out of the clear sky, his opportunity came.

A Southerner, who knew him in South Carolina, came to New York to defend a Negro accused of murder, the son of a slave of their family. Guilty or innocent the loyalty to the old regime brought his champion a thousand miles to fight for his life.

The case had created a sensation in the newspapers. The Negro was accused of killing the agent of a landlord while collecting rents.

Stephens was engaged to defend him. Convinced of his dusky client's innocence he fought the case with fierce energy in every step of its development. He demanded and got a postponement until he could make a thorough study of the evidence. When the case came to trial he tore every piece of this evidence to shreds and made a speech of such strong yet tender appeal for justice to the Negro that half the men on the jury were in tears. They returned a verdict of not guilty in thirty minutes and his reputation was made. The New York papers carried his picture and a two column report of his speech. He had become a figure in the life of the city over night. Of all the messages of congratulations, he prized most a brief telegram from down home:

"Good boy. I knew you would do it. Piedmont is proud of you.
Collier."

From the half million Southern white people in New York the response was instantaneous. He was invited everywhere. And he was rushed with legal business.

From two Negroes he received important letters. Rex Weldon, now a member of the legislature from a Harlem district, wrote one of them, and Craig Willis, the other.

Weldon called to renew his acquaintance and ask him to address a mass meeting in Harlem to demand equal school facilities for blacks and whites.

"You haven't as good schools as the whites?" Stephens asked in surprise.

"Theoretically we have. Actually our schools are poor. I know you stood for fair play in South Carolina. I shouted for joy when I read your great speech. Will you come?"

"Of course, I'll do the best I can for your people."

A Committee expressed, through its Chairman, their appreciation of the brave words which he had spoken, not only for the Negro in the criminal dock, but for the millions of their race whose cause he had defended.

Phil studied DuBois with interest. He had seen his famous rival Booker T. Washington, but he had never before met his radical antagonist. The contrast between the two men was striking. Washington, in spite of the tinge of yellow in his darker skin, was unmistakably African in every line of his face and body. And not of the handsomer type. His hair, inclined to kink in spite of modern lotions, was coarse and plainly Negroid. His large ears were inclined to flop. His nose was large and flattened. His jaw was heavy. Every feature stamped him a Negro of Negroes. Only from his grave forceful eyes flashed the light of leadership. He was heavily built and sprawled Negro fashion when seated.

DuBois, on the other hand, was unlike his rival. There was no trace of the Negro in him except the light tinge of brown in his skin, and that was not marked. A pointed beard, dark melancholy eyes, a quiet man of culture, French looking rather than American, he gave no impression of an African. He could see a striking resemblance to the features of Gabriele d'Annuncio, turned college professor. It was easy to believe that he had taken degrees at Harvard University and in Germany as well. It was difficult to believe that such a man, with a bare trace of Negro in his makeup, should be so fiercely, passionately, and insistently African as to lead a crusade of violence against the white race. Surely it would not be a hopeless task to reason with such a man and through him correct some of the mistakes his associates were making.

"We have come, Mr. Stephens," the Chairman said with grave earnestness, "to ask you to accept a position as counsel on our legal staff."

He paused and waited for an answer.

"I can't do that exactly," the lawyer smiled, "but I'll join you in organizing a branch of the Inter-Racial Commission and co-operate with you in every way possible."

"That will, of course, be the next best thing though I had hoped for more."

Before the night of the mass meeting in Harlem Phil sought the Superintendent of Public Schools, made an individual appeal for backing and won his consent to preside over the meeting.

The rest was easy. The meeting was a success. The press gave a liberal report of his speech and the appropriation was made for a new High School Building. Weldon was elated over both his diplomacy and eloquence and expressed to all his pride in the young lawyer from down home.

When Angela arrived he was an established success. He had kept her posted on his work and she greeted him with enthusiasm.

"I'm proud of you," she smiled. "Above all I'm glad you're here to help me get settled."

"And watch over you a little if I may," he added.

"You may," she conceded.

He went room hunting with her. She didn't like the idea of a rooming house, nor did he.

"You don't want to live like that. We can find an apartment with a good living room, bedroom, bath and kitchen within your means.

"That will be wonderful!" she exclaimed. "I've studied the map of New York and found that Columbia University is on the edge of Harlem. I'd like a place where I could be in touch with both. I'll study on University Heights while I'm carrying on my work below."

They found a place on 121st Street near Amsterdam Avenue.

He took the time to help her buy the furnishings at auction. She was able to do the two rooms in old mahogany. The total cost was less than three hundred dollars. When the last piece of furniture was in place and the rugs laid, Phil sat down by the open fireplace and smoked.

"You can't understand," he said tenderly, "what it means to me to have you here. You've made New York radiant. I may come to see you when I'm lonely?"

"On one condition——"

"Yes, I know. I'm not to make love to you. All right, dearest. I understand."

CHAPTER 22

A few days later Phil received a telephone call from Angela inviting him to dinner at her apartment. She would cook for him an old fashioned Southern meal.

He left his office an hour earlier than usual. Something had happened. He arrived fifteen minutes ahead of time but he rang her bell and cleared the stairs two steps at a time.

"Now don't think silly thoughts, Phil," she laughed. "You should know me better than to think I sent for you to make love to me!"

"I haven't said a word, dear," he protested.

"Not a word. But you look such unutterable things I laugh in spite of myself. Sit down and smoke a cigarette. I've something important to tell you. You remember I wrote you from California about a great motion picture which had been founded on "The Clansman." Every night Clune's Auditorium, seating four thousand people, has been packed. The attempt to suppress it failed. The Court upheld the author's right to free speech and the picture is playing to unheard of business and has raised a storm of excitement. A friend writes me that it will shake the nation. I saw the stage play in Piedmont and it stirred me with greater power, of course, because my Father was the hero of the story. They say the play was a zephyr compared to the picture. If this is true it's God's answer to my prayers—a flaming propaganda for racial purity that will sweep America. My friend in Los Angeles secured for me an invitation to the preview they call it, in New York next week."

"I'd like to go with you," he broke in. "If my crowd are going to fight it I'd like to be in a position to give them intelligent advice."

"I'll get two tickets and we'll see it together. The country is drifting into a deadly apathy on the race problem."

The huge barn of a building, an old skating rink on Broadway, selected for the showing was appallingly large, cold and cheerless. Among the two thousand seats were scattered about seventy five invited guests dimly visible through the darkness. Far down at the eastern end an orchestra was rehearsing the music. Over the incomplete score, the composer was tearing his hair in a hopeless sort of frenzy.

They crept upstairs into a shadowy corner to watch alone in the silence. The last light dimmed, a weird sound came from the abyss below, the first note of the orchestra, a low cry of the conquered South being put to torture. It set their nerves tingling. Then the faint bugle call of the Southern Bivouac of the dead. In it no challenge to action. No trumpet signal to conflict. It came from the shrouded figures of the shadow world. And then the dramatic story enacted in scenes of beauty and reality. Always with the throb through the darkness of the orchestra raising the emotional power of each scene to the heights.

It was uncanny. When the last scene had faded they wondered vaguely if the emotions that had strangled them were purely personal and they hesitated to go down into the little group in the lobby to hear the comments. They descended cautiously, only to be greeted by an uproar from seventy five people. They had not been alone in their reactions. Every one was wildly excited.

Angela succeeded in getting the producer's hand.

"Congratulations on the greatest motion picture I've ever seen. The noblest defence of the South ever given. You remember our meeting in Los Angeles?"

"I'll never forget the impression you made on me. That's why I got you to this preview. Come to see me tomorrow in my office in the Astor Hotel at noon. I want to talk to you."

The Director was not a man to haggle over terms. He wanted Angela on the working staff of the organization and he went straight to the point.

"You are just the young woman we need in the savage fight that the Negroes are making on us in New York. The sinister forces that attempted to close the picture in Los Angeles have their headquarters here. We are up against a serious menace. They have determined to establish a Negro Censorship of the Drama in America. And the suppression of "The Birth of a Nation" is their first planned act of aggression. The threat is real. It is dangerous not only to us, but to the future of free speech in the United States. The Negro forces are led by Oswald Garrison Villard, Editor of the Evening Post, and Morefield Storey of Boston, President of the American Bar Association. They are backed by two powerful millionaires and have unlimited money for their campaign. Will you join our staff as a press representative and a special operator reporting to our President or to me?

Women are our best modern press agents. We can make your salary one hundred dollars a week to begin. How about it?"

"You take my breath away with the honor you do me and the salary offered. You think I can do the work?"

"I know you can. You are not only the daughter of Ben Cameron, our hero, your type has never been seen in a motion picture organization."

Angela walked on air back to her apartment on University Heights. The work appealed to her heart and brain. Her mission was shaping into reality.

She called Phil on reaching her rooms. "Can you come up to dinner again tonight?"

"Can a duck swim?"

"I hope you haven't been consulted as yet about the picture by your new clients?"

"Not yet. But they have asked me for a conference tomorrow.

"You're still free to give me some advice?"

"I'm always free to give you anything on earth you ask."

He brought a box of long stemmed yellow roses. Angela buried her face in them and looked at him reproachfully.

"Surely I may say it with flowers? What's the excitement about?"

She told him of the offer and he sank to the divan and spoke slowly:

"I'm glad you reached me in time. I was so excited over the picture I consulted a friend in the business and got some interesting information today. The Motion Picture Producers at this time are an unorganized little mob of Kilkenny cats. You can't depend on them for any help in the deadly attack these people will make. With them it's dog eat dog and devil take the hindmost. The little Company which produced this film is an independent, has no release for its product, and no affiliation with the big four which dominate the trade. You must seek outside help and it must be a real power."

He paused and rose.

"I've got it," he announced emphatically. "There's just one man in the country whose word could spike the guns of your enemies. Woodrow Wilson, President of the United States——"

Angela laughed. "You didn't have to strain yourself to reach that conclusion. But how are you going to get the President on the job for us?"

"There's a way."

"You don't think I could barge into the White House on such a mission?"

"You may and succeed, too. Wilson is the first Southern man President since Abraham Lincoln. Get his backing and you'll have a powerful weapon with which to fight this sectional conspiracy——"

"Yes, yes, of course, but how are you going to get his backing?"

"I happen to know that Wilson is a personal friend of the Author of this story. He went to Davidson College in North Carolina. His father was pastor of a Presbyterian Church in Wilmington. The Author was his college mate at Johns Hopkins University in the department of history and politics. He went out of his way to have conferred on his friend the degree of LLD when he was but twenty nine years old. I read Wilson's grateful letter of thanks."

"That's an inspiration."

The Director and President of the Company were in conference over the situation when she hurried through the door and laid before them her sensational plans.

They looked up incredulously. "But Holy Smoke, child, that's a pipe dream. It's too big to believe."

"It's not too big to try. The Author's in the next room. Call him in and ask if he'll write to the President."

Without hesitation he agreed.

"The thing to do," Angela said, "is to get the President to see the picture and autograph the programs."

"Go to it and God be with you!" the Director laughed. "We know you can't do it, but we'll hold a prayer meeting! It's too good to happen but we'll sing and pray continuously."

A brief letter was written to the President asking for a few minutes interview. He replied immediately and made the appointment.

"Don't breathe this to a living soul," Angela was warned.

"You're right. I'll keep my lips tight. They say his genial secretary, Mr. Tumulty, has a way of finding out things."

"Freeze him if he tries to pump you."

He tried. But she only smiled. To the Secretary's urgent final diplomatic hints the only answer was still a smile. The appointment was fixed. And no politician could barge in on it. Mr. Wilson received her at his desk with cordial dignity.

"I'm happy to see you," he smiled genially.

Politicians have called Woodrow Wilson cold. To those who really knew him he was always good natured and friendly, though timid socially. From this trait of character grew the legend of his coldness. Nothing could be farther from the facts.

He talked for a few minutes of College days, and then broached the purpose of the call.

She had a favor to ask of him, not so much as the Chief Magistrate of the Republic but as a scholar and student of History and Sociology.

As rapidly as possible he was told that a great motion picture had been made which he should see.

He lifted his head in a moment's thought.

"I cannot go to a theatre, just now. As you know, Mrs. Wilson's death puts the White House in mourning." He was silent for a minute. "But you might set up your machines in the East Room. I'll invite my Cabinet and their families and we will see it here—" he paused and looked at his visitor thoughtfully before going on. "I want you to know, that I'm pleased to be able to do this thing, because a long time ago my friend took a day out of a busy life to do something important for me. It came at a crisis in my career and greatly helped me. I've always cherished the memory of it——"

"But the politicians say you have no sense of gratitude, Mr. President."

"Yes," he nodded. "And they say a great many other things besides their prayers."

"I needn't tell you how deeply we appreciate your generous act," Angela hastened to add.

"You don't need to," he answered briskly. "Just see my daughter, Margaret, before you leave town. She will arrange the date and details. My only suggestion is that you do not allow any use of the event by the press under the circumstances."

He was assured that no announcement would be made and no press reports sent out afterwards.

Angela sent a wire immediately to the New York office that the President had invited them to show the picture in the East Room of the White House and that Miss Margaret Wilson would fix the date and arrange the details that afternoon. An answer came incoherent with joy.

A second message from Angela warned that they must keep the coming event a secret. She had discovered that the enemies in New York, who were busy preparing a coup, not only had unlimited money with which to fight, they had tremendous influence in Washington.

On the night of the showing no more cordial and genial host could be imagined. The President made everybody feel that the White House was theirs for the night and that the Chief Magistrate was honored in their coming.

The President's welcome was more than equalled in that given by the new mistress of the White House, his charming daughter, Margaret. Without apparent effort she made every one feel at home to the last operator and property man of the staff.

The effect of the picture was precisely what had been foreseen. It repeated the triumph of the first showing. The spectators were in a spell, their emotions stirred to the depths, although there had been no interpretive music.

As soon as the applause died away Miss Wilson served refreshments, and the Director received their congratulations. No opinion was asked of the President and under no circumstances would it have been quoted after the understanding about publicity. The one thing wanted of him was gladly given. He was asked to autograph a copy of the engraved programs for the Director, Manager, and the Author. He did it with a gracious pleasure which made each one doubly appreciate the honor.

His signature on the document was a weapon of power in the fight that would be made on the picture by the Negroid leaders who were in conference in New York.

How quickly and how desperately it was going to be needed could not be guessed at the moment.

Emboldened by the triumph at the White House, Angela suggested that while in Washington they make a thorough job of preliminary showings. The Supreme Court of the United States should see it. If they could be induced to accept the invitation the Senate and the House of Representatives could come as the guests of the Supreme Court.

The audacity of the idea appealed to the staff and Angela was given the most difficult task of the undertaking.

To carry out the ambitious scheme it would be necessary to get the consent of the Chief Justice of the Supreme Court, Edward Douglas White,[1] to allow his name to go on the program as the guest of honor presiding over the function. Angela was asked to get an interview with him and secure his consent.

She set about the task with a jaunty air that did not carry her quite through the day. She knew that White was a Southerner, and felt that the task should be easy after the reception at the White House, but the shadow of a doubt kept darkening her mind.

She went to the office of the Secretary of the Navy to ask help in meeting Mr. White. Josephus Daniels[2] and the Author had been friends since early school days. But when told what was wanted of the Chief Justice he laughed aloud.

"Forget it!" he urged. "He'll never consent."

1. Edward Douglass White (1845–1921) of Louisiana served in the Confederate Army, practiced law, served on the Louisiana Supreme Court, was elected to the U.S. Senate, and in 1894 was appointed to the U.S. Supreme Court by President Grover Cleveland. In 1910 President William Howard Taft appointed White chief justice, a position he held until his death. White was the first southerner to hold this post since Roger B. Taney. See Robert B. Highsaw, *Edward Douglass White: Defender of the Conservative Faith* (Baton Rouge: Louisiana State University Press, 1981).

2. Josephus Daniels (1862–1948) was a North Carolinian who in 1894 purchased the *Raleigh News and Observer*. Under his editorship the paper became a voice of Progressive reform, supporting unions and opposing liquor and child labor. President Woodrow Wilson appointed Daniels secretary of the navy in 1913. See Joseph L. Morrison, *Josephus Daniels: The Small-d Democrat* (Chapel Hill: University of North Carolina Press, 1966).

"Why?" Angela faltered.

"Do you know anything of Justice White's personality?" he inquired.

"Nothing."

"Well, he's a wonderful old fellow, but he's a bear. He never goes out of his library. He may see you a few minutes if I ask it but if you don't get out pretty quick he may push you out and slam the door. Do you want to risk it?"

"Certainly."

"All right," he laughed.

In a few words over the phone he got the appointment for the call to be made in thirty minutes.

"If you're late," Daniels warned, "you won't get in."

She thanked him, rushed for a cab and in twenty minutes Mrs. White met her at the door, announced that the Justice was in his library and directed her how to find the room upstairs.

The library was silent and empty as far as could be seen on entering. As the visitor made her way cautiously to the far end she became aware of something moving behind a pile of books and saw a grizzled head set on immense shoulders buried in a volume of sheepskin. The head paid no attention to the intruder who waited for him to lift his eyes. He did at length and they flashed a quick half angry inquiry through heavy bristling brows.

"Well, well, young woman," he growled, "what can I do for you? Mr. Daniels telephoned me that you were coming."

There would be no time for social amenities. She had to talk business and talk it without ceremony or delay. So in rapid sentences he was told that President Wilson and his cabinet had witnessed in the White House the night before a remarkable picture which they wished the Supreme Court to see tonight at a private showing at the Hotel Raleigh.

She was interrupted by an inarticulate explosion of surprise.

"Picture," White cried. "The Supreme Court of the United States see a picture! Of all the suggestions I have ever heard in my life! What sort of a picture?"

She hesitated to say, knowing the answer before venturing to breathe the words ever so softly:

"A great Moving Picture."

"Moving Picture!" he growled angrily. "It's absurd, I never saw one in my life and I haven't the slightest curiosity to see one. I'm very busy. I'll have to ask you to excuse me."

And without so much as a nod of dismissal he buried himself in his law books and forgot the intruder's existence.

She looked at the grizzled head a minute puzzling her brain for the

right word to say to rouse the old bear. There must be a soul somewhere beneath those piles of law books in which he was buried.

She cleared her throat and smiled. The Chief Justice looked up and stared.

"It's useless to say another word. I'm not only busy on a most important case before the Supreme Court but I have invited a distinguished guest from New York to dine with us tonight. I could not see your picture if I wished. Good day!"

She hastened to speak before his mind returned to his studies. Her groping hand had caught a possible key to his interest.

"But, Mr. Chief Justice," she mildly protested. "This is a picture of two thousand scenes which tell a story that will profoundly interest you, because you're a Southerner who lived through the period of Reconstruction——"

"Reconstruction," he muttered. "What has Reconstruction to do with a motion picture?"

The tones in which he had spoken the word "Reconstruction" showed that the quick of his spirit had been touched.

"Everything to do with it," was the hurried answer. "In scenes of vivid life we have told for the first time the Southern white man's story of the crucifixion of the defeated South by the politicians of 1867, the story of the sudden rise of the Ku Klux Klan——"

"You tell the story of the Klan?" he interrupted softly.

"Yes, for the first time."

For some mysterious reason his soul had been found. The visitor waited for him to speak but was not prepared for the astonishing thing he said. He removed his glasses, pushed his book aside and leaned back in his swivel chair. His strong lips contracted and then relaxed into a smile. He leaned closer and said in low tones:

"I was a member of the Klan——"

The big head nodded slowly and a far away look came into his piercing eyes.

"Through many a dark night, I walked my sentinel's beat through the ugliest streets of New Orleans with a rifle on my shoulder."

He paused and looked up with a friendly penetrating gaze and continued: "You've told the true story of that uprising of outraged manhood?"

"In a way I'm sure you'll approve."

"I'll be there!" he firmly announced. "I'll wire Mr. Paul Cravath and make another appointment for dinner."

He asked for more details of the picture. He was told it was not a thing to be described. It had to be seen and felt. He accompanied his visitor down stairs to the door and shook hands with Angela. The scholar and legal thinker was lost in the man. He was genial and friendly and eager to help.

At eight o'clock that night the ball room of the Raleigh Hotel was packed by one of the most distinguished audiences ever assembled at a private gathering in Washington. The Supreme Court of the United States was there to witness a motion picture with the Senate and the House of Representatives as their guests.

The Chief Justice was seated in the place of honor with his accomplished Southern wife. And as Angela turned away she made up her mind that she would not see him again during the evening, realizing that she had perhaps placed the Justice in an embarrassing position as the presiding officer of the highest Court.

The Negro Junta were gathering strength in New York for a determined attack and it was rumored that Mr. Paul Cravath was one of their consulting attorneys. If the attempt to suppress the picture should be pressed with the deadly animosity indicated it would undoubtedly be carried to the Supreme Court for a final decision.

The publicity expert, who had secured the Press Club as a sponsor, was asked to bear this in mind and say or do nothing which would in any way embarrass the Chief Justice. When the invitation had been given him to preside over the showing no one had dreamed that he had ever been an active member of the Klan.

The Chief justice was assured that there would be no attempt to use his name for publicity.

As the little staff who were so vitally concerned watched the excited crowd of Judges, Senators and Members of Congress file out of the hall and heard their tense comments they knew that they were going to surprise their foes when the fight to a finish should be called.

They could not foresee the legal cunning with which their opponents had planned their first attack.

Chapter 23

When Angela reached home she found the greatest difficulty in getting information. The movements of the Negro conspirators were kept secret. She knew but one person who could find anything of their plan of action. Phil promised to talk to her after his conference with the Inter-Racial Commission.

He was introduced to the white members of DuBois' circle and found them very bitter. They were determined to establish a Negroid censorship of the theatre. Stephens did his best to show them the absurdity and danger of such a course.

"We suppressed the play in Philadelphia," the Chairman interrupted.

"Through a politically minded judge, not on the evidence," the lawyer curtly answered. "The proofs of the novel were submitted to John Hay,[1] a careful historian and scholar. He approved every statement in it, wrote the Author a letter of congratulations and asked to keep the proofs in his library as an historical document. Mr. Hay at this time was Secretary of State. As you know he was Abraham Lincoln's private secretary and the author of the standard biography of the great War President.

"I have seen this picture and it is far more powerful than the book or play on which it is founded. You can not suppress it."

"I think we can," the Chairman smiled.

"The only result of your attack will be to give the company owning it millions of dollars worth of front page news advertising that will add to the power of the picture."

"Still we are going to suppress it," the Chairman continued firmly.

1. John Milton Hay (1838–1905), from Indiana, served as President Abraham Lincoln's personal secretary. Following the Civil War he held diplomatic posts in Paris, Vienna, and Madrid. In 1890 Hay published (with James G. Nicolay) *Abraham Lincoln: A History* (10 volumes). He served as secretary of state from 1898 until his death. See Robert L. Gale, *John Hay* (Boston: Twayne Publishers, 1978).

Stephens bowed and left the office. He found Angela awaiting him.

"You can help me a little?" she asked.

"A very little. Naturally after our radical difference of opinion they shut up like a bunch of clams."

"You got no clue to their action that you can give me?"

"One that you may use possibly. They asked my Commission to appear before the New York Police Courts and I refused."

"They'll move through the police then," Angela mused.

"And they'll use money without stint in their first skirmish. That's all I can tell you, dear."

"Thanks ever so much. There's a Police Commissioner in New York who is a member of my Order. I think I can make him a friend and confidant."

She found him and he received her with generous helpfulness. He gave her the complete organization of the police force. The name of every man in charge of a theatrical district and the magistrates before whom trials might be held. In twenty four hours she had met and talked with the men she wished to interview.

When the staff and officers returned from Washington it was but forty eight hours before the opening date set at the Liberty Theatre. The information which she gave was startling and she told the story with an eloquence that drew them into an excited huddle.

"You see, no notice whatever has been served on managers, owners, or the Author. They have reached and convinced a peanut politician in the City government that the picture is subversive of the Republic. This peanut is at the moment rattling around in the office of a deputy police commissioner. The lawyers, or their agents, have easily persuaded him that he has the power to close the Liberty Theatre on the night of the opening, as a public nuisance and a menace to the peace of the State."

The staff engaged one of the ablest attorneys in New York, Martin W. Littleton.

When he had demanded a hearing and it had been granted, he causually remarked to the Magistrate: "I suppose, Chief, you know that this picture was shown recently in the East Room of the White House to the President and his Cabinet?"

Mr. McAdoo[2] answered in mild surprise: "No, I hadn't heard."

"Well, it's so," Mr. Littleton smiled as he hurried back to his office. He had calculated the effect of this remark with care.

2. William Gibbs McAdoo (1863–1941), a Georgian, was a successful businessman and President Woodrow Wilson's secretary of the treasury. McAdoo implemented the Federal Reserve system and supported the new personal income tax and other banking regulations. See John J. Broesamle, *William Gibbs McAdoo: A Passion for Change, 1863–1917* (Port Washington, NY: Kennikat Press, 1973).

Within five minutes, the City Magistrate called the White House on the long distance telephone, and asked Miss Margaret Wilson if the rumor in New York had any foundation in fact.

Miss Wilson promptly replied that it was not only true that the picture had been shown in the East Room of the White House to the President and his Cabinet, but that it had also been seen by the Supreme Court the night following and that everybody had been carried away with it.

When the little deputy began to prance before his Chief he suddenly found himself on trial instead of the picture. He was asked in plain English how it had come to pass that he had issued an order to suppress a play which he had not seen and close a first class Broadway house before it had opened its doors. He was curtly ordered to give the theatre adequate police protection and clear the streets if disturbances appeared.

The Negroid Junta were so stunned by the unexpected outcome of the hearing that they failed to rally to another effort at suppression before the showing.

From the moment the lights were lowered and the first faint bugle call of the crucified South stole into the hearts of the spectators, a tense emotional strain held the first night New York audience. It was a new experience for tired nerves.

The picture became the sensation of the hour. Authors, artists, musicians, teachers, clergymen and producers crowded in line to see it.

Chapter 24

Angela was despatched to Boston to survey the ground. She had no trouble securing an introduction to James M. Curley, the new Mayor. She carried to him a letter from a brother Irishman, explaining the film and its history. She found a keen listener in the man who represented the millions of new citizens who had revolutionized the politics of New England.

The ground was well prepared against the appearance of the agents of the Junta. When Mr. Morefield Storey rose and made peremptory demands the Mayor was not impressed.

To the consternation of the distinguished officer of the American Bar Association, he decided that there were no legal grounds on which such a study of American History could be suppressed and ordered his police to render adequate protection.

Mr. Storey called a 'monster' indignation meeting to protest against the decision. They protested in vain. The New York triumph was repeated.

They appealed to the Courts of the City and asked an injunction. In answer to the assertion of Mr. Storey that there was no occasion for the production of a picture pleading for racial integrity in America, the attorney for the film exhibited a copy of *The Crisis* containing the the poem by James Johnson entitled "The White Witch" idealizing the Negro's passion for white women.

"The poem is a warning against just that thing!" the attacking lawyer shouted.

"Why warn if there is no danger?" the defense contended. "It happens that this warning is expressed in terms that stir the Negro's lust while pretending to warn. A copy was found in the pocket of a fiend who attacked and murdered a Southern girl. Surely the white race is entitled to a hearing on an issue vital to its existence."

Mr. Storey, secure in his fame as a lawyer, wished to argue the case at length. The judges preferred to see for themselves. They saw. And were convinced.

For a moment the cohorts of the Junta were dismayed. But only for a moment. The more fantical decided on a move which they believed would insure immediate victory and close the run of the picture for all time in New England.

They organized a mob of more than ten thousand to storm the theatre, wreck the projecting machines, burn the film and cause a fatal riot. They were absolutely sure that such a riot would settle its fate without discussion of the issues. Their reasoning was correct. If they could do this, they would win without a doubt. But before it could be executed, the Manager of the picture discovered the scheme. Ten thousand Negroes could not keep such a secret. They believed themselves immune from criticism or serious attack in Boston and talked freely.

On the night set for the attack the tall, genial and efficient General Manager stood in the lobby of the Tremont Theatre and saw a mob of ten thousand misguided colored men gather. He watched with a smile of detached pity for their folly.

When the performance had begun, the advance guard of the rioters gave a shout from the Commons and charged the theatre, sure of victory. But they had not gained the center of Tremont Street when the unexpected happened.

Suddenly from the pavements in front of the theatre, policemen rose, a serried line of five hundred, with drawn night sticks. The rioters hardly reached the curb line of the sidewalk. Night sticks whistled in the spring air and the first ranks of rioters fell in a long wave of terror.

The men behind them turned in panic and ran for their lives. The banked thousands on the Commons saw the flash of night sticks beneath the sputtering arc lights and melted into the shadows.

It was a simple work of mercy to gather up the fragments of the mob and lift them into ambulances and police vans. No effort was made to secure sentences against the misled men. The Judge was asked to dismiss them with a warning. He did. And the warning was sufficient.

Their plan had not worked for two reasons. The picture had a level headed Manager. And they did not.

Chastened by defeats, Storey became more careful in his maneuvers. His voice perceptibly softened.

Under the guidance of his skilled and practiced hand a bill was introduced into the Legislature providing that the police power of theatrical censorship now vested in the Mayor should be divided and extended to a State wide sweep. It was necessary not only to stop the picture in Boston, it must be effectively removed from the State, otherwise the youth of the Commonwealth might be indefinitely corrupted by Southern views of history.

The bill accordingly provided that the police power of regulating dramatic and motion pictures should be divided and vested in the Mayor, the Chief of the State Constabulary and the presiding justice of the Supreme Court.

They had sounded the Chief of the State Constabulary and they knew the presiding justice of the Supreme Court. They were sure they held loaded dice before they were thrown.

They marshalled their forces, manufactured a fictitious demand for their bill and drove it through the Legislature of Massachusetts.

It was a strange spectacle to see a cheap act of tryanny pass the General Assembly of the old Commonwealth whose citizens had led the first charge for Liberty in America.

But the deed was done and Mr. Storey's cohorts held thanksgiving meetings of praise to the God of their fathers for deliverance from the threat of an enlightened public opinion.

The legal machinery of suppression had been established. The issue was at once presented to the new Board of Suppression. In common decency they were asked by the General Manager to see the picture before entering judgment. They saw it. And again the miracle happened. They saw and they believed. The new Board *unanimously* decided that they had no right to suppress such a picture!

Four months of frantic agitation, of scheming and shouting demonstrations and feeble rioting had gone for nothing. They had been crushed at last by their own machine. And they had given the picture a million dollars' worth of front page advertising. The New England rights were immediately sold to an enterprising young man by the name of Louis Mayer[1] and a genius was added to the motion picture industry in America. Mr. Mayer welcomed the fanatical tactics of the Junta. When they closed the house he had taken in Springfield, Massachusetts, he pitched a huge tent across the river and packed it full twice a day clearing three times the money possible in the theatre they had closed. Within a year Mr. Mayer was a millionaire and on his way to Hollywood.

Without notice or hearing an order was issued cancelling the license of the company to show the film in the Illinois Theatre. The rent of the

1. Louis Burt Mayer (1885–1957) immigrated to New York from eastern Europe and bought an old burlesque hall in a northern suburb of Boston in 1907. After successful expansion of his movie theater business, he created his own distribution company and eventually founded Metro Pictures in 1915. Mayer later became a leading motion picture producer in California. See Charles Higham, *Merchant of Dreams: Louis B. Mayer, M.G.M. and the Secret Hollywood* (New York: D.I. Fine, 1993).

building was five thousand dollars a week and great sums had been expended in advertising.

The staff employed the ablest lawyer in Chicago and they demanded a hearing but did not get it.

The rent of the theatre, $20,000, was paid for a month until an able and impartial judge sat in rotation to hear injunctions.

Application was then made to William Fenimore Cooper, of the Superior Court of the State, for an injunction restraining the Mayor of Chicago, the Chief of Police and all other officials of the city government from interfering with the showing of the picture.

The injunction was granted and made permanent. In five months from January to June, the men of the Junta, crossing thousands of miles of country in their activities, had not succeeded in closing a single theatre in a large city, nor in doing the picture the slightest harm. They had cost the producers a hundred and fifteen thousand dollars in expenses and legal fees in Los Angeles, Chicago, Boston and New York. But this loss was far more than balanced in the value of the front page publicity the campaign of hate had given. They had created a nation-wide curiosity to see the mysterious force that had aroused such animosity. The carefully laid plans had proved a boomerang. They had helped accomplish the thing they had hoped to prevent.

When the noise of this strange battle had subsided in the latter part of June, Angela saw this message daily received with the laughter and cheers of eager thousands. And the producers waked to the fact that they were the owners of the most valuable piece of dramatic property ever created in the history of the theatre.

Angela never tired watching the showings in New York and Brooklyn. Studying the effects one night in the Greenpoint theatre she saw a grizzled old Confederate soldier, who had seen the play "The Clansman," witnessing the picture version of the story. He had controlled his emotions at the play. But as he sat gazing in rapture at the flashing scenes of the picture, with the throb of the torturing music in his soul, he suddenly uttered the old "Rebel" yell of the battlefield, tore his wooden leg from its straps, and hurled it against the ceiling.

He had not yelled because he wished again to lead a charge against the North. He yelled because the film had given voice to the unspeakable things his soul had felt through the years of bitterness, prejudice and misunderstanding. Now at last the Yankee could see and hear and feel and know his side of the story. It would bring healing and understanding.

Chapter 25

Each day of her life in the North had deepened Angela's conviction that the mixing of the races in travel by the abolition of the Jim Crow car, the crowding of Negroes into white restaurants, the full exercise of the ballot and the assertion of social equality had done nothing to solve the problem of the conflict of color in America. She had not closed her mind but this was an early vivid impression in her search for truth.

The streets were an exhaustless source of human study. The throngs, with the deepening shadow of Negro life from 111th St. to 116th, gave the impression of life in a Southern town except that the Negroes wore better clothes. Some of them sported gay spats and carried gold headed canes. They walked as on parade. Their white teeth in smiles and their jaunty airs suggested the parade of Negro school children at commencement time in Piedmont.

On the way down to the staff offices, her heart rose with a new found happiness in determination to face realities and work out her destiny standing squarely on her own feet. She had done good work for the company and had earned her salary. But her work was done. She would resign now and take up her intensive studies.

She took a week to walk over Harlem and get the feeling of its outer life. A curious development in a great Northern city. More Negroes in one spot than could be found in any Southern city of the Black Belt. These fine brownstone houses, big stores, spacious theatres, churches and schools, had been built by white people for their own race. There was not a building in it that expressed the mind of a Negro. Their coming had simply transformed a section of the city into a huge cuckoo's nest with blackbirds playing in it. It is not a slum. It is located in the heart of Manhattan Island. On the surface of its street life the gaiety was genuine. The high stepping, cane-carrying Negroes were in a happy mood.

They laughed loudly and with real enjoyment. From 125th Street the population darkens until for twenty blocks scarcely a white face is seen. The shops, the jammed restaurants, the theatres, the throngs that pour out of subways are practically all Negroes. They have pushed the white race completely out.

She passed a magnificent church, from which came a congregation of fifteen hundred Negroes who had witnessed a darktown fashionable wedding. The crowd was flashily dressed. From a theatre poured another throng of dark faces. Here was a Negro city in a white metropolis.

Its streets had a distinct movement, a color and gaiety all their own. A procession passed headed by a brass band the loud notes of which drowned all other sounds. A Negro benevolent society was celebrating one of its feast days. Ten blocks farther was another parade jamming the streets from curb to curb. Traffic had been sent on a detour for the occasion.

From the good humor flashed through her mind the hell lit scene that was enacted in her home in Piedmont. Beneath the veneer of supposed culture she could feel the grip of the savage on her sister's throat. She passed a door where a woman stood whispering the signs and pass words of a voodoo ritual. No white man or woman could pass the threshold. She stopped and watched the worshippers enter with furtive glances up and down the street. There could be no question of the descent to elementary savagery within these walls. She had heard of such centers of superstition but had never seen the door to one of them before.

Her suspicions were confirmed by an intelligent looking Negro High School girl with books under her arm.

"Yessum," she promptly replied, "that's a Voodoo Church inside. You better not try to go in. They might kill you. That woman in the doorway is a sentinel. If a white man or woman goes in they stop the services and pretend to be doing something else. Folks in Harlem whisper that they offer children as sacrifices. But, of course, nobody can prove it. Don't you try to go in there, Miss."

"No. Thank you so much, I'll not."

She passed on in somber mood recalling the savage traits of these people, that the study of Anthropology had shown and her own experience in the South confirmed. The precocity of their children, and its collapse at the early onset of puberty, with their failure to grasp subjective ideas. Their overpowering sex impulses. Their herd instincts. These parading crowds, these thronged churches a living sign of it. Their few inhibitions when tempted. Especially their everlasting use of a low type of music. The only contribution the Negro had made to America was the Jazz orchestra and its call to the lower impulses of man. Was Jazz a worth while contribution to music or its degradation to a savage level? Whether worth while or not, it was certainly a direct growth of the African jungle. As their dancing is an expression of sex impulses straight from the tropical forests. As is their low resistance to the poison of syphilis and alcohol, and their easy surrender to the sway of superstition which they call religion. These things all lurk beneath loud clothes. He may wear a Palm Beach suit instead of beads, carry a gold headed cane instead of a poisoned spear, use the white man's telephone instead of his ancient drum, but is his *mind* any the less that of a savage? The mind is the man. As a man thinketh so he is.

What has been his reaction to the high wages, the hiding in crowds, the lack of restraint, the overwhelming excitement which the city has brought? His birth rate is below the Southern. In the North he barely perpetuates himself. The increase is from the new faces that trek from the Black Belt. Harlem is the most crowded section of any city in the known world. Its health is far below the urban Negro population of the South. Its rate of crime from three to five per cent higher than in the South.

She asked herself the question: What problem of race has been solved by the Negro migration to the North?

True, as their writers claim, Harlem is the greatest concentration of every element of Negro life ever seen in the world—the African, the West Indian, the American Negro, the black man of the North and of the South, the man from the city, the town, the village, the farm, the student, the business man, the professional, the artist, poet, musician, adventurer, worker, preacher, criminal, exploiter, social outcast and radical agitator.

And what intellectual contribution to American life had this racial group made? The most important was the founding and editing of a radical magazine called *The Crisis*.

Now that she recalled it, there was something else in that copy besides its marked pages. There was a letter from a Negro pal in Harlem inviting him to come North, promising him a white girl every night if he wanted her. What did this Negro mean by that?

Where could such contacts be made? There was nothing on the surface to indicate such a thing. True she had met one coal black Negro in loud dress, carrying a gilt-headed cane, who walked beside an apparent white girl. There were Negroes who could pass for whites in New York. She had thought of this girl as one who might "pass." Now that she recalled her features and appearance she had distinctly blonde hair. The thought produced a momentary feeling of nausea. But this could not be the thing in the mind of Dan Hose's pal. There must be dance halls, or houses of prostitution, somewhere in Harlem with white inmates. She would investigate them in time.

In the next block she was startled to meet another Negro parading with a white girl. She felt from the first that the throngs through which she was passing were not the ordinary crowd of a New York street on their way to business, to the theatre, to the shop or to meet engagements. This throng of Negroes were exhibiting themselves, their clothes, their escorts. They were on dress parade. And they took time to make the parade impressive.

The white girl who accompanied this Negro was flashily dressed, powdered and rouged and thoroughly brazen. She was the woman of a black man. He took good care of her and she evidently wished everybody to take notice. It was only too evident that she had emerged from the oldest profession known to woman. Yet she was a full blooded Caucasian.

Her proud escort was a little bowlegged black creature, wearing a business suit of incredibly large checks. He had evidently chosen the check to build up his stature. The effect was at once ludicrous and arresting. No eye could pass that suit of clothes without a second glance. And the cloth was chosen for that reason. The shoes were shining patent leather. His tie a flaming red, its loose broad ends flapping in the wind. On his large oblong head sat an immense bowl of a hat, a gray derby. He carried a rattan cane with which he slapped his trousers sharply to attract passing paraders.

His bow legs, diminished size and race horse suit at once stamped him as a track jockey or tout. No jockey of the big circuits would be caught on a public street parading with a white woman. His employers would not permit such action. He was undoubtedly a derelict who had been barred from the tracks and had become a gambler. The thing that surpassed belief was that a sane white woman would parade herself as his chattel. The only explanation was that he had money and spent it freely. In New York she had more than once felt the power of money. There was something obscene in the rites with which the God of Mammon was worshipped. Something that developed the cruel and the sinister in men. She could hear the inner voice of the big town whispering to its citizens: "Get money! Get it fairly. Get it squarely. But whatever you do—*get* it! Nobody's going to ask *how* you got it. All they want to know is *have* you got it. If you have, you're a god. You can do no wrong."

In such an atmosphere this white girl had seen her chance of easy money, and took it. The little black monkey by her side was a nuisance. But you have to pay for what you get in this world—so what'ell! The thought was plainly written on her rouged face as if the letters were etched by a hot iron.

A half hour later, ten blocks farther on, she met the third couple of black and white. This time tragedy was plainly written on the tired face of the white girl. She was a victim whose life had been sacrificed to the greed of foreign parents, or she had been driven into her plight by forces beyond her control. She was the only one of the three seen with Negroes who was not a blonde. Her hair was a deep chestnut brown, whose reddish tints shimmered in the sun. Her hair and complexion were almost a replica of Angela's. The evident shame with which she bore her exhibition was pathetic. Her eyes were open but they saw nothing. Her mind was a thousand miles from the scene through which she was passing. The sight of her all but broke Angela's heart.

Of course, Harlem was not a normal evolution of Negro life. But its significance was striking. It might be a prophecy of a world to come in which white civilization would be sunk in a mongrel breed. These parading thousands had not yet found themselves. But they were on the way to a future whose threat was real. *The Crisis* claimed it was the resurgence of a race. Certainly here could be seen a dramatic glimpse of the coming New Negro—a younger generation already vibrant with a new mentality. Was it possible that an insoluble "problem" was here being transformed into the current of commonplace life?

She had thought of the Negro as a race formula rather than a human being, a social nightmare rather than a normally developing part of humanity. In this parading crowd she felt for the first time the threat of a nation inside a nation under the teachings of radicals whose hatred of whites had become an obsession. Certainly the day of "Mammies," "Aunties," and "Uncles" had gone forever.

Fictions were being scrapped and America must face realities. The Negro was no longer an exclusive Southern problem. The growth of a rabid Negro press and the development of the open highway had brought the North and South into the same world. The migration of hundreds of thousands of Negroes into the North was increasing. The result on the social and political life of the nation could not be gauged at this time.

The radical program was undoubtedly creating a situation fraught with new dangers. Thrown on his own mental resources would the Northern Negro lean toward Communism which promised him full social equality with the free intermarriage of blacks and whites, or would he follow his earlier teachings of democracy and move to the right to support our system of society? A new contact must be found if the white man expects to control the shaping of the Negro mind. The occasional contact of leaders of both races would not answer. The New Negro is demanding less charity and more justice, less help and more intimate understanding. He is already moving toward his own objectives under the ideals of democracy. If he can not get these objectives, what will be his answer to the siren call of Communism?

The longer she walked through these parading thousands the more keenly she realized the growth of a mounting race pride in these black people. A race pride at present being expressed in sullen hatred. The Mulatto radical leaders through their Junta were scouting all panaceas, all solutions of the race problem. They had begun to cast religion into the discard in spite of the crowds that still filled their big churches. How long this leadership will content itself with the ideals of democratic government was doubtful. The Harlem radical was still nominally accepting democracy. But how long would it be before a restless editor would curse all American ideals?

She saw a Negro pass her the second time and look back. She crossed the street and he followed. The next time he passed, his arm brushed hers and he grinned in her face, his bulging coarse lips rolled back.

Her hand had gripped her book in an instinctive movement to slap his face when she saw, to her joy, at the next corner the stalwart figure of a policeman. She had never seen a blue police coat with more pleasure. She quickened her pace and found to her surprise that he was a Negro as black as the one who had been following her. But there was something in his honest rugged face that reminded her of old Nelse. In a moment she had implicit faith in him.

"Officer," she said hurriedly. "I'll have to ask your protection. That hulking brute has been following and passing me for three or four blocks."

She pointed to the man who had annoyed her, and the policeman started for him. He ran toward the crowd and disappeared.

The officer walked back and spoke kindly.

"I can't leave my beat to follow that scoundrel. He's dropped into one of the dens on the next street. We haven't enough cops to man this district."

He paused and studied her a moment.

"You're from the South, aren't you, Miss?"

Angela nodded.

"Lemme give you some advice, before you get into real trouble. Don't you try walking through these Harlem Niggers again without an escort. Promise me?"

"I won't. And thank you."

She stepped into the first gun store on the Avenue, bought a small silver mounted pistol, loaded it, and dropped it into her handbag.

As she hurried home, the weight of it striking a rhythmic beat against her body renewed her sense of uneasiness. Was she really living in a civilized world when such a weapon was needed by a woman to walk the streets in broad daylight?

ROOMS

She passed a curious looking group of Negroes standing on a corner chattering in Spanish.

Tomorrow or day after tomorrow—"Manana manana pasada manana"! Denizens from the realm of San Domingo, admitted freely to our shores while we were excluding some of the best white blood of Europe.

On the next corner she passed another queer looking group of blacks, the women in unusually gay colors. They were talking French. A contribution from the Island of Haiti, where black has ruled white for a hundred years. She had just finished reading a brief sketch of the Haitian Republic, once a civilized country under white leadership, now lapsed into tangled jungle of voodoo cruelties.

A procession of trucks rolled by packed with newly arrived Negroes. From their songs and laughter, their grinning jolly faces it was plain to be seen they were from the South. Twenty trucks passed with an average of forty black men and women standing packed like sardines.

She stopped and asked an Irish policeman on the edge of the Black Town what it meant.

"War time prices of labor it is, Miss. The war factories can't get enough workmen. They're bringin' thousands o' Niggers up here from down South. They've brought ten thousand from the West Indies. And still they come. The Niggers are gettin' rich. Every day now they're buyin' brick and brownstone houses they've been campin' in. The Life Insurance Company that owned the Stanford White Model houses—106 of 'em—built with handsome courts runnin' straight through each block, closed off with big iron gates, have all been gobbled up by the Niggers. Begorry, there ain't an Irish settlement in the town that can hold a candle to it. I think I'll black me face and enlist with the Niggers!"

Chapter 26

The battle waged for an African Censorship of the theatre, was utterly futile. Yet when Professor DuBois was critised his defense was convincing to every man with colored blood in his veins.

"No matter what the outcome in money gained by the owners of this picture we owe it to our sense of manhood to utter our protest. The story is a white man's view of history. We dispute every imputation of its theme and its development."

Phil made no effort to continue the controversy. He contented himself with the suggestion that the subject be dropped.

"You're alienating thousands of your friends in the South," he persisted.

Stephens believed that his first step toward effective action might be to secure a Negro of brains and position to back him on the Board of the Inter-Racial Commission.

The chances were good that Weldon would accept. Too good. He had swept his district for a seat in the legislature and had distinguished himself in Albany in the minds of his people by leading the battle against a bill to forbid the marriage of blacks to whites in the State of New York. The important Negro branch in Albany had been organized as a powerful lobby for more than six years. The Junta now maintained lobbies in twenty-three states of the Union to fight for intermarriage and were planning to organize one in Washington to influence National Legislation.

Weldon had rapidly developed into a serious racial menace, and Phil realized too late that he had made a tragic blunder in backing him.

Chapter 27

Angela's search for an escort in her study of Harlem proved difficult. The courses she was taking in the University were attended by students bent only on meeting the requirements necessary for the degree they expected to stand for.

She sought advice from Phil. When she told him of her first afternoon spent in the streets of the Black Town he was indignant.

"But, my dear," she argued. "Life has warned me and hereafter I go armed. I'll know how to protect myself."

He shook his head in anger.

"With all your bitter experience you are acting like a headstrong child. Will you stop this madness until we can find an escort?"

"All right, I'll go with you, Phil, until then."

"We'll take the evening. Work in the University, library and classes, in the daytime."

"Will you go with me tonight?" she laughed.

"So soon?"

She nodded.

"I've made a discovery. The Tabernacle located in the valley below, on the edge of Harlem, is being run by your old friend the Rev. David Stephens of Piedmont."

"No!"

"One and the same. The son of one of your family slaves, who left home, the friend of every white man and black man in the County. You remember his parting speech."

"Where did you discover this?" Phil interrupted.

"Called the Tabernacle this morning and had it confirmed by the old man. He has an abandoned skating rink that seats three thousand people, conducts a revival of religion and has created a stir. He packs the Tabernacle and the collections more than meet expenses. I am making a study of Negro religion. In Africa religion had no relation to conduct. It was a ceremony of propitiation to angry gods. I'm wondering if the basic fact has been changed by the veneer of civilization."

Phil rose hurriedly and snapped his fingers.

"Wait a minute! Does he call himself, David the Apostle?"

"Yes. He has dropped the name of Stephens."

"Well can you beat it!" he exclaimed.

"Beat what?"

"I've just been engaged to serve a writ of *Habeas Corpus* and get the son of one of our famous millionaire aristocrats out of an insane asylum. He backed their demand for social equality and attended black and tan receptions on Fifth Avenue. He held teas and cocktail parties for the entertainment of his colored friends in his own home. At one of these receptions, his only son, a weakminded loafer, met a sleek young Negress, a tawny specimen of the oversexed Negro female of the species. She made a dead set for the moron son and captured him. He married her in secret, took her to Europe and spent six months in a round of dissipation before his old man found it out. He never learned the facts until he sent a detective to Paris to see what was keeping his son so long. Then he heard the startling truth that he had not only married a Negress, but that she was a vicious vulgar hell cat bent on reducing him to imbecility. She had kept him drunk half the time and carried on affairs with Frenchmen under his nose in their own apartment.

"Naturally the old man and his pathetic wife collapsed. In a moment they forgot their theories of social equality and began a desperate effort to save his ancient name. They determined to dissolve the union if it took every cent of the family fortune. The father cut off his allowance without letting him know that his marriage had been discovered, and he was forced to return to New York.

"Through his connections and his money he has kept the whole festering shame out of the papers. But it has finally reached a point where Sarah, the enchantress, refuses longer to be kept in the background. She demands her rights as the wife of a distinguished son of the aristocracy. She wants a home on the Avenue, with liveried white servants. She has appealed to the Negro Junta to fight for her cause. And they have asked me to get her man out of the asylum."

"You are going to do it?"

"Certainly. These people who preach social equality as a theory should be made to live by it. They are getting only what's coming to them. The fool son is within his rights as a man under the laws of New York which permit intermarriage. He followed the teachings of his weeping parents. And they have no right to hold him in an insane asylum for accepting their ideals."

He paused.

"By the way, is Chloe, the old preacher's wife, helping him in his work?"

"Oh, yes. She's his right hand."

"I'm sorry for him. He's crazy about her and she's a devil. Sarah's her mother's own. I'll stake my life that she was the moving spirit in this romance."

"Shall we go tonight and hear the Apostle preach?"

"By all means. And I hope to see Chloe and Sarah at the close of the service."

"We'll go early and maybe catch them before the singing begins," Angela suggested. "Phone now and tell him we're coming."

He called the office of the Tabernacle and the Apostle answered.

"We'll be glad ter see our friends from de old home town. Come early while I'se healin' de sick an' we'll have more time. Chloe and Sarah'll both be here."

Turning from the telephone he said to Angela:

"It's best they don't suspect you're Marie's sister."

"They wouldn't. I knew them at home only by hearsay. Never spoke to them. They wouldn't know me from Adam's wife."

"All the same we'll be cautious. There might be some one else there who has seen you."

They reached the ante room of the Tabernacle at six o'clock, and found the old man blandly busy with his healing, standing behind a counter in a corner of the room, railed off as a dispensary.

Mose, his sexton, was ushering in the suffering colored folks to whom the preacher ministered. They stood for a moment in the side door and watched before announcing themselves. The old man, wearing enormous glasses, was healing the sick by the laying on of hands and annointing with oil. He slipped in a few pills to be taken on the side.

Jeff, a giant good-natured prize fighter, converted by the preacher, was in charge of the clinic. An ugly grafter attempted to reach the counter, Jeff struck him a blow that sent him against the wall, and then warned in low tones:

"I tole ye ter keep outter here, you plug ugly!"

The Apostle caught the strong arm uplifted for a second blow.

"Now, now, deacon! I know you've consecrated all yer talents to de Lawd. And yo' two fists come in handy at times. But you mustn't overwork 'em. God's power can save the lowest sinner. While de lamp holds out to burn the vilest sinner may return."

"Better put a safety pin in your watch chain and stick it through your vest while dis one's movin' aroun' you," Jeff muttered.

The Apostle ignored the thrust and turned to his sexton:

"Bring another load of sawdust and spread it on the mourners' trail. Last night I could see sinners goin' down to hell jist fur de lack o' more sawdust."

The old man turned toward the side door and saw Phil and his companion. He rushed to meet them.

"Lordee, Mister Phil, I'se sho glad ter see ye. De sight o' you's good fer sore eyes." He looked at Angela and smiled. "And dis is de sweet lady what wants ter ax about de wuk?"

"Yes, this is Sister Angela."

She extended her hand and the old man pressed it respectfully.

"Welcome, sweet lady. An' we hopes you come often and help us fight wid de debbil in Harlem."

He stopped and turned to Phil.

"An' I got somethin' I wants yer ter do fer us right away, Mister Phil. I wuz jist tellin' Chloe this mornin' dat I wuz goin' ter sen' fer ye. De Lawd's House is surrounded by a lot o' debbil dens, dives and dance halls dat's draggin' our people down ter hell. Thar's a big one bout three doors up dis street. I wants a lawyer ter close 'em up and clean dis neighborhood."

"I'll do my best for you," the lawyer promised. "Down home, David, you were an honest, lovable character, deeply religious, truth loving. A man who cherished in his heart ideals of honor, truth, and faith in God. On that record I'll back you here for all I'm worth."

"Thankee, sir," the preacher bowed.

A Committee of leaders in the district called to assure the Apostle of their help in cleaning the town of its disorderly elements.

The old man proudly introduced his lawyer. The Chairman of the Committee warned of difficulties.

"You'll find, sir, that these dives are entrenched in a power as yet unbroken by any effort we have made."

Sarah entered richly gowned, followed by Chloe.

She pushed her way between the Committee and the preacher.

"I've something important to tell you," she whispered. "Get rid of these people."

The Apostle waved to his visitors.

"Thankee for calling, gentmen. We'll let yer know when we're ready to strike."

He turned to Phil.

"That's our glorious daughter, sir. One of de greatest singers in New York. She's jist got home from concerts in Europe."

Sarah nodded to the lawyer and threw him a startled look. The man engaged to free her husband!

Before speaking to Angela she drew Phil aside.

"I know you, of course, Mr. Stephens. You have been engaged to free my husband. My father don't know as yet of my marriage. My mother does but keeps her mouth shut. He couldn't. I'll be obliged to you if you'll not let him know anything until the story comes out in the papers."

She stopped and studied him.

"And, as you're my lawyer, I'll be obliged to you if you can persuade my father to stop his foolish crusade against these dives. His life's in danger unless he does. He has made so many enemies already he should close this place and get away."

She barely nodded to Angela when introduced and launched her attack on her father without delay.

"When I helped you take this place for your revival meetings, I never dreamed you'd jump on the people who own property in this district. You're a marked man. You've got to close this place and get out of here before somebody kills you."

"Close dis place!" the old man cried in anguish. "When de Lawd has blessed me as never before in my life. You can't mean dat, honey Chile."

"I do mean it. And mother will tell you the same thing."

Chloe joined in the demand and the old man stared at her as if he didn't know her as she pushed him to the wall and whispered words of sullen anger. In her fat face there was no trace of revival values. There was but one idea in her head, the glitter of her daughter's wealth and triumph.

Sarah squared herself before her father and threw her message into his teeth.

"For the last time we ask you—will you close the place and go?"

The Apostle's figure stiffened and his eyes flashed.

"I am de servant of de Lawd. I'll stan' my ground."

"All right," his sleek daughter answered. "Goodbye!"

Chloe turned, tossed her head, followed her to the door and snapped:

"Goodbye!"

The old man rushed to her side and caught her arm.

"Why, honey chile, honey lamb, you ain't gwine ter leave me—I cuden't stan' dat—yer not gwine?"

"When you come to your senses, let me know."

The Apostle stumbled back into the room and clutched Phil.

"I got ter do God's will, sir. But my heart's broke. You'll close 'em right away—yessah—right away—de Lawd'll not desert me. I got ter do hit. I got ter do hit."

"Come down to my office at noon tomorrow and sign the papers. I'll have them ready."

"Yassah—yassah," the answer came in tones so low they could be scarcely heard.

On emerging from the Tabernacle, Sarah sent her mother to a hotel and walked the block around the corner to the entrance of her own apartment opening off the main assembly room of the dive, "The House of Salome." In most things she trusted her mother, but she had never let her into the real secret of her life and income. She had told her of the marriage to the white dumbbell who was wax in her hands and she had shared with her the secret of her plans for a mansion on Fifth Avenue, but the source of the princely income which she spent with reckless abandon, Chloe had never suspected. To her a millionaire's son as a husband meant millions to spend.

She sank into a rich armed chair, touched a bell and Eddie entered.

"And what is the queen's wish?" he smirked.

"Whiskey and soda and a minute to look at you as we sip it."

He placed the glasses, ice, club soda and whiskey on the side table between the two chairs and sank into one with contentment.

"Hope you've had a happy afternoon, my love," he sighed.

"I've had a hell of a time."

He sensed her mood and lapsed into silence as they drank.

"Where's Bill?" she asked sharply.

"Taking a nap."

"Sleeps day and night, damn him, unless we drag him out. Well, drag him out. I want him right away. I've made up my mind to do something."

Eddie turned to obey her order. She lit another cigarette and puffed it leisurely as Bill appeared.

"Well, sleepy head, are you awake?"

"At yo service, M'am."

"You know there's a big revival going on at the Tabernacle around the corner?"

The tough scratched his head.

"I seed er crowd er Niggers comin' in and out, but I didn't know what dey wuz doin'."

"You wouldn't. But you do know what a Negro revival of religion is, don't you?"

"Dat I do. I seed 'em down Souf."

"All right. Now get this straight—and don't you come giving me any of your excuses if your job's worth anything to you."

"I'll do what yer tells me. I'se kilt fur ye, ain't I?"

"Well, don't advertise it. Go to the meeting tonight. When the preacher invites the mourners to hit the sawdust trail, you hit it. Make as loud noise mourning as the next one. Get into the thickest of the mourners down front and when things get hot start a fight. His deacon, Jeff, will sock you good and plenty. But you can take it."'

"I'll use mah brass knuckles on him—don't worry," Bill assured.

"Break up the meeting. I'll notify the police. The place will be raided and closed. The more heads broken, the better. You got that?"

"Yas, M'am. Dat's right up mah alley."

The Negro tough paused at the entrance of the Tabernacle and listened to the music for a moment. Old fashioned hymns that stole into the senses with a weird call. Bill took a careful peek inside and saw the figure of Jeff towering among the mourners. He'd have to keep an eye on the deacon. He could swing a nasty fist. The meeting was in full cry with the penitents praying, weeping, groaning and rolling in the sawdust before the pulpit.

The Apostle was standing in their midst calling them to come through and see the glory of the Lord. Mose, the sexton, was lazily scattering more sawdust on the spots that had been kicked bare.

When the preacher called once more for mourners to hit the trail Bill uttered a loud groan and wailed.

"Lawd, hab mussy on mah lost soul!"

He kept repeating this as he pushed his way to the front. Jeff met him at the altar rail, stared at him a minute and drew back to knock him out.

The Apostle caught his arm and repeated his motto:

"No, no, deacon, while the lamp holds out to burn the vilest sinner may return."

He knelt and drew Bill to his knees beside him, while Jeff scowled disapproval. The preacher concentrated on the tough his songs, his prayers, his appeals with one arm around the big shoulders.

"Lawd Gawd Almighty we speak in thy name!" the Apostle shouted. "We lay our hands on this poor sinner an' order de debbils ter depart. Git outen dis sinner, debbils! Come brudders and sisters lay yo hands on 'im and drive de debbils outen him into de swine dat rush in de sea!"

The brethren and sisters crowded about the kneeling figure, laid their hands on his head, shouted and moaned. Poor Bill was drowned in a torrent of emotion contagious, resistless. He "got religion" and, leaping suddenly to his feet, he clapped both hands and screamed:

"Glory ter Gawd! I'se saved! De debbils all gone—Glory ter Gawd!"

The crowd knelt and drew him down to his knees again, giving thanks to the Lord for his salvation. In the excitement Bill seized the preacher's hand and drew him aside:

"I'se saved, brudder, and I got ter come clean. I got ter tell ye de truf."

"What's on yo soul, son?" the Apostle sternly asked.

"I gotter come clean ef hit kills me," Bill cried leaning close. "I wuz sent here tonight ter break up dis meetin', start a fight ter hab de perlice pull de place and shet hit up!"

"Who sen' yo here?"

"Salome, er de House er Salome. She's a callin' de perlice now I specs."

"Purge yo soul, mah son!" the preacher commanded. "Yo wuk fer dis vile she-debbil in de dive roun' de corner?"

"Yassah. But I'se done. De Lawd done save me. Hallelujah! Amen! Glory ter Gawd!"

"Stay here and sing and shout and pray, mah son," the Apostle ordered. "I hab wuk ter do tonight."

He rose and called his first exhorter.

"Carry on de meetin', mah brudder, carry on till I come back ter take yo place. De Lawd call me ter walk froo deep waters tonight. But His hand is holdin' mine. De waters roll ober me. Dey can't drown me. He has call me ter do a mighty wuk dis night. Pray fer me. Tell mah people ter pray. I'll come back in glory!"

The exhorter took his leader's place and raised the hymn "Onward Christian Soldiers Marching as to War!"

Something in his excited voice caught the crowd and they sang with power.

The Apostle drew Jeff aside.

"Come wid me, brudder. Yo hab talents in dem fists an' yo good right arm dat yo can use fer de Glory o' Gawd tonight. We go ter *de House o' Salome!*"

Chapter 28

It was barely ten o'clock but the famous night club dive was crowded with patrons. Its gorgeous trappings glittered under subdued lights set to enhance their sensuous effects.

Sarah, now in her element as Salome, is the presiding hostess of her own shining establishment, happy in spite of the clash with her pious fool father. She had brought him to Harlem at her mother's urging. It was against her judgment, but she yielded. She begged Chloe to leave him and live with her in Harlem. But the eloquent popular husband had become a habit. And the mother feared the possibility of a clash with Sarah's temper. She knew nothing of the dive and had never entered the rich apartment which opened off its main hall. The daughter couldn't quite trust her.

Salome was happy tonight not only because of the crowd which packed her place, but she had assurance from her personal lawyer that Stephens, the counsel for the Junta, would release her husband within twenty-four hours and he would add the prestige of his aristocratic name to her establishment. She would keep him by her side and exhibit to the world her conquest. She would, of course, have to watch his drinking. He was apt to be staggering before midnight unless she held a tight rein on him. His infatuation was so complete he would ask no questions about her affairs on the side, or Eddie, her pampered attendant.

White faces filled her place. She allowed just enough Negro men to furnish dancing partners for the gay white women, and just enough sensuous brown girls to dance and flirt with their escorts.

She specialized in this complete removal of every barrier between the races, and stood at the entrance now arrayed in an evening dress of faultless lines, made in Paris. She called aloud the name of every distinguished man who entered and led the applause which followed. Among her patrons were millionaires, gamblers, race track touts and horsemen, long haired artists and models, society dames and flappers. All mingled in a fast and furious black and tan revel. The food was rich and expensive, the wines the best and the spirit of festival time presided over the palatial hall.

Seamon, the graft collector, called early to assure her safety from the interference of any lawyers. She slipped into her little office for a moment with him to make sure of his protection. When he had received an extra hundred dollar bill as a personal favor he tipped his glass to her.

"To hell with reform! The old fool's Tabernacle has become a nuisance to the community. They shout and yell and sing and pray half the night. Nobody can sleep in three blocks. Leave it to me. I'll pull it on short order."

"They're having a near riot there now, I hear," she laughed. "Pull it tonight."

"No sooner said than done," he answered.

They drained their glasses and Seamon hurried to execute her order.

The first full black and tan dance of the evening was called and her instructions from the dais were explicit.

"In this dance, ladies and gentlemen," she cried, "we are full fledged brothers and sisters of the flesh. All prejudices are in the discard. There must be no white couples, no black couples. Every white man must have his daughter of Salome, sleek and brown. Every white woman must. have a dark mate. Choose your partners!"

The orchestra struck the first notes of a sensuous piece of jazz and the dance floor was filled with black and white couples. They danced with complete lascivious abandon. There was no limit in the pressure that might be exerted on a partner. White men pressed the brown breasts of their chosen sirens without restraint. Negro dancers hugged their white partners in breathless embraces, their legs moving in close contact. As the music ended with a crash, Salome shouted the final command from her dais.

"Salute your partners!"

At the order every white man clasped his Negress in his arms and kissed her. Every Negro held his white girl close, kissed her lips and held them in lingering smothering pressure.

"Atta boy!" Salome shouted.

When the chattering crowd had resumed their seats she lifted her hand.

"An important announcement, my people. I want everybody in this gathering to come tomorrow night and bring a friend. I'm going to give you the surprise of your life!"

A member of the first row answered:

"It'll be some surprise, girlie, if you beat your own record!"

"I'll beat it."

"We'll be here!" the shout came in chorus.

Salome disappeared from the dais through rich velvet curtains and the orchestra began the low throb of an oriental dance.

A semi-nude brown chorus, naked to the waist line, appeared suddenly, their bodies swaying to the rhythm of the music. The chorus weaved an opening in the line and Salome appeared, her body from the waist upward nude, her abdomen and hips draped in veils. Accompanied by her chorus she danced and threw off a veil at each circling of the room. As the seventh fell from her deft fingers she stood smiling for an instant, absolutely nude from head to heel. A wave of excitement swept the crowd and before their breath could be drawn again she had disappeared amid a wild round of applause.

In a moment she reappeared with a scarlet robe of chiffon set with jewels, thrown around her glistening figure. She passed rapidly through the tables and selected a group of the elect. They followed her through a side door which led from the main hall into a palace of mirrors.

Her chosen patrons were seated, all of them white men. She clapped her hands and a chorus of sleek skinned odalisks appeared in the absolute nude. A low murmur of applause came from the circle. Without restraint they gave the *dance du ventre* of Egypt in chorus, each movement so perfectly timed its effect was overwhelming. From sweating bald heads came smothered cries of delight which swelled into shouts of approval that startled the guests in the main hall. Here the first chorus of semi-nudes had slipped all veils except a fiery jeweled loin cloth, triangular in shape, held in place by invisible threads around the lower waist and between the legs. The sparkling crystals on this little triangle were supposed to save the face of the law against indecent exposure of person. In fact the tiny loin cloth had met the requirement in a spirit of travesty and exaggeration. The shining lenses skillfully set caught and imprisoned the light and held it focused on the thing it was supposed to conceal.

The preacher, led by his stalwart fighting deacon, suddenly crashed through the doors before the guards could recover from surprise. He reached the center of the dance floor, stopped and stared with horror.

Two bouncers moved down on him and Jeff moved to meet them, his huge fist clenched, and they rushed into the palace of mirrors to warn Salome.

The orchestra stopped, the nude dancers huddled in a corner in fear, the crowd began to curse and shout and some rose to leave.

The Apostle lifted both hands high above his head.

"Silence, fiends! I have walked but a block from the presence of the

Lawd to find myself in hell. You white men and women have tonight come to mix wid my people. On your lips are words of friendship. But you come here to drag men down ter perdition. Shame on you. The curse of Gawd on you! If dis is de social equality some of our people is ravin' about Gawd save de equality. I want my people to have equal rights and equal justice in all dat can lift their souls and bodies. I want no equality that drags both races into the mire. Get out of here now, all of you! I'll have the law called and close this den of iniquity."

A few men and women were rushing for their wraps. They didn't like the sound of his voice or the message he was broadcasting.

Salome, dressed only in her thin scarlet robe of chiffon that revealed every line of her sensuous body, rushed to the spot and fell back in horror as she recognized her father. She had scarcely confronted him before his mind took in the situation. When she saw the look of anger and surprise on the Apostle's face she cowered for a moment in a panic of confusion. Instead of the torrent of abuse and threats which she had come to deliver, her lips refused to move.

"Go to your room and put on your clothes!" he said in low tones of command.

Still stunned with surprise and confusion she obeyed and led him to her large inner office from which was conducted the business of the place. The deacon followed quietly guarding his leader.

She opened the door and asked her father in. He entered and Jeff took his stand on guard.

She turned to the old man shivering.

"Just a minute, I'll get something to throw around my shoulders."

"Your shoulders don't matter," he muttered, "git somthin' longer!"

She slipped through the door and reached a huddled group of her guards. Seamon who had returned, was with them and slipped his overcoat around her shivering form.

"Listen, Seamon, you've promised me protection."

"And, by God, I'll see that you get it. You've played ball with me. I'll play the game with you."

"All right," she said firmly, recovering her poise. "You're in command now. Everything I've got's at stake in this. We'll give this damned old fool a chance to save his hide if he agrees to leave town. If he don't, have a car outside and four good men in it. When I give you the signal take him out to the woods in Westchester and give him the works. You understand?"

"I understand," was the grim reply.

"First clear my door of that tough he's got outside. Knock him senseless and throw him out of a window in the back."

Seamon ordered two huge blacks to execute this order while she waited for the door to be closed. They sauntered up behind the deacon, knocked him out with brass knucks, tied and gagged him and threw him into the alley. They took their stand by the door to await her signal and Sarah entered.

She found her father gazing in wonder at the magnificence of the place, its heavy scarlet curtains, its vulgar pictures, its nude statuary.

"I can't understan it, Sarah," he muttered. "All dis flash of gold and velvet, dese rugs dat feel an inch thick."

"No, you wouldn't understand if I told you. To begin with I'm married to a millionaire."

"Married?" he gasped, "when?"

"More than a year ago. Six months before I went to Europe."

"He furnished dis place?"

"No. I did it myself, by my beauty and genius as a dancer."

"And where's your millionaire husband?"

"His aristocratic father's got him in an insane asylum. Your lawyer, Mr. Phil Stephens, will get him out tomorrow."

"What has he to do with you?" the old man demanded.

"Nothing personally. He's the attorney for The National Association for the Advancement of the Colored People. They've ordered him to sue out a writ of *habeas corpus*—whatever the hell that is."

"And you earned all the money to furnish this palace of sin?"

"I got it."

He came close to her.

"Oh, mah poor chile. I'se come tonight ter call ye ter repent an' be saved!"

"Save your breath!" she laughed cynically. "I always knew you were a fool."

"You say dat to me, yo own father who skimped an' borrowed an' saved ter gib yer an edication an' send yer Norf ter study music."

"Yes, to you!" she sneered. "I've found out tonight that you're a double damned fool who thinks he can call in the law to run this town."

"Only ter quench de flames o' hell burnin' at mah very doors. I've only begun ter do de wuk o' Gawd."

"Now listen, you old hypocrite. I know you inside and out. You're all alike, you shouting, moaning, hellfired preachers. You call the women to the mourners' bench and get down in the sawdust with them. You do more than pray. You sometimes do a little holy rolling with them on the floor. And your hands are not behaving as you roll——"

"You'se a filthy liar!" he shouted.

"All right. All right. Keep your shirt on when you feel the lash. What I'm trying to tell you is that I'm done with your ignorant religion, your fool God and your stinking piety. There is no God but money. This is his Temple, built to his glory. I'm his high priestess. When I look at you I'm ashamed of my birth and the cheap stuff you taught me as religion. I glory in the world, the flesh and the devil!"

"Stop yo blasphemen!" he growled in deadly menace. "Yer can't forgit when yer wuz a sweet little gal in Sunday School at home. Yer can't fergit when we bought yer fust pretty dress an' sent yer ter High School. Yer can't fergit de nights we knelt by yer bed an' prayed. Yer can't fergit the day we put yer on de train ter go ter college, our eyes blind wid tears. Yer can't fergit de pride and glory in our hearts when we sent yer ter New York ter sing in Opera."

"No. I can't forget, the Opera!" she laughed. "Here's where I sing it every night. The Devil's Grand Opera of Jazz, the naked dance and music that makes you ache for the man in your arms. The world, the flesh and the devil is all I ask of life, my good old man. Your Tabernacle is a nuisance that's got to go. Your voice is just one more stray tomcat yowling in the alley. You've got to go."

She paused and walked close and repeated the words.

"You've got to go!"

"I'll go out of God's house only when his people carry me feet foremost on de last journey." He spoke with a new elation that burned with martyr fire.

"And that's going to be sooner than you expect unless you do as I tell you," she threatened.

"Ye can't threaten me, chile."

"I'm not. I'm just telling you."

"I've got one ob de biggest lawyers in dis town."

"Young Phil Stephens. Bah! I can hire a dozen bigger. Besides when I whisper to the men who have hired him to get my white honey boy out of hock he'll drop you like a hot potato. He'll know which side his bread's buttered on. All lawyers do. He'll not lift his little finger against my business when he knows what he's doing. He didn't know who owned the House of Salome when you asked him to close it—did he?"

"Makes no difference who owns it. He's true. He's honest. He's clean. He'll stand by Gawd."

"Like hell he will," she scoffed. "He's in a conference now with my lawyers and I'm to meet them in his office at ten in the morning. When he learns who Salome is, watch what happens."

The Apostle shook his head.

"God never made a Stephens who was a coward. He'll turn you outer yer gilded hell an' close de place termorrow."

"He'll bring my husband back to my arms and he'll be here at the House of Salome tomorrow night."

Her daring assurance disconcerted the old man and he halted for a reply. Taking advantage of his confusion she launched her final warning.

"There's just one way for you to save your worthless life. Leave New York tonight. Will you do it?"

He frowned and studied her face twisted anew with deadly anger.

"What do—you—mean—by just one way ter save mah life?"

"Exactly what I've said. You may not know it but you've butted into the wrong house tonight. You're on the spot. There's a car outside waiting for me to give the signal for your last ride."

She stepped to the door and opened it in the face of her two guards.

"And what did you do to the big boy?" she asked.

"Knocked him cold. Tied and gagged him and threw him outter the back window."

"Good. Wait for my orders."

The scene was not lost on the old man. He spoke in low strained tones.

"Ye—would—kill—yer—own—father?"

She confronted him angrily.

"No. I wouldn't do that! You're *not* my father, you damned whining fool."

He stared at her in blank amazement.

"I'se—not—yer—father?"

"No. My mother's got more sense in a minute than you'll have in a life time. She fooled you, old man. My father was a school teacher who lived at your house once upon a time. You got jealous bye and bye and ran him off. But he found the way in the back door for five years and dandled me on his knee on more than one fine evening while you were yelling your damned head off calling sinners to repentance."

He seized her in a piteous appeal.

"Take dat back, honey. Yer jist said dat ter hurt me. Yer know hit ain't so. Take hit back. Yer've turned a knife in mah heart. Tell me yer jist foolin'. Take hit back!"

She broke into a hard laugh.

"You poor sap! You thought you could keep on rolling and playing with the sisters in the sawdust and my mother would be waiting to brush off your long tailed coat when you got home. Well she played you for a sucker. And served you right!"

He dropped to his knees, clasped his hands and lifted his eyes to the ceiling.

"Lawd Jesus, come down frum heaven an' help me now. Hab mussey on dis po' lost chile o' mine. Make her ter see de black lie she has tole. Bring repentance ter her soul an' save her frum de flames o' hell. Save me Lawd frum de sins o' doubt an' fear. Yer promise me Lawd. I'm askin ye. Lift de load o' sin frum dis po' lost girl, make her clean an' whole. Thou didst cleanse de leper, cleanse her. Thou didst open de eyes o' de blind. Open hers. Thou didst cast out seben debbils. Cast 'em outter her. Thou didst raise de daid. She's daid in sin an' shame. Raise her, oh Lawd, in holiness an' love."

Sarah suddenly grasped his hair and drew his head back with a sharp jerk.

"Don't waste any more breath on me, damn ye. My men are tired waiting for your carcass. Just one more minute now to make peace with your God before you go. One minute!"

He tried to face her, still on his knees, and sought her eyes in a piteous appeal.

"Ye ain't gwine ter kill me, is you, honey chile?"

Her voice was hard as nails, and he felt the chill of death in them.

"That's exactly what I'm going to do. You've grown too good and great for this world. Get up, damn you."

She kicked him a vicious dig and he rose with both hands gripped on her throat and held her in a vise. Her eyes began to pop, her body to relax, but his terrible steel grip never weakened. There was dead silence inside and outside the room. While he still held his fingers on her throat there was a crash at the door, a body struck the floor, another smash, another crash and Jeff broke into the room, and seized the preacher.

"De Lawd's good ter me, Postle. I knocked dem two niggers cold wid a piece er lead pipe. Dere cords an' gag couldn't hole me. Come outten here quick now fore dey gang up on us."

The limp dead body of the girl slipped from the old man's grasp and slumped to the floor. His deacon took the choking as a necessary discipline and paid no attention to the body.

He drew the preacher through the door and the old man closed it as he passed. It was the work of a minute for Jeff to dear the window through which he had just climbed and draw his partner roughly after him.

The jazz orchestra was still playing in the main hall. An ambitious dance leader had taken Salome's place, and the revelry was again at its height. No one of the dancing chorus of nudes or the dancing black and whites could have dreamed of the tragedy that had been enacted beyond the hallway that separated Salome's office from the main floor. The dead woman lay behind a closed door and the two stalwart bruisers still were unconscious.

At the Tabernacle, the sexton was closing up. The big auditorium was dark save for a single light by the door opening into the dispensary. Mose went in and covered the counter for the night. But few pills had been given out. The healing service had been broken up early by the Committee and the lawyer. He looked anxiously out the front door and shook his head.

"Name er Gawd, why don't he come. Somefin' happen ter him, sho."

Chloe, who had returned to the fold repenting her desertion, had helped Mose extinguish the lights in the big room and now hurried to the dispensary.

"He ain't come yet, Mose?"

"Nobum."

"Whar on earth can he be, do you reckon?"

"Wish I knowed, M'am. De last words I hear frum him worry me lots."

"What he say?"

"He say ter Jeff, 'We go ter de House er Salome.'"

She shook her head angrily.

"Why you didn't tell me this before? Come on, we'll see what's happened to him."

She reached the door dragging the unwilling sexton just as a police wagon passed, the siren screaming. An ambulance was close behind it.

Chloe heard in terror, drew back into the room, closed the door and sent the sexton out to see what it was.

Mose emerged gingerly. Chloe closed the door and sat down in the dark, her heart in her throat.

It seemed an hour before the sexton slipped back and stood trembling.

"What is it? What's happened?" Chloe whispered.

"Dar's a big crowd in front er the House er Salome. De Apostle went dar, you know." His voice failed him and the woman dropped into a chair sobbing.

A crowd was gathering in the street outside.

"It's murder!" a man shouted.

Chloe pressed her ear to the door which she held ajar. The next cry she heard distinctly.

"Salome has been killed in her place!"

She clutched her heart. Sarah had not told her the truth about the dive, but her suspicions once aroused, she had guessed it. Now she was sure that her daughter had been murdered.

"Merciful God!" she breathed to herself. "He couldn't do that. He couldn't. He didn't know. He couldn't have killed his own child because she run a dance hall."

The telephone rang and she grasped the receiver.

"This is Sister Angela," a soft voice called. "I'm with Mr. Stephens. He wishes to speak to the preacher if he's still there."

"He's not here," Chloe gasped. "Tell Mr. Phil to come here quick. Something terrible's happened. Murder's been done!"

Angela drew on her coat and hat and they hurried to get a cab.

A policeman pushed his way into the darkened dispensary, heard Chloe and moved back.

"Turn on that light!"

The light came on instantly and he faced Mose.

"Where's your Apostle?"

"He ain't here, sah."

His wife caught the officer's arm.

"What you want him for?"

"You'll find out in good time. You've hid him here somewhere."

"No, sir. I swear he's not here. I wish to God he was. You can look for him."

"Don't worry. I'll do that."

He pushed his way into the darkened Auditorium and called back through the door to Mose.

"Here you, Nigger, turn on those lights."

The sexton hurried to obey, and the officer searched every nook and corner.

Chloe followed him to the door and called:

"Please, sir, let me know when you find him. He's my husband."

The policeman threw her a sympathetic look.

"All right, I'll telephone. Stand by."

He had scarcely disappeared in the direction of the dive when Phil and Angela stepped from their cab and entered the place.

In hurried low tones Chloe told of her repentance and return to find the preacher gone, his exhorter in charge of the meeting.

"He told the sexton he was going to the House of Salome," she said. "I have been scared to death ever since I hear it. I heard them holler in the streets that Salome's been killed. Oh, my God, do you think he was crazy enough to kill her?"

"It's possible, of course," Phil muttered. "He was terribly worked up tonight. You saw that when you left him."

"I shouldn't have gone—God forgive me. I might a stopped him. He drives me near crazy sometimes but I reckon I loves him. I couldn't stay away. I got back in no time. If he's killed her what'll they do to him?"

"It all depends on how it happened."

"You'll defend him, Mr. Phil, won't you, sir? He's one of your Pa's people."

"You know I will. Stay here until I get back. Sister Angela will watch with you. I'll go to the dive and see what's happened."

He left hurriedly and the two women sat down on a bench used by the patients. Chloe turned to Angela with a long searching look which brought the blood mounting to her face. The darker woman failed to recognize her and she breathed more freely.

"You reckon they'll burn him if he killed her?" Chloe shivered.

"No. I don't," was the quick reply. "The jury will know his character, his work, his piety and the provocation the woman had given him."

"Oh, why wouldn't he do what Sarah and me begged him to do tonight. She's awful smart. She knowed something terrible was going to happen. But he was so bull headed. He'd fight it out. And this is what's happened. If they put him in that chair I'll die. I didn't know how much I thought of him till this come."

She bowed her head in her hands and sobbed. Angela stroked her shoulders tenderly and she cried the louder.

A cab stopped outside and both women rose as Jeff pushed the door open cautiously and entered on tip toe.

"He's in de cab outside."

"Praise God he's safe!" Chloe cried.

"No he ain't, sister," was the low answer. "He's a walkin' straight into de hans o' de perlice an' I can't stop 'im. Fer Gawd's sake hep me."

He appealed to Angela.

"Bring him in quickly," she ordered.

Jeff led the Apostle in carrying part of his weight with an arm under the shoulder. His clothes were torn and bedraggled, his eyes looked dazed and he breathed heavily as if about to collapse.

Chloe rushed to his side gripping his arms hysterically.

"Oh, mah po', po' ole man," she wailed. "You'se hurt, but I'll nuss yer back. Praise Gawd you're alive. I thought they'd kilt you."

He stared at her now with a queer look in his bleared eyes as if he only half heard her voice.

"Thank the good Lawd you're here alive," his wife babbled on. "Tell yo Chloe what happened. Who tried to kill you? And what for?"

He caught her by the shoulders and bored her through with a cold look.

"I kilt a she debbil defendin' mah self and you. Defendin' yo life and mine as real men has always done befo' me down Souf."

"Den it wuz you who kilt her?"

"Yes. The vile keeper ob a den o' iniquity who danced naked befo' men. The woman who tried ter close dis Tabernacle and stop mah wuk fer Gawd."

He paused, drew a deep breath and cut each word with sharp emphasis.

"Your—daughter, Sarah—called in the streets by the name of Salome."

"My gal, Sarah! Hit's a lie—a lie I tells ye. A black hell fired lie. Why do yer say tings lak dat ter me yer wife and de mudder o' yer chile."

In her hysterics she had reverted to the full Negro dialect of her Southern training, shedding the veneer of Northern culture.

"Yer didn't know dat yer brat wuz Salome o' de dive den?"

"An' I don't know hit now. Somebody's lied ter ye. Dat's a lie I tells ye—a lie—a lie—a lie! Dey fool ye!"

"Dere wern't nobody dar ter fool me. I seed her naked wid mah own eyes. She cuss me an' cuss God an' glory in shame. An' what's mo' woman——"

"Hit's a lie, I tells ye," she repeated in lame tones as he began to advance on her.

Sobered by the deadly light in his eyes Chloe backed away in a vain attempt to stem his wrath by denouncing his crime.

"An' you, a servant of de Lawd, stainin' yo hands wid human blood."

Her voice faded into silence before the searching look with which he transfixed her.

"What's de matter wid you?" she gasped. "Is you gone crazy an' you gwine ter try ter murder me, too?"

In silence he gripped her hands and his fingers sank deep into the soft flesh.

Angela sprang to his side and loosened his hands. He stared at her in half apology and turned back to the cowering figure.

"An' you kills yer own chile," Chloe whispered, again rallying to the attack on his sin.

He stared at her steadily.

"Answer me now, woman. Yer knows I didn't kill my own chile. Because she's not mine."

"Who tell yer dat lie?"

"She frew hit in mah face wid de screech o' a cat. Said yer had tole her. Now tell me de truff. Who'se de father o' dat woman we called Sarah an' de slums o' Harlem called Salome?"

His wife suddenly went limp, felt her way to the bench, covered her face and sobbed.

"Yes—yes—I done hit. I fools ye. Her father's de school teacher dat boarded wid us. Yo wuz playin' an' rollin' wid de sisters. I knowed ye wuz an' try ter git eben wid ye."

"Trying ter hide the shame o' yer black soul by lyin' about me? I done nuttin ter dem sisters rollin' in de sawdust cept ter hep 'em come fru."

"Not in de sawdust—no," Chloe countered. "But yer fine de way ter dere houses. Yo beat a path to 'em. Yo knows hit, too!"

"Yo miserable liar!" he groaned turning away and staggering under a spell of dizziness.

Chloe saw his moment of weakness, crawled to him on hands and knees and grasped his legs.

"I done confess mah sin. I'se a lost sinner. Yo hep sabe de odders. Sabe me. Pleze say yer fergives me. De Lawd is slow ter anger an' plenteous in mercy. I hear yer say dat a hundred times.

His anger flamed again at being trapped in his own words and she saw his fists clench.

"Sholy yer ain't gwine ter kill me, too?" she whined, "when I'se in de dust at yo feet."

He suddenly threw her off and kicked her fat hips as she fell.

"No. Yer ain't wuth killin'!" he muttered. "I'se done now wid vain things. Vanity, vanity—all is vanity, saith de Lawd."

At the sound of footsteps approaching the door, Chloe rose as Phil entered. She rushed to his side.

"He kilt her—yer sure?"

"There can be no mistake about it. The two bodyguards she stationed at the door will swear they heard a struggle inside with no cries and little noise. They started to open the door when Jeff rapped them over the head with a lead pipe. On regaining consciousness they entered the room and found Sarah's dead body."

"That wuz Sarah?" the mother gasped.

"Yes. I saw her in this room with you tonight. I identified her."

"They'll burn him fer hit?" she asked dully.

"We'll see."

He turned to the preacher.

"Tell me how it happened."

"She cuss me. She cuss Gawd. She laff in mah face an' tole me she wuz not mah daughter."

"Is that true?" the lawyer asked Chloe.

"Yassah. I confess hit."

"All right, go on."

"I kneel down ter pray Gawd ter sabe her soul frum hell. She grab me by de hair, pull mah haid back an' say she had me on de spot an' gib me one minute mo ter make mah peace wid Gawd, befo' her men take me in a car out in de woods an' kill me. I seed she mean hit. Mah time had come, hit wuz her wuthless life er mine. I grab her by de froat an' chokes her ter death. Hit wuz Gawd's will. I had ter do hit. I'se ready ter die."

"We're not ready to let you," the lawyer said. "We've a good fighting chance to save your life."

"Praise Gawd!" his wife shouted.

Jeff suddenly pushed into the room.

"Ye gotter git a move on ye. Come on, de perlice comin' down de street. I hear de whistle screachin'. Come on, I git yer ter mah place."

The Apostle settled in his tracks.

Chloe added her plea to Jeff's.

"Come on, honey, fly an' sabe yo self. Mah heart's brakin' but I loves ye. Dey shan't take ye. Come on wid Jeff." She broke into sobs at the feel of his stiffening figure.

He slipped an arm around her.

"There, there, now, mah ole gal. I'se always been crazy bout ye. I knows de debbil's in yer sometimes. But I loves ye. I never could hep it. Hush cryin', Mr. Phil's a great lawyer. He'll fight fer me."

He paused and turned to the lawyer.

"I can't run, sah. I'se ready ter meet de Jedge. I'se ready ter meet Gawd, an' tell 'im all. Every thing's a sinkin' under mah feet." His voice failed. He felt himself in utter darkness. There was no truth, no right, no Bible, no heaven, no salvation. His shoulders slumped and the only sound in the room was the low moans that came from his forlorn wife's lips.

The police wagon dashed up, its siren screaming. The men swarmed from the wagon and circled the Tabernacle. The lieutenant entered and arrested the old man.

The lawyer asked for gentle treatment.

"He's all broken up, Lieutenant," he said gently. "There's nothing to get out of him. I have his full confession."

"I'll have him repeat it and swear to it."

Phil turned to the Apostle.

"Tell the officers what you told me, sign it and swear to it. The best place for you in the excitement will be in jail. The toughs who run the dive will try to get you. I'll ask an early trial and defend you."

"Thankee, Mr. Phil," was the pitiful answer. "Yo is one o' mah own people. I trust ye as I trust de Lawd."

An officer drew a pair of handcuffs at sight of which the old man shivered.

Phil touched the Lieutenant.

"You don't need them. He'll go with you. He has said he would, and his word's good."

"Thankee, sah, again!" the preacher nodded.

The Lieutenant hesitated a moment and waved the handcuffs aside.

The bedraggled figure drew erect and he walked from the place with a steady step, his head high, while Chloe continued her low moans.

Chapter 29

When the Negro undertaker came to take the body to his establishment a mob of Negroes gathered at the door. A rumor had spread through Harlem that a white man hired an assassin to murder the dancer.

It was evident from the mood of the blacks that the Harlem Negro thought more of his cabaret than he did of his church. Here white sought black as equals and pals. Here their women of talent ruled as queens of the night. The world came to pay their homage. What she did in private life was nobody's business. Moral or immoral she was their heroine.

Religion didn't enter into the issue. In their inner thought religion had nothing to do with human conduct. Religion was a ceremony. Through their attitude toward religion and conduct suddenly flamed the inheritance of Africa. There religion had never had the slightest relation to conduct. The voodoo priest or priestess demanded sacrifices only to soften the wrath of the gods. When their sacrifices in goods paid to the medicine man, or sacrifices made on the altar of superstition, were sufficient, the safety of the worshipper was assured. It made no difference to this crowd what sort of orgies were held in the House of Salome. She was a priestess of the race.

"She had the right to do as she damned pleased in her own place!" a stalwart black shouted.

"To hell with white men who set themselves up to teach us!" yelled another.

"Kill every damned white that tries to come through this street."

They swung in mass about an automobile in which a Columbia Professor was on his way to his class room, overturned the car, dragged him out, beat him and his chauffeur. In spite of his cries for quarter and explanation of his work they refused to right his car and hustled him from the scene. They beat up a white High School boy on the way to a black and tan school. When the reserves were called out they had formed a division to raid the white settlement but two blocks above.

The time for arguing the application for a writ of *habeas corpus* was set for eleven o'clock the day of the riots. Phil called early to see that Angela had not ventured into the disturbed district. To insure her safety he asked her to act as his secretary for the day. She accepted and came to his office at ten o'clock. The elder Van Vetchen[1] and his wife, heavily veiled, were waiting.

The lawyer received them with scant sympathy and turned to Angela.

"Please get your note book and take the record of our interview."

She hesitated, smiled, got a note book and took her seat beside his desk. His stenographer had been sent to the law library for references he wished to quote.

Van Vetchen scowled at the note taker, but promptly began his plea.

"We have come, Mr. Stephens, a heartbroken mother and father, to beg your help in the postponement of your plea for the writ."

"The poor boy's infatuation for that unspeakable creature amounts to insanity," the mother broke in.

"Yet, madam, your son is of age. Under the law of this State he could marry this woman. You have no legal right to deprive him of his liberty."

"But every moral and social right, sir," Van Vetchen interposed. "Surely, you, a Southern white man will agree to this?"

"Under the present conditions, no," the lawyer replied. "You backed with your money and your good name an Association of Radical Negroes and white associates, who are demanding the marriage of blacks to whites. These white associates hold black and tan receptions in their mansions and practice what they preach. No doubt you joined in this program."

The man hung his head. His wife spoke lamely.

"We only held two such teas in all the past years."

"And at one of these teas in your own home, I understand, this girl danced. Your son met her, became her constant companion, and married her."

"It's true," she sobbed. "I blame myself. But I can't help it now. We are trying to save our son's life and sanity. Please help us by postponing this writ until the woman is buried. The scandal will be appalling when it breaks no matter what we do."

"We only ask two days delay, sir," Van Vetchen broke in.

"I'm sorry. I don't see how it can be arranged. I am acting as an

1. Carl Van Vechten (1880–1964), an Iowan, was a white writer and photographer active in the Harlem Renaissance. Van Vechten is best known for his 1926 novel, *Nigger Heaven*, describing his experience as a white man in the after-hours nightlife of Harlem's clubs. See Bruce Kellner, *Carl Van Vechten and the Irreverent Decades* (Norman: University of Oklahoma Press, 1968).

attorney at law in this case. You will have to secure their consent to a postponement."

"They have already refused it with insults," the father sighed.

The mother turned to Angela.

"Won't you put in a word for me, my dear? You seem so poised. He must think a lot of your opinions. He asked you to stay and make notes. I'm a mother. Maybe you don't understand what that means——"

In spite of an effort at self control, Angela flushed, rose and walked to the window in silence.

"Your appeal to my secretary is beside the mark, Madam," Phil put in with a touch of anger. "The advocates of social equality say that two people who love each other have the right to marry without the interference of outsiders. Now that the thing comes home to you, you awake to the fact that they have no such right. No two people who ever lived had any such right. Marriage is a divine social ordinance. It is the concern of society first, last and always. That's why the law must keep the records. You have imprisoned your son illegally. You are responsible for his marriage. Your request of me to save you from embarrassment by a lie does not appeal to me. I will not ask the Association to permit a postponement. I will not create a legal quibble that may bring it about. I'm sorry. I'll have to ask you to leave. Your appearance in my office is most irregular. For that reason I have kept a witness beside my desk."

"Could we tempt you for a large fee to resign as counsel for the Association and represent us?" Van Vetchen asked.

The lawyer turned to Angela.

"Please make a careful note of the form in which the bribe was offered. My answer is that I come of a race of lawyers who do not stoop to dishonor. Many of them have been poor and died poor. But they never betrayed a client. Good day."

They rose with a sad touch of pride and passed through the door without looking back.

Angela brushed a tear from her eyes.

"You were hard, Phil. Melodramatic for a moment, maybe in your last speech. But it rang true. You're a scion of the old South at its best. The new world has not dimmed your honor or your courage."

He made no answer at once but watched her intently.

"I'm sorry for that question which cut you to the quick. I saw you flinch. Forgive me for dragging you here this morning. It was only because I love you so. You know that, dear?"

She dabbed her eyes with a tiny handkerchief.

"Yes, I know, Phil. I wondered what on earth you staged that scene with the note book for. It wasn't staged. I see now you called me to guard you against a possible slander. I'm glad I was here. Don't worry about the little hurt. I have to live with my memories."

"You don't have to be alone, you know." He spoke his plea in casual tones as he gathered his papers. "We must hurry now to the court."

The room was packed. A mass of struggling men and women overflowed into the corridors. Every newspaper had its crack reporter on duty. There were rumors of a sensation. Not a word had as yet been printed about the Van Vetchen-Salome marriage. It was bound to come out in headlines in the afternoon editions.

Stephens read his petition for a writ of *habeas corpus* to be served on the Superintendent of the Ulster Sanitarium for the production in court of Paul Van Vetchen. When he reached the recital of the fact of his marriage to Sarah Stephens, colored, their flight to Europe, their return and the confinement of the son in the asylum by his parents, the sensation broke. Every reporter jumped for a telephone and the presses hummed with extras. The court procedure was brief. The writ was issued returnable at four o'clock. Phil and Angela hurried to a waiting car and in two hours drew up before the iron grated doors of the "Sanitarium."

The news of the granting of the writ had been telephoned to young Van Vetchen and he had been instructed to be ready and packed for an immediate trip to New York.

The Superintendent, in a panic over the developments, had attempted to make peace with his prisoner. He was allowed the daily papers for the first time and read with horror the story of his wife's murder in the dive which he had helped her refit and finance.

Weakened by his long confinement, the boy collapsed. A doctor revived him and he paced his rooms for an hour in a frenzy of grief and rage. He at once leaped to the conclusion that his father had hired an assassin to kill his wife. He attacked the Superintendent of the Sanitarium as a partner in the crime. He had entered into the conspiracy to imprison him until his wife could be murdered. The Superintendent defended himself. He had been admitted to the institution in the regular order. He had signed his own commitment after a night in the Alcoholic Ward of Bellevue. A judge had agreed to his commitment to a private hospital instead of the public one to which he would have been transferred. He had nothing to do with dives in Harlem. He had never heard of the House of Salome or its hostess.

When the lawyer arrived the boy was still raving his determination to swear out a warrant for the arrest of his father charging him with the murder and one for the Superintendent as an accessory.

Angela succeeded in soothing him. Something in her quiet personality caught his excited mind and helped him.

"You must remember, Paul," she pleaded. "You have a mother who loves you."

"A damned poor way she's been showing it. She worked with my old fool father. They got me drunk and into the Bellevue Alcoholic Ward. She knew I was being kidnapped into an insane asylum. Why the hell, if she loved me, didn't she take my part against the old man?"

"She thought she was saving you from a worse fate."

"Hell!" he exploded. "When she herself introduced us! Now that I've taken their doctrines at their face value I'm insane, and my wife lies dead at an undertaker's."

Angela studied the weak chin and the finer lines of his face with sympathy. He had right and reason on his side in the tragedy which had developed.

He broke down and cried at last, his head in his hands, muttering incoherently.

"No—no—I guess you're right. I must not denounce my mother. The old man's guilty and she is too. But I'll have to bear it. I will if I don't go crazy now sure enough. Come on, let's go!"

"Will you let me talk to the reporters for you?" Phil asked.

"Sure. You're my lawyer. I'll keep my mouth shut."

He kept his word and the lawyer in his presence gave out as dignified a statement as possible under the conditions. The writ was confirmed and the prisoner released. He thanked Phil, called a cab and hurried toward the door where his mother caught him in her arms and held him in silence for a moment before he broke the embrace with a touch of rudeness.

"Please, son, come home," she pleaded.

"I'd sooner be in hell with my back broke than in your house," he answered.

"We'll give you your old allowance again and everything will be as it used to be."

"I don't want your damned money. I've investments in the House of Salome. I can borrow on it if I have to. I'll run it myself now in memory of my wife."

Without looking back he swung through the door and jumped into a cab.

He took charge of the dive and found intact the strong box containing the jewels of the dead woman. They were worth a fortune. He sold them as his own and ordered the most elaborate funeral Harlem or Manhattan had ever witnessed.

The procession was remarkable. Ten brass bands played funeral marches. It required five trucks to carry the flowers. One piece alone filled a float, upheld by two trucks, and cost two thousand dollars. The dusky crowds on the sidewalks gasped as it passed. More than a hundred cars followed through the dense masses of people who lined the pavements and overflowed into the streets.

Phil and Angela watched the procession from an open car parked at a corner.

The lawyer shook his head.

"Only a king of Europe could be buried with such pomp. More than half these flowers were voluntary offerings of the Negro race. The funeral cost fifty thousand dollars. It was not laid out in idle extravagance. It's a challenge of the black race to the ruling whites. It will overawe two hundred thousand black spectators today and fuse their thought into Negro solidarity. They mean it as the prophecy of a new rising power. It is. And it's ominous."

The Apostle demanded through his attorney a speedy trial and got it. The prisoner received no sympathy from the masses of his people. The attendants of the Tabernacle were so stunned by the tragedy and the enormity of their leader's crime, they mourned in silence and he had few defenders among them. Salome was a daring child of genius. They gloried in her fame, her wealth and her triumphant marriage to a white aristocrat.

So hostile were the Negro spectators that Stephens more than once asked the court to clear the room.

Throughout the trial, he studied the preacher with increasing wonder at the contradictions of his character. In South Carolina he had been a man of unusual moral fibre as seen from the outside. His word was good at the bank. He had the respect of both whites and hacks. He left the County with the good wishes of all, his piety unquestioned. Yet this tragedy had developed the fact that, while he was preaching at home with fervor and power, his rolling in the sawdust with women mourners had not been without sin.

That he was, judged by the standards of white world morality, a hypocrite and adulterer. And his wife's life matched his. There had been no connection between his religious emotions and his conduct in life.

There was no connection now between his emotional life in his revivals in the Tabernacle and his act of murder. The murder had in no way dimmed his religious ecstasy, save for a minute of depression on being arrested. His conduct and religious emotions, now on trial for his life, seemed utterly sincere. He had no idea of repentance for his act of murder. He had done exactly right. He hadn't killed his own daughter. He had killed an intruder in his home. This had nothing to do with his religion.

It was necessary again to go back to his savage inheritance from the jungles to understand his religious sincerity and his brutal crime.

Captain Collier came up from Piedmont and testified to the prisoner's character in the County where he had lived. The Apostle grasped his hand and murmured his thanks.

Phil's task was comparatively easy. But for the atmosphere of hostility to the accused from his black brethren in the court room it would have been a thing which required little thought. He denounced the ungrateful daughter with scathing power and killed any sympathy for her that might have been created by the crowds. His analysis of the scene which led to the killing was remorseless in its cold blooded logic. A man has the right to kill in self defense, even if the assailant were his own daughter. In this case she had turned a knife in his heart by proclaiming her mother's sin.

The jury was out but an hour and returned a verdict of second degree murder. It was greeted by hisses from the Negroes and the judge ordered the Sheriff to clear the room.

The preacher stared at the men who had hissed in a stupor of surprise.

The Judge immediately sentenced him to ten years at hard labor in State's Prison. At his age the sentence meant life.

Chloe's shoulders slumped, she leaned against him and uttered a groan. The Apostle drew her limp figure close and whispered: "Gawd'll be merciful to us. Don't cry, chile. It's all right. I'm gwine ter ax de Jedge sumfin."

He rose slowly and faced the Court.

"You axed me, Jedge, if I had anything to say why de sentence should not be said agin me. I didn't speak. May I ax ye somfin now?"

"Certainly," His Honor answered.

"Ef you will des low me ter preach de gospel to de poor convicts in prison I'd be so happy, sah. Ef I can be savin' souls dere won't be no prison walls. I'll rise on the wings ob faith and be in Paradise."

The Judge softly answered:

"I'll ask the Warden to favor you."

"Thankee, sah, thankee kindly."

CHAPTER 30

The sensation of the marriage and murder of Sarah passed quickly. Only the Negro press carried it on. A greater sensation was in the making.

Angela, who had studied at Columbia the science of Propaganda, and knew the deadly menace of its power over the imagination of the people watched with heavy heart the insistent campaign of the Allied Nations to sweep us into the inferno.

The average man and woman who read the war news of the day, and the papers and pamphlets from France, England and Belgium took the stories at face value. The student of propaganda could trace these things straight to their sources. America was deluged with a flood of this stuff which stirred the emotions without the slightest attempt to appeal to reason. To make war possible the emotions of hate and fear must be stirred. It was skillfully done.

President Wilson had fought for three years to keep America out of the War. The pressure was now becoming resistless. Morning, noon and night we read of the violations of the treaties with Belgium and Luxemburg, of atrocities on the French frontier before a declaration of war. We read of the beastly killing of prisoners and the wounded, of looting, rape and murder. Scenes of public assault in the streets of Belgian cities were described in detail amid shouts of laughter of German soldiers looking on, were added to the horror. We were told that women were stripped and had their breasts cut off, and little children were murdered before their mother's eyes by German soldiers.

They used forbidden dum-dum bullets, burning liquids and deadly gas. Whole churches, art centers and the houses of Christ and Science were destroyed with senseless and ruthless savagery.

A young German of culture, sensitive and proud, lived next door to Angela. His former friends turned their backs on him. He was a loyal American. But he shut himself up in his home one night and shot himself before his wife and daughter. He had protested in vain against the lies told of his people. He could not live in the poisoned air.

War against Germany was declared in an outburst of patriotism. We had seen the homes of our ancestors in Europe burst into flames that threatened to destroy civilization. We commanded peace. The belligerent nations of Central Europe scorned our commands. We called to the colors an army of twenty-four million men in a war to end war and make the world safe for democracy. We mobilized our women to raise billions of funds and roll bandages. We marched in endless shouting parades.

President Wilson's voice was one of tremendous power, not only in America where his conservative course had fused all elements into a solid national unity, but in the world beyond the seas as well. We enrolled the greatest army in history and began to drill its millions.

Beneath the shouts and the tumult there were heard rumblings among the millions of Negroes that boded no good for our internal peace and strength. The rank and file of the educated Negroes had taken pride in their race's participation in the Great War. Every Negro newspaper paraded the fact that France had mobilized hosts of coal black Africans, taught them to kill white men and sent them to the front. That England had mobilized hosts of colored troops from India and sent them to the front to kill white men.

In the United States we had registered two million three hundred thousand Negroes as soldiers, and three hundred and eighty thousand of them were drilled and sent into action to kill white men.

No thoughtful man could doubt for a minute the effect of these things on the mind of both races in America. It was an ominous sign of the times. The world in which we were living would never again be the same, whatever the outcome.

Outbreaks of race friction followed in America quickly. A new racial tension was felt in every community, North and South. Six hundred and seventy-eight colored men were trained as officers and given commissions in the United States Army. This should have been a matter of routine incident to the mobilization of hundreds of thousands of their race as soldiers. But the outbursts of race pride from Negro Radicals added fresh fuel to the flames of the growing menace of race conflict.

The first outburst came in the State of Illinois, far removed from the Black Belt of the South. From a comparatively trivial incident a bloody riot broke out in East St. Louis. Six thousand Negroes were driven from their homes, many of them burned over their heads. Scores of blacks were mercilessly and senselessly killed and nearly half a million dollars worth of their property destroyed by fire.

"I've checked carefully," Angela declared, "the list of dead and wounded, and found the facts to be that forty-seven people were killed, 39 blacks and 8 whites. Not five hundred. Many more were seriously wounded, several hundred of each race, and three hundred and twelve houses were burned. Even so, the bloodiest race riot we have yet had in America."

To Phil she wrote a detailed report and gave the true causes which led to the outbreak. During the two years before the riots the shortage of labor in the World War industries had brought up thousands of Negroes from the South. The Negro population had been increased by eighteen thousand. Last year a strike of four thousand white men in the packing plants had brought as many Negroes in as strike breakers. White men were walking the streets in idleness, their families suffering for bread, while their places had been taken by strange Negroes from the deep South who lived in hovels and kept wages down.

The underlying cause of the riot was the conflict of muscle in the fight for a living.

The report was received by radical Negroes with anger. It lacked the inflammatory character which they had expected. They had called a mass meeting to protest against the "Massacre" of their people. On receiving the 'report of the cold facts they decided to let the public statements of exaggeration stand and stage a huge, silent parade down Fifth Avenue with appropriate banners and mottoes.

The silent parade was a success. Nine or ten thousand Negroes marched down the Avenue to the sound of muffled drums. At the head of the procession moved a mass of black children from six to ten years of age, arrayed in white. Behind them marched a phalanx of colored women in white, followed by the rank and file of men.

Just in front of the man who carried the flag of America marched two men supporting a streamer that stretched half across the street on which was written the motto of the day:

"*Your Hands Are Full of Blood*"

Farther down the line was another banner reading:

"*Mr. President, why not make America safe for Democracy?*"

Negro Boy Scouts were everywhere along the line handing out dodgers on which were printed the bitterness of the race. "We march because by the Grace of God and the force of truth, the dangerous hampering walls of prejudice and inhuman in-justices must fall. We march because we deem it a crime to be silent in the face of such barbaric acts."

A few days later an outbreak of Negro soldiers occurred in Houston, Texas, from a battalion of the Twenty-fourth Infantry of the Regular Army of the United States. Sixty-five of them seized their rifles, filled their cartridge boxes and marched from Fort Sam Houston into the city. Without warning they opened fire with murderous effect on the defenseless white people. Seventeen citizens were killed, five of them policemen who were trying to maintain order.

The Negro soldiers guilty of this infamous attempt to incite their race to a bloody insurrection wore the uniform of the American Republic.

Without any question of guilt or innocence the Negro Junta in New York proposed to defend the men to the last ditch.

Eighty-five members of the battalion were arraigned and tried for their lives before a regimental court. Thirteen of them were condemned to immediate death and were hanged at dawn.

A wave of sullen fury swept the radical Negroes of the North at this act which they denounced as a blow at the race by its white foes. At least they should have been shot at sunrise and accorded the death of soldiers, instead of being hanged before day as common felons.

The real cause of the trouble was a rising tide of Negro insolence stimulated by an inflammatory press and a desire on the part of these black troops to avenge their race for the treatment of Negro soldiers at Brownsville a few years before. Brownsville is but a few hundred miles south of Houston on the Mexican border. For a riotous attack on Brownsville a Negro regiment was disbanded by President Theodore Roosevelt and their members denied the privilege of ever again wearing the uniform of the Republic. The radical Negro press of the North had savagely attacked the President for this act and had carried on a persistent campaign for the restoration of these men to the army.

At the second session of the Court Martial five more of the Fort Sam Houston battalion were sentenced to die and fifty-one condemned to life imprisonment. At the third session eleven more were condemned to death.

The Harlem Branch sent a committee to Washington, led by James Weldon Johnson, to present to President Wilson a petition signed by twelve thousand Negroes asking for clemency for the sixteen condemned men awaiting execution.

Johnson, who was an eloquent speaker, made a strong appeal for a review of the case by the War Department. The condemned men had the right of appeal to the Secretary of War, or the Commander in Chief of the Army, the President.

Mr. Wilson gave the committee a careful and respectful hearing and ordered the suspension of executions pending appeals to the War Department.

On final review of the case, he commuted the death sentence of ten to life and sent the remaining six to their death. The Negro Junta continued its fight for the imprisoned men until the entire number were released on parole. There was no question of the guilt of these men. But they were Negroes. And because they were Negroes their release was demanded.

Around every encampment of Negro troops there was trouble. Trouble between white officers and colored privates. Trouble between white and colored officers. Trouble between white civilians and colored soldiers. The bully type of man had his chance to make trouble and he made it.

Chapter 31

It is a curious fact that the enforcement of war time law against treason and seditious utterance was pressed against the white man with far more severity than against the colored.

Eugene V. Debs,[1] a man of saintly character, was arrested, tried and sentenced to a cell in the Atlanta Penitentiary for seditious words. While Dr. DuBois was allowed for months to fill his magazine with efforts to bring into disrepute the cause for which we were fighting.

Stephens tried to stop this. But it continued until a Congressional Committee summoned the editor to explain his actions. Whatever may be said of the new radical leader of the Negro race, who has displaced the careful diplomat of Tuskegee, he is no coward. He answered the questions of Congress with an insolence in every way equal to the articles of which his critics had complained.

"May I ask you," the Chairman put in, "to state in a word what is the purpose of your magazine as at present conducted?"

"To enforce the Constitution of the United States which guarantees to every man under its protection absolute equality without one lying subterfuge."

The editor emerged from his trial a victor. His sincerity and moral courage made new friends and brought confusion to his enemies.

The radical Negro press had filled the minds of colored soldiers with social equality before they sailed for France. That we would have trouble in the Army was a foregone conclusion. And we had it. The truth about the record reached the South before their return. It brought thousands of recruits into the new Ku Klux Klan, and a deep feeling of anxiety to all thoughtful men and women below the Mason-Dixon line.

---

1. Eugene Victor Debs (1855–1926), of Indiana, was a Socialist labor leader and one-time presidential candidate. Due to his outspoken opposition to World War I, Debs was imprisoned in 1918 under the 1917 Espionage Act. See Nick Salvatore, *Eugene V. Debs: Citizen and Socialist* (Urbana: University of Illinois Press, 1982).

The 369th Infantry, the 370th, and the 371st acquitted themselves with credit to their colors. Many of their individuals were cited for bravery under fire. The 371st received the French Croix de Guerre with palm in a special citation which said: "The 371st Infantry displayed in the course of the first fighting in which it participated, all the qualities of daring and bravery characteristic of first rate storm troops. Continuing its advance, in spite of heavy artillery fire which entailed severe losses, they captured many prisoners, besides cannon, machine guns, and important quantities of material."

One hundred and forty-six colored individuals were cited for acts of heroism. The troops of these three regiments were led by skilled white officers.

On the other hand, the 372nd Regiment was commanded in the main by Negro officers. On reaching the front three of them were removed for insubordination. The morale of the outfit went to pieces and the Commanding General recommended its withdrawal until the trouble could be remedied. It was not done. And when the French and white American troops made a successful advance this regiment refused to move and was retired eight miles to the rear.

In a battle of the Argonne colored troops of the 92nd Division were thrown into a panic and ran, and the French Division beside them demanded their retirement from the fighting line. Thirty Negro officers were court martialed on the charge of cowardice. The court martial was composed of officers from another regiment. The first Negro officer tried was condemned to death. General Robert L. Bullard,[2] the high Commander, ordered the suspension of its work until he made a personal investigation. The Court, however, continued the trial and four more men were sentenced to die. General Bullard appealed to the War Department and had their sentences suspended. As a Southern white man, the General did not believe it fair to hold these colored officers to the same strict standard as the whites. All punishment was, in fact, cancelled. They were not even reproved.

The 92nd Division of 27,000 men were a failure as a fighting unit and a disgrace to the American flag. They were too busy discussing their racial rights with white privates and white officers to remember what they were there for. The 372nd Negro regiment was so wrought up over the question of social equality it was utterly useless as a fighting unit.

Says General Bullard in his report: "It is commonly believed among

2. Robert Lee Bullard (1861–1947) of Alabama graduated from West Point in 1885, commanded an African American regiment during the Spanish-American War, and led first a division and later a corps of the American Expeditionary Force during World War I. See Allan R. Millett, *The General: Robert L. Bullard and Officership in the U.S. Army, 1881–1925* (Westport, Conn.: Greenwood Press, 1975).

Americans that French people have no objections to Negroes. This I quickly found to be an error. Little acts that would pass unnoticed in a white man, became with white women a cause of complaint against the Negro. This special Negro Division was charged with fifteen cases of rape. For this reason immediately after the Armistice I recommended that they be sent home first of all American troops. That they be sent in all honor, but above all that they be sent quickly. I was told that they were received at home with great glorification. Yet while its railroad trains were on the side tracks waiting to move to the port of embarkation, a French woman was ravished by five of these brutes wearing our uniforms."

Phil and Angela stood on Fifth Avenue and watched this Division march to the cheers of thousands with a feeling of nausea. A letter from France had given the tragic story of their cowardice, wrangling and brutality. They were marching now to new conflicts of color in America.

Chapter 32

The change in the attitude of the radical wing of the Negro race toward the whites which followed the World War was pronounced. The enrollment of more than two million Negroes in the army of the United States and the actual muster into service of three hundred and eighty-five thousand and their novel experiences in France roused the spirit of the blacks to the point of violence.

These marching Negroes had no sooner returned to their homes than trouble began.

Angela daily studied the news with increasing dread.

The first outbreak occurred at Charleston, South Carolina. A sailor of the Naval Training Station was shot by a Negro. And hell broke loose. The sailors got out of hand, joined with a mob of white citizens and swept the town. Two Negroes were killed and twenty wounded. Eight sailors were injured. Captain Collier mobilized his Vigilante Committee and drove to Charleston in time to join in the heavy policing of the city which followed the riot.

"I knew this would come out of the War," he said to the Commandant of the Station. "Where the hell it will stop remains to be seen."

At Longview, Texas, a black school teacher dared to publish an article in a Negro paper attacking the character of a white woman.

She had been raped and her assailant was lynched. The teacher defended the rapist and attempted to blacken the character of the woman who had been assaulted. A race riot swept the town in which four white men and a number of Negroes were wounded and a block of Negro homes burned.

At Knoxville, Tennessee, a Negro was jailed accused of murdering a white woman. The jail was stormed by a mob of whites, wrecked and sixteen prisoners released. The mob invaded the black quarters of the city. A

Negro was killed and six severely wounded. A white officer of the National Guard was killed and seven white men wounded.

In Washington, the Capital of the Nation, a far more serious riot startled America. The headlines of a newspaper announced in heavy block letters:

> *"The Sixth Attack by Negroes on White Women During the last four weeks."*

And hell was loosed under the dome of the Capitol. Mobs surged through the streets beyond the control of police or guardsmen. The Negroes armed themselves and fought back savagely. On the restoration of order the record stood, seven dead, three Negroes and four white men and hundreds wounded.

Claude McKay,[1] the Jamacian Negro poet of Harlem wrote of the event his famous, biting, defiant lines:

> "If you must die, let it not be like hogs
> Hunted and penned in an inglorious spot,
> While round us bark the mad and hungry dogs,
> Making their mock of our accursed lot.
> If we must die, O let us nobly die,
> So that our precious blood may not be shed
> In vain; then even the monsters we defy
> Shall be constrained to honor us though dead!
> O Kinsmen! We must meet the common foe
> Though far outnumbered, let us show us brave,
> And for their thousand blows deal one death blow!
> While, though before us lies the open grave,
> Like men we'll face the murderous cowardly pack,
> Pressed to the wall, dying, but fighting back!"

It remained for the State of Illinois to again furnish one of the bloodiest riots of them all. On a Sunday afternoon about four o'clock it began in a clash between white and Negro bathers on the Lake shore, spread rapidly over the city and continued for ten days in spite of all efforts of the police to quell the disturbances. White sailors and soldiers in uniform rushed the

1. Claude McKay (1889–1948) immigrated to the United States from Jamaica in 1912. He published several collections of poetry, novels, and essays. His 1919 sonnet "If We Must Die" was a rallying cry for African Americans to resist the wave of violence directed at blacks in the post-World War I years. See Tyrone Tillary, *Claude McKay: A Black Poet's Struggle for Identity* (Amherst: University of Massachusetts Press, 1992).

business section of the loop, killed two Negroes and wounded many. Negro houses in all districts were attacked and burned. The Negroes attacked the Lithuanians near the stock yards, burned forty of their houses and drove them into the streets.

During this time thirty people were killed, five hundred and thirty-seven wounded, thousands rendered homeless and destitute. This in the great Northern City of Chicago, Metropolis of the West, near the site of the Auditorium in which Abraham Lincoln was nominated for President in 1860!

The remarkable feature of this rioting was the dogged persistence and cold blooded ferocity with which the whites of Chicago continued their atrocities. In Southern towns riots flame for a day or a night, and then are over and the white people who take part in them, as a rule, are sorry it happened and set about helping the Negroes to repair the damage. The Northern white man, on the rampage in a race riot, is a different proposition. There is no let up until overwhelmed by force of arms.

But it was at Tulsa, Oklahoma, that a still bloodier and more significant race riot occurred. A Negro bootblack was arrested and jailed for an attack upon a white girl. With astounding swiftness two hundred Negroes, heavily armed, marched on the jail and surrounded it. In a short time their number had greatly increased until a mob of fully five hundred blacks were surging about the place threatening a race war which had not yet been opened.

The story of this sudden concerted uprising spread quickly. It was something new in the South and it brought an increasing crowd of unarmed whites on the scene. When the rumor had been confirmed by the sight of five hundred sullen Negroes, the whites in answer to a single call from their ranks, raided the hardware stores and seized every rifle, shot gun, and pistol with every shell and cartridge to be found.

The white mob, thus armed, swept back to the jail and Court House and confronted the blacks. An officer attempted to arrest a leader of the Negroes and was fired on. A pitched battle immediately opened, no quarter asked or given. The Negroes were finally driven from the jail and the Sheriff announced that his prisoners had been secretly removed to another city.

Through the day and night six battles were fought between the forces. On the next morning the white mob had grown to twenty-five thousand men, hysterical with rage over the killing of nine of their number. They pressed a black gang back into the Negro quarter and when they fought from the houses into which they had taken refuge, the houses were fired. It was the signal of a flaming holocaust which wiped out the entire Negro

quarter of the city, including a new church and school building. The Governor ordered out the National Guard and their Commander proclaimed martial law. Three thousand Negroes had fled the city. The remaining twelve thousand were herded into halls, churches, warehouses and camps and fed army rations. They were quickly released on individual examinations and given badges of ribbons which certified to their character.

The citizens of Tulsa called a Mass Meeting which expressed indignation at the burning of the Negro quarter and pledged the people to assist in its rebuilding.

For three days the front page of every daily newspaper in America carried the sensational story of the bloodiest race riot in the history of the South. Oklahoma was a border state, South Western, and in many ways not typical of the Eastern Seaboard, yet it was classed in the public mind as Southern.

Phil and Angela read the reports with sad hearts. They agreed that sinister influences of unusual character had been set in motion to produce such an outbreak in the South. The lawyer was doubly anxious over the situation in which he was trying to hold the Negroes to a program of sanity. They had shown a curious and confused interest in the events at Tulsa. Their telegrams to the Governor of the State and the President of the United States bordered on hysteria.

"I'm puzzled," Phil said to Angela. "That something unusual is on foot I have no doubt. The riots in Washington and Chicago have produced a crisis which bodes no good for the peace of the country. From undercover men whom I have employed to watch my own clients I have discovered the organization of a secret Negro Society called "The African Blood Brotherhood." From the first I have suspected it to be of a semi-military character. That arms and ammunitions are being shipped into the South for some purpose is certain. Oklahoma would be the ideal spot for the experiment of an armed Negro uprising in a crisis."

"Shall I do some investigating?" Angela asked.

"Not this time. It's too dangerous."

"Nonsense. I can take a room in an obscure boarding house and quietly get the facts."

The first thing of grave importance discovered on settling in Tulsa, she got from an intelligent girl in the telegraph office. She checked on every message going out of the city in the week before the riots and every day during the disturbances.

On the arming of whites, a message was sent to Muscogee, fifty-five miles from Tulsa, asking for the immediate dispatch of five hundred armed Negroes to help those who were holding the jail and Court House. The message was worded in carefully guarded sentences interspersed with code words. Angela had studied the codes and had little trouble in getting at the meaning of the messages.

The coded words clearly expressed the united efforts of the "African Blood Brotherhood." From the use made of this it was evident that a society had been organized and armed over a large part of the State and was ready for action at a moment's notice.

The call for recruits from the near-by city did not materialize. The message was reported to the mayor, and the police closed every road out of Muscogee.

The conclusion was plain that an uprising of Negroes had been planned, and that the arms and ammunition were in the possession of a secret, oath-bound, black organization. And most important that these local units had been acting under orders from a guarded headquarters somewhere outside. The tactics of John Brown to deluge a State in blood by a Negro insurrection were being repeated.

Agitators had addressed secret meetings and open mass meetings of Negroes for several months prior to the outbreak.

"Who were those agitators?" Phil asked of Angela on her return.

She smiled, "DuBois himself made a speech."

"My worst fears are being confirmed," the lawyer muttered. "My uncontrollable clients have, for a long time believed that armed organized resistance is the solution of the conflict of color in the South. I'm sure they picked on the border South Western state as the ground for their first experiment. An organized army with the local contingents of trained Negro soldiers as the nucleus of each group. It was a daring conception. The extreme radicals in the New York organization have believed and preached guardedly that such an attack by Negroes would strike terror to the whole South and produce a revolution in the relations of the races."

It did. But the revolution was exactly the opposite of the one expected. The bloodiest race riot in the history of the South had resulted in twice as many Negroes killed and wounded as whites—the burning of the homes of fifteen thousand blacks. And the inhabitants, good-natured, honest, industrious men and women, were rendered homeless and thrown on the charity of the city.

A local agitator was arrested and escaped punishment, which was to be expected. The real culprits were the radicals, who were preaching race hatred.

The effect of the tragedy was not lost on the Negroes in New York. Their program was softened by a return to legal action. Their first move was for legislation and it was more startling in its import than the plan of an armed insurrection.

James Weldon Johnson moved his headquarters to Washington and began work on a new Reconstruction Bill which would destroy the sovereignty of the States and put the South under the rule of Federal bayonets.

He first appealed to Senator Capper of Kansas, who side stepped the issue in favor of Senator Curtis who was half Indian. Senator Curtis suggested a Congressional investigation of lynchings instead of the drastic revolutionary measure proposed. Johnson refused to consider the compromise and induced Dwyer, of the House, to introduce his bill. Accordingly he presented House Bill No. 13.

The Negroes in New York quickly threw their powerful organization, with every branch in line, behind the measure. Johnson gave his entire time to lobbying for it. He haunted the corridors of Congress and made personal contacts with every member of both House and Senate. Daily he sat in the Senate lobby, sent his card in and got interviews with the men he wanted to contact.

The measure was at last forced on the calendar of the House. Southern representatives, sensing its deadly import, opposed it with savage hostility. Mr. Sisson shouted his challenge to the Negro lobby:

"Lynchings will never stop until black rascals keep their hands off white women!"

The Negro retort that only seventeen percent of last year's lynchings were for rape was answered by the statement that lynching had its origin in the South in the crime of rape and had spread to every clash of race.

The galleries of the House were jammed by throngs of Negroes. Excitement ran high. At one point in a radical speech advocating the bill the Negro crowd in the galleries rose en masse and cheered.

A member from the floor called:

"Sit down, you Niggers!"

A voice rang out:

"You're a liar. We're not Niggers!"

The speaker pounded with his gavel for order and called the Sergeant at Arms.

"On the next outburst from the galleries, clear them. Get your men ready."

The bill was voted by 230 to 119.

A thrill of exultation swept the Negroes of the North. Johnson was in high fettle. The fight in the Senate would be harder. But he expected to win. A majority of the Senate had pledged him their vote.

In the Judiciary Committee the ablest Senator in Congress opposed the Bill on the grounds that it would deprive the States of their sovereign rights and was clearly unconstitutional.

Borah's opposition, backed by a determined group of Southern Senators who resorted to filibuster, shelved the Bill.

It failed of passage, but the bold attempt of its promoters had achieved a moral victory.

Chapter 33

The coming of Judge Rex Weldon into the councils of the Negro organization had been an ugly sensation. He had hoped that Weldon's political caution, his experience in the South and his aspirations for advancement would cause his influence to be thrown with the conservative forces of the race.

But something had happened in the development of Weldon's character. He had suddenly become unapproachable. He refused to interfere with the radicals. He not only refused to give advice that was helpful, he began to side with the extremists and his egotism reached such proportions that Phil decided neither to see nor consult him about anything.

He wondered at the secret of this change. His position as a Magistrate in the City Courts, of course, had given him prestige among the Negro politicians of Harlem. His large salary had brought luxuries to which he had never before been accustomed. But even so there was something still unexplained.

Angela stumbled on the secret in an unexpected way. Bridget, the pretty daughter of the janitress, had become a great admirer of her mother's tenant and haunted her apartment.

She rushed upstairs, out of breath and rapped the brass knocker nervously.

"May I see you a minute, Miss Angela?" she panted.

"Of course, dear, come right in."

"Oh, I'm so excited I can hardly breathe. Viola DeLeon, a High School chum of mine, who used to go to the same Grammar School with Niggers on the edge of Harlem—she's working in Macy's store now—and in love with a fine German boy, tall and slender and handsome, a poet and a scholar if he does work in the shoe department. Well, Viola's father, a big brute of a stevedore, born in Alsace, has sold her to a Nigger and forced her to become engaged to him. The Nigger's a judge with a big salary. He has a fine house and white girl servants."

Viola extended her hand timidly and introduced her beau.

"My friend, Adolph Schultz," she murmured.

The young German caught her imagination. He was tall, blonde, with finely moulded features. In striking contrast to the full figure of his companion. Viola was the Germanic blonde type of Alsace-Lorraine, with honeycomb hair inclined to curl naturally, soft blue eyes of the submissive expression of the European peasant. She didn't look her age. The dimples in her rosy cheeks gave her child-like features.

"How old are you, my dear?" her hostess asked.

"Seventeen, M'am," she answered. "And Adolph's nineteen. We're too young to get married yet but we've been engaged since the first month we knew each other."

"I can believe it. You're so much alike it's weird. Your blue eyes, blonde hair and perfect complexions. After all like attracts like. Red heads generally marry red heads. Blondes marry blondes. That like attracts like is a law of nature and nature's another name for God——"

She paused, took the girl's hand, led her to the couch, sat down beside her, and talked of her tragedy.

"When we got back to the flat," Viola explained, "I didn't want the judge to come up with me. But he pushed right through the door, lit a cigar, drew a flask of whiskey from his pocket and asked me for ice and Club Soda. I didn't know what Club Soda was. Dad always drinks his liquor straight. So I gave him ice and plain water. He flicked the ashes from his cigar, made a wry face with his thick lips and pulled me down on the couch beside him. I drew back but he only laughed.

"'Don't be so shy, honey girl. We're engaged to be married, you know. We must get acquainted.' He tried to put his arm around me but I pushed him away and backed close against the arm of the couch.

"'Your father told me today that we could fix the wedding day,' he said. I told him I was too young to get married and I wouldn't. Then he said: 'Why don't you out with it? You object to marrying a Negro. That's it, am I right?' I told him—yes—that I didn't like Niggers.

"He puffed big rings of smoke to the ceiling, leaned back and said: 'You're too young yet to understand. When you're a little older you'll be proud of my race. Your husband's race. A Negro can live his life in this town exactly as he pleases. He is free to marry white or black. He can gamble, he can drink, he can sport with the best of them. He plays on the athletic teams. He acts on the stage. He sings. He publishes his books. He worships in churches as big and fine as any white man's. He holds high office. I sit on the bench of this city and pass in judgment every day on a procession of white men and women. A black man is a judge in Chicago. A black woman sits on the School Board of Cleveland and lays out the work for white students. Jack Johnson was champion of the prize ring longer than any white man. We've big lawyers at the Bar. We are pushing into the movies. We own millions of dollars' worth of property. We have big colleges. The Nigger rarely kills himself. Twenty thousand white people commit suicide every year in this country. When we're married you'll be proud of me. You've never known anything but skimping and poverty. I'll set you up in a home on the Avenue. You'll have a car and your own chauffeur. I have only white servants in my house. I'll dress you like a queen.'

"I told him I didn't want social gathering with Niggers. He said I'd never seen one. He'd take me to the mansion of Oswald Garrison Villard at his next reception and I'd see what it was like. He said there'd be one next week and he'd take me.

"I told him I was in love with a German boy. He said he had heard about it but it was only puppy love. He'd teach me what the love of a real man means. All of a sudden he pulled me into his arms and pushed his ugly cracked lips against mine and held me there until I thought I would die——"

Angela suddenly went white, walked to the window and opened it.

"I fought loose," the girl went on, "but he just laughed and said I'd get used to a man bye and bye. He didn't mean to go too fast. He'd be more careful. He left then and said he'd call for me in his car to take me to the reception next Friday night at nine o'clock. Said a distinguished Judge couldn't be among the first to arrive."

"Did he fix the wedding date?" Angela asked.

"He said he'd talk that over with my Dad and they'd decide."

"All right, dear, play along with him for the moment. Go to the reception. But let me know as soon as the day is fixed. I'll see what can be done to stop it."

"You *can* do something, can't you?" she asked eagerly.

"I think so. I'll try."

Chapter 34

Weldon decided to play a trump card in an appeal to luxury. He asked the big stevedore if he could fit his daughter out in complete evening dress for a Villard reception.

"Why not?" the father asked. "You've got the dough. She's going to be your wife. Buy her all the clothes you want. She'll maybe loosen up. Never saw a girl yet who isn't daft about clothes."

When the judge called Viola on the telephone and suggested the evening costume she refused to go with him. "No," she said angrily. "I don't want your clothes. I'm not going to marry you. I've told you that a hundred times."

"But your father says you are. He's pleased to have me get you a stunning outfit for the reception. I want you to be the best dressed woman there. I'll send a complete rig with a woman to fit you!"

When her father came home the night of the reception she plucked up courage to defy him. "I'll not march into a crowd of people half naked hanging on that Nigger's arm."

He glared at her.

"What the hell you mean?"

"The clothes he bought don't half cover me."

"Put 'em on and let me see," he growled. "Put everything on just like you're goin' out."

She obeyed and stood before him. He looked at her in surprise. "Damned if you ain't naked," he grunted. "And I will say you're a good looker, if you are a fool. Maybe I'm sellin' you too cheap. If I could get you in the open market, by God, I might trade ye to a millionaire."

"Why don't you wait and try it?"

He shook his shaggy head. "No. I ain't got time to fool with you. A bird in the hand is worth two in the bush. The Nigger'll give me a job for life that will save me from workin' any more."

"I'm not going out with him in this dress."

"You're goin', kid."

"I'm not."

The words had scarcely passed her lips when he slapped her a blow on the side of the head that sent her spinning across the room against the wall. He followed towering over her.

"Do you want me to take a whip to you?" he shouted.

"No," she cowered.

"All right. Keep the dress on then and do as you're told. If he wants to show your naked back to his gang it's all right with me."

When Angela heard the story of the reception it was impossible to keep back the tears at the child's sincerity when she described her shame before the vulgar eyes that had devoured her. She slipped an arm about the girl and drew her head down on her shoulder.

"There, darling, don't cry. I'll help you. You're still determined you'll not go through with it?"

"I'll die first."

"Then he can't make you."

"What'll I do, though, if they rush me into it? My father will kill me if I disobey him."

"All right. There are things worse than death."

Chapter 35

The earth seemed to have opened and swallowed Viola. She had resigned her job at the store and disappeared. The manager was glad to be rid of the publicity that might grow out of her association with a Negro.

Bridget in alarm went to the store and brought Adolph to see Angela.

"What do you make of it?" she asked.

"I think her father has locked her up and she's being guarded. I watched my chance when her old man had gone and tried to get in. A terrible looking woman answered the door bell and without a word pushed me down the stairs. Luckily I got hold of the rail and saved myself an ugly fall."

"Did you go back?"

"Yes. Twice."

"Good boy," Angela smiled.

"I watched the back window of their apartment from a friend's across the well in the rear. The shades were down, but twice I saw Viola's shadow cross. They've got her locked up under guard of the old hell cat. I'm sure of it."

She appealed to Phil over the telephone and asked him to swear out a writ of *habeas corpus* as he did for young Van Vetchen.

"It can't be done, dear," he replied. "This is entirely different. The girl's in her own home with her father. She's a minor. He has absolute power in the case."

"To imprison and torture her if he likes?"

"Not that, no. But you'll have to produce evidence to the court that her father is holding her a prisoner and subjecting her to physical cruelty without cause. If she has disobeyed him he can lock her up to prevent her running away. Who would sue out a writ? You are not a kinswoman. The boy has no claim in law."

"Couldn't I act as her friend?"

"You might if you had any grounds on which to act. But you'd run the risk of notoriety that might seriously affect your life. I wouldn't do that."

"I thought you could do almost anything with a writ."

"You can but this happens to be an exception. If the boy will get someone in the house to swear to the fact that her father is beating and abusing her I could act. Otherwise, no."

"If Adolph manages to get her out, will you help them secure a marriage license?"

"Yes. And I'll give a hundred dollars toward setting them up in housekeeping. It's the only solution."

"You're a brick, Phil! I'll match yours. Two hundred will turn the trick."

She faced Adolph.

"How many feet is it across that well to Viola's flat?"

"Not more than ten."

"All right. Get two of your friends to help you. Push a wide ladder, covered by two boards, across to her window. Have one of your friends ring the bell and try to get in from the front. While the old woman is wrangling with him, you cross over on the ladder and get Viola. Mr. Stephens and I will give you two hundred dollars as a wedding present. Will you dare to do this?"

"And thank God for the chance!"

"When you get her out of the flat, rush her straight to Mr. Stephens—here's his home address. He will send her to a hotel for the night and next morning take you both down to get the license."

Phil called Angela to witness the ceremony at eleven o'clock the following day. Before two they were established in a rooming house in the crowded quarter within three blocks of Macy's store. Adolph returned to his job and Angela promised to get his wife a new position.

Weldon checked on the records at City Hall, discovered the marriage and flew into a violent rage. He rushed to the store and asked an immediate interview with the manager. To his surprise the owner confronted him.

"Well, sir, what is it?" the merchant prince inquired.

"I am judge Rex Weldon of the city courts. I demand the immediate discharge of Adolph Schultz at present employed in your shoe department."

"On what grounds, pray?"

"For abducting and marrying a minor employee of your store, to whom I was engaged."

"A German boy has married a Negress?"

"No. A beautiful white girl whose father had consented to our betrothal. I demand his discharge. I've some influential friends in this town."

The merchant surveyed Weldon from head to foot, suddenly gripped his arm, led him to the door and kicked him through it.

"Tell your influential friends that I turned out to be a white man whose people were born in Columbus, Georgia!"

Chapter 36

A week after the hurried marriage Phil sat in his office thinking of Angela. He saw with increasing clearness that it was the man of direct action who got his woman. The German boy made but a feeble gesture in the struggle for the mastery of Viola's life, until he had put into the fight more muscle and less romantic dreaming.

He asked himself the question of his own responsibility for Angela's broken life. He, too, had played the role of romantic dreamer.

And he had continued his methods of yielding and deference and futile waiting. Was there any sense in it? Years were slipping by. Her state of mind was still a morbid brooding over a past which nothing could change. It was the contradiction in essentials of the religion into which she had grown. Her belief in the presence of God in her daily thought and life was inconsistent with brooding.

He made up his mind to fight for the right to make her happy. To fight her memories. To fight her fixed obsession that she had lived through and beyond the idea of sex. It was silly. She was the most magnetic woman he had ever known.

He began to telephone daily and took her to dinner with increasing regularity. Not a week passed now that he didn't send her flowers.

"You must have a big case, Phil, to indulge in such extravagances."

"I'm working on a big case with those flowers," he said boldly.

"Have we got to go all over that again?"

"Yes, we have," was the emphatic answer. "It's June. These beautiful days stir me. I'm full of speeches you've told me not to make. I can say them in flowers. You love them if you don't love me."

She smiled and remained silent as she buried her face in a mass of yellow roses.

"Which reminds me that you have not had a ride in my new car. I'm a good driver. I want to take you to a road house I've discovered in the Tuxedo Mountains. Shall we go there for dinner tonight?"

"Why not?" she smiled. "I'll be ready at seven."

"Six thirty would be better if you can make it. I haven't yet reserved a table. The place may be crowded."

"Six thirty," she repeated.

She dressed in high spirits. The marriage of Viola, her flight and hiding had depressed her. The memories the affair had stirred were sickening. She welcomed a diversion.

"What's the matter with me now?" she laughed. "Am I getting looney, too?"

Seated in the car Phil pressed her hand and said:

"Relax now and let's have a good time. This is a lark. No serious frowns. No 'Don't do this' and 'don't do that.'"

"That depends," she said, "on how well you behave. I won't ride with a man who drives with one hand."

He laughed.

An hour later they drew up under the porte-cochere of a rugged stone built inn nestling against the foot of a mountain. An elaborate formal garden spread its flower beds and rose banks across a brook.

Angela threw an admiring glance at the moonlit garden before entering.

"It's beautiful. Who on earth could have built such a road house?"

"There's a story in that, too. I'll tell you tonight. It's one of the reasons I brought you here."

The immense dining room was crowded with handsomely dressed men and women.

"Heavens!" Angela exclaimed. "We'll never get a table."

"Wouldn't, if I hadn't engaged one over long distance."

As her escort led her through the throng to a small, reserved table in an alcove, she saw with a shock of surprise that the man she was with was the magnet of every woman's eye in the place. She hadn't thought Phil Stephens so handsome before. When they were seated she took a second look. He had grown into a very handsome and distinguished looking man.

"The girls seem to know you," she teased.

"Never here in my life before."

"I'll bet you come again."

"If you'll come with me."

"You're developing a new technique," she smiled.

"An improvement, don't you think?"

"Maybe. Who on earth built this place? It must have cost a million—this magnificent Club House, with a hundred rooms at least for guests, tennis and golf course and swimming pool. The owner must have money to burn."

"He has. And his life has crossed mine in a curious way. I'm expecting to see him here tonight. I want your impression of him. His name in Antonio Murino, supposed to be of Italian extraction."

He had scarcely finished the sentence when a tall, dark man of unusually handsome features touched Phil's shoulder.

"Delighted to have you with us tonight, Mr. Stephens."

Phil rose and clasped the outstretched hand.

"Miss Cameron, Mr. Murino."

The man extended his hand carelessly until he caught the full view of Angela's face. He stared for a second but caught himself in time to grasp her hand. That he held it in a foolish way was not lost on her escort. And that she was equally surprised and interested still further worried him. He'd put the fellow in his place and tell her all about him before the evening was over. In the meanwhile the owner accepted Phil's invitation, casually seated himself and sent for his head waiter.

When the man had gone to find him, Murino smiled in rapt attention at the most remarkable woman he had ever met, and she had flushed under his steady gaze.

Phil breathed a sigh of relief when he rose and left in answer to a summons from a group of important looking men.

Angela's eyes followed the retreating figure that moved easily and gracefully among the crowded tables.

"A fascinating person," she whispered.

"Yes, very," was the short answer. "He is believed to be a high official in our new secret super government of crime."

"A criminal? That man? Don't make me laugh. I believe you're jealous."

"I was never more serious in my life. This place is one of a chain of luxurious road houses which he owns or controls. Several of them located on navigable waters in touch with the fleet of rum runners that hover off our coast day and night. They say his income was not less than ten million dollars last year and may be doubled this year. For the first time in our history crime has been organized. The authorities no longer cope with the lone wolf, but with a secret organization that makes its own laws and executes them. I've often wondered what will happen to us if the millions of convicts we graduate from our prisons get together with our seven million aliens under the leadership of a brilliant daring mind."

"I thought we were to relax tonight," Angela frowned a little bored.

"You don't take Murino seriously, I see," Phil protested.

"Frankly, no."

"Well, I have to. He came into my office this week and made me an offer to act as their attorney that fairly took my breath. The figure he named as my yearly salary is ten times larger than the sum I'm now earning and the prospects held out for an increase were still more startling."

"And you turned it down, of course."

"The thing that worries me is, I didn't."

"Which proves you don't believe for a moment the man's a criminal."

"A very remarkable one if he is. I promised to consider his offer. I'm ashamed that I did. But it stunned me."

"He must be thinking of a merger," she said as if talking to herself. The idea suddenly started a train of thought destined to change the current of her life, but the man beside her had not heard. At the moment their minds were miles apart.

He had been talking of one thing, thinking of another as he watched Angela.

"Shall we stroll in the garden?" he suggested. "It's an immense affair stretching into the valley. I've something important to tell you."

She rose smiling.

"I thought you thought what you were saying was important."

"Only mildly so tonight. I'll talk to you about Murino later."

They rose and left the crowded room, all eyes following the handsome couple who were leaving so early.

In the valley flooded with silver light they found a seat beside a bank of roses at the brook. The music of its waters rippling over the stones reminded both of a brook in the California mountains.

"You're doing it beautifully, Phil. I hope I'll not be too great a disappointment."

"Don't be flippant—please," he frowned. "I've never seen this place before but it fits my mood tonight. I've formed a plan on which I've set my heart. Nothing can turn me from it. And I don't believe any power on earth can defeat it."

"Pretty sure of yourself."

"Sure of myself," he repeated, "not so sure of you. How long, dearest, are you going to hold me at arm's length?"

"I didn't know you were so close."

"Well, I am. And I'm not going to let you get farther from me again. This attempt on your part to take the veil and yet live in the world can't last. I'm going to wake you out of memories that should have died years ago. God made you to love and be loved."

He suddenly drew her into his arms and kissed her passionately.

"Kisses mean nothing, Phil dear, unless both hearts are in them. I felt no response. It meant nothing. The part of me that should have responded is dead. I couldn't cheat you."

"I'll love the dead heart back to life again. I'll make you forget that night in Piedmont. It was my fault it ever happened."

"Your fault?"

"Yes. If I had been more of a man in my courtship and less the timid dreamer I could have married you and brought you to grace the old Stephens house. As my wife, surrounded by faithful servants, the awful thing that came to you in the isolated cottage could never have happened. I was a romantic fool who stood paralyzed while a red-headed boy walked off with you. I played the role of a weakling and got what I deserved. But I never realized until later that I had allowed you to drift into a position where the tragedy that came to you could have happened. I might have won—yes—even after you turned me down, but for the pride of a sentimental fool. In your heart of heart tonight you know I might have, too. You loved me in the beginning, and I was a damned fool!"

He spoke the last words with a bitterness that touched, Angela.

"Don't say that, Phil," she said. "I think too much of you to allow you to talk about yourself like that."

"You love me but you won't say so."

"I do say so. I love you. I've always loved you. And I always will love you. But not as you want me to."

He smiled.

She looked into his eyes and brushed the hair back from his forehead in a tender gesture.

"I love you, darling!" he whispered. "There's a divine something in you that will hold me forever."

She lifted her head.

"Please don't say any more now, dear. You're fine and generous. In you I see that the Age of Chivalry has not quite passed."

"Let me teach you to live again, dear."

She smiled.

"You are the finest man I know. And I like, you to court me. It restores my self respect."

He laughed, drew her to her feet, led her back to the restaurant and said goodnight to Murino.

"Call at my office at noon tomorrow and we'll talk things over."

"At noon, tomorrow," the Italian repeated.

The lawyer frowned at the eagerness in his eyes as he pressed Angela's hand, bowed and kissed it.

Chapter 37

Phil saw Murino at noon and refused to act as his attorney. A large increase of salary was offered and met with a curt refusal.

"It's not a question of money, Murino," he said stiffly. "You couldn't get my services at any price. You are working outside the law. And it's not for me."

The Italian spread his hands in a gesture of conciliation.

"Then there's no more to be said. I know I can trust you to keep in confidence things I had to tell you about my operations."

"You can trust me."

Within half an hour after Murino had disappeared through his side door, the lawyer received a long distance call from the office of the Attorney General in Washington asking for a conference at the earliest possible time. If the offer he would make was accepted, he said, it would take two weeks to put him in possession of the facts. He was asked to come prepared to spend that much time in the various legal departments if they could agree on the work.

What it meant he could not imagine. But a vague suspicion shot through his mind that Murino was involved in it. The two things came so close together there must be a connection. It was possible that the leader of the Government of Crime had learned through his agents in Washington of the coming offer and made a better one to anticipate it.

He called Angela and broke his engagement for a ride into the country and dinner.

"Why, Phil," she said, "I'm disappointed that your ardor has cooled so quickly. You're talking like a husband side stepping his wife. This Washington business sounds funny to me."

"I swear it's true, dearest," he protested. "I've no choice. I must catch the next train that leaves in an hour. It's something important you can depend on it. I talked with the Attorney General himself and he spoke to me like a brother from the lodge. I'm awfully flattered. Yes—sure—I do think I'm a man of importance."

"And so you are. Hurry to the conference, and hurry back here and tell me what it's all about."

"I will," he said in relief.

He had barely time to catch his train when a glistening Rolls-Royce stopped in front of her apartment. She watched it with a touch of envy, and started when the handsome figure of Murino emerged.

It flashed through her mind that this man knew every step Phil was taking. He timed his call almost to the minute of his departure for Washington.

There was something uncanny about his omniscience. If Phil's belief in his leadership in a vast Super Government on Crime was true, it was easily accounted for. He would have a number of spies under his control. Entrenched in millions he was beyond reach of the law. He directed a Government dependent on his will alone. She had heard the mysterious figure discussed often in the Social Science class in Columbia. But face to face with the ogre, it was too fantastic for words. The man she had met was fascinating. She felt her heart beat quicker at the conquest she must have made to bring this early unceremonious call.

She preened herself in the mirror before answering his rap on the knocker, wondering how he had discovered her address.

He bowed gracefully as she opened the door.

"Pardon my calling without notice, my dear Miss Cameron," he said. "But I didn't have your telephone number. Managed to get your address and here I am."

"Won't you come in?" she smiled.

He entered and presented her a box of orchids.

"For you this evening. I've planned a little dinner in your honor at my country home in Westchester. I want you to see it."

She hesitated and he hastened to add, "I assure you of a chaperone. I've a good stage mother to preside over the festival. She lives there and I spend a lot of time with her first and last. I love the place."

The idea of such a trip in the country with a mysterious stranger whose reputation was a puzzle, was, of course, preposterous. But the spirit of adventure stirred in her. She had lived alone too much. Why shouldn't she go? Surely she would know how to take care of herself. Life had no blacker secrets than those she knew.

She answered with a laugh.

"Your proposal is very unconventional."

"You're not a conventional young woman."

"But how could you guess that?"

"I didn't guess. I knew by intuition. I'm a student of character. I have to be in my business to survive. I knew that you had passed through deep experiences in life the minute I met you. There's a dignity and poise about you."

"I've had experience, yes," she admitted frankly. "My husband and son are both dead."

"You must have married very young."

"At eighteen."

"Come, let's have a little fun tonight. It will do you good."

He smiled in his most ingratiating way and she answered with a smile.

"All right," she agreed. "I'll try almost anything once. I'm in a reckless mood for some reason."

"Good. I'll dismiss the chauffeur and drive the car myself. I love to drive."

The car swept through a side street and turned up Broadway.

"You were born in Northern Italy?" she ventured.

"Milan. How did you guess it?"

"I've intuition, too," she parried.

From a corner of her eye she studied him. Handsome, poised, witty, gracious. His clothes seemed to have grown on his graceful, well set figure. The idea that such a man was a master criminal was absurd.

He watched her, too. Occasionally their eyes met unexpectedly and his drooping lids fell lower. Whether his interest was merely the tribute which every strong man must pay to a beautiful girl, or something deeper she couldn't guess as yet, She couldn't throw off the impression of utter sincerity, which his every move and act gave. He was a new kind of man. A kind she had often dreamed about and wished to know. She was glad she had the common sense to accept his invitation and study his character. She had her chance tonight and suddenly made up her mind to draw him out in a mild flirtation. Phil would resent it, of course, but he had no right to order her life. No man now or ever would have again.

The longer she watched him the more curious she became about his extraordinary personality. Phil's wild theories about the source of wealth was nonsense. This man was born to money and high position.

"You certainly drive like a veteran!" she exclaimed.

"Driven since I was eleven years old," he nodded.

The way he threaded his way through the crowded section of the city was a constant source of admiration. He was part of the throbbing machine that answered his slightest touch with quick obedience.

He slowed down as he passed through a suburban section infested by toughs. Men were staggering down the highway in all stages of drunkenness. Here and there a figure lay prostrate beside the road.

"Mute evidence of a 'Noble Experiment'!" he muttered as the car crept past a crowd bending over a body apparently dead.

A drunk yelled, "We live but once!"

Clear of the ugly place the car speeded through the deepening shadows of the trees and in half an hour drew up before a massive iron grill and gate that opened through a stone wall. A keeper on duty touched his cap and swung them wide. The lights of a house on the hill glimmered through the forests. The car wound its way up the steep grade, shot under the porte cochere and a liveried footman opened the door.

The spacious reception hall hummed with the conversation of fifty odd guests. A maid led Angela to the first room at the head of the stairs where the stage mother received her graciously.

When she returned to the floor below the door of the ball room had been thrown open. An orchestra of sixteen pieces took their places on the platform and Murino faced Angela claiming the first dance.

"It's mine you know, Miss Cameron. The dinner is in your honor."

"I appreciate the tribute," she laughed as his arm encircled her waist.

The host chatted pleasantly with his guests, saw to it his retinue of servants supplied every want, introduced Angela at every turn to groups of admirers, then excused himself for a minute. The men rushed the guest of honor. She danced with half a dozen whose names she couldn't remember.

The three wings of the house were constructed about a magnificent court that had been planned for a formal garden by the man who built the place. The new master had roofed this court with steel ribbed glass and transformed it into a replica of famous houses at Pompeii, with added touches of luxury the Romans had never dreamed.

At midnight the orchestra filed out of the ballroom for their supper and all guests were requested to change their formal evening clothes for one piece bathing suits provided in assorted sizes in each room. An hour's swim was on the program to proceed the banquet at one.

Angela selected an emerald green silk jersey and a darker green beach robe which she carried over her arm. She was surprised at the perfection of Murino's figure when he greeted her. There was a strength about it that suggested enormous reserve power.

Laughing, chatting and a little self conscious, she entered the court and paused breathless at the tropical splendor. The low walls were banks of gorgeous roses in full bloom, their perfume filling the air. In the center stood the banquet table. Instead of modern chairs surrounding it, soft long cushions inclined from the table to the ground. A reproduction of the Roman banquet table at the zenith of Rome's glory. Goblets of solid gold gleamed among garlands of rare flowers, orchids predominating. Murino watched her admiration with a smile.

The attendants were dressed in the costume of Roman servants. The illusion of a leap backward more than two thousand years was complete.

Musicians from a rose bower touched soft stringed instruments with sensuous caress. The place glowed with indirect light softened to the mellow tones of the moon.

At either end of the banquet table shimmered two clear pools of water as warm as the air of the court. Boys and girls were diving, swimming, and splashing in the blue depth, naked limbs glistening in the opal lights.

Angela sat down on a marble bench and watched the fun. Murino joined her.

"Don't believe I care to swim. Do you mind?" she said.

He didn't mind. He curled up at her feet and watched her.

Cymbals sounded and the swimmers rushed the table.

"Goodness!" Angela said. "How do you work it?"

"Recline on the couch, of course," he replied, "as once the ancient Romans did."

He threw himself full length on a cushion.

Angela stretched herself on the one beside him. Awkwardly they managed the first course. By the time the roasts were served and champagne began to flow freely they had become experts. They rolled on their stomachs and reached the plates with sure touch. Rolled on their backs, crossed their legs, and ate with the poise of the ancients.

Swift attendants piled plates with every delicacy money could buy and tempted their palates with the choicest wine from the cellars of Europe. And over all floated the strains of entrancing music.

At three o'clock, through the center of the banquet table a huge pie slowly rose. The crust was suddenly broken from within. A half dozen beautiful girls in costumes of baby chicks leaped out, ran down the couches and did an intriguing dance. The revelers cheered wildly and drank a toast to them.

"Will you give me a cup of coffee in your lovely little apartment if I drive you home now swiftly and safely?" Murino asked an hour later.

"With pleasure."

He studied her room as he sipped the coffee.

"You have perfect taste, young lady," he observed. "There's not a discordant note in your little nest, either of line or color."

"Thanks."

"And now," he began seriously, "I'm coming to the point. I love you and have loved you from the minute we met in the Tuxedo Mountains. And what's more you are the first woman I've ever loved. The first woman to whom I've made that declaration. I confess I've been a cynic. Women meant nothing. Along you came, and in a second bowled me over completely. I swear to you I never slept a wink last night. Of all the forms of love, love at first sight has been the one impossible joke to me. A sex impulse, maybe at first sight, but not love. Yet it came to me with a force that all but knocked me senseless."

He paused and held her gaze for a moment.

"Tell me honestly. You surely felt some reaction to the storm inside me?"

"Yes," she answered candidly. "I did feel strangely drawn to you and for some mysterious reason I was not surprised when your car stopped at my door. Except to wonder where you got my address."

"A little secret of my trade. Can't give it away at once. Otherwise I'm going to make a clean breast of it and tell you exactly who I am. It means too much to me that you should hear the story of my life from hostile lips."

"You can trust me?" she interrupted.

"Absolutely. You're my kind of woman. I ask of you no assurances. You're dead game. I know that by intuition deeper than reason."

He was silent a moment as if feeling for words. What he said was a distinct shock.

"I can't ask you to marry me, because I'm married by the laws of a Church that refuses divorce. Married to a shallow type of girl who will never ask for a divorce under any law. Everything real between us ended while I was fighting in France."

"In France?"

"Yes. One of a thousand idiotic marriages that were made in Great Britain on the eve of leaving for the front. You see, I'm not an Italian. I'm an Irishman, a brother of Dion O'Bannion, the famous bootleg leader who was killed two years ago. I left Ireland under a cloud. My enemies call me a convict. True and not true. In a fight, in defense of my life, I killed a man. A man who attacked me with deliberate purpose to kill. Because of my hatred, which was well known, his rich relatives secured my unjust conviction for murder. I was thrown into a filthy prison for life. I escaped and made my way to Chicago where I served an apprenticeship as a bootlegger under my brother. He was a man of little education, and violent passions. His tragic end taught me caution as the first principle of life. I came here and prospered."

"As a bootlegger?" she interrupted.

"As a bootlegger, first, last, and always—and only as a bootlegger, in reality a wholesale liquor dealer. I have never soiled my hands with one of the rackets that are now gripping this country with iron hands. I loathe the rats who infest our trade and use its millions to organize these gangs. My business is supplying good drink to a thirsty world. I consider it legitimate in spite of the letter of laws the American people despise. There are millions who refuse to believe it a crime to drink beer, wine, or liquor. I sell a supply. Exactly as any other merchant supplies the demands of his customers, I cater to their thirst. There's an element of risk in the work, a daring, a steady nerve in its execution, that appeals to my imagination. It's really a form of sport."

He paused and laughed.

"And I'm going to protect my trade from the wets as much as the drys. I contribute secretly to both forces and watch both with an eagle eye. If the Wets should succeed in repealing the Prohibition Law, my enormous business would be ruined. If the Drys could enforce the law, they would ruin me. I play one against the other and stand pat. Ten years more and I'll be set for life. I'm not boasting. I've more money now than I can count. The people of the United States are spending money, twice as much, for drink as they did before Prohibition. I'll get my share of the two billions that pour annually into the hands of the bootleggers. It'll be a lion's share, too. I'm not the 'Master Mind' they talk about. There's no such animal. But I am one of ten or fifteen men who control the liquor trade in America. And there's no power on earth or in hell that can break my control as long as the Prohibition laws stand. And believe me we are doing our part to make them stand. Last year I gave a million to the Drys. In ways, of course, that could not be traced. Why not? It's a hard boiled business proposition."

He stopped abruptly and took Angela's hand.

"I'm going to clear out of this insane country and settle in a quiet spot of the old world where people know how to live. I'm desperately, hopelessly and for all time in love with you. Could you like me?"

"You're a very handsome, likeable young man," she fenced. "Easy to look at. How well you'd wear I couldn't say."

"With you, I'll be a slave. I'm not a rounder with women. I've never been. I've had light experiences, that meant nothing. You are the only girl who has ever gotten under my skin. You're the kind of girl I've always dreamed at the head of my table,—yes, and—well—rocking babies to sleep for me."

She pursed her lips and interrupted him.

"A rather reckless dream for a man who can not marry, don't you think?"

"Well, now, is it?" he drawled. "As a moden woman look the thing squarely in the face. I can't marry without committing a felony called bigamy, a serious prison offense. But I can pledge you my love and protection for life. And if I'm ever free, I'll beg you to marry me. You will be independent. I'll never intrude in a way that will embarrass you. I'll guard your welfare——"

She laughed heartily.

"You have an uncanny knowledge of other people's lives. Will you be frank with me if I ask you a plain question? Have you any knowledge of my personal life before I came to New York?"

"None whatever, I swear it. I haven't the remotest idea where you were born and lived. I know, of course, you are a Southern girl. Your soft sweet accent reveals that. No matter where you come from, no matter what your rearing, you are today a modern of moderns. In your heart you don't stickle for conventions. You leave me the impression of a mind that could despise the whole rigamarole of social taboos. You certainly flout the law in a night club and speakeasies. Very unconventional. Why not play the big game? You would grace any court in Europe and be its sensation. We live in a new world. Your grandmother's has passed. Conventions, laws, customs pass and make way for new ideas. Marriage is one of the customs that may pass in time, though I don't think so. Love is the one force that will survive all change and make new laws. How about it?"

She faced him squarely.

"You're a very persuasive young man. I'll think it over in the cold light of day after I've slept ten hours."

"You don't refuse me?" he asked eagerly.

"Nor accept you," was the firm answer. "Your dead earnestness, and sincerity, your plausible way of looking at life, I confess, have startled me. I must have scoffed at law and conventions and invited this sort of proposal or I would not have ventured on that dinner with you tonight. But I don't think I've ever scoffed at marriage. I've always thought of it as the one folly we wish our daughters to commit. Defiance of law may have become with me a mental habit in a topsy-turvy world. But to scorn marriage is a rather stunning thing for a girl to face in a moment, isn't it?"

He pressed her hand as he was about to leave.

"You don't have to decide in a moment. May I see you tomorrow night?"

"Surely."

"At seven?"

"Seven," she repeated.

Chapter 38

Angela, thoroughly tired, fell into bed and was soon asleep, firmly closing her mind against all thought of the startling events of the night. She had gained this mastery of mind within the quiet walls of the Order at San José. The most valuable lesson she had ever learned in life. A moment's touch of an idea could do no harm. It was the harboring of poisonous thought that struck to the depths of being.

She rose at noon, refreshed by six hours sound sleep. Rose with a quick sense of new interests that excited her to her finger tips. The experience through which she had passed had widened her horizon. She realized for the first time the narrowness of the life she had been living. There was a new sense of freedom and power. A few days ago the remarkable man whom she had met was going the even tenor of his way undisturbed by the thought of a woman, his dangerous trade absorbing every talent.

His eyes had looked into hers and the purpose of life had been changed. He had lived to amass millions for their power over men. He was living today with but a single thought, the winning and possession of a woman. He was still fighting for wealth but not for its mere power over men. He would have millions because with them he could make happy the woman he loved.

There could be no doubt about this transformation of character. Every word he had spoken, every act, every gesture confirmed it in the cold light of morning.

Under the laws of convention most women would have gone into hysterics at the offer of an establishment without the ceremony of marriage. She wondered for a moment what had come over her that she had felt no such indignation as the occasion called for. What had come over modern society to make her attitude possible? The foundations of the social, economic, and moral world had been undermined by the World War—

certainly—but had this sinking gone to the point of submergence of character? She asked herself the searching personal question. In her case the tragedy which she had suffered might account for anything. Except for the fact that her life had been saved and rebuilt on stronger foundations by a grasp of the new philosophy taught her by Ann Lovelace and the Order at San José.

The new freedom which she felt fully for the first time had its roots deeper than the effects of any event that was purely personal. It grew out of the swiftly changing standards of a new age dawning in the world. An age in which the power of woman would be raised to the nth degree.

Woman had always played a greater role in human history than its record showed. Historians were loath to give to Eve's daughters their due. History is not a science. It is merely the light from a lantern held in the hand of an individual writer. What we see depends on the steadiness of the hand that holds this lantern and the angle at which it is held. Most historians have been men of narrow minds, of a limited sense of sex, of singleness of purpose in presenting a partisan view.

In spite of this, the record of woman's influence over men has been a startling one. No great man has ruled the world at any period free from her influence. The greatest statesmen have often been putty in her hands. The keen mind of France, long ago, worked out the formula for the solution of every mystery of life—"Look for the woman!"

Woman's Suffrage so far had been a dismal failure because she had found no expression of the mysterious power of her sex at the ballot box. She had in fact lost power, instead of gaining it. The ballot has simply been multiplied by two. How long this anomaly could last would depend, of course, on the possibility of woman's leadership. Once conscious of both her full personal and civic power, woman may yet dominate human society.

She felt this morning a throb of this new inheritance. What she would do with it was as yet in a mist. But the miracle of it stirred her imagination. Yesterday she lived a narrow life in comparative poverty. Today every luxury of which her mind could dream was hers for the taking.

She dressed with care, humming a song of her childhood. Could it be that this adventure had brought a rebirth of her conscious woman's life? A thing she had counted as dead. Might not a new girlhood have grown in her being and found in this excitement the expression of a new womanhood? The idea was fantastic, of course. Yet we are the sum of the life we have lived and the new impulses born of that life.

She made no effort to solve the riddle the adventure had raised in her mind. But she realized sharply that life had suddenly broadened, become more interesting, more exciting, more worth while. She thanked God for it and faced the future with a smile.

When her telephone rang she knew instinctively who was on the line. Murino's voice was low, but clear and full of a subtle quality of emotion that she caught instantly.

"I hope you've quite recovered from last night's shocks?"

"Oh, quite," was the prompt answer. "In fact I'm cheerful and stronger than usual."

"Would your strength be equal to a dash out to the end of Long Island with me for a good dinner and another mild adventure?"

"It would," she laughed.

"Fine. The chariot will be at your door promptly at seven."

"I'll be ready."

Clearing the traffic of the first forty miles, Murino gradually increased the speed until the dial registered eighty miles an hour. She wouldn't have known it save for the telltale hand. In an hour and three quarters they drew up under the marquee of a Country Club on the water's edge at Montauk Point. Again a crowded dining room of well dressed people. The table he had reserved looked out over the waters of ocean and sound where they mingle tides at the tip of Long Island. The moon flooded the water with an indescribable brilliance.

"This is the finest place on the Island, you know," he observed as he settled in his seat.

"And you own it, I suppose?"

"Not exactly. But I control it through a partner who owns it. I'm going to let you see the wheels go round in one of the big machines of the modern world tonight, if you like."

"I'd like it very much. You've roused my curiosity."

The dinner over, he finished his cigarette and they rose.

"If you're ready we'll stroll along the beach until we see the big water wheel go round."

He led her through the moonlit grounds to a path that skirted the shore line. They followed it for a quarter of a mile and entered the shadows of a scrub oak woods of more than usual density. In the woods they passed a line of trucks without drivers, parked two abreast. There were at least a hundred of them.

A little farther on he stopped and listened.

"Do you hear anything?" he asked.

"Yes. A sound of water rippling against the bow of a boat."

"You have keen accurate ears," he remarked laconically. "You'll see her hulk in a minute as she docks!'

"But there's no dock. I can see the water rippling against the shore line."

"That's her dock. There's sixty feet of water here and a shore line so straight up and down that a twenty thousand ton steamer can land and unload on the bare ground."

The low call of a boatswain's whistle sounded off shore and in a minute the black form of an ocean going steamer pushed her nose in and eased her side against the shore. Her ropes were made fast to trees and a crew of two hundred men swarmed ashore.

Her hatches opened almost without a sound, the derrick swung and landed its load of whiskey cases direct from Scotland. A truck picked them up and moved swiftly toward the highway. They watched for half an hour the clocklike work.

"Before two, a half million dollars' worth of the best Scotch from the British Isles will be under cover in my places of distribution. There's a profit to me of three million dollars in this cargo—barring accidents, of course. Sometimes a truck gets knocked off, but not often. Many of these Government sleuths are good friends of mine. Many of them are in my employ. It's a great system when you know how to work it."

They walked back to the Club and paused at the entrance.

"Are you game for a real adventure, tonight?"

"Try me."

"All right. You may have read in the morning's papers that Henry Dickman was found dead in a car pear Coney Island last night?"

She shook her head.

"No, of course not. The name would mean nothing to you or the general public. He was one of my inside organization. The brains of the Brooklyn division of the liquor trade. In spite of all I could do to keep him straight he got into two dangerous rackets."

She lifted her hand.

"Wait a minute. I need a blue print to follow you. In spite of your efforts to keep him straight he got into two dangerous rackets. Aren't you in a racket?"

"Far from it," he firmly asserted. "A racket is a private tax levied on legitimate business by strong arm men who use bombs and pick axes when there's any back talk. A strong arm gang decided to levy a tax on the garage business in Brooklyn. They organized their racket as "The Garage Protective Association," and invited all the owners in town to join. They guaranteed to stop cars from parking in the streets of the district. They do that much. They send out squads of men armed with ice picks and rip open every tire standing by a curb until the cars hunt for garages. For this service they charge an initiation fee of thirty-five dollars and monthly fees of five dollars. It means half a million income for the racket in that district. If

the garage owner gets funny and won't join, they blow up his place and beat him into insensibility. The racket is a game I loathe. It is growing daily and is a menace to the existence of a democratic republic. They are collecting now more than two hundred millions a year in New York City alone. I hate their vicious work, but men are making so much money in the liquor trade they have begun to use it to finance rackets."

"But what has this business to do with you?" she asked with a frown.

"I must first see the man in charge of Dickman's funeral. Your question will answer itself as we develop the adventure tonight."

He settled in his seat, headed the machine for Brooklyn and resumed his talk on the rackets.

"In spite of warning from "The Garage Owners Association" Dickman thought he saw a chance to clean up half a million a year on his own account by organizing the "Chauffeurs League" and levying on the drivers. I begged him to keep out of it and stick to his business of supplying decent men and women with good liquor. But when he had salted down a couple of millions and began to drive two or three big cars he thought he owned the earth, organized his own racket and the men who had warned him put him on the spot."

"Another blue print," she interrupted. "Just where is the spot?"

"They condemned him to death. And executed him after a secret trial at which the accused was not allowed to appear. People call these executions murder. By the letter of the laws of the State, they are. But you see these men don't live by State laws. They have sworn allegiance to another form of Government where they make their own laws and each man swears obedience to a super government of the strong. They have four offenses that call for the death penalty—double crossing, squealing, poaching and welching.

"No help is asked or permitted from the police. To call the police is to squeal. To squeal is to die. We must give the devil his dues. The men found dead, as Dickman was found on a lonely roadside, are not murdered by private malice. They have been executed under laws of their own making. As a rule they never squeal on the man who sends them to eternity."

"You trust me with these deadly secrets?" she broke in.

"Certainly without hesitation. I am going to be on the level with you. I have been from the first. I have never been so interested about anything in my life as I am about you. You could do anything with me you like, even to reforming me if you should get tired of excitement. I need you. I'm one of the loneliest men on earth. This thing in Brooklyn is one of the ugliest jams I've ever been in. Will you stand by for a day or two and see me through it?"

"Your life is really in danger?" she asked.

"It's always in danger, but a lot more so just now than usual until I convince the men who executed Dickman that I had nothing to do with financing or directing his rackets. His letter files will show this, if they haven't been destroyed. When I've given an order to the funeral director I'm going to his home with one of his executioners. Your presence in the car will be a guarantee of my safety until I get home in New York. Will you go through with it?"

"I'm not a quitter. Of course, I will."

In half an hour the car stopped in front of the funeral parlor where Dickman's body had been embalmed and placed in a silver casket.

Murino entered and in five minutes returned with a man who took his seat in the rear. He was not the dark skinned thug she expected to see as one of the executioners, but a stalwart youth with blonde hair and deep blue eyes of the North of Europe.

When they reached the stately home which Dickman had recently bought and furnished with a luxury that had given the yellow journals more than one exciting article, Angela whispered:

"Shall I go in with you?"

"Would you if I ask it?"

"Certainly."

"Good, you're a brick! Just sit in the car until my friend and I return. There'll be no monkey business while I'm with you. If I find my letters to Dickman I'll come out of this with more influence than ever. If I can't find them, they'll demand an explanation. Don't worry. I'll do the worrying."

In ten minutes the two men emerged from the house and returned to the car. Murino opened the door and showed Angela four letters bearing the imprint of his Fifth Avenue home, addressed in his handwriting.

He handed them to the blonde gunman who gave a receipt.

"Take them to your headquarters and tell your Chief I wish to see him at my home in New York at ten o'clock tomorrow morning."

The fellow nodded, placed the letters in his pocket, and stepped into the car in stolid silence.

Murino returned to the funeral parlor, the man got out and re-entered the establishment without a word. Murino drove rapidly to New York.

Angela was sobered. She had seen the wheels go round in the machine of a super government of the strong. And it was weird. It sent a shiver down her spine. She began to realize her position with conflicting emotions. The thing that now startled her most was the certainty of Murino's love. She had not before faced it quite frankly or sincerely. It had been a lark. It frightened her a little to realize how deadly in earnest this poised man could be. His confidence was distressing. Yet he had been so serious and frank it had been impossible to repel it. She saw at once that her life was beginning to be entangled with his in a way that might make retreat difficult. At the same time she saw his work touching the race problem in a way that all but stopped her breath with its tragic possibilities.

She fixed him with a smile.

"You are getting me terribly excited, young man!"

"And you are getting me more hopelessly in love with you every minute," he answered soberly.

She opened her lips for light banter, frowned and remained silent. There was something about his love making that couldn't be laughed off. It got under the skin.

Chapter 39

Angela slept late. The pace of the night before had kept her restless for hours after she had gone to bed. An unusual occurrence. For the first time since the development of her new powers of mental control an attempt to exclude thoughts had failed. It was not the result of the over fatigue nor the excitement of the long ride. This she could have thrown off with slight effort.

It was the grave possibilities Murino's description of racketeering had opened that set her mind spinning. These racketeers used sub-machine guns and powerful bombs. Bombs that had the destructive power of heavy artillery. She wondered how many of these desperate groups of criminals there were in New York and the other great cities. She wondered what might happen in a crisis if these machine guns and bombs were massed behind a Negro insurrection. When sleep came at last it was disturbed by high tension, ill defined dreams.

She awoke with the clear impression that an event of grave importance had happened. Her mind went back immediately to the racketeers and focused on them. She would find out their present strength, equipment and possibilities. Murino would tell her.

She dressed leisurely and sipped a cup of coffee. As she was musing over the man's deep emotions and the infatuation to which he had surrendered, her knocker sounded. She went to the door and was surprised to see Murino's dapper chauffeur standing cap in one hand and a note in the other.

He handed her the note.

"I'm to wait for an answer, Miss Cameron. I'll see that the kids are not smothering my car and be back in five minutes."

She read the message in the fine clear handwriting of the man she had been thinking about.

Her eyes danced with amused surprise and pleasure as she read:

"My dear Miss Cameron: I have been called to Chicago this morning following my ten o'clock conference on Dickman's end. Still greater possibilities open for me. My trip will be triumphant—not dangerous, but will keep me for a week. I know you love a good car. It seems a crime to put mine in the garage and let my chauffeur loaf while you are walking. Please honor me by using the car and man during the week I've gone. I've instructed him to report at your place every morning at eleven unless you forbid it. Murino."

She hesitated for a full minute. The use of the car would put her under obligations which would still further entangle her life with his. But what of it? He had made this offer without conditions. He was waiting an answer to his proposal of an unconventional alliance. She could guess the inspiration which came to him. A week's luxury in his Rolls would be a good beginning in the intensive campaign which he had mapped out. The sense of possession and well being the car would inspire would be preparation. It would be senseless to refuse. She couldn't argue the question with him. He had gone. She could use it without comment. Stephens was in Washington. There was no vulgar monogram on the shining body. His chauffeur was well dressed. He wore no livery and would attract no attention.

Her quick mind had covered every detail of the plan and she laughed heartily.

"Another adventure!" she exclaimed. "And I can hear Phil begin his futile quarrel—shucks, I've missed something along life's way. Why not?"

For a week she swept the highways a hundred miles in all directions, exploring Long Island, Westchester, and up to Albany. She took tea one afternoon at the stone road house in the Tuxedo Mountains and lived over again the exciting night of her meeting Murino and of Phil's love making. She grew to love the low rumble of the big machine's heart as it rolled smoothly over hill and valley with exhaustless power. She took Mary and Bridget for long rides. And Adolph and Viola were her guests on a lovely moonlit night. The car was a loan and she asked them to help her enjoy it. Never before had she realized that she might have wings and annihilate space in ease and perfect safety. The imported machine and the expert service of a man trained in Europe caught her imagination and filled it with dreams of world travel.

When she picked Murino up at the Grand Central she dazzled him with a gracious smile. He had wired her that he had been called home a day ahead of his schedule.

"A very subtle young man!" she murmured. "You've spoiled me completely with this car and the young magician who drives it. I'll never again get used to a Dodge."

"Why should you? I shouldn't drive the same car too often in my business. I'm going to use my runabout for three weeks. Please keep this one."

She lifted her hand.

"Couldn't. Three weeks more of this and I'd find myself in a scandal."

"Who'd know it?"

"I would. I appreciate this lovely week's outing. It's enough."

"At least you'll dine with me at my home tonight and keep the car until you come at eight?"

She nodded.

"We'll compromise on that."

She had never seen his town house, and wondered what it was like.

Her host proved himself, in the conventional surroundings of his home, a model of good manners and hospitality.

She noted the quiet taste of the furnishings with a little surprise. The pretentiousness of his road house and country place had led her to expect something different. A little vulgar display. But the place had been decorated and furnished by a master hand. The library was inspiring in its solemn beauty. Books lined the walls to the ceilings except when panels revealed a painting by an artist of international fame. Above the mantel hung an oil portrait of Marconi. On the wall opposite, set in a panel deep among books, was a steel engraving of Napoleon. A bust of Dante, and a Knight in armor completed the ornaments of the room. Four foot lengths of wood were heaped in the open fireplace. She studied the dark beauty of the place. The house had been built by a multi-millionaire miner, to whom books had no appeal, but he had spent twenty-five thousand dollars on the rich tooled bindings. The new owner had added a collection of his own to the library, sold all the gilded junk of the Westerner and refurnished the home.

The dinner was served in a state dining room by quiet servants who seemed to have been born in the place. As Murino handed her into the Rolls to drive home he smiled and nodded toward two undercover men who carelessly strolled past.

"Please note my guards of honor."

"Your what?"

"Two men from the District Attorney's office greeted me at the station. Two men are watching my house. I forgot to tell you of the honor the authorities have been paying me for some time. But I've gotten used to it. Every movement I make now from the time I rise at eight until I say goodbye to my guests is completely recorded. My association with you I hope has been set down to my credit."

She said goodbye beside the car.

"Thanks for a wonderful dinner in the most perfectly appointed house I have ever seen."

He bowed over her hand.

"It's yours when you wish to step into it."

When Phil arrived the next day he called her in excited tones and asked if he might see her at once. She knew intuitively that in some way he had heard.

He was beside himself with anger and uneasiness. The moment he had discovered from the reports of undercover men that she had been Murino's companion on drives and at dinners during the two weeks he had been in Washington, his alarm was roused. That Murino would dare to follow his introduction so swiftly was ominous. He hurried to her apartment but before taxing her with her indiscretion he would pave the way by telling her of his important work in Washington.

"I know you'll be glad that I've been offered and have accepted an important position in the Department of Justice," he said with a touch of pride. "The Government is alarmed by the rapid growth of crime and the secret power of organized criminals. They are determined to throw the full strength of the law department into the fight to stop their atrocities. I have been appointed a special counsel by the Government with extraordinary powers which I'm going to use. The first step I'll take is to get Mr. Murino."

Angela broke into a laugh.

"Come now, Phil, be honest with yourself. You say he's a dangerous criminal?"

"In my judgment the most dangerous in America today."

"If so, why hasn't the District Attorney's office with an army of detectives, backed by twenty thousand police, gotten him before this? Your accusation is fishy. I've been with him almost every day for the past two weeks. I find no sign of a criminal. He's a fine looking young man, well groomed and well bred. A man any girl will look at twice. You're jealous. And you have reason to be. I've taken a new lease on life since meeting him."

"I can't believe my ears when I hear you say that. The Department of Justice have convinced me that Murino is the master mind of a conspiracy of racketeers in America."

"Nonsense. You know as well as I do that he is a liquor dealer and not a racketeer."

"It's coming to mean the same thing, my dear. The country is drifting into a desperate situation through opposition to the enforcement of Prohibition in the North. A nation of lawbreakers is a nation doomed. The determination of people to enforce their views of drinking on millions who do not agree with them is creating a spirit of defiance that may sound the death knell of all law. Law defiance is becoming a deepening menace to the nation. It creates an atmosphere of passion, hatred, unreason and violence. It expresses an emotional attitude toward life that smacks of insanity.

"Half the energies of the National Government are being expended in an effort to enforce this law. And unless we enforce it we approach the moral bankruptcy of democratic society. We have scores of holdups in every big city night after night. Our officials are sinking in an ocean of graft. Only through graft can this city support fifty thousand speakeasies against nine thousand saloons under the old regime. The net result seems to be the saving of a few more bums by the Salvation Army, while thousands of our finest boys and girls are being plunged into hell."

She looked up slowly recalling the scene in the Westchester country place.

"And you hold Murino responsible for this?"

"He certainly is building a career upon it. We know that the big bootleggers back Prohibition. They must. Otherwise their trade would be destroyed. According to figures in Washington, we are consuming about three hundred million gallons of hard liquor this year. Nearly three times the total drunk annually before 1920. And the stuff costs three times as much. Our savings accounts are down and the death rate from alcoholism higher each year.

"And we are losing our self respect. For this there can be no compensation. We are fast becoming a nation of liars and hypocrites. We are fast becoming the laughing stock of the world. Once we were a model. We are losing all influence in shaping the development of human rights and liberties. The humbler people of the world scorn today our claims of leadership.

"We have raised a bigger question than drink. One that involves our worthiness and life as a nation."

He stopped and mopped the perspiration from his forehead.

"I know I'm making a stump speech, honey, but I'm crazy with grief over your association with this man. You can not join the forces that are degrading our life."

"I resent the suggestion, Phil. Murino is no more responsible for this than you are."

"You know that he is a master bootlegger. Fleets of heavy laden ships hover off our shores. Smuggling is one of the easiest tasks of the adventurer."

"You think that I know of his smuggling?" she broke in with a curious smile.

"Personally, no. Of course not. I mean that with our thousands of miles of shore to attempt to stop it with our little Coast Guard is to try to bail out the Atlantic with a pint cup. They are proposing to increase the force and use a quart cup. It won't help much. They can not seize one ship in ten that unloads on our shores. And if every ship were caught the supply would still be exhaustless. Dr. Doran, our Commissioner of Prohibition, declares he is destroying one still in ten. Last year he smashed two hundred and fifty thousand of them. This leaves two million three hundred thousand illicit distilleries running. Can't you see that unless a solution is found we are facing the greatest tragedy in our history? A nation of liars and hypocrites, we have now become drink crazed and drink conscious. We have forgotten decency and principle. In the daily scenes of law defiance we may be hearing the death rattle in the throat of our race. I'm calling you, dear, to join with me in this crisis and help save our society."

"It doesn't appeal to me, Phil," she declared firmly. "I've mapped out a life work to which I'm going to stick. I'm more and more convinced I have a call."

"But you mustn't be seen with this man again!" he said.

She flushed and faced him.

"I mean it, dear. You *must not* be seen with this man again. I positively forbid it."

"Since when have you the right to forbid me anything?" she answered hotly. "From the time of my recovery of sanity in Piedmont I have been conscious of a voice of freedom within. It may be the voice of intuition. It may be a sixth sense. It may be a flash from the infinite. It is not something to be explained. It is an experience. I hear with the heart. I am calm, strong and serene. I am the mistress of my life. You can not dictate to me."

He lifted his hand in a futile gesture, tried to speak and lapsed into silence, and then spoke with finality.

"I'm going to send this man to the electric chair. If you are seen with him again, our association will end, desperately as I love you."

"It's incredible that you should take such a stand. I'm amazed at you."

"I've taken pains to make clear the big issues that are back of my position."

"And this you call a love that's bigger than life or death?"

"Yes. My decision cuts to the depth of life and character. I can't compete with such a man for your favor without conscious degradation."

She smiled.

"You must love me, Phil, or you wouldn't be so crazy!"

"But you don't love me," he answered sadly.

"I don't know. You've always seemed a part of my life. I'd miss you terribly. Yet I must keep my self respect. I, and I alone, will decide my associates."

"You must know that an alliance of any kind with this man and his underworld will destroy your life."

"On the other hand it has given me a new and broader outlook and truer perspective. I live with more intelligence and less conscious personal emotions. I have finished my first big search. It has led me to a trail at the end of which is the death of our nation or its rebirth. I'll begin to-morrow a new study that may change the current of my life."

"If Murino suggested it, I've no doubt you'll find that so."

"He didn't suggest it. But I'll ask his advice and help."

"Then you'll not need mine," he said with anger, seizing his hat and hurrying through the door.

She heard his foot fall on the stair with surprise and hurt, but with renewed determination.

Part III

THE SOLUTION

Chapter 40

Angela's reaction to the breach with Phil was a vigorous reassertion of her complete personal liberty. She had broken with her childhood playfellow. Phil's accusations of crime against Murino had made no impression.

He had been wise enough not to ask for an immediate answer to his unconventional proposal. He knew instinctively that he would get the answer when she had played fully with the idea. That she was playing with it he never doubted for a moment. Her gaiety and good fellowship, her graceful acceptance of his gifts of daily flowers, all convinced him of that. Whether it was a mental tack she was exploiting as a pastime or a genuine test of character he had been unable to determine.

He was in no hurry to put it to the test. He was more than usually quiet for a week. He announced his departure for Chicago again, but she discovered, quite by accident, that he had merely moved down to the Plaza Hotel for a few days, and smiled at his deception. He had felt the decision in her tones the last time he had called and announced his summons to the West with a renewal of the offer of his car. She had declined it with an emphasis that made him regret the offer. He dreaded the meeting they must have with premonition of the verdict.

But he took the plunge on the day he had announced for his return.

"Will you take dinner with me tonight?" he asked immediately.

"With pleasure," she answered gravely. "I've a lot to tell you."

"You'll honor me with another evening in my home?"

"Delighted. Send for me."

"I'll call if it's just the same."

"Better still," she laughed.

Tonight he had an orchestra hidden in the conservatory that opened off the state dining room.

"I hope this evening will be a memorable one. I want the vision of this room and the strains of the music to haunt you."

"I see," she said evenly.

At the close of the dinner he looked at her quietly and both remained silent for a moment. He spoke finally with a touch of sadness in his tones.

"I've anticipated what you are going to tell me tonight."

"You have guessed it?"

"No, not guessed. I've a sixth sense that tells me things. You have the same. I've often felt it. You have made up your mind and I have lost. Don't tell me. I don't want to hear it. Let us part tonight without a break. I understand. And I love you all the more for it. But I don't want to hear you say it, that's all. I accept the situation and go on hoping for every hour I can have of your time and every thought I may inspire in your heart. Give me what you can, when you can. I'll be overwhelmed with the biggest plans of my life in the next four months. I'll never be too busy to come at the slightest hint that you wish to see me. But I'm not going to intrude for a while. You'll understand if I don't call you?"

"I'll understand. And I marvel at your wisdom. You are used to having your own way. Your deference to my feelings is very sweet. I can't tell you how I appreciate it."

"Just one thing I'm going to ask you," he said with a penetrating look. "You won't let Stephens cover me with infamy without giving me a chance to defend myself?"

"No," she agreed emphatically. "We have had a pretty severe break. I may not see him again."

"I'd say thank God, but I'm too polite, and, if you'll let me say it, a little too wise. He's a childhood friend. We don't sever such ties in a hurry. He'll come back bye and bye and you'll see him again."

"I don't think so."

"I know it. And I prepare myself for the battle he is going to open on me. He's going to give no quarter and ask none. Unfortunately I can't fight him with such bitterness. I don't blame him for loving you. I admire his good taste. I respect him for his desire to protect and defend you. He's a foe worthy of my steel and I'll fight fairly. I doubt if he will be so scrupulous. He thinks I'm an outlaw. Just one thing I beg of you," he urged tenderly. "If there comes an hour when I can help you in any way, you'll call me?"

"If such a time comes I'll call you."

"There's nothing so important that I'll not drop it instantly to answer."

She began next day the studies destined to change her plan of work. She had announced it to Phil. In a class in Social Science the teacher had uttered a sentence about the rapid development of Communism in America which decided her to begin at once an intense study of its methods, status in the world and its ultimate purpose.

She found it a tremendous subject with historic roots in the building of modern society she had little dreamed. Through a Russian student she met Maurice Hindus whose great novel on the Soviet Regime was in manuscript and he was kind enough to let her read it.

She was swept away by its brilliance and power. The picture drawn was so vividly realistic it was difficult to exclude its thoughts at bed time.

"I can not understand," she said to him, "how a man of your genius, your kindly sympathies, your evident love of humanity can tolerate the cruelties of Soviet Russia."

"What do you mean?" he asked seriously.

"You record in your story the "liquidization" (murder) of six million five hundred thousand Russian peasants and workmen who helped in the revolution, yet were killed because they employed a helper in a shop or a single workman on their farms. This is the most terrible massacre in all human history."

He nodded. "Communism has no sentiment. It is a merciless system of logic. It's either right or wrong. The men who have established it in Russia believe with every beat of their hearts, it's right. It teaches there are but two classes of mankind—the exploiter and the exploited. The man who profits by another's labor is an exploiter. Whether he hires one or a hundred. The exploiters must be liquidated. Six millions die that 160 millions may live. It may not be merciful but it is logical. It is scientific."

Her studies were suddenly broken by a tragedy in her building. Bridget went out to work one day in a Department Store in Harlem and did not come back to her dinner at six thirty. Mary, her mother, waited impatiently until seven thirty and called the store.

Only the night watchman was on duty.

"No, M'am," he said. "Everybody left here at six o'clock. There's no extra work. Nobody here."

"Do you know my daughter, Bridget O'Brian?"

"I'm sorry, M'am, I don't."

She hung up the receiver with a forlorn gesture. The dinner was already spoiled. She couldn't touch it until her girl got home. She only lived for her. She had opposed her marriage too soon. As a matter of fact Bridget was already three years older than she had been at her marriage. The truth was she couldn't give her up.

She called every friend whose telephone number could be found. Not one had seen her.

At eight thirty she rang Angela's bell and asked her what to do.

"Was she well this morning when she left home?"

"Never looked better in her life. She's never sick. Never saw a healthier girl in all me life."

"All right. We'll go to the police station and get help."

They went to the district police headquarters and reported the case.

The Irish Sergeant said: "Go home, little mother, wait by your telephone. If she was hurt we'll find out by calling every hospital."

"You think she's maybe knocked down by a car or a truck?"

"It might be. We'll find out in a few hours. Go back and sit by your phone. She may be telephoning now."

Through the long night the two women watched and waited in vain. Near dawn Angela gave the distracted mother a sleeping tablet and put her to bed, promising to return when she had gotten a few hours sleep.

At nine o'clock she returned. Mary, wide eyed, met her at the door.

"Mother of God, Miss Angela, what'll we do!"

"We'll get an officer to go with us and search every street in Harlem."

"You'll—go—with—me?" Mary moaned.

"Yes," was the quick answer.

For two days and a half they searched. Angela made Mary stand by the telephone while she went on secret missions alone. She found the Captain of the Precinct and asked his theory of the disappearance.

"I haven't any theory, my dear young lady," he answered sadly. "These disappearing girls are the unsolved riddle of police life. Hundreds of them drop out of sight in this district every year. Where they go and what becomes of them, God only knows. There's too many such cases in Harlem lately. We've got to get at the bottom of it. I've asked a big increase in our undercover force. She's been kidnapped, you can bet on that. But by what sort of outfit, we haven't an idea."

"You think she might, be held in one of those Nigger "Heavens" of Father Divine we hear so much about?"

"Not a chance. The little Nigger preacher isa fanatic, maybe crazy, when he shouts that he is God, but he's trying to do good in my opinion."

"Could her mother and I get into his places and look through them?"

"Certainly. I'll give you a letter to the preacher's secretary, who will open every door unless I miss my guess."

"Thank you," she murmured.

The letter was written and she hurried home to find Mary sitting in a chair beside the phone, her bloodshot eyes closed in fitful sleep.

They found a beautiful special built car in front of Heaven No. 1 awaiting Father Divine's orders. Angela had read a description of his car designed by the white playboy, John H. Hunt, called "St. John the Revelator." The touring church was a sensation in auto design. Hunt had built it with an extra long wheel base. On the rear seat were two upraised "Thrones," a wide arm rest between them. A hand microphone was attached to the arm rest through which Father Divine gave orders to his driver who was shut off from the throne room by a heavy glass panel.

"They say the man who built this car for the Negro," Angela observed, "has lured a 17 year old girl from home and has paraded her in the country as the "Virgin Mary." We may get a clue here. We'll leave no stone unturned."

They were welcomed by the little Negro's white secretary who detailed an attendant to show them through each of the "Heavens" in Harlem. No trace of Bridget was found in any of them. The practice of full social equality Angela found to be a fundamental requirement of all the "Angels" who inhabited the places. White men who enter a "Heaven" sleep with Negro men in the same room. And all eat at a common table in the same fashion.

Angela paused on the sidewalk and looked back at the building. It was hard to realize that she was living in the 20th Century in the greatest city of the modern world. Behind those walls was a little black man who had proclaimed himself God. Thousands of Negroes acknowledged the claim and worshipped him. They were giving their goods and chattels, their houses and lands, their souls and bodies into his keeping.

A Negro Cult which proclaimed little George Baker[1] none other than the Lord God Almighty come to earth! That some of his white followers were merely after the loaves and fishes and scraps that fell from his table, and others were lecherous scoundrels who scented opportunities for sex indulgence, was true. Yet the fact remained that the emotional imbecility of the cult appealed to a few white men and women who had become abject slaves of Baker. A strange world this enlightened progressive age!

Newsboys were calling the evening papers of the metropolis. A long line of cabs moved by the curb signalling for fares from "Heaven." A stream of thousands of blacks sprinkled with whites filled the sidewalks.

They walked back to the apartment in silence. At the door Angela pressed Mary's arm.

"I'm going to call on a man who will know what to do. Antonio Murino knows New York as no other man in it, perhaps. He has asked me to call him for help if I need it."

1. George Baker (Father Divine) (ca. 1880–1965) was born in Maryland and became a cult religious leader in New York City. Members of Father Divine's Peace Mission Movement believed that he was God, and they followed him blindly in the quest of health, prosperity, and salvation. See Jill Watts, *God, Harlem USA: The Father Divine Story* (Berkeley: University of California Press, 1992).

"Call him right away!"

"I will."

"Thank you, darling, thank you. I don't know how I'd have lived through this without you. I know you'll stand by me until we find her."

"Depend on it."

In half an hour the big Rolls stood at the door.

"I'm going to his house, Mary. He has sent the car for me. He was tied up in conference and couldn't come here. As soon as I've talked with him I'll let you know. Cheer up now. I've a hunch we're going to have some powerful help."

The doorman, following instructions ushered her into the library. It was half an hour before Murino came out of his sanctum with his friends, bade them good night and hurried to greet her.

"So sorry I couldn't drive to meet you. We'd have swung out to a good Road House and dined. It's been a month since I saw you."

"I've been awfully busy," she smiled. "And the business I've come on tonight is so sad and urgent, I couldn't have eaten at a Road House."

He drew his chair close and devoured her with his eyes. She felt her influence over him and thanked God for it. In a rush of impetuous words she related the story of Bridget's disappearance and their vain search.

"Why didn't you come to me sooner? I think I can locate her in twenty four hours."

"You think so?"

"I'm practically sure of it. A new racket has been established in the greater cities of the North by the devils who deal in white slaves. They are establishing groups of prison houses in which they confine kidnapped white girls for the exclusive use of Negroes. I've an idea that the large number of missing girls in New York can be accounted for in this racket."

"Can such a thing be possible in our civilized nation?"

"Civilized or uncivilized, the thing is here. The White Slave traffic is no new thing. It has been an international scandal for years. But the catering to the black man's lust for white women is a new profitable twist to the business. I suspect it has political significance when you get all the facts. I'll take you home and spend the night among the racketeers. If I locate the girl in one of their places do you wish to call the police, raid it and send the keeper to prison, or get the girl back to her mother in the quickest time possible?"

"Oh, get her back quickly," was the tense answer.

"You see," he went on, "the minute you call in the police, there's always a chance these people have a spy at hand to tip them off. The girl may be removed and we'll find nothing. If you want quick action I can buy her for a lump sum from the skunk who controls the house."

"You'll do this generous thing?"

"For you, I'd do anything in my power. I've missed you, dear girl. Please let me see you often now."

"Get Bridget back to her crazed mother, and I will."

"It's a bargain. I'll hold you to it."

"I'll make good. I promise."

Murino pulled the strings of his organization, gave every intelligence man in his assorted employ a description of the girl and located her in the next eighteen hours. She was an inmate of a row of three brown stone houses in the heart of Harlem.

The keeper of the place called the manager for the conference.

The black bristling eye brows were lifted at sight of the distinguished visitor who had been admitted by a letter from headquarters.

"What do you want with the little hell cat? She's no good and never will be. We've had to beat the stuffin out of her. She's been here a little over a week and she's a wreck already. No looks, no pep. She's what we call a dead flop. What do you want with her?"

Murino pursed his lips.

"Just a fancy of mine. I saw her once and took a shine to her. Didn't have time to set up to her. And now that she's had a little experience I want her."

"Sure you want this particular girl? Her name at school was Bridget O'Brian?"

"That's her."

"All right. It will cost you two grand. Got the money?"

Murino handed him two one thousand dollar bills.

"I'll blindfold her. She came here blindfolded. I'll set her free at the corner of Amsterdam Avenue and 117th Street in half an hour. Be there to pick her up."

"I'll be there."

When the bandages were removed from the poor girl's eyes and she was set out on the sidewalk at noon, the brilliant sun blinded her for a moment, and she stumbled to the wall of a building.

Murino slipped quickly to her side, and seized her arm.

"Why, Bridget, you're ill."

"Yes, sir," she muttered, "I'm awful sick, Mr. Murino. I'm so glad to see you. I'm trying to get home."

He led her to his car.

"Come, child, I'll take you right home."

Her mother heard the crunch of the car's wheels at the curb and rushed to gather Bridget in her arms, too excited at first to notice her condition.

When she saw that one eye was blacked by a blow, both of them bleared and bloodshot, she fell in a faint at the girl's feet and was helped into bed by Angela who had just rushed into the room.

The girl refused to talk. She had been a prisoner in hell and there was nothing left to live for. She spoke in dead sodden tones. When Mary revived, she drew her head down on the pillow and crooned over her.

Bridget rose, turned her bleared eyes toward the window, walked to it, and looked out on a group of curious children who had gathered on hearing of her return.

"For God's sake drive those kids away," she begged her mother. "I'm not a freak in a side show. Maybe I am, too."

In vain Angela tried to comfort the mother who finally led her to the door.

"Go get some sleep now, dear. I praise the Mother of God for you and your good friend. You've saved my life and the life of my girl."

But she hadn't. Two hours later a shot rang out from the basement rooms. Angela heard it. Bridget had found the revolver her mother had kept since the abduction and blew her brains out.

Murino sent a trained nurse. Together they saved Mary's reason.

Depressed over the tragedy, Angela suddenly decided to make up her quarrel with Phil.

"I'm so happy to see you again, darling," he said with a mist in his eyes, as he grasped her hand.

"I've missed you, too, Phil," she responded cordially. "We'll bury the hatchet, if you say so, and be good friends again."

"Good friends again," he echoed. "You should have called me in to try to find Bridget."

"Don't start something again," she warned. "Murino did that job so swiftly and perfectly I wonder at his genius and generosity. He bought her release for two thousand dollars."

"No doubt he knew exactly where to find her."

"I'll ask you to go if you make another crack like that."

"All right, dearest," he smiled. "We'll call a truce on the gentleman. Though I must have you know that I am still camping on his trail as an attorney of the U.S. Government and I expect to get him."

"All right," she answered, "I've been devoting myself to the study of Communism. The thing is in the air."

"I trust your sympathies are not interested?"

"On the other hand, I have been stirred to deepest antagonism. I am interested in the attitude of your scholarly editor, DuBois, the most powerful leader the Negro race has in America. He has not only destroyed the prestige of his old rival, he has a hundred followers to every one who gives his rival lip service. Washington won white friends by the genius of his diplomacy. DuBois has won the black race by his daring and dangerous doctrines. I'm meeting his influence at every turn in my study."

"I'm not surprised. America is yet to hear from this firebrand. He has only been playing with fire so far. When he is ready for action, history is going to be made."

She dismissed her old friend early pleading important work. He held her hand with lingering tenderness.

"But I'm on the old footing. You've forgotten my foolishness and dictatorship?"

"Of course. You can even send me flowers and make love to me. I've been lonesome."

He walked down the two flights with buoyant step and she listened with a thousand memories crowding her heart from the past. She wondered, after all, if she didn't love this man. The curious thing was that her association with Murino had stirred her to a new feeling of tenderness for Phil. She was grateful for the new horizon the other man had opened to her vision. He could be of enormous help in her work. She proposed to use him. He had let fall a hint of possible political significance in the growth of the White Slave traffic for black men of Harlem and the big cities of America. The declaration of the lecturer in Columbia on the rapid spread of Communism kept echoing in her mind. And now came Phil's striking statement that DuBois was headed for Moscow. She determined to follow each of these leads and see where they ended. Murino held the key to the most baffling and exciting idea of the three. She would first find what possible political connection a chain of White Slave prison houses held. She called Murino and asked him to take her to dinner the next night.

"I'm perfectly shameless in my suggestion," she laughed. "I've got to pump some information out of you on a theme I'm studying. My motive is selfish. Can I depend on you?"

"To the limit, my dear. I'll buy a cap and run errands for you if it will only bring us together."

"You'll send the car at seven, then?"

"At seven. And I'll be at the wheel."

Chapter 41

Angela dressed for dinner in an evening gown that displayed her lovely figure in all its charm. As she studied herself before the mirror she laughed at her new interest in the male of the species.

And her revived interest was due to the man with whom she was going to dine. Something in the strength of his mind and body and driving personality stirred her. She was going to use his keen intelligence and his wide knowledge of social, economic, and political affairs to-night for her own purpose, sure that she could gain valuable information.

"Is that all I want of him?" she brooded. "No, it's not," was the honest answer. "I'm more keenly interested in my conquest of him as a man than in the information which I'm going to get out of him. Why? Would I marry him if I could?"

Across this thought flashed the tall handsome figure of Phil—and his devotion. If she ever married again—which she wouldn't!—Phil should be the man unless this fascinating devil should supplant him! Curious she had never paused to weigh the question of money. There was a time in her life when millions did not appeal to her imagination except as an added responsibility in life. Phil Stephens had an ample income and it was growing daily. Yet the luxury which millions would bring was, after all, a fascinating idea . . . and with it the thought of herself in a strong man's arms. Arms stronger than Dave Henry's. Arms that would throb with mind and imagination!

She found herself flushing under the idea.

"Thank God I'm human again," she breathed.

She watched the street for Murino's coming.

As she settled in her seat beside the driver, he bent close.

"You won't mind a little spin on the South Shore of Long Island for dinner at a new place, would you?"

"I'd love it."

Again the low rumble of the big car stimulated her. She glanced at the handsome profile of the man by her side and laughed softly.

"A penny for your thoughts!" he said.

"Cost you more than that, young man. I'm deeper than you suspect."

They passed through the stately iron gates of a beautiful country estate and swept down the long drive shadowed by waving poplars.

"You don't mean to tell me that you've gobbled up this mansion or a Road House?"

"We have," he smiled. "Eighty guest rooms make it a fair sized hotel. Admirably adapted to our work."

They dined alone on a veranda overlooking the silver mirror of the Sound, across which lights blinked from the houses on the other side. The wind was from the south and the low roar of the surf made the music of the orchestra superfluous.

The smell of salt water raised Angela's spirits. It always did. It brought dreams of strange lands and people beyond the sea. She spoke in brisk tones:

"Shall we transact the business first for which I inveigled you into this dinner?"

"By all means."

"You told me quite incidentally the other day that you suspected a political motive behind the development of the White Slave traffic in Harlem and other cities. Would you mind telling me on what you based such a suggestion?"

"If you don't mind my discussing an ugly and similarly disgusting parallel fact?"

"Its not a very pretty subject at best. I'm ready for plain facts. I want to know the truth about it."

"The reason I made the remark was that only the day before yesterday I stumbled on an unbelievable condition of affairs in Harlem. Through a smart young reporter from one of the dailies I learned that the Communists have organized an intensive campaign in Harlem. They have selected a Harlem Negro for their candidate for Vice-President."

"Vice-President of the United States—a Negro?"

"Exactly. This Negro is the leader of Harlem. They are making a tremendous bid for the Negro race. The amazing thing is that they have enough white girl volunteers to supply mistresses for every Negro politician of any importance in town."

"White girls are going to volunteer to give themselves to Negroes to lead them into this fanaticism?"

"They have already volunteered and have established themselves as housekeepers, stenographers or secretaries to their black politicians. It's a subtle scheme. It seems these Northern Negroes are obsessed with the idea of possessing white women. The moment I encountered the fact that there is a chain of prison houses where white girls are held as slaves for Negroes, I put two and two together. The same forces that have sent these volunteers to work for politicians—giving themselves literally soul and body—the madness capable of this would not hesitate to imprison white slaves for the use of the black rank and file, as a political maneuver."

"I can understand how white slavers could kidnap and hold in prison girls for such a purpose," Angela said. "But that any sane white girl could volunteer for such service is incredible—utterly beyond human belief."

"Suppose I put you in touch with some of these girls?"

"Could you?"

"I'm sure the reporter knows more than one and he'll introduce you. It would be necessary, of course, for you to cultivate the girl, win her confidence and then find out the truth about it."

"You can send the reporter to see me tomorrow?"

"By three o'clock."

"All right we'll forget business—let's talk about us," she laughed.

"If you'll be serious for a moment I'll tell you of a conclusion I've reached. If you'll marry me I'll leave my church, join yours and get a divorce."

She flushed and held his gaze.

"You do love me, don't you?"

"More than you can ever dream. Can you give me an answer now?"

She shook her head.

"Not tonight. There are two reasons. I've work to do before I can consider marriage. And there's another man I like."

He took it without flinching.

"Stephens?"

"Yes. Boy and girl sweethearts, you know."

"You'll outgrow it!" he sighed in relief. "It's not settled?"

"Far from it."

"Does my trade handicap me?"

"A little. Yes."

"I'll give it up the minute you accept me."

"That's a good one!" she cried. "I don't know how I resist you."

"Don't, please."

The reporter called promptly the next afternoon.

"Could you put me in touch with one of these girls?"

"Half a dozen if you like."

"One's enough, if she will talk."

"She will if you win her confidence. They are perfect specimens of the modern female fanatic."

"They must be."

"What shall I tell her you want with her? It must be perfectly definite and along the line of Communism."

"Tell her the simple truth. I'm a young woman studying her religion at Columbia University. I've heard of her work and wish to know her. You might hint that I'm a possible convert."

At five the next day he called with a plump little Syrian girl of twenty-three—she had lovely eyes and brown hair of the same shade as her own. As they entered the room Angela was impressed with her common place type. There was no sparkle of madness in her eyes, no mannerism that betrayed the fanatic. A girl you could pass on the street and never give a second look. It was incredible that she had chosen a martyrdom of the repulsive type under discussion.

"Allow me to present Miss Mona Lucas of Greenwich Village, Miss Cameron of Columbia."

The hostess extended her hand in a cordial gesture accompanied by a smile that won her visitor at once.

"If I'd had time," the reporter said, "I would have picked a blonde Amazon from an outlandish neck of the woods in Central Europe. The dark boys also prefer blondes. But the little Syrian is all right, well reared and smart as a whip. Please let me help you in your work. I'm a bright lad. I recom end myself highly. You have my telephone."

"Yes. Run along now. Thank you very much. I'll call you again."

He left with a jolly wave of his hand and she returned to her guest.

"You were born in New York?" Angela asked.

"Yes, indeed. In the outskirts of darkest Brooklyn twenty three years ago. I don't look of that ancient vintage, do I? It's the dimple in my left cheek that saves me."

"It does make you look the school girl rather than the serious student of social science which our friend tells me you are."

"A student, yes, and serious, I hope," she agreed. "He tells me that you too are a student of the religion of Communism. It is the world's last divine revelation, you know."

There came a flash from her brown eyes that completely obscured the dimple.

"I am profoundly interested in it," Angela acknowledged. "I've been studying it intensely in the morning for the past six months. I've been a student of Social Science for seven years. I am eager to learn about your work and your principles."

"I maybe ought to be more close lipped in what I say to you," the girl mused.

"I'll appreciate the utmost frankness," her hostess broke in. "Our friend tells me that you have with others of your group, undertaken a special mission in Harlem."

"Not in Harlem only. But in all the great cities of America. I may be ordered to Detroit tomorrow. We have each taken a vow to give ourselves to the Cause body and soul. And that's not a figure of speech. We practice what we preach, as surely as any nun from a convent walks into the battle lines to nurse wounded soldiers."

"Would you tell me about your work in New York?"

"I'd give a lot if I could win you to our Order," was the low response.

"What do you mean by your Order? I know that Communism has become a passionate religion to many of its adherents, but I didn't know it was yet divided into orders."

"We have established the first Order of women. If I tell you the secret name I'm sure you will respect it and not use it in print? I've never given it to that impudent reporter. I wouldn't trust him as far as I would throw a cat. But you. There's something about your personality that calls me. That has completely won my confidence. The name of the organization reveals its sublime purpose, 'The Sacred Order of Monna Vanna.' I have changed my name to hers."

She paused and looked at her hostess for appreciation of her secret. She got no answering look of understanding.

"You understand?" the girl inquired.

"I'm afraid I don't."

"Surely you have at some time seen Maurice Maeterlinck's great drama 'Monna Vanna'?"

Angela blushed.

"I'm sorry but I haven't. I was born in the South and saw very few good plays."

"You'll go with me to see one of our performances?"

"With pleasure."

"We play it every Saturday night in a Jewish theater down town. It always draws a crowd. With us it's a religious ceremony. Monna Vanna, you will see, was the woman who volunteered to give her body to save her country. Men give their lives, why shouldn't women give their chastity if called on? I have been assigned to service with a Judge, a man who will take a leading part in the revolution when it is launched."

"Would you mind telling me his name?"

"Confidentially, no. Judge Rex Weldon of the city bench."

Angela felt the name coming before she pronounced it. But she felt her heart beat a little faster when her intuition was confirmed.

"You will, of course," she warned, "not mention my name to him."

"Certainly not. I've let you into my innermost secrets. I don't know why. But I'm sure I can trust you"

"Your present campaign is the opening of a determined drive to capture the Negro race in America, you say?"

"Yes. You haven't seen our Manifesto addressed to the Negroes?"

"No."

"It is published in full in the *Crisis* magazine. I've a copy in my purse. I'll leave it with you."

She opened her handbag and gave to Angela a neatly printed leaflet containing the full text of the appeal to the Negro Race.

"THE WORKERS PARTY TO THE NEGRO RACE OF AMERICA."

"We demand:

1. A Federal law against lynching, and the protection of the Negro masses in their right of self-defense.
2. Abolition of the whole system of race discrimination. Full racial, political and social equality for the Negro race.
3. Abolition of all laws which result in segregation of Negroes. Abolition of all Jim-Crow laws. The law shall forbid all discrimination against Negroes in selling or renting houses.
4. Abolition of all laws which disfranchise the Negroes.
5. Abolition of laws forbidding intermarriage of persons of different races.
6. Abolition of all laws and public administration measures which prohibit, or in practice prevent, Negro children or youth from attending general public schools or universities.
7. Full and equal admittance of Negroes to all railway station waiting rooms, restaurants, hotels, and theaters.
8. Abolition of discriminatory practices in courts against Negroes. No discrimination in jury service.
9. Abolition of the convict lease system and of the chain gang.
10. Abolition of all Jim Crow distinctions in the army, navy, and civil service.
11. Immediate removal of all restrictions in all trade unions against the membership of the Negro workers.

> 12. Equal opportunity for employment, wages, hours and working conditions for Negro workers and white workers. Equal pay for equal work for Negro and white workers."

"This platform we are going to put into the hands of every Negro in America who can read and write."

"You'll have trouble doing that in the South, won't you?"

"You'd be surprised how rapid our progress has been in the South. The Negro Junta are established in every Southern State. In North Carolina they have eight strong branches. We distribute our literature, through them."

At the door she whispered, "We are launching a big drive into Southern industry next week for the capture of both the textile operatives and the Negroes. You'll hear from it."

Long after she had gone the sentence lingered ominously in Angela's memory.

Chapter 42

Her first thought on awakening next morning brought Angela out of bed with a bound. How could a common place girl deliberately give her body to a Negro politician for a Cause! Surely there was no Cause within the range of her knowledge of history, past or present, that could make such a thing conceivable. Here was a devotion to principle, a madness unparalleled in the history of America. The Red following had surely become a religion, a dangerous one. The kind of religion for which followers glory in death. These were glorying in worse than death. The rise of such a cult in an age of gross materialism was stunning. It was a sign. A grim portent. These people were in dead earnest. They would stop at nothing to gain their ends. With them the end justified the means.

What did the girl mean by a rapidly developing plan to invade the South? She must have been mistaken. Yet her statement couldn't have been simpler or more emphatic. Could it be possible that the South was open to such an invasion? The South, the home of American conservatives. The South, whose fathers created the American Republic. She had always thought of its great States as the bulwark of the nation's liberties. Had its character been debased to the point of giving welcome to these people? It was unthinkable.

She must find where Mona got such an idea and what was back of it. The resolution had just crystallized in her mind when the phone rang and the girl's voice called pleasantly:

"This is Mona Lucas."

"Yes, Mona."

"I've just learned that a special performance of "Monna Vanna" will be given by our unit tonight. Will you go with me?"

"I'll be delighted. Where shall I meet you?"

"At the old Yiddish Theatre on the Bowery. Think you can find it?"

"Yes, of course, but a better plan will be for you to meet me for dinner at Luchow's and you can show me the way."

"All right. I'll be in front of Luchow's at seven."

Angela ordered a dinner of sauerkraut and imported frankfurters which delighted Mona.

"You'll find the theatre a dirty old hole," the girl laughed. "But the acting will give you a thrill. You know some of the greatest actors in America had their start there."

When the beautiful performance of Maeterlink's masterpiece had gotten underway, Angela forgot the shabby walls, the rickety seats, the dirt and the grime of the place. She was back in the fifteenth century in Pisa witnessing the tragedy of a little Republic. In the rich sentences of Marco she felt the pulse of its culture and its dreams. And heard the cries of its beseiged starving people. Princevalle at the head of an army of savage soldiers, wearing the uniforms of the Republic of Florence, had ringed the city with death. The Conqueror sent word to the Council of Pisa that he would spare the city and send in train loads of food for its starving people if the beautiful wife of Guido, the Commander of its garrison, would come to his tent alone that night and submit to his will.

Vanna approaches Marco and says:

"Father, I will go tonight."

The old man kisses her forehead.

"I knew, daughter."

And at the end of the scene Guido in desperation sweeps her into his arms crying:

"Come to my arms, Vanna. It is there that you will live!"

Her body suddenly becomes rigid as she repulses him:

"No, no, Guido—I know—I can not speak—all my strength fails me if I say one word—I cannot. I would only—I have reflected well. I know. I love you, I love you. I owe all to you. I may be vile and abandoned—and yet I must go—I must go."

As she goes the distracted husband staggers and supports himself against a marble pillar while she passes out slowly, alone without looking at him.

A sob caught Angela as the curtain came down softly.

"Isn't it great?" Mona cried.

"The most wonderful acting I've ever seen!"

When in the Conqueror's tent, Princevalle reveals himself as the boy who once played with her at the fountain in Venice, who kissed her once and loved her always. He asks nothing now except to counsel with her how he may save her life and the lives of her people.

Angela let the tears roll down her cheeks without shame.

Vanna had made the sacrifice in spirit. A boy's love had saved her from the physical shame. A beautiful romance. But this little dimpled girl from Brooklyn was living the hideous shame daily with a Negro!

Throughout the last act Angela found herself watching the girl by her side out of the corner of her eye. Surely here was a force of stark fanaticism the defenders of the old regime must meet!

When she left for her uptown home, Angela pressed the girl's hand.

"I'm deeply grateful for the treat, Mona. It has been a wonderful experience. I'll never forget it."

"You could do something that would more than repay me if you would."

"What?"

"Come to one of our social hours with me and meet some of our boys. A few of them are in Columbia."

"I'll go if you'll do something for me," Angela fenced.

"What is it?"

"Tell me about the plans for the invasion of the South."

"All right. The next time we meet, I'll give you the literature of our coming political campaign. You'll see how it grows out of it. Call me soon."

Chapter 43

The next morning, Angela walking through 116th Street, found a gang of Negro workmen building seats in an immense old warehouse. They were rushing it with such enthusiasm she asked what was going on.

A coal black foreman tipped his hat: "We belongs to the Universal Negro Improvement Association. We've outgrowed "Liberty Hall." Our President, Marcus Garvey, speaks to the people here to-morrow night. Come, Miss."

She thanked him and made up her mind to call Phil. She had heard with interest of Garvey's scheme of an African Republic. Phil came with alacrity. He too was anxious to hear the new leader, now being bitterly opposed by The National Association for the Advancement of Colored People.

They found the place packed with five thousand cheering Negroes, the vast majority of them full blacks. There was something electric in the spirit of the crowd. They sang with a lilt of triumph that was contagious. The ushers walked with impressive dignity. Whatever this man Garvey was up to, he was breathing a new spirit into his race.

They finally found seats near the platform which was decorated profusely with flags and bunting.

"The thing that is stirring the Radical Wing of the Negro Party in bitter opposition," Phil said, "is the rapid spread of this movement. Garvey claims a membership of over four millions. And he has in the field between nine hundred and a thousand orators stumping the country . . ."

"Sh . . ." she warned, "here he is."

The leader suddenly appeared from the rear and stood for a moment under a brilliant light. He was a man of striking personality, a coal black whose face bore the lines of a born fighter. He was dressed in a black robe and gorgeous sash. The length of the robe exaggerated his height and gave him an impressive appearance. The moment he appeared the black throng rose en masse and shouted and cheered for full two minutes.

He was presented to the audience by one of his lieutenants in a few glowing words:

"Ladies and gentlemen: I present to you the new Negro Moses of the world, Marcus Garvey, President General of the Universal Negro Improvement Association and Provisional President of Africa."

His first sentences stamped the man as a born orator. There was a force back of his speech, a reserve power that caught every listener and held him.

"My People," he began evenly. "The Negro now stands at the cross roads of destiny. He is at the place where he must either step forward or backward. If he goes backward he dies. If he goes forward it will be with the hope of a greater life."

"Forward!" shouted a stentorian voice from the center aisle. There was something new in the ring of his word. It was not the typical Negro response of religious ecstasy. It was the voice of a man who was coming to himself. A man whose shout rang with the consciousness of self respect.

"We are either on the road to higher racial existence or racial extermination. The political re-adjustment of the world means that every race must find a home; hence the cry of Palestine for the Jews, Ireland for the Irish, India for the Indians and simultaneously Negroes raising the cry of Africa for the Africans, those at home and those abroad.

"As far as the Negro race is concerned, we find but few real men to measure up to the standard of the creation, and because of this lack of manhood in the race, we have stagnated for centuries and now find ourselves at the foot of the great human ladder.

"Negro leaders have advanced the belief that in another few years the white people will make up their minds to assimilate their black populations; thereby sinking all racial prejudice in the welcoming of the black race into the social companionship of the white. Such leaders further believe that by the amalgamation of black and white, a new type will spring up, and that it will become the American of the future.

"This belief is preposterous. I believe that white men should be white, yellow men should be yellow, and black men should be black in the great panorama of races, until each and every race by its own initiative lifts itself up to the common standard of humanity, so as to compel the respect and appreciation of all, and so make it possible for each one to stretch out the hand of welcome without being able to be prejudiced against the other because of any inferior and unfortunate condition.

"The white man of America will not, to any organized extent, assimilate the Negro, because in so doing, he feels he will be committing racial suicide. This he is not prepared to do.

"God Almighty created us all to be free. That the Negro race became a race of slaves was not the fault of God Almighty, the Divine Master, it was the fault of the race.

"Sloth, neglect, indifference caused us to be slaves.

"Confidence, conviction, action will cause us to be free men today.

"Some of us believe that this slave race of ours will live here and in the future again become law makers for the white race, our masters of sixty years ago. Nothing of the kind has happened in all human history. There is not one instance where a slave race living in the same country, within the same bounds as the race of masters that enslaved them, and, being in numbers less than the race of masters, has ever yet ruled and governed. It has never been so in history, and it never will be so in the future.

"For five years the Universal Negro Improvement Association has been advocating the cause of Africa for the Africans. That is, that the Negro peoples of the world should concentrate upon the object of building up for themselves a great nation in Africa.

"It is clear that the question of African nationality is not far-fetched, but is as reasonable and feasible as the idea of an American nationality. There is no other way to avoid the threatening war of the races that is bound to engulf all mankind, which has been prophesied by the world's greatest thinkers. There is no better method than by apportioning every race to its own habitat.

"The time has come for Asiatics to govern themselves in Asia, as the Europeans are in Europe and the Western world. So is it wise for the Africans to govern themselves at home, and thereby bring peace and satisfaction to the entire human family.

"The answer to the lie that Negroes will not return to Africa is the fact that we have enrolled four millions who are ready to go tomorrow. Let the great white nation, which our courage and muscle has helped to build, lend us a friendly hand and we'll build a mighty republic in our Motherland, that will be your glory and ours, the glory of the world!"

He suddenly took his seat and the black mass seethed with hysteria. Men and women leaped on the wooden benches, shouted and yelled, cheered and sang. They shook hands and threw their arms around one another.

Above the roar, the tumult, the shouts, Garvey's name rang out and was repeated a hundred times.

Settled in the cab, Phil's hand sought Angela's and he held it in silence during the drive to the apartment, each mind busy with the significance of the scenes they had witnessed.

"Come in and chat a while," she invited.

"I wondered if you'd ask me—" he grinned.

He left his coat in the foyer and went into the living room. Angela slowly drew off her gloves.

"You know, Phil," she began hesitatingly, "Garvey's the greatest Negro I've ever heard speak. He has elemental manhood. He stands squarely on his two feet. His words ring true. And he has character. It's the one thing that impresses you from the moment he speaks. You feel it with redoubled power in the last word he says. Didn't you feel it?"

He nodded slowly.

"I felt it as keenly as you. Except that the futility of his scheme, now and then, destroyed for me the illusion."

"Why say the futility of his scheme? I'm absolutely convinced tonight that it is the only solution of the race problem. And remember it was long ago given us by the two prophets of American democracy, Jefferson and Lincoln. All through Garvey's dignified speech I heard the quiet voice of Abraham Lincoln saying: "There is a physical difference between the white and the black races that will forever forbid their living together on terms of social and political equality." This man is voicing the inspired soul of the Emancipator."

"But the scheme's impossible. Why discuss the impossible?"

"Nothing could be more practical. A hundred million dollars from our treasury would start the movement and settle the first contingent on African soil. Another appropriation would move the four million Negroes Garvey has enrolled. In a hundred years we could help the Negro build a nation of his own in Africa. The races can not live here in physical touch with one another. It's a violation of law. God's law—who made of one blood all the races of men and *fixed the bounds of their habitation*. Africa is one of the richest countries of the world."

"The Negro won't go," he interrupted.

"But Garvey has proven that he will go. It's curious how the bold assertion of a lie can be repeated until millions of people will accept it. Lincoln asked General B.F. Butler[1] to devise and report to him a plan to colonize the Negro race. Butler, hostile to the idea, hurriedly made his famous, false and facetious report, that ships could not be found to carry the black babies to Africa as fast as they were born. Ships have brought to

1. Benjamin Franklin Butler (1818–1893) was a lawyer, Civil War general, and Massachusetts governor noted for his advocacy for the rights of blacks, women, and labor. In 1892 Butler claimed that in 1865 Lincoln discussed with him his plan to "get rid of the negroes," notably "those whom we have armed and disciplined." Historians consider this allegation to be spurious. See Mark E. Neely Jr., "Abraham Lincoln and Black Colonization: Benjamin Butler's Spurious Testimony," *Civil War History* 25 (March 1979): 76–83.

our shores seven million emigrants in six years. They could take as many back. Yet this Butler lie is still being repeated.

"Why not face the question squarely? We are playing with it. Our educational schemes are make-shifts. We could establish a colony of half a million Negroes in two years. They could lay the foundations of a Black Republic which would solve the problem on the only rational basis—friendly colonization.

"We owe this to the Negro. We're deceiving him and allowing him to deceive himself. He hopes and dreams of assimilation. Our attitude of hypocrisy is inhuman and brutal toward a weaker race——"

She paused, took a book from the table, slowly turned its leaves and said: "I wanted to show this to you to-night, a most remarkable and illuminating study of the Negro by Major Earnest Sevier Cox of Richmond, Virginia, a brilliant explorer, who has spent years in Africa, India, China and South America, studying this question at first hand.

"Race traits," he declares, "were determined at a remote period when races were young and plastic. Succeeding centuries have but accentuated the differences. We must accept the races, as such, sharply distinguished from each other, and conditioned to development in accord with their respective instincts and tendencies. We can not act toward the Negro as if he were a white child, for he is not a white child, but a full grown black whose hope for the future lies in his development of himself as a Negro, and not in his pathetic and ludicrous aping of the white man.

"From the study of history we are safe in assuming that if the white race were effaced from the earth, civilization, as we know it, would perish. The insane desire of colored people to blot out the color line and bridge the chasm between the races by intermarriage ignores the fact that the white race, as white, is the source of progress. If the Negro in America boasts his boxers, athletes, artists and singers let him remember that they are each and every one of them the product of white teaching and training. Not one of them ever came out of the jungles of Africa.

"The white man, during the first three thousand years of Egyptian history built the great civilization of the Nile. In daily contact with the dark hordes of Africa, the barriers of race were at last broken down and a Mulatto ascended the throne of the Pharoahs. And from that day Egypt began to die. Her civilization was not destroyed. It perished.

"Scientific research has established three facts . . . 1st, The white race has founded all civilizations. 2nd, The white race, remaining white, has never lost civilization. 3rd, The white race, become hybrid, has never retained civilization.

"Negro blood made the proud Egyptian a mongrel. For the past three thousand years the same Nile has flowed, but Negroid Egypt has known no progress. We are struck with awe when we consider their three thousand years of progress. We are no less struck with awe when we consider the completeness of their decay. White nations have made great contributions during this period in the persons of governmental officials, educators, religious instructors, merchants, agriculturists, artists and explorers. But their coming did not impart life to the dead body. It remains a Negroid quagmire which engulfs all agencies of progress, a little more slowly, but quite as hopelessly as does the Negroid quagmire further south in Equatorial Africa.

"Long continued race contact, throughout human history, is written large in one word . . . AMALGAMATION. The Negro problem is not essentially that of Slavery or Freedom, but one arising from the physical presence of the Negro. Slave or freeman, there will always be a Negro problem so long as the two races remain together. It is not the subnormal white man, sinking to the level of the Negro in producing Mulatto offspring, who gives the greatest impetus to race amalgamation, but the abnormal sympathizing whites who encourage them in this degradation.

"North America is nine tenths white, one tenth colored. South America is nine tenths colored, one tenth white. Ninety per cent of all births in South America are illegitimate. North America possesses a vigorous, expanding, self sustaining civilization. South America has a puny, restricted, dependant culture which is receding before a terrible hybridism.

"The white South must realize that it is confronted by a situation that threatens its existence. The future must witness in the United States, either a white nation or a Negroid nation. If the South becomes Mulatto the North will become Negroid. The question before the white people of America is whether they will give the Negro a home of his own, or incorporate his blood.

"It is the mission of the awakened South to lead in removing this danger of the centuries from our people, and at the same time atone to the Negro for centuries of wrong done his race. The white people of the North will quickly support our efforts to solve the problem by the separation of the races, knowing that the issue is really the future of America.

"The South of ideals and of hope must crush now beneath its heel the greed that counsels delay. It must crush beneath its heel the race perverts who ask for intermarriage. It must deal patiently but firmly with the "New Southerners," who, in a spirit of abject meekness, say weakly that separation can not take place and amalgamation must come.

"The Southern people who wish the Negro to remain in the South to use his cheap labor have the same selfish ends to serve as our fathers who established the Negro in Slavery. We protest against any yielding to these greedy few.

"The most subtle and by far the most dangerous amalgamation trend in the South at this time operates under the cloak of Christianity. In the face of a great biological problem, that has nothing on earth to do with religion, this branch of the Church falsely proclaims that it has a solution. No such problem has ever been solved by religion. If we should build up a population of 50,000,000 Negroes, all good Christians in the South, would the conflict of Color be solved? It would be immeasurably aggravated. The Church, of all our institutions, should support the Negro in his aspirations for separation and national freedom. It can not do this and at the same time cater to the greed of a few whites who demand cheap labor——"

"But they'd fail miserably," Phil broke in. "The Negro has no capacity for colonization or self government."

"We'd help them. Help them with millions in money and intelligent teachers. They couldn't fail with our staunch backing."

"They've failed in Liberia. Gone back to savagery and slavery. There are two hundred thousand slaves of black masters in Liberia today."

"We haven't backed them. We have dumped a few of them on the shores of Africa and left them to die or go native. We must sponsor their nation with men and millions until it is established."

"The Negro, I tell you, is not a colonizer. He is by nature a dependant."

"But you heard a new leader tonight. You heard their answering shouts. He is sincere. He is honest. He tells you that four millions are now ready to go. Why not back Garvey with all our energies, our money and leadership?"

The lawyer rose, walked to the window, looked down on the street traffic, turned back and spoke thoughtfully.

"Because, my dear, Garvey is doomed. A powerful conspiracy has been formed by his enemies to drive him from America and destroy his work . . ."

"It's infamous!" she cried.

Chapter 44

The conspiracy to destroy Marcus Garvey and his work developed with a ferocity that surprised Phil Stephens, although he knew in a general way that it had been in preparation for two years. The Radical Negroes had developed, early in the fight, a slogan on which they rang the changes . . . "Garvey must go!"

Certainly, either the Universal Negro Improvement Association must go, or the Junta fighting for intermarriage as the solution of the problem must go. They stood for ideas as far apart as the poles. Garvey had built his Association squarely on the principles laid down by Abraham Lincoln. And DuBois was fighting these principles with every energy.

The conspirators had first moved secretly against Garvey's most ambitious and vulnerable company, The Black Star Line. They bored into this organization, seduced a large number of its employees and began to sabotage the whole enterprise. No convictions could be gotten against them. They induced corrupt officers of the Company to pile up thousands of dollars of debts without the knowledge of the Corporation owners or its President. And they systematically damaged the ships at sea.

When Garvey dismissed these men, they openly joined his enemies and demanded his destruction. His most savage fight developed with a group of militant Reds who had joined his workmen as spies and organizers of strikes and riots. Garvey loathed this crowd and all they stood for. He denounced them as anti-social vermin, hunted them out relentlessly and quickly combed his organizations free of them. Which, of course, brought down on his head every Communist in New York, black and white.

The conspirators finally succeeded in alienating a number of the high officials of Garvey's Association inducing them to sue for overdue salaries. The leader had called a convention of all the Negro peoples of the world, from whom these officials had been elected. Twenty five thousand delegates had packed the Madison Square Garden to hear his eloquent address. Many of these delegates, comparative strangers, were easily influenced to attack Garvey when the large salaries promised had not been paid.

His enemies played their trump card, however, in the preparation for their final assault by the wide circulation of a vicious and dangerous lie accusing Garvey of being a member of the Ku Klux Klan! This came on the heels of a national campaign to destroy the Klan, led by Mr. Pulitzer[1] of the New York World.

Nothing could have been more utterly absurd than such an accusation. By its very constitution, no Negro could become a member of the Ku Klux Klan. Yet this lie was so widely and persistently circulated in the daily press, the Negro weeklies, by letters, circulars and handbills, and by stump speakers . . . that millions of people accepted it as a statement of fact.

No deadlier blow could have been struck below the belt. For the entire population of Manhattan Island were hostile to the Klan. When the time came to move against Garvey in the Courts the masses from which a jury must be called would be his enemies through the circulation of this lie.

The stage thus set, the conspirators went into court, and secured Garvey's indictment on a trumped up charge of using the United States mails to defraud the purchasers of stock in his Black Star Line, though not one of them had complained.

Garvey's first mistake in the crisis was to act as his own counsel and defend himself. The real reason for it lay in a supreme consciousness of innocence and the feeling that he could not possibly be convicted in an American Court of Justice. He knew that the essence of fraud is intent. He knew, and the world knew, that the purpose of his work was to build a great free republic of Negroes in Africa. He was the logical successor of Lincoln and Jefferson in this purpose. The stock had never been offered to the public. Every dollar of it had been sold to the members of his Association who believed as he did. Thus secure in the consciousness of innocence, he walked into a deadly trap that had been carefully prepared for him.

The first feint of the conspirators was to secure the postponement of the trial every time it appeared on the regular docket of the United States District Court, over which a distinguished and impartial Judge presided.

A great lawyer, of the calibre of George Gordon Battle, who came into the case on appeal, would have seen through this subterfuge immediately and called a halt. He would have demanded and gotten a hearing

---

1. In 1923 and 1928, respectively, the *Memphis Commercial-Appeal* and the *Indianapolis Times* received Pulitzer Prizes for their exposés of the Ku Klux Klan. See Kenneth T. Jackson, *The Ku Klux Klan in the City, 1915–1930* (New York: Oxford University Press, 1967), 47, 160.

before Judge John W. Knox, presiding Justice of the District. Garvey, a layman, unacquainted with legal procedure, suspected nothing. Until he was suddenly arraigned for trial before a judge whom his bitter foes had selected, the Honorable Julian W. Mack. And when a gentleman with the significant name of Mattuck appeared as the Assistant United States District Attorney conducting the case, the cast of actors in the cooked up anti-Ku Klux Klan farce was complete.

Julian W. Mack was once a regular presiding justice in the Commerce Court until it was abolished. Since that time he has maintained offices both in Chicago, his home, and in New York, and takes odd assignments in the United District Courts as they are offered. . . . A bitter partisan critic of Garvey, he was the last man in the Federal Courts who should have been allowed to sit in judgment on this case. But he took the assignment and, arrayed in the robes of his high office, sat down on the Bench of the United States District Court of the Southern District of New York, and rapped his gavel for order.

Early in the trial, badgered and insulted by both the Assistant District Attorney and the Judge, Garvey realized that he had been betrayed, and boldly demanded the resignation of Judge Mack from the case. The wily Jurist denied the motion on the ground that the technical form of the affidavit was not properly drawn! He did not deny that he was a member of the organization seeking to destroy the prisoner before him. He merely asserted that he could try the case without bias! Had a good lawyer been in charge at this juncture, Judge Mack would have been forced to retire.

The conduct of the trial was, in fact, unique in the annals of court records. The presiding justice permitted the Assistant District Attorney, Mr. Mattuck, to shout "Liar!" into the face of the prisoner defending himself before the jury. A juror was allowed to leave the box, walk up to the judge, and receive whispered comments or instructions, and then look at Garvey and laugh to the amusement of the jury and all spectators. This happened, not once, but many times during the trial.

At the conclusion of the evidence, His Honor delivered a hostile charge to the jury, they retired, and to Mack's amazement remained hung for eleven hours. Without any request for further instructions the Judge sent for the jury, made another speech against the prisoner, and sent them back demanding a decision. In thirty minutes they returned a verdict of guilty against Garvey . . . NOT GUILTY against three associate officers of the Company. If one was guilty all were guilty. The indictment was against all four officers of the corporation.

The Judge immediately sentenced Garvey to the extreme limit of law, five years in Atlanta Penitentiary, and denied him the right of bail, pending an appeal, and left on the next steamer for Europe on a vacation of three months! These three months imprisonment he knew would be long enough to wreck every enterprise of Garvey's Association, if he never served another day.

George Gordon Battle valiantly fought for Garvey on appeal. But so many technical errors had been made at the trial that the appeal was denied. And the grim gates of Atlanta Penitentiary closed on the greatest Negro of the modern world.

Chapter 45

The revelation of the activities against Garvey which developed in his trial shocked Angela and intensified her interest in the vital theme she was studying with so much interest.

She arose early and decided to telephone the girl, who had said that she arrived at Weldon's house at sunrise every morning, went directly to his bedroom, took his order for breakfast and served it to him in bed.

The morning paper revealed that the Red organizations had called a strike in the Textile mills of Piedmont in an effort to establish a radical union of cotton workers in the Carolinas. The strike had dragged through weeks until a militant group had arrived in Piedmont the day before. The newcomers demanded direct blood stained action. They threw a line of armed pickets around the headquarters of the strikers. Their sawed off shot guns were loaded with buckshot, and the strikers, in groups of more than a hundred, were ordered to picket the mill in North Piedmont of which John Lovelace was foreman. A clash of armed forces was expected daily. Angela knew instantly that the program of which Mona spoke had been put into operation. She caught the first express train to Spartanburg without a word to anyone, wiring Ann to meet her train. Her friend held her in her arms a long time in silence, tears blinding them both.

"I'm so glad to see you, darling," the older woman said. "You're looking so well and happy. I'm proud of you."

"I owe it to you, dear. But for you I would have run away from life. I'm so grateful. I've come to see if I can help John in his fight."

"He needs you," was the gentle answer. "Never before did he have any trouble with his people—any real trouble. He always gave them concessions, bettered their conditions and they always went back to work in a happier mind. Now the Devil's loose in Piedmont. A strange foreign devil imported from the North. They don't want reason. They don't want compromise. They want bloodshed. They want the front page of every newspaper in the South and their leader knows that he can get it by a bloody riot. And they are going to provoke one. John hasn't slept for two nights. Every day he expects the worst. And, of course, it will come. We always get what we're looking for. He won't listen to me when I tell him to take the thing to God. To leave it in God's hands. To know that God is really in the hearts of the strikers too. But he always shoots back at me—'But not in the heart of the devils who come down here to shed blood.'"

They drove by the mill and Lovelace came out, his hair disheveled, his suit grimed with grease and lint.

"Excuse me, Angela. I can't shake hands. I've been mending machines all morning. I'm having one hell of a time to keep my wheels going and prevent a clash. It's coming though. I feel it in the air."

A scout from the mills dashed up.

"Mr. Lovelace, the strikers are marching on us again. A hundred strong, every one of them armed."

The foreman sounded his whistle and four officers on duty answered the call.

"Lieutenant, go down the road, meet the armed fools who are marching on us, tell them we are armed too and they'll get trouble if they're looking for it. Ask them to go back to their headquarters, lay down their guns, put their demands in writing and disperse."

"If they won't go?" the officers asked.

"Call the Sheriff to go with you to their headquarters and ask the fellows who are running it what they want. Ask them to put their full demands in writing that we may consider them."

The officer tipped his cap and the four uniformed men marched up the road to meet the strikers.

"You drive on home," he signalled to his wife.

Angela stepped from the car.

"Park it, Ann. We're not running. We'll help John."

"I don't want you, honey," he protested. "You can't help me and you may get hurt."

"Give me a gun, John Lovelace," the younger woman said. "I've had to practice shooting in New York."

He smiled and handed her a revolver which she slipped into her handbag.

He offered one to his wife.

She answered with tears.

"You know me better than that, John. I trust in God, not guns.

"So do I," he answered, "but I keep my gun ready."

He paused and looked down the highway at a car coming on at high speed.

"Get inside. That's the Sheriff on his way to their headquarters. The men I sent have called him."

In five minutes a fusillade of shots came from the strike headquarters.

"My God! They've opened fire on the Sheriff. I must go."

He rushed to the car, but both women beat him to it.

"Get out!" he shouted.

"Don't strain your voice, John," his wife said gently. "I'm your wife. My place is by your side."

"You'll be killed."

"No I won't. God is protecting me. You may be shot. You expect it. I'll be there to help you."

"Please, Angela, make her stay and you stay with her!"

"No. I'm with you. I can fight if I have to. Drive on."

He threw up his hands, got into the car and speeded to the scene of the shooting. Three of his men were lying on the roadside wounded and the Sheriff was leaning heavily against a fence.

"I'm done for, John," he said. "The other boys are hurt but not fatally. Get me home or to the hospital, will you?"

Lovelace lifted the Sheriff into the car and Ann held his head on her shoulder.

Angela refused to go to the hospital but found the Lieutenant and asked him what had happened.

"You never saw nothing like it, Miss," he said. "We got the strikers to come back and it set the gang wild at headquarters. I tried to go inside to talk to 'em. But they shoved us back with the muzzles of their guns in our stomachs. 'Get out, damn you!' the leader yelled. 'We don't need you. We're running this strike now.'

"The Sheriff walked up and said: 'What's the trouble, boys? I've come down to help you when they called me. What is it?' 'None of your damned business!' the same fellow hollered. 'Get away from our headquarters!'

"The Sheriff's a mighty quiet man, a good deacon in his church. He nodded to me: 'Come up the road, boys, and we'll decide what's best to do.'

"He walked away and as he did they opened fire on us with sawed off shot guns. Every door and window in the place blazed. They put a load through the Sheriff's back. He can't live. Three of my men are wounded with buckshot. It's all the work of damned Communist devils from the North who've come down here to stir riot and bloodshed!"

The Sheriff died at six o'clock, and by eight the streets were packed with excited men. Captain Collier addressed them and rifles were dealt out to five hundred picked members of the crowd. They were sworn in as deputy sheriffs. By twelve o'clock the strike headquarters had been raided and every Communist in town was lodged in jail and sixty strikers with them. All charged with murder. Governor Gardner[1] of North Carolina, in whose territory on the north side the mills were located, had not sent troops. The Mayor had not requested it. The Governor had mobilized two companies of the State guard in the earlier weeks of the strike, overawed them, and the ringleaders had awaited their withdrawal before calling in the radicals from New York for the purge of blood. The citizens of Piedmont under command of the gallant old Confederate Captain had armed and taken drastic action.

Every train entering the station was watched and no man was allowed to stop who was under the slightest suspicion of radical connections. Guards were placed on every highway leading into town, every car stopped and searched and every occupant had to give an account of himself or go to jail.

An able array of lawyers appeared in the prosecution of the accused, led by the distinguished attorney from Shelby, Clyde R. Hoey. The strike was called off. The mills resumed full operation and the plot to organize the textile workers of the Carolinas as a Communist unit collapsed.

Angela called on Captain Collier.

He greeted her with deep feeling.

"I can't tell you how proud and happy I am to see you looking so well. It's an honor to be your friend. When I think of what you lived through and conquered I'm ashamed to whine over my little troubles."

She leaned across his desk.

"Tell me, Captain Tom, is this the first attempt of these invaders to influence the South?"

"The first I know of. But believe me, unless all signs fail, it will not be the last. Take a look at this."

He handed to her a map of the Southern States showing in deep shadow the Black Belt stretching in solid mass from Washington, D.C., through Virginia, North Carolina, South Carolina, Georgia, Alabama, Mississippi, Louisiana, and Arkansas into Texas.

"In this vast territory," he said, "there are nine million five hundred thousand inhabitants, a majority of whom are Negroes. They are now flooding the South with inflammatory leaflets, pamphlets, and books calling on the Negroes to rise, and take this land by force of arms. They are told it all

1. Oliver Maxwell (Max) Gardner (1882–1947) of North Carolina was an attorney and later was governor of the state from 1929–1933. In response to labor unrest, in 1929 he called out the National Guard to suppress textile strikes in both Gastonia and Marion. See John A. Salmond, *Gastonia 1929: The Story of the Loray Mill Strike* (Chapel Hill: University of North Carolina Press, 1995).

belongs to them. That the United States Government promised it to them in 1867, and it was stolen by their former masters. They are told the time has come to build a great Black Republic out of this part of the Southern States."

He paused and took up a leaflet printed in bold faced type.

"Listen to this from one of their new teachers:

"In the Black Belt of the South full equal rights for the Negro can mean only one thing—the right of self determination. The Civil War did not fulfill the tasks demanded by history. The revolutionary proletariat finds one of its most important allies in the Negro people. And the Negro people can find their only dependable and most powerful ally in the Proletariat.

"The plantation unit is situated precisely in the area where the Negroes are a majority of the population. The revolutionary governmental power which is created in the Black Belt as the result of a democratic revolution, would of necessity be in the hands of the workers and the peasantry. In such a government, from the local administrative units to the top bodies, the Negroes would be greatly predominant, because they form the overwhelming majority of these classes in the area where such a transformation would take place. They constitute the chief revolutionary sector of the plantation."

He paused.

"Have you ever seen this stuff before?"

"No. But I've a pretty clear idea where it comes from. And it's giving a new purpose to my work. Here's the big threat against our life, Captain. And the South may yet save the nation."

"If our people wake up. But, honey, they're peacefully sleeping at present. The shots that rang out from the strike headquarters at John Lovelace's mill will wake a few of them. We must stir the whole South. This same bunch of Reds are now using the Scottsboro case to inflame the minds of the Negroes."

"Yes, I know. I'm going to Scottsboro from here. May I take this map and pamphlets?" she asked.

"Yes. But you get into their headquarters in New York and give me their latest. They're bringing out something new every hour now. Keep me posted."

"I will," she promised.

He walked with them to the door.

"By the calendar I'm a little older. I don't feel it inside. It's glorious to be alive and play my part in the big drama. We're living in tremendous times."

He turned to the other woman.

"Thank you, Ann, for bringing her to me. It's good for sore eyes just to look at her. I've ignored you in this talk not because I don't trust you. But because I'm aware you don't trust me."

"My trust is in God, Captain——"

"Oh, I trust in God, too. But it makes me awfully nervous sometimes. Get Angela to the train as quick as you can. The devil may break loose here any minute until we hang a few of the boys we've got in jail. They call themselves a Party, these Communists. Party hell! They're a gang of revolutionists. If I had my say I'd line every damned one of them against a wall tomorrow morning at sunrise and shoot them. They hope to do as much for us some day." He paused and looked at Angela with a frown.

"But the thing that sickens me worst of all in this crisis is that our people are losing their sense of values. Our own party, under new sinister influences, has begun to coddle the Negro voter. The dominant party of the South will always be a white man's. The minute we begin to hug the Negro we are waltzing with Death and we're on the way out. The damned fools who are now running the State seem to have forgotten this."

She seized his hand.

"As long as the South has men of your clear vision, the thing you fear can't happen."

The old man bent low, kissed her, and murmured:

"Goodbye, honey, God bless you.

As her train swept through the Black Belt of the South to the little town in Alabama, now the mecca of Reds from every State and nation, she tried to imagine this vast rich territory transformed into a Black Republic with the Negroid fanatics in New York directing its offices. The scenes of carnage and tyranny that would be enacted! That it would be transformed into another Haiti, where black men rule whites, would be a tragic certainty, unless the white race should rise and drive out the blacks.

Arrived in Scottsboro she sought the seclusion of an old fashioned Southern boarding house and began her investigation of the activities. The task was easy. The shrewdly managed "International Labor Defense" had gotten the consent of the parents and ousted the great lawyers, Arthur Garfield Hays and Clarence Darrow. They had been supplanted by a Mr. Liebowitz from New York, engaged by the Communists.[2]

2. In 1931 the famous attorney Clarence Darrow (1857–1938), along with Arthur Garfield Hays (1881–1954), a prominent civil liberties lawyer who had defended the Gastonia strikers, agreed to argue the appeal of the "Scottsboro boys"—nine African American youths convicted of raping two white girls on a freight train in Alabama. The two lawyers withdrew from the case, however, because of internecine conflicts between the International Labor Defense Committee and the National Association for the Advancement of Colored People. In 1933 the criminal lawyer Samuel S. Leibowitz (1893–1978) agreed to defend the "Scottsboro boys." See Dan T. Carter, *Scottsboro: A Tragedy of the American South* (1969; reprint, New York: Oxford University Press, 1971), 97–98, 181–82.

This new shrewd lawyer, did not enter into the public controversy. He sat back and let the other fellows rave. He won an appeal for a new trial for the eight Negroes accused of mass rape on two white prostitutes and a wave of enthusiasm swept the Negro millions in America. No matter what the merits of the case, it was white against black, and the black man had won a legal victory. Communism became, overnight, a magic word among the Negroes of the South.

And they were taking advantage of this enthusiasm without delay. A Negro agent was in Birmingham organizing black cells among the miners. Another was in Georgia circulating seditious leaflets and calling his black comrades to organize.

Angela stopped off in Atlanta and attended the trial of the Negro agent sent into Georgia. He had been arraigned under an old law of the Reconstruction period forbidding seditious speech and writing.

The court room was packed with perspiring Negroes and excited whites. The Red organizer who had come to test the temper of the South was sentenced to the chain gang.

Angela took the train for home assured of one thing. The South was in peril.

Chapter 46

Upon her return Angela determined to carry out her plan of cultivating the Communists. She would join the Party and learn their last secret. She telephoned Mona and made an engagement to attend a Party reception the following evening. Mona was in high spirits. She introduced Angela to her friends as a possible convert whom she had partially won. Her culture, and personality created a mild sensation. But she would not rush her plans. They required timely development. She cultivated the men and women she met purely on a personal basis. She found herself always a center of interest with a circle of four or five hovering about her.

Two or three young men were too attentive to suit Mona. She drew her friend aside.

"Don't pay any attention to these poor saps here tonight."

"Oh, I enjoy talking to them, they're good listeners."

"But don't take any of them seriously. They've got no brains. A month from tonight we have our annual meeting. The most brilliant leader of the Cause in New York will be here. I've picked him for your first victim. He boasts that he never looks at any woman twice. I'll be close by when he meets you."

"So I'm to save my ammunition for him?"

"By all means. Don't give these fellows a second thought. You're making a hit tonight. You're a man's woman and a woman's woman."

Mona introduced her to a group of The Sacred Order of Monna Vanna, all of them goodlooking girls from eighteen to twenty five. She stared at them still with unbelieving eyes. It was grotesque—this fanaticism that could send hundreds of handsome young white women into Harlem daily to win Negro leaders to accept their Cause. This madness was surely a dangerous force in a world of flabby faiths and selfish indifference.

On parting Mona obtained her promise to attend every weekly meeting possible and come to the annual gathering loaded for bear.

"We dress that night, you know!" she laughed.

"I'll come armed for the fray," Angela promised.

Her plans of investigation rapidly formed and Phil must do his part. She telephoned him——

"Where on earth have you been these past three weeks?" he asked.

"Took a flying trip down South. Saw the folks in Piedmont, hugged old Captain Tom and saw John Lovelace's strike settled."

"Hope you were not there the day of the battle."

"Right in the thick of it."

"I'll have a guardian appointed for you. And bribe the Judge to appoint me. I'm working late tonight. Can you meet me at the Lafayette for dinner, say at seven thirty?"

"With pleasure."

"Don't be late. I'll be there at 7:30 on the dot."

"On the dot."

The dinner was a success. The oysters were fresh. The frog legs delicious and the breast of Guinea Hen done to the king's taste. They talked of personal things and when Phil's cigarette was lighted she broached the big theme.

"I've come back from the South, Phil, with a sense of uneasiness, overwhelmed with the conviction that our people are standing at the cross roads of a new destiny. And I'm frankly frightened. They have won easily the first skirmish with the Reds in the Textile strike—too easily. I've no sooner reached home when I read in the morning's news dispatches from Chattanooga an account of the Southern States Conference of the Communist Party. A hundred and thirty delegates from eleven Southern States, Negroes and whites, men and women, sitting side by side, plotting the overthrow of our civilization."

"It's amazing," Phil agreed.

"What's come over the South that they permit these desperadoes to hold a meeting under the shadow of Lookout Mountain?"

"There's but one answer. The Old South is breaking up. A New South is shaping that is forgetting what their fathers lived for, fought and died for."

"And the tragic thing is," he added, "that the Negro already holds the balance of power in the elections of the great industrial States of the North. If the Reds dare to strike in a crisis——"

"We've got to do something," Angela broke in.

"I've been dreaming and working on the plan for a big national Patriot Union to meet this threat. Are you interested?"

"Am I?"

"Its purpose is the preservation of the American form of Government to drive out seditious influences and propaganda from our schools, colleges, Labor Unions, relief agencies, churches and all civic bodies. To be effective this Union must be secretly armed and drilled. The plan calls for a working unit in every County of every State which will unite all veteran organizations. Every post and patriot society in each County will be brought in until every election district is organized. Every County chairman will receive his appointment from headquarters here in New York, directed by a Legion of Valor. These men must swear obedience to the orders of the general staff. Each election district will have a chairman elected by the district, but approved by the County chairman. Every member will be given a job to do as a working American patriot. The press, the radio, the pulpit, the platform will be used daily. The outer form of the organization will be political. In essence it will be a patriot army that can be mobilized over night."

"The Communists are arming and drilling."

"And the essential thing we don't know is the day that will be fixed. That we must have!"

He studied her face and quietly said:

"It's going to take big money to launch this ambitious scheme. Fifty thousand at least to start it. Several millions to work it. Where's the money coming from?"

"We'll begin with a contribution of five thousand from each of us."

"You can put in that much?"

"Yes. And I know you can. That will start enrollment. We'll accept money only from men and women who have taken the oath and from those whose loyalty can be vouched for by at least two of your County chairmen. There are two of us here now. I'm going to ask you to let me raise the first fifty thousand dollar contribution."

"Murino?"

"Yes. Why not?"

"I'll never agree. I won't associate with criminals. You're mad to suggest it."

"You're mad with jealousy to refuse it. You can't understand that Murino is an exception. He is no gangster. To call him a murderer is nonsense. He only sits as a judge and sentences men under laws which they have established themselves. He was a bootlegger only by a miscarriage of justice. He made his millions in the illegal liquor trade—yes. But repeal now makes his acts fair trade. There are many men in the liquor business in America who will fight for their country. George Washington, you know, was a distiller who sold liquor. We still count him a pretty good American.

Don't be childish. Murino has never soiled his hands with a racket. Mark my word, when trouble comes he'll be one of the most powerful allies we have. Be fair. You're not fair because you happen to know that he likes me. We have no time to split hairs on fine points of prohibition ethics. I'm going to ask Murino for a contribution."

"And should I refuse to work with him?"

"I'll go my way and you can go yours."

"All right, you win. Ask him. I think you're a little overconfident, myself."

"Maybe."

Murino answered her call enthusiastically, and Angela asked:

"Where do we go?"

"To my house. Your boy friend is watching me so closely I'm afraid of the road houses."

When they entered the house and the butler had disappeared she sank into a deep chair and laughed.

"What's the joke?" he demanded.

"Well, Phil insists that you couldn't elude him so successfully unless you have a secret passageway into this beautiful house. I wonder if you have?"

"What do you think?"

"It's possible, of course."

"Would you like to take a peek before dinner?"

"You're joking!"

"I'm not," he smiled, "follow me."

He led her into his luxuriously appointed office opening on the street by a side door.

"This," he said, "is my office for transacting business with the outside world."

"Perfectly appointed."

"Now I'm going to show how utterly I trust you without a pledge of secrecy. Why is it I know that such a pledge is not necessary with you? I trust you with my life without a minute's hesitation."

He paused and walked toward a life sized portrait of Lincoln's full figure standing. It reached from the baseboard to a height of ten feet.

"You would never suspect this rather commonplace painting of the great President of concealing the door to my inner room and passageway out to the side street. It doesn't, in fact, conceal the door. It is the door."

He touched a gilded knob of the immense frame and the picture dropped three inches from the wall. He pressed the portrait covered door back and she saw the entrance to a narrow hall.

"Enter, M'moiselle!" he bowed. "And mind your step—one inch up to clear the baseboard."

They entered the hall, he closed the door and led her through the passage to a narrow stairway leading to a lower level. At the foot of the stairs he took a key and opened a steel plate door. Ten inches beyond this outer door was another heavier panelled backing that yielded to a different key. The door closed automatically behind them and he switched on the lights. They stood in a spacious room of heavy steel construction with a single large flat top double desk in the center, a swivel chair on either side and half a dozen small metal chairs scattered about the place.

The wall on one side of the room was lined with filing cases and the index drawer was half open.

He waved an arm carelessly toward the cases.

"Here are kept the records of my business. Naturally they are not for public inspection. I needed a retreat from the detectives on my trail. This is my sanctuary. Here I meet the leaders of my trade and here we make our deals. Usually alone. Occasionally a committee of two or three. The small chairs are for the small fry."

"You allow a secretary or stenographer to come in here?"

"No. That wouldn't do. Occasionally when there's a lot of bookkeeping to complete I bring an expert of our organization for a day's work. Otherwise I keep all records. I'm a pretty fair typist."

He touched a drawer on the right of his desk and a section swung open revealing a small typewriter. He touched the left drawer and the outer section moved showing two telephones and a Morse telegraphic key.

"You send and receive telegrams, too?"

"Yes. A precaution for emergencies. I've never used it yet. Might come in handy some day. The point is I've put my wires to these phones into heavy tubes that lead to the mains under the street. They can't be cut or tapped by troublesome undercover men from the District Attorney's Office."

He paused and crossed to the wall opposite and opened a panel without a key. Inside was a complete radio room containing sending and receiving sets.

Angela smiled in approval.

"Efficient, I must say."

"Isn't it? I can get London, Berlin, Rome direct from that chair and talk any time day or night—to say nothing of every town in North or South America."

"It's wonderful."

"Now," he said smiling, "I'll show you the way in."

He led her through another double door entrance into a hall opening on the side street through a servant's entrance level with the pavement.

"I own this house, too, and allow only our own people to occupy it. That is, their mothers, sisters and aunts. No males and no servants. I stroll by the place, if no undercover men are watching, drop into the servant's entrance, the door you see is ten feet back in the shadows of a narrow hallway. The District Attorney may suspect this but he has not, as yet, been able to locate it."

He stopped and looked steadily into her eyes as he offered her a set of keys but she shook her head.

"I wouldn't dare."

"Why not?" he asked. "I had them made for you. You might sometime be of the greatest service to me as well as yourself."

Seated beside his desk she studied his face and asked frankly:

"Why all these extraordinary precautions?"

"You understand, of course, that my business requires the utmost secrecy."

"Certainly. But not all this steel clad protection. You seem prepared to stand a seige."

"I am. It may come to that before we're through with the crisis we are approaching. You are studying Communism. So am I. When I delve into the plans of these gentlemen I find I am an ultra conservative member of modern society. There are big schemes afoot in Harlem and lower Manhattan. Have to keep myself informed on every move of the political chessboard and the latest moves have disturbed me."

"What moves?"

"The program of the Reds in particular. My agents report that their coming ticket will carry two ominous names for President and Vice-President. Your brilliant District Attorney calls me a dangerous criminal."

"But I know better!"

"Of course, you do, but a lot of people don't. My nightmare today is this movement among racketeers, gangsters, and desperate criminals for organized action. If the criminals in this country ever effect a full national organization, God help our moron society! I've shown you how I'm fighting racketeers. But they're gaining in numbers and power daily. We have seven million aliens in this country, two thirds of them with criminal records. Do you know that our prisons are discharging convicts at the rate of a million every ten years? Think of pouring these millions into our social organism in the past twenty years.

"Have we absorbed all this poison? We have absorbed it all right. But we have not assimilated it. There's now a criminal population in this country of more than two million racketeers and desperate men born in America who lie awake nights thinking up schemes by which they can destroy your society. In the past the criminal was a lone wolf and you merely kicked him

back into prison. But there are men of brilliant minds now among these racketeers. Last year crime levied a tribute of thirty billions on the citizens of the U.S. What it will be in ten years more, God only knows, if these crime leaders really organize."

"But how can they?"

"That's why I'm studying Communism. They are hatching a scheme in Harlem to nominate for the President of the United States, an ex-convict, representing over seven million criminals and a coal black Negro for Vice-President representing the twelve million Negroes they're determined to capture."

"You think such a combination possible?"

"We are living in a crazy world, today. Anything's possible. You've probably read their manifesto."

"Yes. "

"They have preached social equality and fought for the intermarriage of the races before every legislature that will give them a hearing.

"They are reaping what these radical Negroes have sown. They must now outbid the followers of Karl Marx or quit the field. The power behind this political move may be a combination of Communists, Organized Criminals and Negroes. If they name an ex-convict for President and a Negro for Vice-President my worst fears will be realized."

"Then we agree on the real issue," Angela interrupted. "The important question is how to meet the threat."

She outlined fully Phil's plan and gave him credit for its conception.

"A great idea," was the quick comment.

"We need fifty thousand dollars to launch the organization of the Patriot Union——"

Without a moment's hesitation he opened the strong box in his desk and handed her the amount neatly fastened in five packages of ten thousand each.

"It's a privilege to do this. Come back when you need more. Count on me. You're late in starting but you're on the right track and may be in time to stop the big push."

Her eyes were sparkling as she rose, put both hands on his shoulders and kissed him. He held her close for a moment and she could feel the pounding of his heart.

"You're a great man, Tony!" she cried.

"'Tony' to you from now on?"

"And always."

"You'll accept the keys now, I hope. They may prove valuable to your Patriot Union."

"Yes."

"Is there anything else I can do?"

"I must learn to drive a car again. This terrible traffic bewilders me. You might loan me your roadster."

"I'll do better. I'll have you to brush up on your driving and present a new one as a contribution to the Cause. I'm going to fight with you. War makes strange bed fellows, doesn't it? I've a sneaking idea, of course, that this association will bring us closer together. I've never wanted anything in this world as I do that. When I look at you, my wealth, my success seem futile because I can't get the one thing I want most. But I'll keep on hoping and waiting. I almost said praying—maybe I can pray—who knows?"

She looked at him gravely: "You can."

"Let me be your driving instructor?" he asked suddenly.

"I'd love it," she laughed. "You're the best driver I ever saw."

"All right. Meet me at the Packard place on Broadway at ten tomorrow morning, select your car, and I'll give you the first lesson."

The telephone rang.

"The butler says we are spoiling a good dinner."

"Does your butler know about this room?"

"No. The same phone rings in my office."

Early the next day she called on Phil before his office hour. When he heard the news of Murino's gifts, his face was a puzzle.

"That's great. We'll thank God and take courage. I'll give the devil his dues. There's more to him than I thought."

They quietly opened offices in the Rockefeller Center and provided for their enlargement as needed. Angela puzzled Phil by refusing to take a desk for herself.

"No," she said emphatically, "I must not be known in the organization. There's a reason—a big reason for this. There's something I must do alone—something of the utmost importance."

"But this organization is half yours," he protested.

"No. You're elected chief. Get to work. You'd better consult me at my apartment—never over the telephone. I'll report to you when my first job is done."

He grinned happily.

"There'll be a lot of consulting!"

"I expect and welcome it. Your name is Old Reliable now."

"We should have every Sunday afternoon to outline the week's work," he suggested.

"Good. We'll begin Sunday with dinner at one o'clock."

Chapter 47

Mona came to the apartment the night of the annual meeting and gave final instructions.

Angela had moments of repulsion for the girl that she tried to overcome. She attempted to think only of her faith in a Cause. To this girl's mind the Cause of human redemption.

But when she remembered that she had yielded herself to a Negro, she felt a deep sense of revulsion. No such sacrifice should be asked of any white girl God ever made. How dare the fanatics at their Headquarters work up this infamous scheme! Her impulse was to draw back and cut her life free of such associates. But she, too, had made a vow to consecrate her life to a Cause, the sanctity of a race. Nothing could be more certain than the extinction of our civilization if the black man mixed his blood with the white. And a thousand influences were now at work in America to break down all barriers. She must pocket her own feelings and forget the sordid details of the personal lives of these people. She had work to do. She must do it. In this case the end would surely justify the means.

There was a certain compensation in the devotion of Mona. It was genuine. Her admiration knew no bounds.

"I'll be proud of you, tonight," she said. "You'll knock 'em all dead. But the one I want you to slay without mercy is our hero leader, john Allen, the scion of an old patriotic American family. He's a graduate of Yale. A gentleman if there ever was one. He takes particular pride in his contempt for the charms of a mere woman. Every girl in our group is crazy about him. He don't know they exist except as units of our scheme. I thought he gave me a second glance once and my heart missed a beat. He failed to see me the third time. Think some cat in our crowd tipped him off that I was a member of the Sacred Order of Monna Vanna. He worked out that title for us, too. He even made a swell speech at the dedication of our old theatre. But I'm afraid deep down in his soul he holds a secret contempt for every one of us. We are used as pawns in a game—that's all. When he meets you, he'll take more than a second look. He'll mark you as a possible convert and leader. Play the role. It's worth while. He's the smartest leader we have in America and he's marked for the highest honor in the new Soviet Republic we're going to establish."

"He's of the inner grand council of the party, then?" Angela asked softly.

"One of its highest officers."

"I hope he will like me."

"He'll like you all right. I've heard him describe the ideal woman—the impossible woman. His description would make a good sketch of you . . . and tonight's the night!"

When Angela drove into the line of cars and cabs approaching the International Assembly Rooms on 2nd Avenue, it had begun to rain. They called a boy to park and watch the car.

The ball room was already crowded.

"I'll show you the big shots, first," Mona said in low tones."The swellest of the bunch is young Gordon Perry. You've heard of him, his father's a big banker. It's funny to find him here. But there he is, bursting with pride and importance. He's a Red writer now. Specializes on preaching atheism. He thinks he's sincere. But he's not. He's just a silly person who thinks that he thinks. There's always a gang of "Yes" men around him. I honestly believe he hires them as chorus boys to play the scenes with him. You remember the kind of boys who used to run up and down on the stage and get in the way of the chorus girls? That bunch of rioting college boys beside him are harmless. They are just playing a part. I hate to think what John Allen will do to him and his bunch the morning after the revolution breaks. Would you care to meet him?"

"No thanks. Just to see the miracle of a Wall Street magnate's son playing at this game is enough."

"There's some more swells over there on his right. They're saps who pride themselves on being broadminded, liberal, and progressive. Not one of them has the remotest idea of what Communism means. They work merely to show their liberty in opposing and offending conventions.

"The funniest people down here are a lot of clerical morons who leave their pulpits to mingle with the radicals and show their rapture over the coming of a new world without the profit motive. They draw fat salaries, too, some of them. They don't realize that the purpose of Marx was to destroy all religions and exterminate the clergy as social vermin. It's enough to make a cat laugh!"

Mona drew her forward.

"Comrade, John Allen, allow me to introduce a student of Social Science from Columbia University, Miss Angela Cameron."

Holding her with a steady gaze, Allen extended his hand and grasped hers in a sort of daze. He quickly recovered, frowned and said:

"You are the student of our Cause of whom Mona has been boasting, I assume?"

He asked the question with a serious tone that brought the color to Angela's cheeks.

"Mona is far too generous in praise of her friends, I'm afraid."

She paused and turned toward the girl to find she had joined another group.

"Shall we find a seat and have a little chat?" he ventured.

"By all means," she nodded.

He led her into an office, and offered her a chair while he drew one near hers.

"We'll be undisturbed here. It's the manager's office and I believe I'm the boss tonight."

He spoke with a quiet egotism that ruffled Angela from the first sentence.

"You'd make a star leader of our woman's division," he remarked looking at her with critical eyes. "I've been looking for some time for a Joan of Arc type to make a grand tour of the United States."

"Aren't you assuming a little too much? I'm only a student of Communism."

He smiled.

"I'm already booking your dates in my mind."

"You think I could hold an audience?"

"No doubt of it. Once we've grounded you in our principles."

His easy assumption of her conquest roused her fighting spirit. Her first impulse was to slap his face.

"There are a few things you will have to explain, before I can join your cult."

"For instance?"

He asked the question in a way that presumed an answer was superfluous. Her anger rose again and she cut each word of her reply into sharp edges.

"It has always seemed to me that your philosophy is a fanaticism in many ways unparalleled in history. A war against a sane social system. A war against civilization itself. But more. A war of the hand against the brain of man. For the first time since man emerged from the cave and stood erect there is a breach between the head and the hand. You are a leader.

Why? Because you have a better trained mind than your comrades. Yet you would ignore this fact, the basis of all possible progress. The idea shocks me. You have made no provision for intelligence."

He stared at her in surprise. He was not used to such talk from a mere woman. It struck him as an impertinence. Yet he must waste a little breath in replying.

"You misinterpret our principles," he condescended. "We honor intelligence as no other system. The difference is we require the man of brains to give his talents a free offering to humanity, and for his reward receive their love and admiration, not hard earned dollars."

"And howl down all distinctions between men, the dignity of labor lighted by intellect and spirit, for the glory of a thing you call the dictatorship of the proletariat."

"But only that we may make equality a reality, not a mere word."

"Yet if your equality is the common level of a pig pen with one big trough filled with black bread and water in which all thrust their noses, I fail to see how it's worth while. You propose to destroy all classes in a holocaust of murder, not merely the idle rich, but the whole upper and middle strata, the landowner, the country farmer and the thrifty and skilled workman. In short, all except those who work with bare untrained hands. Isn't this the complete tyranny of the ignorant and anti-social elements? Will not humanity sink into the depths of a degenerate barbarism under such a system?"

He smiled with condescension.

"Far from it. Civilization will rise to unheard of heights of achievement. The human mind, freed from the tyranny of the struggle for bread, will soar in its search for the riches of the spirit. In Soviet Russia there is no poverty, no unemployment."

"Certainly no unemployment," she smiled. "Because every man and woman is compelled to work at a task assigned by an overseer. This is involuntary labor. It used to be called Slavery—whatever you call it, in your new jargon."

"But not for the profit of an individual. For the good of the whole."

"What does it matter for whose good it is decreed, if it means slavery?"

"We have universal human slavery under the Capitalist system now. For the profit motive, men and women are ground to powder in the machine. We propose to better their condition and build around them a new world of comfort, contentment and happiness."

"Yet you form a fanatical international party which in Russia where it is supreme, indulges in mass starvation for millions of peasants and workers, mass executions without public trial, the suppression of free speech and assembly."

"Only that the people may ultimately rule in a real Democracy."

"I can't understand a man of your intelligence talking about democracy in a system that allows but one party who must vote as they are told or face a firing squad. To spread your propaganda here, you appeal to our guarantee of free speech which you would destroy the moment you gain power."

"Well," he smiled, "you either believe in a program or you don't."

"Certainly," she countered. "Civil liberty is the right of all free men. But a man is free only when he wants freedom, for himself and all others. A man who would take freedom from the rest of the world is not fit for civil liberty."

"I thought you were at least a sympathetic student of the Cause. I seem to have caught a Tartar."

"You rub me the wrong way."

"Sorry I can't compromise," he laughed in a superior tone. "You'd as well understand the fundamentals of our system in the beginning. Karl Marx taught that there can be but two classes of human society—those who own property, business, investments and hire labor. These are the exploiters of mankind. And those who own nothing but the labor of their hands. These are the exploited whom we propose to exhalt to the dictatorship of the proletariat. Marx's manifesto ends with words that are burning themselves into the souls of millions today:

"The Communists disdain to conceal their views and aims. They openly declare that their ends can be obtained only by the forcible overthrow of all existing social conditions. Let the ruling class tremble at a Communist revolution. The proletariat has nothing to lose but its chains. They have a world to win. Workmen of all countries unite!"

"You propose in your plan to do away with all private property?"

"Absolutely. That is just what we intend. Our whole thought may be summed up in the single sentence—ABOLITION OF PRIVATE PROPERTY."

Angela saw that'she had so enraged the leader he no longer attempted a sympathetic teaching of principles. They were quarrelling. Her plans were going awry. She put into her next question a gentler tone.

"And you would abolish the family?"

"Certainly," he snapped. "On what foundation is it based? On Capital, on private gain. In its completely developed form the family exists only among the bourgeoise. This type of family will vanish as a matter of course. The bourgeois claptrap about the family and excitement over the hallowed co-relations of parent and child becomes disgusting when we see the actions of modern industry, see family ties among the poor torn asunder, and their children transformed into articles of commerce and instruments of labor."

She broke into a hearty laugh.

"That is a literal quotation from Karl Marx, I believe. I don't think you hold that as a personal creed."

He flushed and stammered.

"Yes—yes—I do—really—I do."

"I don't believe you," she said smothering him with a gracious smile into which his frown gradually melted.

"Well, if you've quarrelled enough," he said evenly, "shall we dance?"

"With a mere bourgeoise woman who may still believe in the family?"

"Certainly. You're mighty in an argument. But a very charming young woman to look at."

They danced and then he introduced her to a group of society people, left and went the rounds as host. She found the conversation so vapid and futile it was not to be endured. Catching Mona's eye, she signalled her.

"Let's run up to Luchow's for a bite and get out of this mob."

The girl showed bitter disappointment.

"You want to leave so soon. What's got into you?"

"Seven devils, I think. And Allen's egotism is so colossal I had to take him down a peg or two. What did he say to you, just now?"

"That you were a hell cat. That he hoped he'd never see you again."

"My, my. As much as that?"

"And then some. I haven't told you anything."

"Well, he must have been shocked. At least that's something."

"Something I'll always regret. I'd set my heart on you two making a go of it."

"He danced beautifully."

"Shall I call him back?"

"Don't you dare!"

"I gave him a piece of my mind. Sometimes he can be ugly as hell. He's really an idealist and dreamer. A man of beautiful spirit and high thinking."

"You must be in love with him." Angela laughed.

The girl nodded.

"Sure. We all are."

The doorman signalled for the car and when it slipped up beneath the awning the rain had stopped and the stars were out.

"After supper," Mona sighed. "I'll have to return to the Assembly Room. Our black assignments will hold the center of the floor at twelve. A special dance has been arranged for them. We swap partners for the dance. Some of us will swap assignments."

The announcement took Angela's appetite. She had ordered a welch rarebit, but only nibbled at it. Mona ate heartily and was dropped again at the Assembly Rooms. As the new car moved through Fifth Avenue, the owner wondered how long it would be before heavy hands knocked on the doors of its mansions.

What a strange development of the life of a great nation, conceived in liberty and dedicated to the freedom of the individual man, the talk she had heard to-night! The amateur, slum explorers from these palatial houses had no real conception of the drift of modern life. They were stupidly re-enacting the scenes which preceded the blood purges of the French Revolution when aristocrats condescended to patronize the radicals until their heads were suddenly chopped off. She glanced at the iron gratings of their doors with a feeling of contempt. They would get only what they deserved when the revolution broke. It was a waste of energy to pity them.

The strange thing about the evening's experience was the anomaly of a man of John Allen's antecedents leading such a cause. Here was a man of the finest New England stock—the stock which had made the largest contribution to our ideals—the stock which had created a national character that furnished standards of conduct by which others set their course, as stable in its action as the needle that points to the North star. We know that without such standards man feels himself a mariner without a compass. The loss of national character is a calamity beyond calculation. Here was a man of family, of traditions, of the highest ideals who had deliberately thrown his compass away for the guidance of crackpot theorists of a foreign nation! It was an amazing thing. She wondered if he really believed the stuff he professed, or was it an unconscious pose that grew out of the boredom of life since the World War.

CHAPTER 48

Murino heard with mixed feelings Angela's report of her first encounter with John Allen.

"You quarrelled, you say?"

"Regular cat and dog fight."

"Over his creed?"

"All evening."

"Allen is the High Priest of their inner circle. His fine old American name is an important asset. He has ability of a high order. I'm surprised that he lost his temper in a tilt with you over principles."

"I lost mine first, perhaps."

"All right. We'll attend their National Convention in Madison Square Garden next week and see if they really pull the purpose of naming a Negro and an ex-convict on their ticket. The Negro is a certainty. James W. Ford was their candidate for Vice President during the last campaign. His renomination is a certainty. He drew thousands of reckless young Negroes into the organization. The only question is whether they will dare to nominate an ex-convict for the first place. It's hard to believe they will have the audacity to do this, but they may."

He paused and studied her a moment.

"Allen has made no effort to follow up his meeting with you?"

"Ignored my existence."

"Again I'm surprised. He's the kind of man who would appreciate your possibilities, personal and political."

"He did say I'd make an admirable Joan of Arc."

Murino laughed.

"You'll hear from him again."

"He'll probably be on the platform of the Convention next week?"

"He'll be there but not on the platform. The leaders of the inner circle of the Party do not parade themselves as political leaders. Politics with them is wearing a mask. They put forward their smaller fry."

"Will you take me to the Garden that night or shall I drive the Packard?"

"Neither. We'll jump in a cab and dismiss it a block from the building. You couldn't manage a private car in the mob that will jam the Garden inside and out."

"Really?"

His prediction was accurate. They arrived half an hour before the time set for the opening and a crowd of twenty-five thousand people, black and white, packed every approach.

Murino got a policeman he knew to open the way to the side entrance his tickets called for. He had reserved seats just behind the voting delegation on the ground floor. Near enough to hear the speakers' voice without the relay of an amplifier.

Every seat in the arena was filled before the gavel of the temporary Chairman, the distinguished jail-bird, William Z. Foster,[1] struck the desk. Angela's eye swept the sea of faces with increasing amazement. One half of them were Negroes. Such a convention in the greatest city of the American republic was a thing to shock the imagination of the stoutest patriot.

They settled to business in short order, in sharp contrast to the usual dawdling tactics of the old parties. With scant ceremony the Chairman introduced the key-noter.

While the speaker was pushing his way-to the front through the crowd on the platform, Angela nudged her escort.

"Will you look at that?"

His eye followed hers.

Across from them sat a blonde white girl of the college type, wearing a squirrel coat. She was being ostentatiously pawed by two Negroes seated on each side of her. She returned their caresses. Just beyond sat an older white woman with a bored Negro companion. She put her arms under his and nestled close, in vain. He watched the platform and paid not the slightest attention to her.

"You'd think that she would pick a more responsive Romeo, wouldn't you?" he laughed. "They make a point of these scenes of practising social equality in their public meetings. There's a special Committee in charge of the demonstrations."

1. William Z. Foster (1881–1961), was an influential leader of the American Communist Party, running three times (1924, 1928, 1932) as its standard-bearer for president. In 1932 Los Angeles police arrested Foster on suspicion of "criminal syndicalism." See Edward P. Johanningsmeier, "William Z. Foster: Labor Organizer and Communist" (Ph.D. diss., University of Pennsylvania, 1988).

The speaker arranged his manuscript, stepped before the microphone and began his speech.

Before he had finished his incendiary address he had worked his ten thousand Negro hearers into hysteria. At its close they formed resistless columns and marched up and down the aisles cheering and yelling themselves hoarse.

Order restored, the call for naming candidates for President of the United States brought to the speaker's stand but one nomination. The Candidate had been agreed on. He had no opposition and on the utterance of his name the Convention rose and named him by acclamation—"Mr. Earl Browder,[2] the John Brown of 1936!"

"They've dared," Murino smiled grimly. "Browder is an exconvict from the Leavenworth Kansas Penitentiary."

On the Chairman's announcement of his unanimous nomination for President of the United States again pandemonium broke loose. An organized gang of toughs led the marchers up and down the aisles yelling and shouting for twenty minutes.

When order was restored, James W. Ford, the Negro standard bearer of 1932, was unanimously named for Browder's running mate as Vice President. The roar of marching fanatics filled the building. But it was not until they sat down and Browder rose on the platform, put his arm around Ford and shouted: "I am proud to be on the same ticket with my friend and comrade, James W. Ford," that the crowd went wild. Negroes embraced white men, white men hugged Negroes, sang and shouted until it was necessary to adjourn the meeting. No other business could be transacted.

The brief nominating address by a shaggy looking old white woman, "Mother Bloor," rang out in every ear and broke up the meeting.

"The Communist Party," she shrieked, "stands squarely for complete and unconditional equality for the Negro people. We do not propose equality in a vague and limited sense. We do not say the Negro is all right "in his place." We say that any place open to a white man shall be open to a Negro. We stand four square for full political, civic, economic, and especially *social* equality!"

This sentence was the match that exploded the powder magazine. Back of it the frowzy old woman had put the energy of a brave revolutionary mind. It was contagious. It fired every Negro's heart. No matter how old, she was a white woman calling the Negro to her bed—for herself, her sisters, her daughters.

2. Earl Russell Browder (1891–1973) followed William Z. Foster as leader of the party. He ran unsuccessfully for president in 1936 and 1940. In 1940 the U.S. government convicted Browder of passport irregularities and sentenced him to a four-year prison term. See James G. Ryan, *Earl Browder: The Failure of American Communism* (Tuscaloosa: University of Alabama Press, 1997).

As they stepped into a cab, Murino said:

"Would you mind going by my house for a little supper?"

"I'd love it. I've had enough of crowds for one night."

"I've a possible message waiting for me on my desk, and I want to show you something."

He ordered the cab to stop in the side street a block away from the entrance. She wondered at the precaution.

"You don't happen to have your set of keys with you?" he asked, alighting.

"Of course not," she laughed.

"We'll use mine. I got to thinking the other night that unless you were sure of those keys and where they belonged, you might fail to get in if you ever tried. We'll kill two birds with one stone tonight. I'll show you how to use these, pick up my message from the desk and enter the house from the inner room"

They walked down the Avenue to the next crossing, turned into the side street and paused before the open hallway leading into the passage to his house. He glanced up the Avenue, and through the side street.

"Not a single undercover man on my trail tonight. The Convention threw them off. Step lively now."

They entered the open hallway, he switched on a light and showed her the bunch of keys.

"You see they are numbered from one to six—that's reaching from this entrance. Coming the other way from the office and lobby, they run from six back to one. Insert each key as numbered, counting this front door number one."

She took the keys and opened the first door. He switched out the light he had turned on, and pressed the switch for the inside light. At the end of the hall she found the second key, inserted it, opened the outside door, inserted number three and opened the inside one. Each door closed automatically and they stood within the steel clad inner chamber. The room was in total darkness and she gripped his arm.

"There's some one in here," she whispered.

"How on earth could you guess that?"

"I don't know. But I'm sure."

He flashed a tiny pocket light on the desk and revealed a figure slumped in his swivel chair, mouth open, dead asleep.

"Asleep at the switch, Henri," Murino said.

"Just dozed a minute, Chief. Got so tired waiting. Not a peep our way tonight, sir."

"No word of any kind from London?"

"Not a thing."

"All right. You can go for the night.,"

Angela noted the man's well cut suit, his slightly foreign but cultured accent.

When Murino had opened the two doors leading to his outer office he turned back into the main room and the doors softly clicked in closing.

"I'm puzzled," she said, "to know why you thought it important to rehearse me in the use of those keys tonight?"

"Frankly a sense of uneasiness which got me as I sat in that damned Negroid-Criminal-Communist convention. They've named an ominous ticket. Not ominous because they can elect it but for its threat of the future. Browder is not only an ex-convict who will solidify two million cell mates from the prisons and five million alien criminals of America as well, he is a fanatic from the bloody ground of John Brown of Ossawotomie, Kansas. Old Brown, you know, sang hymns to God while he crept through the forest to murder the innocent victims he had selected for sacrifice. They call Browder another John Brown. He has the temperament. He's from Kansas. If he succeeds in drawing many of the Negro race into his camp things are going to happen.

"Ford is a formidable running mate. He was born in a mining town of Alabama. He has served an apprenticeship in Soviet Russia and other nations of Europe. His race is proud of his achievement of a Vice Presidential candidacy. No such honor has ever before been offered a Negro. His nomination for the office confirms as in no other way possible their plan of equalizing the races. They are boldly proposing to enforce sex equality, and rob mankind of the birthright of race, as well as the individual father and mother, while they destroy belief in God. And note that no country has ever been sold on Communism by a campaign or educational process. They have won always by direct bloodstained action through a crisis of surprise."

He led the way into the library, rang for his butler and they ate a delicious meal prepared by the master artist in his kitchen.

"Your house is an Aladdin's palace!" she exclaimed. "Your chef is a great man."

"So I've told him. He ought to be. I pay him the salary of a United States Senator. If you want to hear an explosion ask him what he thinks of Communism!"

The next evening Angela was just finishing dinner when her phone rang. She was surprised to hear the voice of John Allen.

"I saw you in the Convention last night," he ventured.

"But I couldn't find you."

"You looked for me?"

"Naturally as a leader of the inner circle I thought you should have been there."

"I had to hang on the side lines. But those things tire me. They are all cut and dried. Arranged beforehand you know. I'm just finishing work. Is it too late to ask you to dine with me and give me a chance to apologize for my boorish conduct the other night?"

"I'd like to, but I've just finished dinner. If you'd care to come to my apartment, I'll fix you a little bite here."

"That's more than I deserve. I'll be there in a jiffy."

In less than thirty minutes she welcomed him.

He held her hand a moment and gazed at her with undisguised admiration.

"How becoming that costume! You look the high priestess of an ancient temple!"

"Thank you. I like it. I bought it in California."

"But I thought you were from the South?"

"Why did you think that?" she countered.

"Your accent, of course. And Mona told me."

"Yes. I was born in South Carolina, but my mother was from Quaker Pennsylvania. "

"What a marvelous combination. No wonder you're what you are!"

"And what is that?" she asked with a touch of banter.

"I'll be frank with you. The reason I was rude that night at the Assembly Room was that you completely bowled me over. I had been immune until I met you. I resented the shock you gave me. I found myself drawn to you in spite of all my resolutions of devotion to a *Cause*. It's funny!"

"What's funny?"

"I don't know. I feel like forgetting parties and battles and rivalries."

She led him into the dinette, sat opposite him and sipped a second demitasse while he ate with gusto. She led the conversation around to him and finally he was talking of his family.

"I imagine your mother was a wonderful woman in spite of your scorn of such bourgeoise ties."

"She was too," he acknowledged. "A tall stately woman of your type. Plain of feature but with the bearing of a queen. I confess I worshipped her to the day of her death."

"Then how could you swing to the extreme of Marx: Contempt for home and motherhood?"

"Who said I had at heart? Marx is a great philosopher. But he was not infallible. I can punch holes in his ponderous philosophy and yet believe enough of it to make me a revolutionist."

He paused and smiled.

"Do you think you could learn to like me in spite of my inconsistencies?"

"I might in time," she laughed. "You're a very charming young man when you're yourself."

"I'm going to be myself with you if you'll let me see you occasionally. May I?"

"Certainly. I've a sort of radical salon here. All sorts and conditions of people from all sorts of trades honor me with their friendship. I'll be happy to include you."

He scowled at her banter.

"You'll find me very much in earnest I'm afraid. And I'm going to take infinite pains in giving you the reasons that have led me into the enterprise I've embarked on. I'll do my best to win you to my way of thinking. And I'll promise never again to throw brick bat questions from Marx or any other expounder of Communism at you. What an ass I was!"

"All right, sir, in view of the circumstances all is forgiven. From tonight we're friends at least—comrades, if you can persuade me your creed—is right."

"You're splendid!" he exclaimed. "I had an idea if I was frank, you—would be just like this. It's a curious thing! A short time ago I didn't know you lived in the world. Tonight here we are together! Sure now you won't hold the boorish egotism of that first meeting against me?"

"It's forgotten."

As he ate, laughed and chatted she watched him with secret satisfaction. She would use deliberately all of her powers to gain through him the date of the coming revolution.

Chapter 49

Phil Stephens found his position as associate of the Inter-Racial Commission practically impossible after the Presidential election of 1936. The amazing growth of Communism in this campaign had upset all calculations. No effort was made by Browder and Ford to pile up a record vote for their Party. Their sole aim was to conceal their strength, bore into other organizations and make ready for a bigger event.

Browder had proved himself a master strategist. He slipped in his radical friends as electors on the Republican ticket in the West, on the Democratic ticket in the East. He persistently and effectively bored into the Army. And organized his first secret cells in the Navy.

And most amazing of all, he secured a footing in the National broadcasting of propaganda. His voice was heard by millions in radio hookups from coast to coast. The nation listened to the ominous note of a traitor's voice speaking into American homes doctrines that would destroy the home itself. All in the name of free speech which he proposes to suppress the moment he attains the power.

In the South, Ford was greeted with tumultuous audiences. Under the spell of his name a Radical Sharecroppers Union was organized.

The struggle of the Red leaders for control of the race threw the amalgamation Junta in New York into a panic of fear for their future. DuBois met the situation by a sharp turn to the left in his writing and speeches. The Russian Government was praised, our own denounced. Atheism was lauded. Denunciation of the white race of the South increased in violence. Every device of insinuation and direct attack was now used to stir the hate of Negroes against the Southern people.

The Editor dared to publish in double leads a bold prophecy of Negro World supremacy:

“AS THE EAGLE SOARS

“All things have their rise and fall. The black man had his day of supreme power and glory. Black generals from Egypt, Carthage and Babylon once swept the plains of Europe and conquered the white peoples inhabiting the continent.

“The white man succeeded the black and today he still rules supreme. He still dominates and tyrannizes, he still looks down on all other races as inferior. But the day will come when the whites will also bite the dust and taste the bitter fruit of tyranny. Then will come the brown man’s turn. He will hold the world in his hands and rule supreme over all other races!”

Under the influence of these teachings a series of books whose purpose was to cover the white South with infamy began to pour from the press.

Stephens devoted days and nights to their study.

A volume bearing the specious title *Let Me Live* got his attention tention first. On page 159 of this infamous volume Phil read:

“Beginning August 3, (1931) the bloody reign of terror raged in Birmingham for a full month. Seventy Negroes of both sexes paid with their lives. Blood and more blood was demanded by the white butchers.

“No one in the South ever saw so much blood flow. It seemed as if the white Protestant churchgoers, who sang with piety “What a Friend we have in Jesus,” on every occasion now tarred and feathered Negroes and roasted them alive over the scorching flames. And every moan and groan of Negro martyrs aroused in them neither human compassion or shame. The lynchers went wild in convulsions of bestiality. They howled with glee, and going insane, burst into a perfect frenzy of obscenity.”

Stephens called the attention of the public to this libel on the people of Alabama: “I am informed by a citizen of Birmingham that this statement is a lie out of whole cloth, a filthy invention. No such thing happened. Not a single Negro was killed in or near the city during this period.”

CHAPTER 50

When John Allen had given Angela the thrilling episodes in the history of his hero leaders and asked many stimulating questions he urged her to begin a three years' course of intensive study.

"You're not afraid of the truth?" he sternly asked.

She repressed the smile of triumph in the development of her plan and firmly answered:

"Never."

"Your old time religion says: "Ye shall know the truth and the truth shall make you free." I dare you to honestly and earnestly study Communism, its history, its ideals, its methods. At the end of a course of three years you will stand by my side, my comrade in arms."

"I'll make the study if you'll give me enough of your time to guide my work intelligently."

"I'll do that! And you will be inspiring me before the study is done."

He gave her every Monday evening in her apartment to discuss the reading and study. She paid her tuition with a dinner which he ate with boyish relish. She made rapid progress. He was extravagant in praise and elated over her advancement in the ideals which had become with him a madness. She watched his deepening interest in her with a cold intelligence that at times shocked her inner sense of fairness.

After they had been studying and working together for six months he took her hand one night at the end of a conference.

"It's getting very hard for me to be with you."

"What do you mean?" she asked seriously.

"I swore I'd be careful never to say a word that might jeopardize the happiness I've been dreaming—but it's no good. I can't go on blithely this way as if nothing had happened to me. For something has. You must know this."

"How could I?"

"In spite of all resolutions and theories, I'm in love—I want to marry you."

She threw him a sharp look, held her silence for a moment and spoke slowly:

"I don't know what to say."

"All right, don't say it then! Just let things drift a while and think it over—will you?"

His sincerity and reserve was a new experience for Angela, accustomed to Phil's flow of romantic words and Murino's matter of fact poise. She couldn't be flippant in her reply.

"I'm sorry to have to say it, John, but I'm not interested in marriage."

"Because of the principles I've taught you—that's a good one on me, I must say!"

"No, it's not that. Let's just go on as we have for a while."

"All right," he agreed. "Just as we have for a while longer. And that brings me to an important matter. Four Scottsboro Negroes, whom our shrewd lawyer Leibowitz has released, will arrive at the Pennsylvania Station tomorrow at three o'clock. Unless I miss my guess there'll be something doing in that neighborhood as the train pulls in. Would you go with me and see it?"

"If we can see it from the side lines. I don't care to meet the Scottsboro boys."

"Certainly, from the side lines. I'll call for you at two. We'll go into the Penn Station from the Subway and have a better chance to see the show."

They entered the Subway at 116th Street and Broadway and found the trains jammed with Negroes who were using both lines, from Harlem and Washington Heights.

"Never could understand the Jim Crow car idea down South," he remarked.

"No, you wouldn't," was the quiet answer. "You never lived down South. These New York Negroes are decently dressed. They use bath tubs. The English philosopher, William Archer,[1] studied the problem with great care and wrote the conclusion that the separation of the races in travel in the South was wise, fair and inevitable. It's all in the point of view, you know. Born a New Englander with your, Abolitionist inheritance you can only see one side."

---

1. William Archer (1856–1924) was a British author and drama critic. In 1910 he published *Through America: An English Reading of the Race Problem.* See Peter Whitebrook, *William Archer: A Biography* (London: Methuen, 1993).

A huge perspiring Negro woman suddenly crowded in beside Allen and pushed him out of her way.

Angela laughed.

They found difficulty in getting into the main hall of the station. The police reserves had been called into action an hour before. The main hall had been roped off and an impassable crowd jammed every approach from the streets, a mob of hysterical Negroes.

Every Negro workman down town had thrown his tools away and come. Every maid and bell-hop, bootblack and elevator boy who could escape by hook or crook was there.

Allen had passed the guards but suggested that they watch the reception from the balcony and avoid the crush. It was a wise decision. A roar came from the lower level of incoming trains.

"They're getting out and the special committee of reception is welcoming them," Allen interpreted.

The black torrent poured up the stairway and hell broke loose on the main floor. The mob surged toward the exit, seized the four Negroes, lifted them on their shoulders and paraded around the vast room, yelling, shouting and cheering. Above the din came the wild shouts——

"Our heroes from Scottsboro! The Scottsboro boys! Glory to God! We've won! We've won!"

A leader leaped upon the information counter and led three rounds of cheers that shook the girders. White men and women were trampled by the insane rush and four ambulances were called to carry them to hospitals.

Allen hustled Angela into a cab and yelled to the driver.

"Get in line outside and follow the crowd to Harlem."

He managed to slip into line at the exit of the South side of the station. As far as the eye could see surged the black waves. The scene inside was repeated outside. They carried the lawyer and his clients on their shoulders again before they were allowed to take their places in the open cars. Along Broadway and Fifth Avenue the black tide roared.

Through every passion torn shout rang a single thought, piercing Angela's soul:

"These four black brothers of the blood have each raped a white woman and gotten away with it!"

She felt as if she were suffocating.

Turning to Allen she said through pale lips:

"The thing sickens me—this crazy mob."

"There's not the slightest danger," he assured. "I wish you would see it through. There are forces behind this mob that the world little suspects. It marks an era in the development of the conflict of color in America."

"Still I'll ask you to get me home. I'm not feeling well."

He dropped out of line and had the cab rush to her apartment.

Allen was bubbling over with an elation she never understood until a blinding flash from hell revealed its meaning later. There was a strange look in his eyes as he slowly spoke:

"It's impossible to estimate the tremendous effect of this event . . ." he grasped her hand, suddenly coming back to himself . . . "I've an appointment in Harlem. See you again Monday night."

For the next three weeks she was reminded every day as she read her little paper from Piedmont, that millions of Negroes had gotten a tremendous impulse from the event which the radio had carried to them.

Following the triumphant reception of the Scottsboro boys in New York, the "Piedmont Herald" recorded in twenty-one days the rape of fourteen white women by Negroes in the Carolinas alone! One of them a twelve year old girl on her way home from school near Marion, North Carolina.

"They keep careful record of all lynchings," she muttered. "There hasn't been a single case in six months. There are no statistics kept of rape. Why? Because now there are five hundred assaults on white women to every case of lynching. . . ." Her mind came back to the thought that had haunted her since the tragedy at Piedmont:

"We are not living in a civilized world!"

Chapter 51

Murino surprised Angela by a sudden call in person on Monday morning. He was under excitement of an unusual nature. He glanced at the street from her window as if expecting to be followed.

"I'm sorry to leave you," he said. "But I'm catching a steamer for Europe within two hours. The risks here are more than I care to take for a while."

He paused and searched her eyes.

"My life's in real danger from a gang of racketeers. I have refused to contribute a million dollars to their cause. You have the keys to my house. Use them when you like. I've told my butler you'll call and check his accounts each quarter and report to me. Will you do this?"

"Gladly."

"How goes your work?"

"I'm making progress."

"Need any more money?"

"We've still half of your funds in the bank."

He handed her a card with his London address.

"If you need anything, cable me."

"Thank you, Tony. I'll miss you."

"Really?" he asked softly.

"Really."

As he kissed her a tender goodbye he said casually:

"I've important business over there I'll tell you about when I come back."

When John Allen called for their conference he, too, was excited.

He paced the floor for three complete turns before speaking to Angela.

"Great events are coming swiftly to a climax, my dear!" he exploded.

"It's astounding the progress our Party is making. We, the leaders, have been expecting a sudden blooming for years and yet we stand amazed."

"All of which means nothing to me," she interrupted. "I don't know your plans, I don't know your progress. So I decline to get hysterical. If you'll explain what you mean to me I might respond with some intelligence."

"You are grasping our principles with deeper sympathy and understanding daily. You've studied nearly three years to good purpose. I'll soon be able to take you completely into my confidence. I'm to be sent to Europe on a most important mission. I want you with me."

"I'm taking no wild chances, young man," she answered gravely. "If you are to be my comrade in the truest sense of the word, there can be no secrets between us. I'll know when you go, where you're going and why. I'll know when you're coming back and why. Frankly your secret meetings and your alliance with blood purging Russia leaves me cold. I don't know you."

"If you'll marry me your life will be bound with mine forever. There could be no secrets between us. Where I go, you go."

"I'm, not ready for that. I've more studying to do on your plan and your philosophy of life. There must be perfect unity of thought and faith and purpose or there can be no true comradeship—you know that."

"Yes. I know," he said sinking to a seat and drawing her down beside him. "But you are making progress in understanding our principles and purpose?"

"Great progress. When I met you, I didn't like your Cause, I didn't like you. Now——"

"Now?"

"Your Cause seems reasonable. You have become quite human and likable."

"Then I'll smile and wait a little longer—shall I?"

"I'm afraid you will have to."

"All right. It's only a question of speed in your study. I'll make good my promise. We'll be comrades in the truest sense. A sense that cuts to the deepest meaning of life. I've sworn it and I'll make good."

She studied him with a feeling of elation. He could not conceal from her the approach of the crisis that would mean the lighting of the torch, and she would stand by his side when the momentous decision was made!"

She called at Phil's downtown office and found him buried in reports of Red agitators in the South.

"Since DuBois resigned to write the amazing book which he outlined to me," he began with a gesture toward the pile of papers on his desk, "I've been pretty busy. My touch with his organization will probably end with the issue of his message, and I'm finding out all I can of the inner workings of Negro agents in the South. I may be all wrong but I've an idea that the greatest Negro leader the race has yet produced in America is heading directly for the Moscow camp if he is not already a secret member of their inner council."

"Which tallies with my findings. There's a big event pending. I'm on the track of it. When the trap is sprung I want you to be near, Phil."

She spoke with such seriousness he lowered his voice.

"I've told you there was grave danger in this boring into Communism which you have undertaken."

"It's necessary. We must know the date they set. Events which I am watching are swiftly developing. The thing will break soon."

"All right," he assured her, "you'll find me doing business at the old stand when you need me."

"It may come in six months. It may be a year. It can't be longer."

I suppose we'll have to save the darned old world before I can save myself—so far as you're concerned?"

"It looks that way now, Phil. But you never can tell."

He laughed heartily.

"You're a conscienceless flirt, honey, but I'm hopelessly in love with you and always will be."

Eighteen months slipped by swiftly with neither man gaining in his pursuit. John Allen was awaiting the big crisis before he spoke again. Murino lingered in Europe and wrote fascinating letters. Phil caught at every engagement he could wheedle out of her.

And then the first break of events came. An advance copy of the DuBois book from the press of Harcourt, Brace and Company reached the lawyer's desk. Its contents stunned him. Stephens sternly faced the Board of Directors of the Negro Junta:

"Unless you repudiate this book we can no longer associate with the Inter-Racial Commission.

"Dr. DuBois challenges the veracity of every historian of the Reconstruction period. He glorifies the rule of the Negro over the white man of this period in terms that will not bear discussion. His position is so bitterly partisan it has no value as an historical document. His theme is that the Negro made in the tragic fiasco of Reconstruction a noble record. That his white rivals of the South were his inferiors.

"His discussion of the economic problem involved is a specious plea for the philosophy of Karl Marx. The Father of Communism is referred to in almost every chapter with bated breath, until, in his most important conclusion, he boldly proclaims the Dictatorship of the Proletariat as the only solution of America's problems.

"In his treatment of the white people of the South he loses all sense of proportion in the virulence of his hatred.

"*Black Reconstruction in America* is a firebrand hurled into the imagination of our twelve million Negroes. Its preface informs us that the money needed to write it was contributed by the Rosenwald and Carnegie Funds.

"Dr. DuBois is the foremost Negro scholar in the world. Yet he hurls his firebrand without a minute's hesitation. It is in no sense a history, in spite of its jumble of irrelevant and worthless quotations. It is a call to race riot by a man who has become a monomaniac in his hatred of whites. In every line one feels the passionate desire of the author to slit the throat of every white man in the world. His theme is merely the platform from which he rises to harangue the mob and excite them to violence.

"The old South," he declares, "turned the most beautiful section of the nation into a center of poverty and suffering, of drinking, gambling and brawling; an abode of ignorance among black and white more abysmal than in any modern land. . . . Southerners who had suckled food from black breasts vied with each other in fornication with black women, and even in beastly incest. They took the name of their fathers in vain to seduce their own sisters."

"In a chorus of woe he bemoans the failure of Thaddeus Stevens to carry his bill to confiscate the land of the ruined people and give it to the Negroes. Rejoicing in the Black Legislature of South Carolina he cries,"I have more respect for the golden spittoons of the freed Negro lawmakers in 1872 than for the entire chaste elegance of the colonial mansions of slave drivers in 1860."

"Toward the end of the volume we begin to get its purpose.

"There is no doubt," he admits, "that the object of the white and black labor vote (in Mr. Stevens' regime) was gradually conceived as one which involved CONFISCATING THE PROPERTY OF THE RICH . . . and it is quite possible that long before the end of the 20th Century the deliberate distribution of property and income by the State, on an equitable and logical basis, will be looked upon as the State's prime function.

"In the final paragraph of his chapter on Counter Revolution we get the full statement of his creed: "The rebuilding (of America after the Depression), whether it comes now or a century later, will and must go back to the basic principles of Reconstruction in the United States during 1867–1876—Land, Light and Leading for slaves, black, brown, yellow and white *under a dictatorship of the proletariat.*"

"Your National Association for the Advancement of Colored People is now taking its stand boldly for the amalgamation of the races. Even so conservative a writer as your James Weldon Johnson, has issued a pronouncement which proclaims amalgamation as the coming fate of America. After declaring the most beautiful women in the United States today are Mulattoes, he says:

"The result of these forces will, in time, be the blending of the Negro into the American race of the future. It seems probable that instead of developing them independently to the utmost, the Negro will fuse his qualities with those of the other groups in the making of the Ultimate American people; and that he will add a tint to American complexion and put a perceptible permanent wave in America's hair."

"It should be obvious that if you follow these teachings you must alienate your friends of the white race, North and South. Continue on this course and any further cooperation from the Inter-Racial Commission will become impossible. I am a member of that organization of liberal white Southerners. We have prevented hundreds of lynchings in the past ten years. Everywhere we have preached kindness, toleration, understanding between the races. There can be no understanding if you follow the new doctrine of race hate, and Communistic teachings.

"The one sensible thing you can do today is to ask for the suppression of the DuBois book."

He sat down amid a tense silence. A member arose and spoke with indignation. The meeting ended in a near riot.

The lawyer left with a feeling of deep discouragement. He had taken up the work of advising this dangerous organization with the belief that he could serve both races. The Association had finally taken the bit in their teeth and bolted for a straight stand up and knock down fight for social equality and intermarriage. This had led their ablest leader into the camp of militant Communism, and Dr. DuBois had become the bold champion of the Dictatorship of the Proletariat.

Chapter 52

The Junta, freed from conservative advice, lost no time in reintroducing into Congress their so called "Anti-Lynching Bill."[1] This time with the distinguished sponsorship of Senator Wagner of New York, a powerful member of the New Deal bloc in the Senate.

On paper the arguments used were plausible. Lynching *is* a disgrace to civilization. No one disputes it, North, South, East or West. No one, however, seriously asked the question whether such a bill would stop lynching or aggravate the evil. Pot house politicians vied with each other in catering to their Negro friends. Senator Wagner claimed a majority in the Senate for the Bill and it was jammed through the House without debate of a serious character. As Wagner was a spokesman of the Administration in Congress it was assumed by many that the President backed the measure, though he remained silent.

When Phil and Angela met in his office they agreed that the situation was tragic. Such a measure passed by Congress would put the South under a cloud, demoralize its people and provoke outbreaks that would send the army into its territory exactly as its sponsors hoped. In answer to a telephone call from the Senior Senator of South Carolina, Phil left for Washington and took Angela with him.

"You can help me, honey," he laughed. "You'll make a great lobbyist."

"I'll do my best," she agreed.

Phil interviewed every Southern Senator and Angela first cultivated the three women, Mrs. Graves of Alabama, Mrs. Huey Long of Louisiana,

1. In 1934 Senate Democrats Edward Costigan (Colorado) and Robert F. Wagner (New York) proposed on behalf of the National Association for the Advancement of Colored People an antilynching bill that would levy a $10,000 fine on any county in which a lynching occurred. The bill passed the House of Representatives but failed in the Senate. See George C. Rable, "The South and the Politics of Antilynching Legislation, 1920–1940," *Journal of Southern History* 51 (May 1985): 201–20.

and Mrs. Carraway of Arkansas. They were staunch in opposition. But agreed that the majority for the Bill would be heavy.

The question of a filibuster of Southerners that would stop the wheels of Government was a serious one. They had killed the bill once by a filibuster. Whether the Senate would vote cloture and put the measure on passage was the real question. A second filibuster to delay all legislation would antagonize many Northern men and rouse a wave of sectionalism that might have serious consequences.

A caucus of Southern Senators and party leaders was called and Phil was asked to address them.

"I can't overemphasize the gravity of the situation," he warned. "The radical Negro groups in New York are struggling through their press, through books, through incendiary speeches to cover the white South with infamy. And they are doing it. Their power is formidable. This measure which they drew and introduced through Senator Wagner will play into their hands in the most dangerous way. Behind the movement there are sinister forces at work that are seeking to destroy our Government itself. I haven't time to go into that. But they must break the backbone of the South before their plot can succeed. This Bill will break its back. I beg of you to fight it with every ounce of your manhood and womanhood."

The caucus unanimously resolved to use the filibuster again, and kill the bill.

The battle began. The three women in the Senate made effective speeches against it. The men followed and all business of legislation in the upper house came to a dead stop. The administration leaders gave notice of a motion to end debate. The motion was lost and the filibuster continued. Again the Junta demanded a motion of cloture. To pass it would be to strip the Senate of its dignity and power and reduce it to a rubber stamp. Enough men, who were for the measure, joined its opponents to defeat the motion the second time. The filibuster continued until the bill was shelved and twenty-five million Southern people breathed freely again.

Chapter 53

Phil had just lighted a cigarette after luncheon and lazily dropped on the couch in Angela's living room when the telephone rang.

"Who dares to interrupt our conference before it has begun?"

He got no answer. The man on the other end of the line kept her busy.

"But I can't see you now.—No, not even for thirty minutes.—Why? I've a friend to luncheon—I can't send him home. I've important things to discuss with him.—Who? My lawyer, if you must know.—All right, come at four.—I'll see you then."

She sat down beside Phil.

"Who on earth was the persistent pest?"

"The man from whom I'm going to get the date of the uprising. Something's happened that he can't come tomorrow." She spoke as if talking to herself.

"Your Communist leader?"

"Yes. I must see him."

"I suppose nothing could persuade you to drop the dangerous game you're playing?"

"Nothing. We must have the date."

"Well, I've learned my lesson with you. I'll say no more."

They talked for another hour, a few very important details were settled, and the appointment of two more members of the General Staff were confirmed. One of these, a commanding General of the World War.

At four John Allen came. He entered the room with a boyish haste out of keeping with his position as the most important leader of revolution in America.

"It's come!" he exclaimed. "My summons to Moscow for last instructions."

"For the day?" she whispered.

He nodded. "And for the confirmation of my position and authority here."

"The day has been fixed?"

"It can't be, until the crisis here reaches an acute stage. That will be decided by a meeting of the inner circle in New York when the hour has struck. We depend on surprise."

He paused and watched her in silence. She wondered if he had guessed the secret of her real purpose. It couldn't be possible. His love had become an infatuation. Reassured, she asked:

"What is it?"

"I can't leave you here. These hours together have grown to mean more to me than anything else in life. Marry me and sail for Russia tomorrow. I may be gone more than a year. It will be a glorious honeymoon. You'll see a mystic's ideal become reality on earth. You've studied enough to see it now with sympathetic eyes. Don't say no. I've secured funds enough to cover our joint expenses—will you?"

"Now, John," she protested. "You must know in your heart that I couldn't do so mad a thing. Marriage to me is not just a honeymoon trip. If I ever marry again it will be in a church with all due ceremonies. To rush off to Russia on an hour's notice—don't be foolish!"

He dropped to a seat forlornly.

"I knew you'd say something like that. But I had to come and try. I can't postpone my sailing. It's an order from Grand Headquarters."

"I'll be right here when you return."

He took her in his arms and kissed her.

"Au revoir. Not good-bye, mind you, just au revoir."

She repeated the words with a little smile playing around the corners of her eyes.

It was snowing next morning. Having no engagement for study, she turned over and slept until ten o'clock. When she awoke for some reason her mind was full of Murino. His letters had been guarded, but she had read between the lines the ever living fact of his love.

He was fine in his personal character, generous and chivalrous. Again and again she asked herself the question why she did not marry him. She had felt in their parting the beat of his heart. And something within her had answered.

Her telephone rang and she rose to answer it indifferently expecting to hear Phil. She was surprised by Murino's voice.

"Hello, darling," he greeted jovially. "How are you?"

"When did you get back? And why didn't you cable so I could meet you?"

"Would you have met me at the pier?"

"I'd have hired a tug and gone down to Quarantine. Why didn't you cable?"

"A little too risky. I had important business to look after the minute I arrived. Before my racketeering friends could possibly know. I've been here for a couple of days in fact."

"Oh, you mean thing!"

"I've called you the minute I finished the troublesome business. It's done now and I want to see you right away. Shall I run up and bring you down here for luncheon, dinner and an evening together?"

"Couldn't please me better. Hurry. I'll be ready. Come right on up stairs."

When he entered the room he caught her in his arms.

She looked up tenderly.

"Tony, you're the most wonderful man I've ever known. I've missed you terribly. I'm awfully afraid I'm falling in love with you."

"That's wonderful news," he smiled. "The most wonderful I've had since we parted an eternity ago."

She led him to the divan.

"Sit down and tell me what you've been doing all this time."

"To begin with I spent six months in Ireland, quietly looking up old friends and relatives and trying to help them. It was a tough job. They were all ready to leave the old country and come to America with me. I had a time convincing them that Ireland might be a much safer place to live in for the next two years than the United States. Of course, I refused to let one of them come on here. And that's a strange thing when you consider how well I've done for myself. Naturally I couldn't walk around in the open over there with a prison record to my credit and an escape to add to its horrors if taken. But I managed to see them. The Irish are born conspirators. They can keep dangerous secrets. I gave the grim old prison in which I lay for dreary months a wide berth. There are things in our lives sometimes we can't look on with our own eyes. The horror of that prison is one of mine. The memory of its cruelties, its bread and water days, its ugly beatingss with which they tried to break my spirit and murder my soul—" he paused. "Let's forget it and go down to my house," he urged. "I've had a wood fire built for you in the library. We'll sit beside it, watch it snow through the windows and dream. Besides I've a reason for wanting you there to-day."

"A special reason?"

"Yes."

Never had the rich beauty of the library glowed with such subdued

splendor as to-day. With a snow storm raging outside and the glow of the big fireplace lighting its shadowy recesses. She spread her hands before the burning logs.

"This is the most beautiful room I've ever been in!" she cried. "Rich, quiet, in perfect taste, and so restful."

"I'm glad you like it," he said with a slow emphasis. It was not a conventional phrase. There was a meaning behind the words.

"Tell me what else you did in Europe?" she asked. He sat beside her a moment before answering and then spoke carelessly.

"Oh, I bummed around a while in London. I love the old place. Always wanted a town house in its mysterious sombre heart. Revelled in Paris, Berlin, and Rome. Paris always amuses me. Even in the old days Berlin irritated me with its damned signs forbidding everything, leaving politics out. Of all the European cities Rome fascinates me most. The continuity of its life stretching down into human history from three thousand years grips my imagination."

"Is Europe drifting into another War?"

"Not half as fast as this country is drifting into a possible Civil War."

"If we are vigilant we can prevent that!" she interrupted.

"If we are—yes—but will we be? I don't think so. Nothing can equal the ignorant complacency of the average American. He refuses to see what he doesn't want to see. He won't look at it even when you push it under his nose. Remember the country drifted into its Civil War of the sixties with nine people out of every ten, North and South, refusing to believe in the possibility of such a thing. And when it broke, these same complacent people said it would all be over in three months. It took three years to reach its bloodiest days! People are now busy poohpoohing the danger of serious trouble in this country, and they'll keep it up until the thing breaks over their heads."

He took her hand and pressed it.

"I can't say this too emphatically and I want to get you out of it in time. I've invested most of my fortune in Holland. Half of it in bank deposits. A fourth of it in good securities, the other fourth in gold coin. I'm closing out all my holdings in the United States. I made the last sale yesterday. I've bought an ocean going steamer. She's lying at a pier in Brooklyn ready to sail when I'm ready. I want to take you with me, dearest. I've bought a little island off the coast of Italy that's a natural fortress. A place of inconceivable beauty. I looked for it a year. A sparkling jewel set in the deep blue waters of the sea. I want to take you there in our own ship and spend six months resting and dreaming before we sail again. I came over to tell you this and ask you to marry and go home with me."

She drew a deep breath and would have spoken but he lifted his hand.

"Let me finish telling you something before you say anything. I talked last night with the most remarkable Labor leader this country has produced. He has brains, he has daring, he has had many bitter experiences. John L. Lewis is not a beauty to look at but he is a tremendous personality. He is usually alive with faith. He has seen a vision lately that has completely changed his outlook on life. And it's an ominous thing. Let me read you an article he has just written. If you believe this you're going to sail the seas with me until we find a sane world.

"Says Lewis: "There are thirteen million Americans now out of employment. And their number increases as the nation drifts with terrifying and deadly sureness into financial bankruptcy, economic collapse and human tragedy. What that human tragedy really means I'll come back to in a minute. And this is true in spite of the fact that our Government has dipped into its Treasury to grant huge subsidies to industry, agriculture, banking and finance.

"These grants have already mounted to the enormous total of twenty-two billions. Our national economy has so nearly collapsed that no major enterprise can longer survive on its own resources.

"The banks are supported by Federal funds. The shipping industry, since the World War, has squandered nearly three billions given it by the Government. In addition it has sunk its own resources and its capital assets. A recent Government report shows its complete financial ruin.

"Agriculture is a beggar living off direct Government aid. The railroads are rushing toward financial collapse. They demand higher rates for freight and passengers and pile their burden on the backs of the people. Every dollar added to freight, increases the price of food. There's scarcely a business that is not receiving larger loans from the Treasury than could be obtained at any bank. They will never be repaid. While the banks are glutted with money which they are afraid to invest and on which they pay no interest.

"Since 1933 seven billions of Government money has been paid to the unemployed in direct or work relief. This vast sum has trickled through the tills of merchants and thus has become for them a necessary subsidy.

"America is moving backward, not forward. We are in reverse gear. Our consumer goods slowed down in '33. The big industries quickly followed. Since then the whole trend has been downward. Shut downs in industry are the order of the day. Thousands of human beings are thus thrown again into our bread lines.

"Neither industry nor Government has come forth with a sane proposal to meet the problem of this depression. Congress in continuous session has failed to devise or enact a single law that would give a gleam of hope to the millions of despairing Americans. In the meantime we have coveting and confusion without end. Our statesmen are reviling each other in anger and bitterness that defiles, scars and destroys. While our population suffers in silence and a creeping paralysis impairs their minds.

"What is to be done?

"America is menaced, not by a foreign foe that can take over forts and sink our ships, but by the more fearful enemy of domestic strife, savagery and incompetence."

"The picture is not overdrawn, my dear. I sent you a second contribution for your Patriot Union before you asked for it. But you're late. An uprising in America, bloody and relentless is swiftly approaching."

"I believe that, too," she broke in. "Our organization will be armed and placed on a military basis. We'll raise a fund of ten million dollars with which to do it."

"Which can only mean one thing—a civil war on the model of the hell now raging in Spain."

He pressed her hand again.

"Come, let's get out of it, dearest. Life's too short for more blood and strife. It's just long enough to love. Will you come?"

"How can I run under fire?"

"You're not fencing because of Phil?"

"No," she answered firmly. "You're the most fascinating man I've ever known. But I've begun a tremendous thing here. I must carry on."

"If I stay and help you at the risk of losing this precious life of mine—what then?"

"You might win," she smiled. "I don't quite know my own heart—please stay—will you?"

"With the hope you hold out—yes. If hell must be braved, it must. But I'm not going to live in this house any longer. I couldn't. The boys who are after me would get me here. So when I got back I made out a lease to you for the house and all its furnishings and established a trust fund sufficient to keep it up during your life time. Will you accept it? I knew in my heart you wouldn't sail with me—not just yet."

He handed her two legal documents—a lease and a Trust agreement.

She held them a moment in silence gazing at them through tears.

"You take my breath," she murmured. "How can I accept such a thing and give nothing in return?"

"You've already given more than you know. Don't hesitate to take it. I'm moving out tomorrow. I hate to leave. It will make it easier if I know you're here. This house expresses the best that's in me. You should make it your personal headquarters. You may find that steel clad room below the street level exactly suited to your needs when your Patriot Union is on a military basis."

"Dear Tony," she answered with difficulty, "you overwhelm me. If I were flippant about it I'd accept it as another contribution to my cause. That, deep down, would hurt my vanity. Facing the issue squarely I find I'm vain. I'd like to think you do this because you love me—not because I've chosen a cause."

"Please look at it that way—it's true—and you know it. Only love could inspire such a gift. I mentioned the other things to give your mind little excuses."

"I don't need them," she interrupted. "And I won't have them. I'm going to accept the use of your house because you love me, and, I'm fair enough to say with the hope that I may yet love you in a way worthy of your generous heart. But you're old enough to know that we love just because we love. You make me very happy and very proud when I realize what you've done. Thank you, dear, with all my heart!"

Her eyes suddenly sparkled.

"Let's call Phil to have dinner with us here tonight and let me give him the lease to record for me tomorrow."

"How did you know I'd want it recorded?"

"Because your enemies should be informed. Will you call Phil now?"

"If you won't let him stay too long."

"I'll pack him off after he has smoked two cigarettes with his coffee."

He looked at her steadily.

"You won't let him change your mind about this?"

"No. But I'll feel better when I have his blessing on it. He's my lawyer, you know, and my oldest friend. It will make me happy to see you two men shake hands."

"All right," he nodded. "But you call him. Here's the phone." He handed her a movable telephone and she rang Phil's office over his private wire and he answered immediately.

"It's clear. I'm alone, honey. Shoot."

"I'm at Tony's house having luncheon with him. He wants you to come up to dinner tonight—just we three."

"Oh, my God, Angela!"

"What's the matter?"

"You don't mean you've accepted him and are asking me to celebrate with you?"

"Oh, you poor fool—no. Certainly not. It's a little celebration—yes—but not that kind."

"All right, if you say so. I'll pocket my pride and come just to please you."

"Don't be late. Promptly at seven. I've a surprise for you."

"What did he say in that first crack he made when you called him a fool?" Murino asked.

"You'd never guess."

"And you won't tell me?"

She shook her head.

After lunch they looked the house over in all its conveniences luxuries and appointments.

He glanced at his watch.

"Would you mind spending the afternoon here getting acquainted with the chef, the butler and the maids while I take a little whirl down to Wall Street?"

"It'll be wonderful to walk around and try to realize all it means. I'm afraid I'll wake up and find it a dream."

"Enjoy yourself," he called from the door. "And if our friend arrives before I do, receive him, will you?"

"You won't be very late?"

"No. I'll do a day's work in the two hours left of the afternoon."

A subtle man, she decided when he had gone. Alone she would revel in the sense of possession until no power could loose her hold.

It turned out as he had foreseen. Phil arrived first and when Angela received him, she acted the part of the hostess with such unconscious perfection it cut him to the quick. She seemed to have passed completely out of his life and had become a part of the furniture.

He scowled and asked.

"Our host is not here?"

"Detained at his office. Asked me to offer you his apologies."

"I must say I think it rude. I'm not going to recognize you as hostess, by a damn sight."

"Now, now, Phil, you mustn't swear in the presence of a lady!"

He grinned. "Sorry. You know how I feel."

"Well, you shouldn't."

Seated before the glowing fire, his mind softened with memories of his childhood.

"Doesn't the fire remind you of a thousand beautiful things down home, dear?"

He stopped and flushed at sight of her face.

"Yes. There was a wonderful fireplace in a little home I built—once."

"Forgive me, darling," he pleaded. "I should have had better sense."

"Why should you? We can't jump out of our own skin, can we? The past is part of us. And to me it will always mean one thing. We are not living in a civilized world."

She stopped abruptly and smiled at him.

"But away with sad thoughts. I'm happy tonight."

And then in a rush of words she told him of Murino's offer of marriage, a home in Europe on an enchanted isle, her refusal, and his gift of the use of his house with a trust fund to run it. He rose pale and trembling.

"But, my God, Angela, you haven't accepted it?"

"Yes."

In a counter rush of passionate pleading he told her how impossible it was to take such a gift except as a marriage settlement.

"Damn him!" he groaned. "He knows that, too. If you accept the lease of the house endowed for your use, you are going to accept him. You may not know it, but you are."

"Am I?"

"Well, you'll move into his mansion without batting an eye!"

"I had to. He was so wonderful about it. Besides we'll need it for our work."

"Do you know what this house and its furnishings are worth?"

"Haven't an idea.

"I thought not. It's worth a million. The lease and funds to run it mean fifty thousand a year. I can't believe my ears when you say you'll accept it."

"Oh, yes you can, Phil. You know that if this gift came from an old maid friend you'd rejoice with me. It's terrible because it comes from Tony—a fascinating man—to whom I owe more than I can tell you."

"Other rich gifts on the side?"

"Other rich gifts—but not on the side—on the inside. Brace up now. Play the role of a Southern gentleman and at dinner drink a toast to Tony. Can you take that order?"

"There's nothing else to do. You leave me no choice."

"Shh—he's coming. Chin up!"

Murino entered and extended his hand.

"You've heard the news?"

"Yes. And I needn't tell you that I'm shocked that Angela puts herself under such obligations. It's not quite fair under the conditions, do you think?"

There was a cold ring in the words that was not lost on Murino.

"I think it's fair. You see, Mr. Stephens, you had the advantage of me in the start. You've had a beautiful boy and girl love affair that never quite ended. Frankly, I envy you. I'm going to fight for her with every power I can swing."

"All right," Phil smiled. "We'll shake hands on that—and—" he paused looking at Angela— "And may the best man win!"

"May the best man win!" came in echo.

Angela presided over the dinner with grace and tact. When they took their coffee and cigarettes into the library before the cheering fire, the two men talked as friends.

When Phil rose to go at nine, she handed him the documents.

"Have these recorded for me tomorrow, please."

"Certainly, dear. Shall I give you a lift to your apartment?"

"I'll take her home later," Tony broke in. "I've a lot of details to go over with her about the management of the house. You can understand that?"

"Quite."

He bowed and pressed Angela's hand.

"Goodnight."

His host followed him to the door.

"I'd like to see you in your office for a confidential talk tomorrow at eleven, if I may?"

"I'll be glad to see you at eleven," the lawyer answered in crisp business tones.

Chapter 54

When Murino was shown into Phil's office at precisely eleven o'clock, the lawyer looked at his watch and smiled.

"Have a seat."

A strained silence followed. Murino broke it in friendly tones.

"Come, now, Mr. Attorney, let's forget personal differences for a moment. I've matters of grave importance to discuss with you and a proposition to make."

The lawyer relaxed.

"What's on your mind?"

"More than I can tell you in the hour at my disposal. But I'll give you a general idea. Enough for you to decide yes or no on what I suggest. This country is in a far more serious crisis than you, or any other men not inside the radical circles, can conceive. I'm in a position to know things you can not know. I'm going to give you the benefit of that knowledge."

"Thanks. I'll appreciate it," Phil interrupted in more cordial tones. He saw that the man was in dead earnest. He couldn't doubt his sincerity in spite of the knowledge of an adventurous past.

His caller leaned back in his chair, blew a ring of smoke toward the ceiling and went on.

"The Communists hold the key to the situation. And that's the most ominous aspect of it. They have bored into your Labor organizations until their agents control at least four million members of the Unions. They have bored into the farmers until they control the Western divisions. Few people in this country as yet know enough about this cult to gauge either its power, or its menace. Mental disorders are now the despair of the medical world. There are more people suffering from diseases of the mind than all other ills combined. There are five millions at present confined in asylums. There are five millions more, outside, as crazy as those inside. But there is no room for them. Communism is the collapse of the human mind under the pressure of modern life. It is a malignant, contagious, mental disease now sweeping the world as the Black Death swept Europe in the middle ages. Its victims can see but one way to safety. A return to the herd life out of which an intelligent humanity grew. This impulse to touch shoulders with the herd, to sink back into the mass for food and shelter, means the end of all progress and the death of civilization itself. The mind once broken by this disease cares nothing for society, country or race. Its only thought is food and shelter with the least possible exertion. Man must live by bread—there's nothing else to live for! So the hand arrays itself against the brain and drags the human race down into the dirt. We are living in crazed times. The foundations have broken up. It may astound you when you put it to the test, how many weaklings with diseased minds are ripe for the new fanaticism.

"Here lies the danger of their coming uprising—the stampede of millions back to the herd when their masters give the call.

"The Communists in America are building a People's Front as in France. They have already issued the call for their political convention for the coming Presidential campaign. With them, of course, political campaigns are conducted merely to throw sand in people's eyes. They hold all of your political machinery in utter contempt. They play politics only to prepare for direct blood stained action when the time is ripe. We must find the date which they fix. The possibility of stopping them depends on this.

"On the combination of the forces that will make up the revolutionary uprising they depend for success—always on the element of surprise.

"Few men in this country have any conception of the wide spread and deadly activities of the Reds. They have divided every large, city into districts and sub-divided them into sections, consisting of shop, neighborhood or street unit. Every member is assigned a specific task. It may be to provoke a riot or spy on his employer.

"The general purpose of their program works in a hundred ways to destroy society. They support every government undertaking that promises extravagance enough to weaken faith in our political and social system. They support any labor agitation that will slow down business, create unemployment and misery, postpone recovery and promote class hatred. They support in its wildest extravagances every relief system, national and local. They tell every dependant that his position is one of honor, that it should be better paid and by all means be made permanent. They thus seek to make our relief burdens ruinous, and every man on relief a revolutionist.

"They support at the polls every political wrecker of whatever party, and every program which promises to be destructive. They have even begun already to seize the machinery of our government. There are many parts of the United States where it is now impossible to get on the pay roll of the WPA without first joining the Communist Party, or its puppet The Workers Alliance. They have established units in the Postal Service and organized their cells in the Post Office. Their Army Unit dares to publish a seditious sheet called "The Soldier's Voice." The Naval Unit issues "The Shipmate's Voice" which glorifies Soviet Russia and urges American workers and sailors to follow in the footsteps of foreign fanatics. In our Navy Yards they publish "The Navy Yard Worker" which preaches the most violent class hatred. The deadly import of these Navy units scan be grasped when we remember that one man, with technical knowledge, can put a great battleship out of commission, or sink it.

"They specialize on printing seditious sheets in the shops in which they work. They issue one of these filthy shop papers within the walls of a utility company which supplies light and power to one of the largest cities in America. "They have their tools in every newsgathering agency and newspaper in the United States. The NEW YORK TIMES, our conservative leader, determined to preserve its editorial integrity, has been honeycombed by traitors who take orders only from Moscow. They publish a vicious shop sheet called THE NEW TIMES for the sole purpose of ridiculing and injuring their employers. In every great newspaper these shop sheets are used to stab their employers in the back. One of our big publishers declares that he can not print a news story unfavorable to Communism without risking an attempt to destroy his plant. He says that there are more of these people now on the pay rolls of our great metropolitan dailies than are on the staff of their own organ "The Daily Worker."

"They have kidnapped and held for ransom" says Congressman Hoffman, "great industrial plants until workers and owners have met their demands. To General Motors they caused a loss of forty million dollars in forty days. To this must be added the loss of six millions to retail merchants and eight millions to wholesalers during this strike. Like foraging armies they seized and held possession of executive offices, hotels and barrooms and helped themselves to food and drink. They seized railroads and stopped the movement of freight in interstate commerce. They shot down airplanes carrying food to beseiged workers. They destroyed the rights of private property by organizing the refusal to pay rent. Peaceful workers have been assaulted, peaceful homes picketed, courts defied. In the labor movement they claim the right, and use it, to beat workers, destroy property and escape all punishment. They have interfered with the United States mails and cut off light and power in large areas, endangering the health and lives of millions.

"They have even dared to take possession of the Capital of a great

State, where they created flying squadrons armed for acts of violence, stopping traffic and business, driving busses and taxicabs off the streets, closing newspaper plants, barbershops and restaurants.

"They are now moving on the railroads with deadly purpose, organizing new units, especially in the terminals of great cities. They are making a determined drive on the trackmen, workers who carefully cover every mile of track daily. If these men should strike, all trains must stop. They could blow up every bridge and wreck every tunnel in America in an hour. With transport, communication and utilities invaded these conspirators could stop all traffic and supplies on orders from Moscow.

"One of their most successful tricks is to disguise their work behind high sounding words. The Youth Congress Movement is theirs. The Workers Alliance is theirs. The American League against War and Fascism is theirs. The American League for Peace and Democracy is theirs. The Civil Liberties Union is theirs. A dozen other patriotic high sounding associations are theirs. They recently invented a brand new philanthropic title under which they invaded the South . . . The Southern Conference on Human Welfare. Under this specious appealing, name they induced the wife of the President to appear in Birmingham and speak from their platform. Not one item of real human welfare received any attention. It finally developed that the sole purpose of The Southern Conference on Human Welfare was to stir in the deep South the ugliest phase of the Negro Problem by a brazen demand for social equality. The Conference was completely dominated by six hundred Communist delegates who threw off their disguise in the last sessions and took complete charge of the stinking affair. It developed that the money to finance this remarkable Conference had been furnished by the Communists. The same social uplifters were there who had been taking groups of Negroes from Atlanta, Birmingham and other Southern cities to New York and Chicago and quartering them in the homes of white families that they might be sent back to the South enthusiastic advocates of social equality.

"Wars and revolutions are psychic epidemics. Such an epidemic is sweeping the world. Millions are succumbing to its delusions. Here is a power, once in motion, that surpasses all the powers of earth. Communists believe that the hour is rapidly approaching when they can grasp the power of these delusions to launch their uprising in America."

Murino paused and fixed Phil with a steady gaze.

"The proposition I have to make to you is to swear me into your Patriot Union and put me in absolute charge of the forces that will fight the Criminal Division of the People's Front. It's a dangerous job, but my training has prepared me for it."

"Would you undertake it?"

"That is my proposition. I will find out how far the organization of two million ex-convicts and racketeers and five million alien criminals has gone and what part they are to play in the proposed uprising."

"You will take a desk at the Headquarters of the Patriot Union?"

"No, but I'll keep in touch with you by phone and in person."

Phil studied his visitor and slowly said:

"I can't tell you how you've surprised me, and how pleased I am at your proposal. With your old organization you can render invaluable service."

"Not through the organization I once controlled. It died with Prohibition. Most of my men have surrendered to the racketeers. There are enough of them, however, who like me personally and believe in me, to form a nucleus in the Patriot Union in the big cities. The great cities of the thirteen industrial States will be the first object of attack. On their fate depends the fate of the nation!"

At the close of the hour's conference, the lawyer took Murino's hand.

"My apologies for a lot of hard things I've said about you. There's no longer a gulf between us. There's a bond. I admire your good taste in loving the woman I love. On that issue there can be no compromise. It's a fight to the finish, on all else, friends."

Murino nodded.

"I'm leaving town today for a survey of Chicago, Cleveland, and Detroit. I've asked Angela to keep her apartment for appearances but take immediate possession of the house. You'll help her I hope?"

"I'll have to, of course," he frowned.

"Don't frown, my friend. There's a private entrance to that house and an inner room, she may yet use in an emergency."

Phil laughed.

"I've always suspected that."

"But you never discovered it. She can show you now."

Phil winced but smiled a good natured parting.

Angela piloted him the next day through the double doors into the steel room.

He gazed at its perfect appointments in amazement.

"What a college of intrigue the Emerald Isle has given the world!" he said casually.

"You know that he is an Irishman?"

"For some years. He's the brother of Dion O'Bannion of Chicago, who was killed by his rivals."

"You know that he served a prison term in Ireland?"

"But unjustly convicted on perjured testimony. I've never held it against him."

She took his arm and held it firmly.

"Why Phil, I'm just beginning to know you. I had no idea you were so human!"

He smiled and re-inspected the radio room with its double sets.

"I've an idea we're going to need this, and need it badly," he said gravely. "Our big danger will be the cutting of the lines of communication. We'll have the Patriot Union set up a secret amateur radio set in every city district and every town in America. This room will command them all. Murino must have had this steel nerve centre in mind, when he turned this house over to you. We'll make it a workshop the next few months."

"Would you like a set of keys to the private entrance?"

He turned them curiously in his fingers.

"Not a bad idea. I suppose you've had a set for a long time?"

"He gave them to me before he went to Europe, but I've never used them. Shall I show you the way in from the side street?"

He nodded.

When she had led him to the entrance and back into the chamber he said:

"This will also fit into a plan I am developing for defense and aggression when the uprising breaks. I'll go over it with you when the plans are complete. We're going to need a lot more money in the Treasury of the Patriot Union."

"Let's go to the men and women who have it and get it now."

"You're game for a canvass of funds?"

"Ready to start tomorrow morning if you are."

They covered the financial centre of New York, Philadelphia, Boston, Cleveland, Detroit and Chicago in eight weeks intensive work and secured in cash and pledges ten million dollars. When the situation was explained, cash subscriptions were given with enthusiasm and the promise of more when needed. A few very rich men pooh-poohed the whole idea of trouble as fantastic.

Angela developed a speech of farewell to these men that brought more than one belated check.

Looking the ostrich men squarely in the eye she said:

"When they knock on your door and demand that you give a reason for your existence, remember the warning I've given you and the opportunity to defend yourself which you have neglected. Goodbye and good luck!"

It was the subtle meaning she threw into the last words which found their nerve centres, when she had gone, and brought the check.

When they were back in New York and had their first dinner alone in the great house, Phil lit a cigarette and said:

"I'm ready to go over the plan of defense with you. Let's get into that inner chamber."

Again in the secret room he reexamined it with care, sat down at the desk and smiled.

"It's perfect. Couldn't be better if we'd built it ourselves. A couple of months ago while New York was racing on its way, millions of people sipping their drinks, dancing and rushing the theaters, I was in the office of the District Attorney with whom I was associated for several years. I found him suffering from a case of nerves. The power houses that supply the current for subways, L roads, street cars and electric lights reported that men had been prowling around their plants, day and night for a month. Two of these prowlers had been arrested.

"For an hour the men were grilled with merciless skill. To no purpose. Not a thing could be gotten out of them.

"It was not until my friend explained the arrest of a man loafing about the telephone exchanges, that my suspicions were confirmed. These fellows are already at work, mapping their plans of assault on the big cities.

"I tried for a week to convince the Police Department of the threatened danger. They couldn't see it. The Chairman of the Commission was indignant at my persistent warning.

"What the hell's the matter with people today?" he asked. "Everybody's got the jitters. An appropriation of public funds for an imaginary emergency? Rats!"

"What's your plan? I'm eager to hear it," Angela urged.

"That a plot is on foot to capture first the big cities is confirmed by these prowlers. That they will try to paralyze the transport and lighting systems and at the same time seize the telephone exchanges is clear. We must prevent the possibility of a seizure of the means of communication between the units of the Police Force. I propose to install a siren set in tall towers in each district. And, on the siren, place electric lights of enormous candle power, red, white, and blue colors, for use in a code of signals. This code must be in the hands of every Police Captain and he must understand the meaning of the alarm. At its call he would mobilize his men and concentrate them on the point menaced, or a rendezvous agreed on.

"The locations of the sirens and signal lights will be kept a secret from the public. In case of an unrising, each watchman in charge of a tower will know instantly what to do. What do you think of it?"

"The Mayor and the police must accept the plan and agree to act on it, of course."

They secured an appointment with the Mayor, laid the plan before him and he agreed to order the full cooperation of the Police Department.

"That a group of madmen," he smiled, "will attempt an attack on New York is highly improbable. In the insane times in which we are living, however, almost anything is possible. I appreciate your zeal and the great expense you are willing to bear. We have no funds that could be directed to such a thing, but I assure you of full cooperation. Give your signals and instructions to the Chief of Police and each district Captain. The Reds are always uttering threats. If they act some day instead of talk, let your sirens give the alarm."

Phil ran up to Albany, conferred with the Governor and asked his cooperation in case of emergency.

"I don't want to call out a division of the State guard except in a grave crisis. You understand that."

"If we call on you," the lawyer answered, "it will be the greatest crisis the State and the Nation has faced since the Civil War."

He quickly extended his system of warnings to Boston, Philadelphia, Cleveland, Detroit and Chicago.

Chapter 55

The Communists held their National Convention again in the Madison Square Garden, New York City.

Angela wondered at John Allen's long absence of more than a year. She had not expected a letter. He had warned on leaving that the censorship was tightening daily and that letters would be impossible. But she had expected him to attend this convention as he had the last one. True he had not taken a leading part except behind the scenes. But she had not dreamed of his ignoring it. He had hinted then that this might be the last Convention held under a Capitalistic regime. Which meant, of course, that the uprising would occur within the next four years.

"What do you make of it?" she asked Phil.

"His absence is far more significant than his attendance would be. The big plan is being matured in silence. The political hue and cry is all for the morons who don't think. We should be there, however, tomorrow night and feel the pulse of the meeting. I've gotten two tickets. We'll go early. It may take an hour to maneuver our way through the crowd."

They took dinner in Angela's apartment and joined a group of students from the University at the Subway. They fought their way through a dense mob at 42nd Street and finally got to the entrance on Eighth Avenue. The mob in the streets was twice the size of the one that jammed it four years ago, and more than half of them were Negroes. It looked as if the whole population of Harlem was trying to get into the Garden or fight a way to a loud speaker.

The Garden was packed and the flags of the Reds waved from every staunchion, beam and girder. There was a curious tension in the crowd. They hadn't come to hear politicians rant. The feeling of crisis and of direct action was in the heavy beer-laden air.

When the Executive Secretary of the Party, ascended the platform holding the arm of his Negro running mate of the last campaign, pandemonium was loosed. The crowd became a mob of howling, screaming, shouting hysterical fanatics. In vain Browder pounded for order. Every time he lifted his hand for silence it was the signal for a new outburst.

At last he took his stand before the microphone and sternly demanded silence. The tumult died away and he introduced the resolution which exploded the bomb the mob had sensed in the offing.

From a grim silence, his voice rang in clear bugle notes to his twenty-five thousand hearers inside the Garden and a hundred thousand who were listening around ten loud speakers set on the corners of the surrounding streets.

"Whereas a call has been issued for a Union Convention of the People's Front to meet in Minneapolis, Minnesota, three weeks from today.

"Resolved that this National Convention of the Communist Party accept the invitation and withhold all nominations at this time."

The resolution was seconded. There was no debate and it was carried by a unanimous rising vote followed by another demonstration led by New York's black district leaders.

Chapter 56

When John Allen returned from Moscow in the spring the savage three cornered Presidential struggle of 1940 was in full swing.

Allen called Angela just as she was about to get her car for a round of secret organization work for the Patriot Union.

"Well," she answered banteringly. "I thought you had decided to accept a life job in Russia!"

"Not me, my dear. I've just landed—not through the customs yet—and I'm calling you. I've big news. May I come right up to your apartment?"

"Yes. Right away. I'm so anxious to see you!" She threw into her words a studied tenderness.

"Would you mind," he added, "if I brought my bag with me? I have no hotel or room as yet. And I would like to talk to you about the location."

"A little unconventional that would be, don't you think?"

"We are not conventional people."

"All right. Bring it along."

"It's not large. It will not excite suspicion."

The bag turned out to be a small trunk with a handle used in valise fashion.

Angela laughed heartily and had him put it out of sight in her closet.

"A very small trunk!" she smiled.

He grinned.

"Thereby hangs a tale. I had to use a little diplomacy before telling you the big news."

He paused and studied her intently.

"You stood the test. You took my trunk into your apartment.

You couldn't have done that unless you love me. You're glorious!"

He caught her in his arms and kissed her passionately.

"You're for me now a hundred per cent?" he asked tensely.

"I don't think I'd have allowed that trunk in here unless I had been, do you? It's probably full of secret documents that may hang us both."

"Exactly. That's one reason I wanted to bring it here. It will be safe. I'll trust you to guard it." He paused and smiled——

"The big thing is on. I come from Russia with the full power to act. I have called the Inner Circle of our revolutionary army to meet day after tomorrow."

She held his gaze a moment, thinking with lightning rapidity. The Inner Circle had been called to act. She must be at that meeting. Could she risk the suggestion that he make her a member and give her command of the Women's Division? She felt his hand trembling as it held hers. His love had surely mastered. Her decision was quick. She would risk all on the bold stroke.

"You are going to make me the leader of the Woman's Division?" she asked gravely.

"Will you accept the appointment?"

"Yes."

"You would have to join our Inner Circle immediately and pledge your life without reservation to our Cause."

"Of course."

"All right. As Chief of the Party I appoint you my first aide in command of the Woman's Division of the United States."

He extended his hand and she seized it.

"It's done," he smiled. "I'll put your name on the list of the Inner Circle in time for admission. And you'll go with me to the meeting."

Angela's heart leaped at the thought of her triumph.

"I'll call for you at six thirty on the day," he added. "Fix a bite for us here. We should be at the place at eight. A little before would be better."

Chapter 57

The next day Murino appeared at Angela's door.

"Why, Tony," she cried in surprise. "I didn't know you were in town——"

"Rushed here from Chicago when my men reported the date of your fateful meeting of the Inner Circle. Do you happen to know where it will be held?"

"Not yet. John will call to take me there."

"Well, I got that for you, too—a thing of tremendous importance—which brought me by plane from Chicago to warn you. The meeting will be held at the headquarters of the NAT TURNER Branch of the Communist Party in Harlem. Does the name NAT TURNER mean anything to you?"[1]

"Frankly—no—it doesn't—though I have heard it somewhere."

"I was afraid of that. Sometimes a foreigner has to instruct Americans in their own history. NAT TURNER is the most ominous and infamous name in the story of the South and of the Negro race in America. He was an ignorant semi-insane preacher in Southampton County Virginia, one of the blackest Counties of the Black Belt. He conceived the idea that he was called of God to raise a Slave insurrection that would exterminate by fire and sword the entire white population. He claimed to hear voices and see visions. A sign would be given him. The eclipse of the sun in February 1831 he accepted as the sign, but he had such difficulty in getting followers that his plans did not mature until August 13th. He believed that the black

1. Nat Turner (1800–1831) was the Virginia slave who, inspired by a religious vision, led the August 1831 slave rebellion in Southampton County that left more than fifty whites dead. The ensuing fear of mass rebellions plagued white southerners for decades, led to a tightening of slave laws and racial repression, and disinclined white southerners to open discussion about slavery and race. See Peter H. Wood, "Nat Turner: The Unknown Slave as Visionary Leader," in Leon Litwack and August Meier, eds., *Black Leaders of the Nineteenth Century* (Urbana: University of Illinois Press, 1988), 21–42.

masses would answer his call, follow his example and sweep the Black Belt with blood and fire.

"Gathering only five companions he finally began near Cross Keys on Sunday night August 21st by killing his master's family while they slept. He was joined by a few recruits and forced others to follow until they numbered fifty three. He swept with death the surrounding farms, killing in cold blood every man, woman, child and babe in arms, and burning their homes. He continued his murders into the next day and butchered the teacher and every child in the neighborhood school house before the whites gathered and drove him and his men into the swamps. Several companies of militia from Virginia and North Carolina and a detail of marines from nearby Fortress Monroe hunted him as a wild beast for six weeks. In the twenty four hours of his operations he had killed fifty seven men, women and children, and burned scores of homes.

"His plan failed for the same reason that John Brown's invasion at Harper's Ferry failed in 1859 when he attempted to drench the South in the blood of a servile uprising. The slaves of Southampton refused to rise and do his bidding. Instead they joined the masters in defending their homes.

"Turner was hung with but seventeen followers. The rest of the fifty three proved that compulsion had brought them into his ranks.

"The name of this fiend has never before been used by any organization in the history of America. It is amazing that Negro Communists dare to adopt it as a slogan to-day. The fact is a complete avowal of their bloody purpose.

"That the meeting of the Inner Circle to decide the question of a national revolution is to be held in the NAT TURNER headquarters is an endorsement by the whole Party of the life and purpose of this devil. It surpasses belief but for the fact that the American people are asleep and the Reds know it. Be on guard for your life if you go there to-morrow night. There will be no friendly slaves to defend you."

"I haven't the slightest fear."

"Don't say that, dearest!"

"I haven't really. Allen is their supreme leader. He vouches for me. He has made me his aide in charge of the Woman's Division of the Soviet Republic of America . . . and a full fledged member of the Inner Circle itself."

"All the same I am warning you. Few people have any idea what is going on between the Communists and the Negroes. In the past five years thousands of young blacks have been graduated from the Moscow Institute and sent back here to secretly organize the revolution. Phillip

Randolph,[2] President of the Brotherhood of Sleeping Car Porters, at the Negro Congress in Chicago boldly declared:

"The time is ripe for a great movement among us. Revolution must come. Physical force is self defense. A bullet is more convincing than a hundred prayers!"

"I must attend the meeting," she interrupted.

"All right. I'll be waiting outside with a guard to see that you get home."

"Thank you, Tony. You are very sweet."

"Call me at the Waldorf if you need me . . ."

"I'll be all right. Don't worry."

2. Asa Phillip Randolph (1889–1979) founded the Brotherhood of Sleeping Car Porters and Maids in 1925. He created a powerful nexus between labor and civil rights that led President Franklin D. Roosevelt to promulgate Executive Order 8802 (June 1941), leading to the establishment of the Fair Employment Practice Committee. See Paula F. Pfeffer, *A. Phillip Randolph: Pioneer of the Civil Rights Movement* (Baton Rouge: Louisiana State University Press, 1990).

Chapter 58

John Allen arrived at Angela's apartment at six thirty and they ate a light meal in strained silence.

"We'll walk to the meeting," he said. "I'll go ahead. We'll not be seen together on the way. I'll meet you at the corner of Lennox Avenue and 134th Street, upper West side of the Avenue. Remember now. Speak to no one in the meeting. Refer all questions to me. Just say, Mr. Allen will tell you. Speak casually."

She smiled.

"Just ask Mr. Allen, please!"

"This meeting," John went on, "is the biggest event in the Western World since the Declaration of Independence. It will reset the history of humanity. Once in the saddle, America will give Moscow some points. If they vote revolution tonight, I'll emerge the most powerful figure in the Nation. The fact will not be long kept a secret. Be careful in the preliminaries to express no surprise or concern at the appearance of any of them. There will be three Negroes there. One from the Industrial North, one from the South and one from New England. You're Southern. Don't betray it by the slightest frown or suggestion of repugnance if one of them should sit down beside you."

"Must you leave me?"

"Not for a minute. But remember that you and I now live under the Dictatorship of the Proletariat. We're one class. All are equal."

"I'll use my brains."

They reached the entrance to the meeting place at eight o'clock. A sentinel recognized Allen at the corner and gave him the salute, which Allen cautiously returned. Angela watched him closely and repeated his actions.

The door was guarded by a stalwart Negro and a queer looking foreigner with a head like Rasputin.[1] He, too, was a giant. He spoke no English but took his cues from the black, who recognized Allen.

"Your wife?" he asked brusquely.

"No. A new member of the Inner Circle whom I have appointed Commander of the Women's Division of Soviet America."

The sable guard nodded and admitted them to the first passage way which led the entire length of the building to another door in the rear. The ceremony was repeated and they entered a narrow hallway leading down a flight of stairs to a basement.

The room was dimly lighted with shaded electric lamps. A small table was placed on a low platform over which hung a heavily shaded drop light.

Allen gripped Angela.

"He's here! The man at the table. He came over on the same ship with me. The Ambassador from the Russian Government of the Third Internationale to the new Soviet Republic of America. He will preside tonight, present the issues, take the vote and call the Master of the World in Moscow who will say the final yes or no. He's a man of culture. A diplomat and linguist who speaks English without an accent. He was in London for four years. He looks like our Emperor Stalin—only his mustache is heavier. He's talking to Stalin in Moscow now. You see him bending over? The transmitter is concealed in the table at which he sits."

The three Negroes were stepping lively over the wide concrete floor space of the room.

"Better meet the Negro Comrades first," he whispered. She steeled her nerves and shook hands with each. The last one, a dapper looking little coal black, wearing spats, flashed her a look of surprise, held her gaze a moment and passed on. She had seen him somewhere, and began to tremble. Where? She cudgeled her brain. Sure! She remembered now. It was on her first long walk through Harlem. She whispered to Allen:

"Stick close, dear. I've seen one of those Negroes before and I don't like him. I'm afraid he recognized me—the little one."

Allen studied him a moment and shook his head: "He couldn't know you. He's Northern born from Detroit. Never was South in his life."

"He gives me the creeps. Don't you dare leave my side a minute."

"I'll not. I want you to meet the man we're depending on for some of

1. Grigori Yefimovich Rasputin (1871?–1916) was the mystic credited with healing Czar Nicholas III's young hemophiliac son, Alexei. A group of his political enemies, distrusting Rasputin's sway over the czar and his family, killed him. During the revolution of 1917, Rasputin's body was exhumed and burned by rebel soldiers as a symbol of political corruption. See Bryan Moynahan, *Rasputin: The Saint Who Sinned* (New York: Random House, 1997).

the most daring work. The leader of two million ex-convicts and five million alien criminals. He leads the army of the outlawed into our ranks."

The man was strikingly like in features the rugged face of John L. Lewis. His eye brows were as heavy, his shock of black hair equally unruly. In striking contrast his voice was smooth. There was a vibrant quality in it that gave warning of reserve power. He looked at Angela with keen interest and turned to Allen.

"The girl you've been raving about, John?"

"Did I overdraw the picture?"

"You couldn't," he smiled. "The half of her has not been told. I congratulate you. And I congratulate the Cause. She will become a great leader of the New Regime."

Angela flushed and lifted her hand in a gesture of depreciation.

John caught the eye of the Ambassador, shook hands and introduced her.

"Welcome to our ranks, beautiful lady. We need women of your type. And I know your wise young mentor will see that every power of your magnetic personality counts for the Cause."

Angela bowed.

"Thank you."

When they had passed on, Allen saw the Chairman watching her out of the corner of his eye with a touch of suspicion. He was not surprised to receive a summons from his secretary.

"You're doing an unwise thing, Comrade, to bring so beautiful a woman to this gathering."

"I'll stake my life on her loyalty. She's now a free member of this circle, in command of the Woman's Division."

"She's the only woman here tonight. A mistake might cost us our lives."

"I understand."

CHAPTER 59

All lights in the big bare room were extinguished but the single shaded one over the table at which the Ambassador presided.

Angela shivered to think the fate of a great nation might depend on the decision of the group around this little table. They were few in number but they represented the rulers of a hundred and sixty millions in Russia, a hundred and fifty millions in China and as many scattered among other nations. They had engulfed Mexico. They were rapidly advancing in Brazil and reaching strong hands to grasp power in other countries of South America.

The grim man presiding represented the brains and the will of the world revolution which his group in Russia had plotted since the triumph of Bolshevism during the World War. The fact that their Eastern attempts to stir the wider revolution in which their regime must ultimately rest had failed was not to be wondered at. They attempted to overthrow the government of other nations, among them our own, before they had consolidated their power at home. That work had now been completed. They had decreed blood purges until every faction had been exterminated. In Russia, they had deliberately murdered six million five hundred thousand of their own people who had helped to win the revolution. These poor devils were the ablest men in their ranks, thrifty and careful peasants and workers who had saved a little. The Proletariat under Stalin's iron hand was now supreme. At least Stalin was supreme. His word was undisputed law for the millions of the new religion. When he promulgated a new Constitution, the unanimous vote of millions were recorded for it. Not a single ballot in opposition was thought of, cast or counted. Their standing army is the most powerful in the world. Their air forces outnumber any other single power. They can put into the field the largest army the world has ever seen. And it would be led by fanatics as desperate as the first conquering heroes of Mohammed.

Their Treasury bulges with gold, which they are using for propaganda in every nation. They are at the moment supporting four daily newspapers and hundreds of weeklies in the United States. They represent the mightest single force of revolution ever set in motion in human history. She had all this from John Allen's own lips. It was beyond question.

Angela could see from the first that the Ambassador regarded the vote to be taken as merely a formal endorsement of plans their supreme master in Moscow had already perfected. The vote would be taken after reports had been made—yes. But the decision would be unanimous as the election had been in Soviet Russia.

The circle of men around the foreign leader watched his face with tense interest. Not a word or the lifting of an eye brow escaped their attention. They listened in a dead silence.

"I am happy to announce to you, gentlemen," he began evenly, "that the occasion is an auspicious one. I bear greetings to you from the most powerful leader the human race has ever known, the coming master of the world."

The circle rose and came to a salute.

"Good. I like your spirit. Resume your seats."

The thing had taken Angela so completely by surprise she had not moved as quickly as the others. Her delay had not escaped the keen eye of the Ambassador and she felt his displeasure.

Allen leaned closer.

"Watch your step, darling. I'm afraid you're under a little suspicion."

"I'll be careful."

The leader resumed: "Let me remind you of what was done in Russia at a meeting similar to this, held in a basement around a single flickering candle. The Bolshevists numbered less than 70,000 men. But we were determined. We were united. And we were armed. By a surprise blow this little army of seventy thousand overthrew the Kerensky Republic, wiped out the last vestige of the old regime and completely mastered the lives of a hundred and sixty five million Russians. An armed determined minority, choosing the supreme moment for a surprise attack, can overthrow any government. The United States is the most vulnerable of all because the people are ill-informed, complacent, egotistical, unsuspicious. When we strike it will be like taking candy from children as you say in this country."

A ripple of laughter ran around the circle in which Angela managed conspiciously to join, thus gaining a point in the favor of the leader. For again his eye had rested on her.

"Of course," he went on, "it's unnecessary for me to explain to you that we are not a political party except to take advantage of the system of free speech and free press which our enemies have invented for our use. We are a Revolutionary Junta, with direct blood action as our method. We are in politics only so long as we can use the politician and his votes for our purposes. You have done superb work in America in spreading our propaganda through the newspapers, the pulpit, the platform and the radio. When I was told in Moscow that you had been assigned time on the radio by which you could speak to millions, I couldn't believe my ears. I never quite grasped it until last night I listened to Earle Browder talking to millions over a coast to coast hookup. The American gods have been good to us.

"I am glad to report to you tonight that our fighting ranks have been crowded during the past four years by the enrollment of more than half a million new names. I mean that our secret revolutionary forces have been thus increased. We can count on these half million men and women to move as one man at the word of command. And they are all armed with rifles, sub-machine guns and T.N.T."

A round of applause greeted the statement.

"Such a force," he went on quickly, "choosing its own hour of surprise, will be resistless. Back of this disciplined army of five hundred thousand, against Lenin's bare 70,000, we have more than five hundred thousand picked men from your outlawed or criminal population who each owns a machine gun. Their spokesman is here tonight."

Nickolas Adams, the leader of the convicts, waved his arm.

"We've more than five hundred thousand. We're much stronger. And we have planted thirty thousand men in the army and navy sworn to execute our orders."

"The most remarkable group of all, perhaps," the Ambassador hurried on, "is the contingent of three hundred thousand armed Negroes, picked men of the race."

The little black man who wore spats lifted a hand.

"You can double that estimate, sir. We'll put into the field the night of the uprising more than five hundred and fifty thousand armed men. DuBois is the greatest leader we have ever produced in America. His book advocating the Dictatorship of the Proletariat has become what he designed it to be, the Bible of the Negro. We'll give the Southerners the biggest surprise of all."

The Ambassador smiled.

"Still I'll have to remind you of Dr. DuBois's statement that across our path the South stands with flaming sword. The South I count our weakest spot. Your armed black men, most of them, are in the North. In the great cities they will do yeoman work when the hour strikes. What we must provide is more rifles, sub-machine guns and bombs for the Black

Belt of the South, to keep the white South from marching on the cities of the North which we will capture."

As he paused, Angela felt a chill. The hard boiled ruthless precision of his plans made her shiver.

"Everything depends on the possibility of a complete surprise! Is the time ripe for this? The coming campaign by the head of the People's Front is, of course, a mere paper feint. We have no intention of electing their distinguished nominee our President. Such a victory would be a hollow one in so far as we are concerned.

"I've carefully considered the hour for the surprise. The system of Presidential Radio chats hands it to us without much mental exercise. Two weeks from to-day the President will give his great broadcast. While a hundred million complacent Americans are listening in rapture to his charming voice, we will strike!"

The circle rose in excitement with low cries.

"Good!"

"Great!"

"A master stroke."

"It can't fail!"

Allen whispered to Angela: "I handed the old coot that idea. But he gives me no credit. I wonder why?"

"Jealousy in heaven!"

"While the hundred million Americans listen to the voice, the one thing furtherest from their imagination will be the danger of a direct revolutionary uprising. Their only thought will be the joyful counting of ballots on election day. The ballot is God in America. They think it the cure for all ills. They never stop to think that a dozen men in each party meet and decide on the candidate they shall vote for and the platform on which he will take his stand. What will be done after the election, they will decide later.

"This sense of security, this colossal conceit, this unbounded complacency of the American masses will make our success sure. Nothing could convince the American masses of any danger from our armed forces. The element of surprise will dominate the situation. While morons listen spell bound to the voice of their leader our armed hosts will strike at the heart of every great industrial city, capture, loot and burn them if necessary. A picked force will seize the Government buildings in Washington.

"The moment we have taken the air ports needed we will call on Russia for pursuit planes and bombers. The Soviet Republic has the greatest air force in the world to-day. It will be at our command.

"This is not guesswork. The armed forces answerable directly to our orders will number more than two millions. We will capture every armory of the National Guard in the great cities, seize its artillery and equipment and in six months disarm the population of every state. Once disarmed, we are their masters for all time. We have bored into both army and navy with enough men to neutralize their forces. Heavy attacks from them will be as futile as the White army of Russia, once we are in power. The army and navy do not move on their own initiative. They take orders from the Government. We will be the Government.

"The question before you first is the one of time. Is this the hour or shall we wait four years more until another Presidential campaign? It's now, or later. Our ultimate triumph is sure!

"My own feeling is that delay would be a mistake. At this moment there are about fifteen million people out of work. That means, with their dependents, forty millions of the population are desperate. They have nothing to lose. We can count on their joining us. Organized labor is in an ugly mood. The stopping of production has paralyzed their power to strike. We can control the C.I.O. machine when we rise. No matter what their conservative leaders may say the rank and file will always follow the radical leader in a crisis. They strike without orders today. They refuse obedience to their chosen officers the moment caution is advised.

"It seems to me that the hour of all hours has struck. If we had asked it made to order it could not be more favorable for surprise. Now let me hear from you. Is there a flaw in my argument? What say you, John Allen, Chief of the American forces?"

"The hour is now. Your argument is without a flaw."

"So say you all?"

The circle rose and gave their salute.

"All right. Is the hour of the Presidential broadcast the right one to strike—what say you, American Chief?"

"An inspiration!" Allen declared.

"You should agree!" the Ambassador smiled. "For you suggested it."

"Hurrah for Allen."

"Good for our leader!"

"Good boy—we're proud of you."

"So am I," the Chairman smiled. "And so is the Master in Moscow. He comes back to you from Grand Headquarters with the highest honor, clothed with supreme power in America when the revolution has been launched. You will give him perfect obedience."

Angela pressed his arm and he smiled proudly into her searching brown eyes.

"So say you all?" the Chairman cried.

Again the circle rose as one man and saluted.

"Now for the O.K. of the Master of the World in Moscow and the decree will be final."

He paused, made the connection with the Capital of Russia.

"Your Majesty, we have unanimously agreed that the hour of the uprising shall be fixed at the precise moment of the next Presidential broadcast when a hundred million Americans will be eagerly listening in, unconscious of danger—what say you?"

"Perfect."

He turned from the phone, his eyes sparkling.

"Your supreme ruler has issued his decree fixing the hour you have chosen. It is so ordered. If we encounter unforeseen difficulties we will cancel the decree and bide our time. Our ultimate triumph is just a question of time, crisis and surprise."

He stopped, seized the telegraph instrument and called Chicago, Boston, Detroit, Minneapolis, Milwaukee, St. Louis, Atlanta, New Orleans and San Francisco. To each he gave the identical signals and each replied with their O.K.

"It's done, gentlemen. It can't be undone. The revolution is in motion. Every leader in each branch is now busy issuing orders which will not be revoked. I must warn you that our Cause and our lives now depend on keeping the hour of the uprising a secret. I will ask each of you in a moment to answer individually on this point. Let me refresh your memory with the first official order of action agreed on in Moscow and communicated to each branch. The moment you are in power in any community, city or State, your first work is to liquidate the undesirables in our own ranks. There must be an immediate blood purge that will insure our perfect unity. We can have no factions, no arguments, no wrangling of any kind. All possible discordant elements must be eliminated by drum head court martial. You will not wait for the formality of sunrise executions. Get out of your mind all personal favoritism. Some of your very brave friends may be among those who must be sacrificed for the Cause. Communism is not humanitarian. We scorn the word and the idea. It is merciless, logical, scientific. Karl Marx poured out his scorn on all Utopian and Humanitarian dreamers. Remember now the minute you have the power—not the next day—but the minute you have the power, execute without mercy or discussion every officer of Government, County, State and National, every policeman, every political leader, every preacher and priest, every Pink Communist or Socialist, and every lawyer. Such material can not be used in the new order. Too many of them would expect office and power. They would try to control your organization. Death is the only remedy. Apply it remorselessly. You are scientists not sentimentalists."

He paused and held Allen's gaze with a steady stare that sent a chill down Angela's spine.

"And now," he went on. "I must examine all of you individually on the question of the secrecy of this meeting and the possibility of a betrayal of the Hour. What say you, Chief John Allen?"

"I can vouch for my comrade present here tonight. She is new to most of you. But I have personally instructed her for the past three years and chosen her for the leadership of the women of America. She will be the Joan of Arc of the new era."

"What say you all to the statement of your Chief?"

There was a moment's silence. And then the little dapper coal black leader rose and stared coldly on Angela.

"I am sorry," he began venomously, "to differ with John Allen. I was surprised to see him enter the meeting with this woman. I happen to know that she is Southern born, and for that reason is unfit to sit in this circle. I happen also to know that for several years she has been closely associated with Antonio Murino one of our most powerful enemies."

"Mr. Chairman, I object to this senseless abuse. I hold myself responsible for her loyalty."

"Your objection is overruled," was the slow answer. "You must answer those charges. Has she been an associate of Murino?"

"Before I met her, Murino paid court to her beauty, and offered her his hand in marriage. She turned him down and chose me for her mate and our Cause for her life work."

The dapper Negro lifted his hand and jumped to his feet.

"I swear to your Excellency that the colored elevator boy in the apartment on 121st Street from which she came here told me that Murino called on her yesterday and this afternoon as well. He spent an hour with her yesterday and half an hour today."

The Ambassador turned directly to Angela.

"What say you to this, young woman?"

She rose promptly with uplifted hand and faced the Chairman.

"It is true, your Excellency. I have known Mr. Murino for several years. He has repeatedly asked me to marry him. I have always refused. He called for another talk with me to ask that I marry him."

"You knew of this?" the Chairman asked Allen, who lied without batting an eye.

"Of course, I knew of it. She was perfectly frank with me, about it."

"I am sorry, John Allen, that I must in the name of our Cause pronounce sentence of death on the woman beside you. We cannot risk her knowledge of our secret and the tremendous issues involved."

He rose and drew his automatic.

Allen confronted him with a steady stare.

"You dare to execute your order in this summary fashion here tonight?"

"Here tonight, at once!"

John covered Angela and squared himself before her executioner.

"I deny that you have authority to put to death a member of this meeting without a fair trial with evidence presented in full."

"I have the right to execute any man or woman in our organization if I believe in their betrayal or possible betrayal of our secrets. I have that authority in writing from the Master in Moscow."

"I demand to see it—as Chief of the American Division."

The Ambassador drew the document from his inner coat pocket with his left hand, his right still gripping the pistol.

Allen read it—and frowned.

"I appeal from this act of tyrannical power to the authority of the Supreme American Soviet assembled here tonight. If the Ambassador can do this to me, he can shoot each one of you in turn before he leaves the room. We are not going to use such methods in America—not while I remain your Chief. I love this woman."

"Communism has nothing to do with love. It is an economic science!" growled the Chairman.

"I appeal to my comrades who have chosen me as their leader. I brought this woman here tonight to secure your consecration of her beauty and brains to our Cause. She came at my suggestion, not her own. I'll not see her shot in cold blood. I ask you to hold her a prisoner under guard every hour until the night of the uprising—Promise me, Comrades!"

The Ambassador moved a step closer.

"Stand aside, John Allen! I know nothing of love or lovers. I do my duty to the Cause."

Allen suddenly whipped a pistol from his pocket but before his finger tightened on the trigger the Russian fired and he dropped in his tracks.

Angela sank by his body.

"Oh, John, John, they've killed you!"

The circle closed in, each man with drawn gun. The gesture was not lost on the Russian.

"What is this, a mutiny at our first official meeting?"

There was no answer.

The silence was broken by the dying voice of Allen.

"I beg of you, my Comrades, spare the life of the woman I love. Put her under heavy guard. Keep her secure day and night to insure your safety—yes—I beg of you—will you?"

"By God we will!" answered the stalwart Nick Adams. "If Allen dies, I succeed him. I'm second in command."

"Promise me, Comrades," Allen pleaded with an ugly rattle in his throat.

"Yes! Yes! Yes!" came from every member of the circle save the three Negroes.

The Ambassador glanced at the pistols gripped in each hand and said sharply:

"Put up your weapons. It shall be so. We'll carry out his last order. And I'll appoint his successor before we leave the room."

"You mean *we* will select our leader and you will O.K. him!" the stalwart from Chicago corrected, his gun still held fast.

The two men glared at each other and the Russian yielded.

"If you wish to vote on it—good—it shall be so."

Allen's arm stole around Angela as he gasped:

"Forgive me, darling, for bringing you here tonight——"

His head sank, she lowered it to the floor and threw a light shawl over his face.

She rose and fixed the Ambassador with a steady gaze.

He turned to his orderly.

"Detail a guard of six men to take this woman to your headquarters prison and keep her under guard day and night until I order her release."

Again the stalwart confronted him.

"I'd say out of respect to our brilliant ex-chief and to avoid arousing suspicion that we send her home, secure his papers from the trunk he left there, and keep her under guard in her own apartment. We can cut her telephone wires and she'll be perfectly safe."

The two men confronted each other again and once more the foreigner yielded without appeal to the circle.

"All right. Give the order to the guard. First see if we are being watched."

The orderly passed quickly to the outer door and returned running.

"The outer guard reports that our entrance and the rear exit are guarded by a force that may attack us!"

Chapter 60

The circle tightened around the Ambassador and the stalwart who had been confirmed by unanimous vote as the American Chief.

The Russian waved them back.

"Sit down. Mr. Adams and I will decide on a plan of action."

"They'll not attack if we are ready for a fight," Adams said. "I'll order a machine gun car to lead and one to follow our car. Two machine gun men will ride with us. I'll command the guard and deliver her safely to her apartment. The minute they see that she has been taken there, they will not attack our men. They'll throw their own guard around ours. They know that a clash of forces at this time would upset their plans of defense. I'll stake my life on it."

The Ambassador nodded.

"All right, your life is on the issue. See that your plan succeeds."

Adams drew himself erect and faced his superior.

"Is your Excellency threatening me?"

"Certainly not. I'm just warning you to be careful."

"Good."

"Open the trunk. Get every scrap of paper inside and return it for a conference with me. See that every telephone connection is cut."

Adams gave a short laugh.

"I'm not a child, your Excellency. You'll find that out I hope at an early date."

The Russian bristled.

"You're not by any chance now threatening me?"

"No. Just reminding you that I am Chief of the American Forces, and I know my business."

"I've heard your experience is broad," his superior answered. "Order your cars and machine gun guard."

"My adjutant heard my suggestions and they are on the way, sir."

A younger member of the circle tipped his cap in confirmation.

"They'll be at the door in five minutes, Chief."

Adams turned to Angela who sat between two men guarding her.

"May I speak to you a minute?"

She started, rose quickly and followed him to a corner of the room.

"You've heard my name, no doubt?"

"Yes, Mr. Adams, I heard it just now."

"And you know that I was second in command under John Allen—now his successor?"

"And I am grateful to you for your help."

"You mustn't be. He was the best friend I ever had. He secured my release from prison before I had finished my sentence. He had a mind big and broad enough to know something of my character and ability in spite of prison records. I'd have gone through hell for him. And I'm ready to go through hell now to save you from these damned fools. But you've got to help me or I'll fail. Will you help me?"

"Certainly," was the prompt reply.

"I'm going to count on that now. I'm the commander of the American Forces, but I can't save you if you attempt to escape or communicate with our enemies. An armed guard must stay in your rooms day and night. I'm sorry for this intrusion on your privacy, but it can't be helped. It was either this or your imprisonment in a foul Harlem basement. The guard will sleep on your couch. He will be a man you can trust."

"Thank you."

But remember. He will be armed with an automatic in each pocket of his coat and a tear gas bomb in his belt. One move to escape or communicate with the outside world and you will be shot instantly. I don't want to hurt you. I loved your friend. I'll guard you with my life. You'll not attempt to escape for the next two weeks?"

"I'll stay quietly in my rooms. I promise you."

"Your friend Murino is the only man who would have the brains and the nerve to surround this meeting place. He'll not attack us when he sees it will precipitate a battle. He knows that you would be shot instantly and he knows the battle would cause his own plans to go wrong at this juncture. I know that he is at work on a scheme of defense. He and I watch each other pretty closely. I'll go with you to the apartment and get John's papers. Not a word now from you when you see Murino's men."

"I promise."

Adams' adjutant reported the three cars at the door.

"All right," was the quick answer. "Tell the captain to place machine gun men on each side of the car we'll use. Let the men who are watching us see the guns. And tell the machine gunners in the car in front and the one following to get out and show themselves."

The man saluted and hurried out.

"Just a minute to give time for that order to be executed. Murino's a dangerous boy. He might rush us unless he sees those guns."

"Your guard is ample?" the Ambassador asked.

"Ample!" was the quick retort.

"Come back here with the papers at the earliest possible moment."

Again Adams held the Russian with a stare.

"I'll bring them. Never fear. But I am John Allen's successor in command. I'll not surrender his papers to any one except The Master."

"I haven't asked you to surrender them. I'll have the Master on the wire when you return."

"Good. I'll make my report to him direct about what happened here to-night. And I'll ask your recall."

"You'll waste your breath."

The two confronted each other, and the tension relaxed as Adams took Angela's arm. His adjutant signaled the guard was ready and they started to the waiting cars.

As they emerged, Angela saw the single figure of Murino standing under a strong electric light but a hundred feet away. There were no others in sight. She knew at once that he had realized her danger and called off an attack.

She breathed a prayer of thanksgiving and tried to get her message across the air to him without word or gesture. She evidently succeeded. For he turned in his tracks, waved an arm in friendly farewell and walked toward Lennox Avenue.

The engines of the three cars rumbled in chorus and they started at the same moment. The machine gunners assigned to her car had climbed into the front seat with the driver and the procession dashed through the thinning traffic of Harlem and in ten minutes drew up at her apartment. On alighting she turned sharply at the sound of a fourth car which stopped suddenly and discharged five men, who quickly disappeared.

Adams' eye caught the move of his enemy and he issued a quiet order to his adjutant.

"I leave you in command of our guard. Not a shot from you or a hostile move except in self defense. They are going to watch only. They'll not attack you."

He saluted and placed his men in strategic positions commanding every approach to the apartment, both through mist Street and along

Amsterdam Avenue and Broadway. All were quickly instructed to make no assault, or fire except to defend themselves.

When they had entered the apartment, Adams immediately cut the telephone wire and smashed the receiver. He handed the pieces to a guard.

"Wrap these up carefully and take them with you."

He found that John Allen had locked his trunk and the key was in his pocket.

"You haven't a key?" he asked Angela sharply.

"No. He opened it only for a minute to change his clothes, locked it and put the key in his pocket."

He got a chisel from the handy kit of the guard, broke the lock and took out all papers. He found but half a dozen which he placed in his inner coat pocket. One of them he showed to Angela. It bore the great seal of the Soviet Republic.

"John's appointment as American Chief," he pointed out, "and my name as his second in command and his successor in case of death in action. I'll try to have the dog who killed him recalled to Moscow."

"There's no time to replace him before the date of the uprising," she warned. "And an uglier man might be sent by plane."

"You may be right."

"I'd not attack the Ambassador. Better cultivate him a little. He's afraid of you."

"That's so, too. You've a brilliant mind, young woman. I hope you can forget the tragedy tonight and work with us."

"I'll have to forget it."

"And work with us?"

"Of course," was the firm reply.

Adams' keen eyes bored her through as she made her reply. She wondered if it had been a little too firm. Apparently not, is for there was no suspicion in the tones of his voice when he spoke again. With a quick movement he crossed the room and drew down the shades of the windows looking out on the street.

Angela asked quickly:

"Don't you think that unwise?"

"Why?"

"Mary, the janitress, is a friend of mine. She'd be sure to notice that. She knows I haven't left town. It would excite suspicion."

"Right again. Everything must go on as usual. Who is your grocer?"

She gave him the address on Amsterdam Avenue.

"I'll send their boy for your order, and you can tell him what hour each day to come for it. He will not see the guard, but the guard will see him and you. No message can be passed. Have your order written and the guard will O.K. it before the boy comes. I can't make it too clear, young woman, that if you attempt to escape or get a message to Murino or any friend, it will mean your death."

"I understand."

"Don't make me your executioner. I saved your life once. Play fair with me."

She made no reply and he moved so that he caught the expression of her eyes.

"Your mind's miles away! You didn't hear me."

"I heard. You warned me of certain death if I tried to escape or communicate."

"Then you're two people in one. I'd swear your mind was not on what I said."

He studied her carefully.

"Well, I've done all I can. Your life is in your own hands. Goodbye."

He left hurriedly and the guard took his seat in an easy chair. Angela studied his face for the first time. He was a giant blonde of distinct European type.

"I've seen you before, young man," she said pleasantly.

"Yes."

"I can't recall the time or place."

"You will in a minute."

"Sure. I remember. You were detailed to go with Mr. Murino to a certain house in Brooklyn and get some papers from him afterwards."

"He opened them and you O.K.'d them," he nodded.

"I'm glad I have a friend for a guard. You must be hungry. I'll fix you a bite with what's in the ice box."

She fixed a ham sandwich and a glass of milk and brought the tray to him in the living room. He had followed her into the kitchen and came back, his actions dog like as he trailed her. He gulped the milk and munched the sandwich hungrily, and as he chewed remarked coldly:

"It won't do you any good to try to soft soap me, just because I've met you once in the course of business. I've never trailed with Murino. Always been on the other side. I don't like him or his gang. If they'd taken my advice he'd have croaked long ago."

There was no mistaking his hatred or his deadly purpose to guard her. A hope she had cherished for a moment faded.

Her mind was working now clearly, testing every possibility of escape or communication. From her windows she could see men on guard. It was impossible to tell for whom they were working, Adams or Murino. She finally recognized one of them as a man who had entered the first car in the procession that had brought her a prisoner to her apartment. She stood at the window and saw Mary coming up from Amsterdam Avenue. The janitress saw her at the window and waved a greeting. Her first impulse was to answer with a friendly gesture. On second thought she remained motionless. Her failure to answer might excite Mary's suspicions and she'd climb the stairs to see her.

Her thought proved correct. Mary's faint footfall echoed on the stairs.

"It's the janitress coming up to see me. What'll I do?"

"Tell her you can't see her."

"But she saw me at the window and I didn't answer her friendly wave of her hand."

"All right let her in a minute and tell her you've important business with me."

Mary started at the sight of the tall blonde guard and Angela hastened to say:

"I'm busy, dear. Come later."

The janitress nodded and hurried through the door, but not before she had caught a flash of anguish from Angela's eyes.

The guard had watched his prisoner with a cold stare, his fight hand on his automatic.

"All right," he said, "handle 'em all as slick as that and you'll not get a scratch. You saw my hand in my pocket?"

"Yes. I saw it."

Her knocker sounded loudly.

"Who the hell's that?"

"The grocer boy. I know his knock."

"Tell him to wait a minute. You're in the tub. And write out our order."

She called from the bath room door.

"In the tub, Johnnie. Wait a minute."

"Yessum," came the faint answer.

She threw a negligee on over her dress, drew off shoes, put on per slippers and went to the door.

"Don't let him in," her guard ordered.

She astounded her favorite grocer boy by giving him a writen order at the door.

He stared at her in dumb surprise and she frowned for silence. He knew that somebody was in the room. It had happened before. But it had always been Stephens, Murino, or Allen and they were his friends handy with tips. This was something new and ominous. His surprise and horror were plain. She couldn't be sure what the horror meant. He might think her in a compromising position with a man. Maybe now in the bath room. She frowned again for silence and he took her order with a hurt look and hurried down the stairs.

The temptation had been strong to whisper a word. She hadn't dared. The guard was close again at the door, towering over her, and she knew his hand gripped a gun.

"I don't like that kid coming here twice a day to deliver and take orders."

"We must eat, you know."

"Yes, I know. But I'm going to have one of my men take these orders and deliver the goods. I'll signal him from the window. Give me the address of the grocer."

She wrote it on a piece of paper and gave it to him.

"When the boy brings the stuff, tell him you're changing grocers. He needn't come again."

"That'll bring the grocer."

"All right, tell him the same thing and no back talk."

When Johnnie delivered the groceries she shocked him by a curt dismissal and asked that her bill be mailed. In breathless distress he mumbled:

"Looky, Miss Angela, I never seen nothin' and I wouldn't open my mouth if I had."

"That's all, Johnnie. Goodbye."

He saw a tear in her eyes and retreated forlornly. In fifteen minutes the grocer came and was more curtly dismissed.

"My man'll still trade with him, strictly cash," the guard said.

Angela settled to the routine of her prison with a firm grip on her mind and nerves. She would fight this thing to a finish. It was her wit and Murino and Phil against her captors and their secret power. The thing that appalled her was the certainty that they would spring the revolution as planned on the night of the President's broadcast. Every cell of their far flung conspiracy was now stirring with preparation. And her Patriot Union was helpless because the date could not be known. She must get word to Phil or Murino! A hundred plans flashed through her mind. None would work. She wondered what they were doing. Murino knew of her imprisonment. He would confer with Phil.

They were in fact in conference at that moment in the inner room of the Fifth Avenue house. They had called over their radio every important unit of the Patriot Union and warned them of swiftly approaching action. The warning would cause haste in preparation but no definite orders could be issued, without the date. Angela had the date. She had been imprisoned by John Allen as a precaution.

"I can't understand," Murino said, "why Allen did not come out of their headquarters and take her home himself. The placing of her under his own guard would have been simpler and easier in every way.

"Something may have happened to Allen," Phil returned.

"That's exactly what's on my mind. Adams, the leader of the criminal division which he is summoning into action took her to the apartment. I'm puzzled. Adams is intensely loyal to Allen. He's an able lieutenant. He has spent fifteen years of his life in prison and educated himself. He is an authority on the history of political economy and the technique of conspiracy. He has a better education from his prison reading and study than if he had graduated from Harvard or Yale. He's a far more dangerous man than John Allen. I don't like his sudden assumption of power."

"All the more reason we must rescue Angela at the earliest possible moment."

"But the moment must be carefully chosen. When we move we will be sure of success—no matter how many days or weeks we must wait."

"My God, man, don't say weeks. We must act."

"But don't you see," Murino said, "the moment our guards close in she will be killed? The mystery of mysteries is why they haven't killed her already if she knows the date of the uprising. Something happened at that meeting. Something big and ugly in their own ranks. I've tried my best to get in touch with John Allen. He can't be found."

"Thank God for this inner room you built with such care. We're in touch with our people every hour, day and night."

"But all we can say is, get ready, get ready—more machine guns, more rifles, more ammunition. When they ask what hour, we can only reply it will be given you. Get ready. But unless we know the hour of the uprising the element of surprise may give the conspirators their victory."

"We'll wait a week, and then, by God, we're going to bring Angela out!" Phil cried.

"A week should give her a chance to communicate with us."

"That's so, too."

"They've got a circle of guards a rat can't slip through. But Angela's a bright girl. She may outwit them."

"We'll wait six days and no more," Phil conceded.

"Not another hour," Murino confirmed.

Chapter 61

Adams entered the headquarters in Harlem fully decided to take Angela's suggestion and cultivate the Ambassador.

"You succeeded?" he inquired.

"Certainly. The young woman is safe in her own apartment, guarded by our faithful men, inside and outside. She will give us no trouble."

The Russian fumbled his beard.

"I wish I was as sure of that as you seem to be. Give me a daily report of the situation."

"In person after my men have reported to me."

The Ambassador noted the conciliatory tone in which Adams spoke with satisfaction and met him half way. He dropped into the attitude of comradeship.

"You wish to speak to the Master in Moscow?"

"No. We'll work in harmony, I think."

"You got all the papers?"

"Every scrap of them. Allen was too wise to carry many documents about with him."

He laid six folded papers on the table and said casually:

"Look them over."

The Ambassador noted the contents of each and handed them back.

"You know how dangerous one of these documents is, carrying the Great Seal?"

"I'll guard it."

The Russian studied the American closely and spoke with ill concealed irritation.

"I can not make it too plain to you that my consent to the arrangement you suggested for guarding the woman in her own apartment was given under duress. I didn't care to precipitate a pitched battle at our headquarters. I hope that mature thought will convince you that the arrangement is unwise and extremely dangerous."

"I'm sorry we can't see alike on this, Your Excellency. Had you put her in a basement prison, her friends would have given the alarm and we would have had the entire police force of New York and the detectives of the Federal Government on our trail. We must be free from such annoyances in the crisis. The fact that Murino knows she is safe in her apartment releases us of embarrassment. Surely you can see this?"

"There's something in what you say, of course, but the thing of supreme importance is to see that she does not communicate with her friends. She looks to me a dangerous young woman, brilliant, poised, capable of anything."

"I'll guard her. She can't escape, nor can she get a message through the circle I've drawn around her."

"You're sure she hasn't an amateur sending set?"

"I'm sure of it as I live. But I'll make another search."

"Do this without delay and confer with me daily on her condition. I'm uneasy. You can rest assured Murino is not idle."

"He has too much sense to imperil her life. He's in love with her."

The Russian shook his shaggy head unconvinced.

Murino and Stephens were wrestling with the problem at the same time. They could only wait for developments. Each man felt sure that Angela would find a way to get a message through. They stood by the telephone and radio in the Fifth Avenue house receiving daily reports from Murino's guard.

On the second day Mary called and reported the strange situation in Angela's apartment.

Phil laughed for joy to get word direct:

"You saw her?"

"With me own eyes."

"How did she look?"

"Scared nearly to death. The big blonde fellow sitting on the couch glared at me and she asked me to go and come back later."

"Good," Murino put in. "Go up every day. As long as they'll let you see her. Make some excuse. Take her flowers one day, fruit another."

He handed her some money.

"And report to us the minute you can get a phone. We'll depend on you for the latest real news. We'll work through you."

On the sixth day the two men were making final preparations for the rescue at ten o'clock the next morning when Mary rushed into the library past the butler, her face flushed, her hair dropping in strands, her voice so thick with excitement she could hardly speak.

"Oh, Holy Mother of God," she gasped. "Ye must come quick—right now!"

"What's happened?" Murino asked.

"They've fixed to take her away. When she opened the door I saw two men inside instead of one. The place was all torn up like they'd been searching it and they were fixing the telephone. She was bending over one of her big bags, packing it to go. She looked at me, as if she'd die. She dasent speak. I could see one of the men with his hand in his pocket on a pistol."

"We've not a minute to lose," Murino whispered. "They're repairing the phone to clear the way. Your guns ready?"

"All set. And a suit for her?"

"In this bundle which I'll have to carry. No time to put it on."

They hustled Mary into a waiting cab which Murino owned and drove for University Heights.

"Step on it, boy. Step on it!" Phil begged the driver.

"But no accidents," his master warned.

They stopped at a florist's on Broadway and bought a bouquet of roses.

"You'll go up and take the flowers, Mary," Murino said. "We'll follow right behind you and when the, door is opened, duck. There'll be a fight."

They reached the door without challenge and Murino spoke to his man.

"Keep your engine running and when we step into the car, start off slowly at first and when you turn into Broadway for home, give her the gun: You understand?"

The man nodded.

"Take it easy now," he warned Mary. "No excitement. Walk slowly. Hold the flowers well up."

Mary led the way, rapped the knocker and a man's voice called roughly:

"Who is it?"

"It's me, Mary the janitress. I've got some flowers."

The guard turned to Angela.

"Let her in and get rid of her quick. The telephone connection is ready and we're waiting orders where to take you."

The rescuers drew their guns and gripped them firmly. Murino whispered to Phil: "Take the man on the left. I'll take the one on the right."

Angela opened the door, they brushed her aside, sprang into the room their guns leveled, spitting fire. The guards fired at the same moment but both sank to the floor.

Murino handed Mary the bundle of clothes. "Help her into this suit, quick."

"I must tell you," Angela cried. "Tell you quick—something might happen to me. The hour is the Presidential broadcast tomorrow night!"

"Good," Phil answered. "We understand. Tear your dress off and get into that suit—hurry! The guard didn't hear the shots . . . or mistook them for the back fire of an automobile . . ."

"Wait a minute," Murino broke in. "They've come to take Angela away. We'll change overcoats with the dead guards, hustle her into our own cab, and get through without a scratch."

While Angela and Mary waited impatiently, they changed into the coats of the men they had shot.

They called Angela who kissed Mary goodbye.

"Thank you, dear. You've saved my life. Lock the door and go back to your room. Then in half an hour come to the Fifth Avenue house. It will not be safe for you here."

The three stepped into the waiting cab, which rolled leisurely into Broadway and then shot down the street at a dizzy speed.

"Easy now," Murino warned. "Don't get pinched, for God's sake."

They reached the house without accident or interference.

Inside the library Murino gripped one of Phil's arms and one of Angela's.

"Quick now, into the radio room and begin calling your mobilization. You've not a minute to lose. Give them the hour and ask for an army of two million men with the National Guard artillery to move on the cities of the North—quick. I saw a man waiting for me at the end of the hall. I'll join you in a few minutes."

Angela inserted her key and opened the first door. In a moment they were both in the steel clad room and the signals were flying.

They worked in tense haste for an hour, when Angela looked at her watch.

"Heavens! We've been here an hour and Tony hasn't come. What could be keeping him?"

"Go and see," Phil said. "I'll stand by the radio."

She hurried through the heavy doors and saw the butler standing in the library, his eyes blurred with tears.

What is it? What's happened? Have they attacked the house?"

"No, Miss," was the low reply. "Mr. Murino was shot during your rescue."

"Why, he said nothing."

"No. That's like him."

"Where is he?"

"The doctor is probing for the bullet. It lodged near his heart. His condition is very serious."

"Take me to him."

"The doctor has locked the door. No one can see him until the probing is done."

The doctor walked into the library.

"You are Miss Angela Cameron?"

"Yes."

"Mr. Murino is calling for you. I found the bullet and it has been removed. He has scarcely a chance. Don't talk to him long."

She followed the butler into the stately bed room, rushed to his side, took his head in her arms and kissed him tenderly.

"Oh, Tony, darling, you must live. Live for me!"

"I'll try, dearest," he answered in low tones. "I must tell you some things of utmost importance while I can."

She put her hand over his mouth.

"Sh—don't talk—nothing matters now but your life. Please live."

He gently removed her hand.

"I must tell you some things I've just learned from that courier in the hall. They have detailed men to kill the President and every high officer of the Government in Washington to-morrow night. They have men planted in the Army to shoot their officers and men on our warships to sink every one of them the minute they move against the conspirators. Negro criminals have been detailed to fire every Southern city, rape every white woman who can be taken, and blow up the armories. Put the South on guard quickly. Unless they move to the rescue, the great Northern cities will be lost. And if they are, the nation will be disarmed and enslaved. Quick . . . now . . . get back . . . to your radio . . . and mobilize the South! Some of the great cities will certainly fall. New York first."

His eyes blinked and his breath was labored.

"Don't talk any more, darling," Angela begged, holding him close.

"I . . . must . . . I . . . love . . . you . . ."

His head suddenly sagged. His heart had ceased to beat.

Chapter 62

Angela gazed a long time at the handsome features of the man whose last word was a tender declaration of love. When she could no longer see through her tears she called the butler and quietly ordered him to have the body prepared for burial.

"We've no time for ceremonies," she said. "A few friends may wish to see him for the last time. We are in war—the opening battles of a bloody revolution. He was the first to fall in the front ranks. Call the library telephone when you need me. I will be in an inner room below."

The butler nodded his understanding.

At the door of the Lincoln portrait Angela called back to him:

"I am expecting General Ambrose Wheeler and his staff. Call me the minute they arrive."

On entering the armored room, she called Phil from the radio.

"It's important—yes—come quick."

He rose from the instrument, his hair dishevelled, his eyes red.

"I've ominous news from the big cities."

"And I've ominous news here. Tony is dead."

She swayed against the desk and Phil caught her in his arms.

"Why, darling, it can't be possible. Did they get into the house and assassinate him?"

"No. He was shot in my apartment by the man he killed. You all fired at the same instant."

In a rush of broken words she repeated Murino's last message.

A sob caught her voice.

"Oh, Phil—I loved him!"

"Yes, dear; I know. You love me, too. I know now that it's possible for a woman to love two men at the same time. If we come out of this alive we'll cherish his memory—you and I."

He seized the telephone and Wheeler promised to report for duty immediately.

While they were waiting Phil opened the drawer and saw a folded document marked:

"The Last Will and Testament of Antonio Murino."

He drew the paper out and studied it a moment.

"A will in his own handwriting, dated yesterday."

He read it slowly:

> "Grateful to Almighty God for the saving of my soul through the love of a beautiful woman I appoint her, Angela Cameron Henry, sole executrix of this will without bond.
>
> 1. I give and bequeath to Angela Cameron Henry my home on Fifth Avenue with its furnishings and five million dollars from my estate.
>
> 2. I direct my executrix to divide another equal sum among my lawful collateral heirs in Ireland.
>
> 3. I further direct her to organize the Marcus Garvey Colonization Society, establish its work on a trust fund of ten million dollars, and ask its trustees to elect Philip Stephens President of the society with a salary of fifty thousand dollars a year. I ask Mr. Stephens to join with my executrix in devoting his entire time to the peaceful, voluntary colonization of the Negro race.
>
> 4. The remainder of my estate, I bequeath to the faithful butler, chef, maids and servants who have so faithfully served me in this house, with the hope that they may continue to serve its new owner as faithfully as they have me.
>
> Signed Antonio Murino
> (family name) Michael O'Bannion."

Angela lifted a tear stained face to Phil:

"His spirit's with us here now in this room. I feel it. He's telling us to fight a good fight. Yes, Tony, we will!"

The telephone rang and she answered.

"Tell the General I'll see him immediately."

"Put them in command," Phil said, "I'll hop a plane for Washington. We must give Tony's message to the President. I'll be back tonight."

When he reached Washington Mr. Roosevelt was in conference and his secretary refused to interrupt him.

"But, my God, man, I have discovered a plot to assassinate the President and his cabinet."

The secretary smiled.

"We hear such stuff every day. But it never happens. Excuse me, I'm busy."

He reached the Secretary of War and told him of the threat against the life of the nation, of the traitors who had bored into the ranks of the Army and what they proposed to do.

The Secretary of War was not only incredulous, he was indignant.

"How dare you assert that Communists have bored into the rank and file of our Army? Tell your informer he's a cheap liar. The Army of the United States is above suspicion, sir."

Phil shook his head sadly.

"So John B. Floyd, Secretary of War in Buchanan's cabinet, laughed at the man who rushed to inform him of John Brown's plot to invade the South and deluge it in the blood of a Slave uprising. Nothing was done. Brown captured Harper's Ferry, and the Civil War had begun. History repeats itself. Good day, sir. God help you—when they strike!"

He seized his hat, hurried to the airport and reached New York in deeper alarm over the ugly situation.

After greeting Angela he found General Wheeler and his staff busy with reports and orders over the radio.

"What's the situation, General?" Phil asked tensely.

"The news from Philadelphia and Boston is hopeful. The latest reports from the other great cities are ugly. They couldn't be uglier. The enemy are secretly moving bodies of men, their arms concealed, on the systems of water works, transportation, power houses and the telephone exchanges and light systems. It seems impossible now to save them from capture. I've no doubt they are mobilizing to-day in New York at each of these strategic points.

"The South is a puzzle. Our leader in Atlanta has just phoned in that the Carolinas are mobilizing with swift sure movement. But that Atlanta, New Orleans and San Antonio refuse to take the rumor seriously. He believes two million white men will be under arms by the time the President makes his broadcast to-morrow night . . ."

Phil lifted his hand in sharp interruption. "The President's advisors have received our warnings as the ravings of lunatics. They have scorned any suggestion of caution—all but threatened me with arrest."

"We have bad news, too, from the Mexican border," the General added. "A Communist army is secretly mobilizing close behind the line. A bloody invasion is a certainty. We have had great difficulty in getting action down there on our side. They are as incredulous as the officials in Washington."

"What is your plan of military action?" Phil asked.

Wheeler took a sheet of notes from his adjutant.

"Spent all last night developing them for every emergency I could figure. Here is my suggestion. Send three divisions to meet the Mexicans as they cross the line. Cover the armories of the South with men enough to save every piece of artillery and every shell in their arsenals. Above all things we must save every tank and see that it is equipped with ammunition for its cannon. This fight will be won in the streets by infantry and mechanized cavalry. The airplanes can't be used in such a Civil war with any intelligence. We are mad to send planes over our cities to destroy them. We've got to go in and dig the devils out, retake the water works, telephone exchanges, and power houses when they are captured and defend them from recapture. We'll need tanks and artillery to do this. We must move half a million men on each of the great cities threatened, Chicago, St. Louis, Cleveland, Detroit, New York. If these cities fall they will capture the thirteen big industrial states. With this power in men, money and equipment they can take the nation."

"How can you move your division quick enough to save the cities?" Phil asked anxiously.

"By the mobilization immediately of the Railroads. Their officers are patriots to a man. Their now swift streamlined trains will lead with the staffs and light artillery. Behind them will run the heavier trains with big guns. The Railroads can save the nation in this crisis."

He turned to his adjutant.

"Get every official on the radio. Tell them I ask the immediate commandeering of every train and engine in their service. This is a secret order. It must not be known until the conspirators rise tomorrow night. But they must be ready to move on an hour's notice. Order every division of the Patriot Union to place immediately a strong guard over every railroad bridge, tunnel and terminal, segregate and conserve the food supplies."

Angela placed the room in charge of the General and staff and their orders were sent to every branch of the Patriot Union with all speed. An amateur radio set had been established in every County. The telephones and old fashioned telegraph instruments proved valuable aids.

She turned anxiously to Phil.

"You think they may capture New York?"

"They may. There are more alien criminals here than in any city of the United States. The Negro Red unit in Harlem under Ford's direction, is the strongest in the country. We know they are armed with rifles, submachine guns and bombs. Headquarters are here. I can feel their men creeping to their appointed tasks to-day. New York will be the heart of the revolution as Paris was in the French holocaust of the eighteenth century. THERE ARE 810 COMMUNIST CLUBS IN NEW YORK CITY, EACH ONE A REVOLUTIONARY CELL!"

"While the Generals are sending their orders," Angela said, "we'd better inspect the New York branches of the Union."

They received a shock at the headquarters of the City Hall unit. The place was tight closed and only a boy left in charge.

"Where's Andrews, your boss?" Phil asked.

"Left last night to get more men. He'll not be back until tomorrow night."

"That's funny," Angela muttered. "He should be on his telephone every hour today and tonight. The conspirators have gotten to him. He's a deserter. We'll put a man in his place and make these telephone lines hum."

The phones were in working order, but not a single officer of the unit could be reached. They were all out of town.

"My God, how many more of our units have been captured by treachery?"

"I don't believe another one," Angela declared. "But this, of all stations, is most important. If they take the City Hall, their command of the whole town will be almost certain."

They spent two hours reorganizing the station. An amateur radio set was part of its equipment. A new unit had to be created. Men were detached from uptown centers, hurriedly installed and heavily armed. Not a trace could be found of a single officer of the original unit.

Phil shook his head.

"If this has happened in other big cities we're in for some surprises. Thank God the sirens and light signals are installed."

Chapter 63

Every order had been sent over the radio that could be dispatched until the uprising should break or fail to materialize.

General Wheeler spoke with nervous tension.

"They may find our defenses so strong the revolution will be postponed."

Angela shook her head.

"Nothing will stop them. The final orders were given two weeks ago. I heard the Russian Ambassador to the new Soviet America issue them to every branch of the conspirators."

"The broadcast will tell the story," General Thomas, the adjutant, put in. "If they strike tonight they'll assassinate the President while he's speaking."

"I don't agree with you," General Wheeler objected. "That would give them away in a minute. If they carry out their plan of liquidating the Government in Washington tonight, it will be done after the broadcast is over and everybody is discussing it."

He looked at his watch.

"The hour is here. We'll know in thirty minutes."

The radio announcer in Washington made his stereotyped introduction.

"Ladies and gentlemen of the radio audience, I present the President of the United States."

The familiar voice came over the radio clear, good natured, persuasive. They listened intently, some of them expecting each word to be his last. There was no pause, no crash. He finished in fine form and the announcer made the closing statement of station and speaker.

The lights in, the room suddenly went out. Angela sprang to her feet with every man in a circle about the desk.

"It's come!" she breathed tensely.

"You've candles?" General Wheeler asked.

"Much better. An emergency lighting system in the basement. I'll switch it on." She felt beneath the desk, threw a switch and the lights flashed on in full power.

"Marvelous!" General. Thomas exclaimed. "You've thought of everything."

Angela seized a telephone. The instrument was dead.

"They've captured our telephone exchanges. We've still our radio sending sets. Phil, call Chicago."

Stephens entered the radio room and quickly returned with blanched face.

"There's no answer. The whole big system is out of commission."

"Depend on it," General Wheeler said, "they've not destroyed the stations. They've taken them, if they don't answer. Try other cities."

He tried St. Louis, Cleveland, and Detroit with the same result. Not a word in reply. Only Boston and Philadelphia answered.

"Try the amateur stations we've concealed outside the cities," Angela said.

"Your own current is intact?" General Wheeler asked.

"The emergency set supplies it now. We should reach any city in America."

Phil called the amateur stations and got replies. Chicago, Cleveland, Detroit and St. Louis were in darkness, terrific explosions rocking the earth. The water supply in each city had been cut, all transportation stopped. The NAT TURNER LEGION was rapidly mobilizing.

"Try that faucet over the wash basin!" Angela called to the generals.

Thomas turned the faucet.

"There's no water!"

"They've beaten our guards," Phil cried, "and captured the Water System."

Washington was shrouded in silence. When the amateur station finally answered, the man at the radio was gasping for breath.

"I couldn't answer before. Our Unit's been wiped out. We saved this station. They never found it. I crawled here on my hands and knees. I'm pretty well washed up. They say the President and all the Cabinet members have been captured. The Commanding General of the Army and the Commanding Admiral of the Navy, too. The Justices of the Supreme Court have formed a Committee of Public Safety and barricaded themselves in the basement of the new Supreme Court building."

Phil called the amateur station at Old Point Comfort. The fleet had tried to put to sea and five ships had been blown up. The others, fifteen or twenty, had anchored.

He tried in vain to reach the Governor of New York at Albany. The radio station was silent. The amateur station was silent. Both had been captured.

He rushed from the house, seized the wheel of his car and tried to reach an airport. The tunnel and bridges were held by the enemy. He circled on a rapid tour of inspection.

Governor's island had fallen. The commanding officers had been shot and revolutionists from the ranks had marched the garrison into New York City and joined the Division at the City Hall. The Patriot Unit had been wiped out after a bloody skirmish.

The police barracks were blown up, their machine guns and artillery put out of business. Every armory had been taken without a shot. Communists had bored into the ranks of the caretakers, secured the keys and marched in. The City Hall had been captured, all systems of transportation and communication were paralyzed.

He drove back to the house for the latest outside news. It was ominous.

"Fires are raging in every great Northern city," Wheeler said, "with bloody battles in the streets . . . now breaking out in Boston and Philadelphia. The South is fighting to save Atlanta, New Orleans and San Antonio. The first clash with the Communist army of invaders from Mexico will come to-morrow morning. In South Carolina, Mississippi, Alabama and Louisiana the NAT TURNER LEGION have begun a reign of terror—burning, murdering and raping. The Home Guard of the Patriot Union is everywhere engaging them in battle. In spite of their troubles at home the South has promised to send a million men, artillery and tanks, to the big Northern cities. The American Legion are answering to a man and their troops are moving to the firing line. . . ."

A terrific explosion drowned his voice, followed by another and another—three from the direction of Times Square, one from down town and three in Brooklyn.

"That's strange," Wheeler said. "I expected the first big explosions would be aimed at Police Headquarters."

"We'll see what's going on in the streets," Phil said.

He rushed upstairs followed by Angela and the staff.

They opened the front door at the moment the shriek of a siren hurled its long cry over the darkened streets. A minute and another joined. And then another and another until the din was a steady staccato roar. A red light suddenly shot two miles in the sky and stood trembling.

"Your plan is working, Phil," Angela whispered.

"Yes," he nodded.

The shrill cry of a newsboy rang from the side walk.

"Extra! Extra! The new *Soviet Herald*—only newspapar in New York. The rest blown up! Extra—extra! The new *Soviet Herald*!"

Phil bought a copy and they read the proclamation of Nickolas Adams,

Chief of the forces of the Revolution, in big black type across the front page.

"We command the people to stay in doors until order is restored. The Soviet Republic of the United States now rules the nation. The National Government in Washington is in our hands. The Army and Navy are taking orders only from the Government. Loyal citizens will submit to its authority. All men bearing arms against it will be shot as traitors. No newspapers will be printed except those authorized by the Soviet Republic."

"Our first big surprise!" Phil exclaimed. "They have bored into the newspapers offices and destroyed their plants. There can now be no expression of public opinion, and they'll strangle the nation with their damned *Soviet Herald*. It's an appalling calamity. They've wiped out every daily in the United States!"

He anxiously faced General Wheeler.

"What are the chances, sir?"

"It all now depends on the quick transport of men and guns over our railroads. If their trains move swiftly and surely we may go in with tanks, artillery and infantry, recapture the great cities and save the country."

"The issue is in God's hands, Phil," Angela whispered tensely.

"Let's pray He keeps the railroads open and their trains running full speed——"

For a long time Stephens stood staring over the heads of the group around General Wheeler.

He spoke, at last, as in a dream:

"You know, dear, something Tony said keeps haunting me——"

"What was that?"

"*Communism is the collapse of the human mind under the pressure of modern life—a malignant, contagious, mental disease now sweeping the world as the Black Death swept Europe in the Middle Ages.*"

Angela answered tenderly: "All right, Phil, we'll just play our parts. It's glorious to be alive and have the chance!"

The two clasped hands in a warm pledge of faith, courage and love.

The End